Alexander Smith, Patrick Proctor Alexander

Last Leaves

Sketches and criticisms

Alexander Smith, Patrick Proctor Alexander

Last Leaves
Sketches and criticisms

ISBN/EAN: 9783337011437

Printed in Europe, USA, Canada, Australia, Japan

Cover: Foto ©Andreas Hilbeck / pixelio.de

More available books at **www.hansebooks.com**

LAST LEAVES

SKETCHES A

ALEXANDER

AUTHOR OF " A LIFE-DRAMA," "DREAM

Edited, with a Memoir, by

PATRICK PROCTOR ALEXAN

AUTHOR OF " MILL AND CARLYLE," ETC.

EDINBURGH:
WILLIAM P. NIMMO.
1868.

MEMOIR.

IN superintending the issue of this selection from the Essays of my friend, the late Alexander Smith, it has fallen to me to write, as Preface to it, some little account of him as he lived. It is a task which I would willingly have declined, as knowing its extreme delicacy; also, as well knowing that I shall not succeed in doing it as I myself should wish to see it done. Not the less, on other grounds, I am frankly willing, and, in some sort of sad fashion, pleased, to do the best I may in the matter. What I have to write I shall write very simply as it is given me, believing that that will be best; except as I should be sorry indeed that the book or the memory of the man should suffer through any *bêtise* of mine, not too curiously concerned, as I proceed, as to what may be thought of my performance, and especially indifferent to possible charges against it, in parts, of the *egotism* which, I trust, will be seen to be pretty much in the nature of the task itself, as I conceive it.

Alexander Smith was born at Kilmarnock, in Ayrshire, on the 31st December 1829. He was the eldest born of his parents—excellent people both, who lived to take just pride in the world's recognition of his genius, and, more lately, to have life saddened for them by his too early death. Some few years after, the family removed to Paisley, and thence, in a short time, to Glasgow. Of the education which he there received it seems scarcely necessary to say anything. I should suppose it to have been a fairly good one, including, as it did, with the three indispensable *R's*, some tincture of Latin and mathematics. His knowledge of these two latter branches he did not much air in his later time; perhaps because he really knew them; more probably, because he had forgotten them as completely as if for some years of his life he had studied them diligently at a University. Properly, his education may perhaps have amounted to this, that he was thoroughly well taught to *read;* and—the key thus put into his

hands which unlocks all the wards of knowledge
—he proceeded to make pretty good use of it.
With a fair round of general information, taken
on his own special topics of English poetry and
the *Belles Lettres*—English literature, I may say,
in extenso—he was always to be held, as it
seemed to me, an unusually well-read man,
even among men professedly literary.

The boy early gave evidence of talent; and,
at one time, it was proposed to educate him for
the ministry. It is, perhaps, no mighty matter
of regret that this project, for some reason or
other, was abandoned. Undoubtedly, as a
parson, he would have been much beloved by
his parishioners; but there seems no special
reason to suppose he would have shone as a
pulpit orator. He would scarcely have written
the "Life Drama," or writing, could scarcely
have published it; and, instead of "Dream-
thorp," etc., the world might perhaps have been
favoured with some volumes of dull discourses,
which would not, by comparison, have enriched
it. Mr Smith, senior, was a pattern-designer;
and by this accident, as I imagine, rather than
any special leaning or aptitude that way, the
junior was determined to the same employment.

If—as he used to tell—great part of his early poetry was composed by him over his work, it may be surmised that the design, taking shape under the hand, would not exceedingly profit by that intense pre-occupation of the head. In after life, he was never, that I heard of, known to touch a pencil; a fact which, of itself, may be held conclusive, as showing that, in his choice of a pursuit, he was ruled by no depth of natural tendency. Still, the designs — such as they might be—were, no doubt with perfect regularity, produced; and, along with them, much of the poetry which afterwards, as the "Life Drama," became famous. Certain of his verses appeared from time to time in the *Glasgow Citizen*, edited by Mr James Hedderwick, a man of the nicest literary taste, "an accomplished journalist, and poet of no mean order,"* with whom he was thus brought into friendly relations. Naturally, however, the "Poet's Corner," after his first flush of young fool's delight in seeing himself actually in print, came to seem to him a somewhat restricted field; and, with a view to a wider publicity, early in 1851, he forwarded a selec-

---

* "Summer in Skye," A. Smith.

tion of his pieces to the Rev. Mr George Gilfillan of Dundee, asking his opinion and advice.
From Mr Gilfillan he had instant and generous
recognition; and shortly, through his kindly
furtherance, the poems began to appear, by
regular instalments, in the London *Critic*, a journal then of wide circulation, with which he was
connected as contributor. There and elsewhere,
moreover, he expressed, in no stinted terms of
eulogy, his sense of the power and promise of
the "New Poet" he had thus had the luck to
unearth. That in the first instance, and as gain-
ing him the ear of the public on the instant, Mr
Gilfillan was of much use to Smith, he himself, as the last man in the world to forget a
true kindness done him, always continued to
acknowledge.

The interest excited in London literary circles
by the poetry, as it thus appeared, was something quite unusual; and—as then living in
Glasgow—I very well remember the curious
speculation which was rife as to what kind of
strange bird *this* might be, beginning so to pipe
in our midst. Soon, through his friend Mr
Hedderwick, who asked me to meet him of an
evening, I had the pleasure of making his ac-

quaintance. Considering his youth, and the somewhat exuberant cast of the poetry, I confess I expected to meet a more or less flighty kind of blockhead, whose gyrations in the direction of the Empyrean it might be not unamusing to watch. With a considerable shock of surprise, and possibly—the amusement being looked to—of something very like disappointment, I found myself face to face with one of the most simple, quiet, modest, and unassuming of men. He did not gyrate in the least, and seemed to indicate, indeed, an entire, and even helpless, incapacity for that kind of performance. He did not speak overmuch ; rather showed a considerable talent for silence, which—except in the entire unreserve of intimacy, not even in which was he wont to be specially voluble—he continued through life to cultivate. Anything he did say was closely pertinent to the matter in hand—plain, shrewd, sensible. What, at first meeting, struck me as remarkable about him, besides this unexpected quiet sense and solidity, was his *forehead*, which really, I think, *was* remarkable—a fine square block of brain, such as I have not often seen the like of, with dark hair massed heavily over it. Otherwise—except, for something of a squint, a little startling at first, but which afterward you would not have wished away—his face, though comely and expressive, was not such as to strongly arrest attention. Afterwards, as the years dealt with him, he changed somewhat in appearance. As he neared middle age, face and figure became fuller, and the first, as the fashion of the day suggested, was improved by a moustache and an ample beard, brown in colour, and of almost exceptionally fine proportions. In himself he changed not a jot; remaining throughout, and to his last hour, precisely the same simple, quiet, unassuming, undemonstrative man who met me that first evening; without a suspicion in him of anything like small affectation; averse in his own person from every form of self-exhibition, and with a humorous and kindly contempt for that vanity as it showed itself in others. This *identity* was, perhaps, even curious, and of itself might be held to illustrate the truth and sincerity of his nature. Most of us may have known people who seemed to us, on the first blush of acquaintance, of something like ideal excellence; but by and by we found them out: and even if the excellence remained, it shrunk, and seemed more and more short of the ideal at first suggested. The man who has hitherto shone in your eyes as the very soul of easy gene-rosity, is precisely the person who is sure not to have the necessary £5 when you wish to oblige him by borrowing it. The only certain truth as yet known in ethics is this—that it is good to believe in human virtue, and better still, as a rule, not to test it any way severely. Nobody better than Smith stood the test which is neces-sarily furnished by a long and intimate acquain-tance. He did not in the least strike you as ideal, to start with, but as something very genuine and real; and more and more you found that he *was* so. He was eminently *good wear*, so, in some rough and ready way, to phrase it.

To Smith, as to myself, this evening could not fail to be memorable, if only as for both of us the commencement of intimacy with a most interesting, and, in some distinct sense, remark-able, man, by name Hugh Macdonald. Hugh was one of the best and most curious specimens of a class of men which this curious country called Scotland produces, in perhaps somewhat exceptional numbers. The famous " Parochial

System "—now on its last legs, they say—has had something to do in the production of them ; but much more Robert Burns, who has simply, for the humbler grades of the Scottish people, done the work of a legion of schoolmasters. (It is not, of course, to be forgotten that Burns was himself an *effect*, and in this relation must figure as *con*-cause, rather than accurately cause.) Originally a factory operative, Macdonald had developed himself into a poet (*of course*, with Burns as the god of his idolatry); a naturalist of no ordinary accomplishment, more especially in the branch of botany ; and a writer of really good and eloquent prose,* with, perhaps, just the least little tendency to become at times *too* eloquent—Burns, perhaps, being his theme, the *Osmunda Regalis*, or some other of the botanical hobbies on which he was wont to career about with astonishing vigour and enthusiasm. In virtue of all this, he had come into contact with Mr Hedderwick—to whom, in that metropolis of cotton, anything literary

---

* His two books, " Rambles Round Glasgow," and " Days at the Coast," are really, in their kind, of quite superior excellence, and, as Guide Books to the whole district, attained a great popularity.

seemed by natural necessity to gravitate—and was at this time employed as his sub-editor. The three of us going away together, as we did, naturally enough met again at my room the evening after. As the first of many such evenings, I infer it must have passed, on the whole, pleasantly; and some sort of comfortable intimacy was pretty rapidly established. Smith had afterwards many friends, and of these an unusual proportion, his relations with whom were close, cordial, and even to be called endearing; but scarce any of them was ever his *bosom*-friend (to use an expressive, if somewhat gushing phrase) in such sense as Hugh Macdonald. The two speedily become so inseparable that almost on meeting one of them, you would look about in some puzzled way, as if expecting the other. And the men were so utterly unlike, that there conjunction had in it a positive element of the ludicrous. Macdonald, though born in Glasgow, and essentially a Lowland Scot, was a Celt, as his name implies, and some portion of his boyhood had been passed among relations in Mull. Though this had left but little trace in him, there could be no mistake about the *breed.* He had much of the Celtic vividness, vivacity, enthusiasm; "the flash and outbreak of the fiery mind" was perpetually expressed in his speech, and his various odd modes of procedure. Smith, on the other hand, fronted the world, as I said, as quiet an embodiment as may be, of the right Saxon sense, shrewdness, and solidity. The contrast was fundamental ; and at almost every point of detail it was so marked as to make the friendly amalgam of the two amusing, not to say absurd. Most pleasant comrades each apart, together they were really incomparable ; and when I used to expect them of an evening, one or two congenial spirits would probably be asked to drop in. Do ever any of my friends in the West recall these *Noctes cœnasque Deorum ?* I should think it not improbable ; for—the omens being reasonably propitious—there could scarcely be better entertainment. Our "Society," whether or no to be held "good" in the paltry, and, perhaps, rather idiotic sense, was as good as any I have seen, or much care to see ; and almost immeasurably better, for any rational purpose of either instruction or delight, than other societies I have seen, which would have been shocked to hear they were considered not quite unimpeachably "*good.*" By virtue of his real conversational power, Macdonald, on his own topics, would have shone in any society in which, as thoroughly at home, he felt himself free to develop it. Smith, who had afterwards fair opportunities for testing ability in that kind, used always to say, that for vital force and brilliancy of talk he had not met any one quite equal to "poor Hugh" at his best. (He died some few years after this, but never ceased to be affectionately remembered, and every now and then referred to.*) Also, he had considerable powers as a vocalist, and held himself frankly ready to sing at a moment's notice. Burns was his general stand-by ; and failing the songs of Burns, he was partial, I think, to *his own*, which he gave with fine, wild, masterly effect, to any tune or none, as it might chance. Nice *connoisseurs* among us would hint that generally, in this matter of *tune*, Hugh was the least thing shaky or so. As myself unfastidious in such matters,—which Smith most distinctly also was,—I could never rightly see their objection, and rejoiced in the bursting *soul*,

---

* Some tender reminiscence and account of him will be found in the Glasgow section of Smith's "Summer in Skye."

and genuine lyrical impetuosity of his performances. Afterwards, when these nice *connoisseurs* would show us in another company how
the thing should scientifically be done, I missed
the lyrical impetuosity, and found the science an
indifferent substitute.

But these are by comparison poor and trivial
accomplishments. What on such occasions
very particularly endeared him to us was this—
that, with the warmest affection for Smith, as a
man, he combined a resolute contempt for him
as Poet, to which he never hesitated to give the
very broadest Doric expression.* "I like ye

---

* It was one of Hugh's whims, which aided the quaint effect of
his conversation, that, though he could speak very good English, if
he liked, it was a point of honour with him not to do so. Smith,
though a good Scot, was never specially to be called *Scotch ;* he
did not, that is, "glory in the name of Scotchman ;" his love of
his country was pretty much like his love for his mother, a feeling
to be understood as existing, but with which he did not think it
necessary to rush clamorously into the street. He had, moreover, through literature—which in its essence is life—very strong
English sympathies ; and even thus early Chaucer was, I think,
more eminent with him than Burns, whom yet, of course, he
knew most thoroughly. With Macdonald, on the other hand,
Scotticism was a fiery and irrational passion, which in every
way he held himself bound to assert ; and *this* was one of his
ways of doing so. For all English sophistications and refinements of what he held to be the primitive speech of mankind,

weel, Sandy," he would say, "an' that ye weel
ken ; but as for yer *poetry*, as ye ca't! sae help
me God! I mak' but little o't. It *may* be poetry ;
I'm no sayin' it is na ; the *creetics* say it's
poetry, an' nae doot *they* suld ken ; but it's no

---

he professed a great abhorence in his friends ; and, for himself, as
religiously eschewed them as an Israelite the unclean thing.
The words Papa, Mamma, in particular, always comically excited his antipathy ; and they could scarcely be used in his presence without provoking some wild explosion. "Pap*aw!*" he
would say, "mamm*aw!*" with as great a length and breadth of
scornful emphasis as the broadest Scotch tongue could convey.
"What ails ye at faither and mither as ye hae them gi'en ye i' the
Scripters ? But folk hae a' gotten sae *fiine* noo, that God's ain
Scripter's no guid eneugh for them. Pap*aw*! I scunner to
hear't. Lod ! if ony bairn o' *mine* was to ca *me* pap*aw*, I think I
wad jist fent (faint). I *daur* them to dae sic a thing!" And so
forth.

   If, any time during summer, you chanced to be wandering about
Loch Lomond, or any where in the beautiful Highland district
which the Firth of Clyde lays open with its branching arms, you
were nearly sure to spy on the deck of some steamboat, a quaint
little figure in a huge old rusty pilot coat, crowned with a Glen-
garry bonnet, jauntily set on one side, in which a considerable
sprig of heather was always defiantly stuck, as making a testimony to all men. This was Hugh Macdonald on one of his
perpetual "Rambles." The sprig of heather, on such occasions,
was never in his toilet omitted ; his Scottish dialect he wore
somewhat in the same way, at once as ornament, testimony, and
defiance. So much in explanation of the savage jargon—as
needs it must seem to many readers—he is, in the text, reported
as speaking.

my kind o' poetry. Jist a blatter o' braw words, to my mind, an' bit whirly-whas, they ca' *eemages !* Damme if I can mak' either head or tail o't." (With this he invariably concluded ; and, in fact, it is not to be denied that the good Hugh shotted his speech at times—a sin, it may be hoped, forgiven him, as never in the list of the deadly ones.) Here, at least, was what could not but commend itself to Smith, as clearly a " candid opinion." It became part of the regular programme, at some time or other of the evening, to skilfully lead the conversation up to a discussion of Smith's claims, when Macdonald never failed *in effect* to deliver himself with trenchant emphasis as above, however the tune might be played with lively and ingenious variations. Smith seemed always to enjoy quite as heartily as any one else what should have been his own discomfiture ; and shortly after, the two oddly-assorted companions would go off into the night together.

The truth was that, in his fanatical devotion to Burns, Macdonald could not, except in the most grudging way, be got to concede merit to any other poet whatever ; somewhat as a

knight of old, did his eyes but chance to
stray to a rival beauty, might suspect in himself dereliction, and some dishonour therein
done to his own peerless Dulcinea. "Shakespeare?" he would say, dubitatively; "Weel-
a-weel! Shakespeare! Nae doot a vera great
poet! I wadna just ventur to say oor Rabbie*
could hae written 'Hawmlet;' but there's aye
twa ways o' puttin' a thing. Honestly, div
ye really think, noo" (with a twinkle in the
keen grey eye of ironical humour, pre-
sumably, more probably of intense conviction), "Shakespeare *could hae written 'Tam o'*
Shanter?' Deil the fears o' him!" Shakespeare's superior claims were thus to be considered neutralised, if not entirely disposed of.
Lesser and later men were much more per-
emptorily set aside. Keats was "a puir bit
penny-whustle o' an English cratur! 'Endee-
mion,' say ye? There's naething in't to *get a*
grip o'. I canna get *a haud o't,* Sandy, ony mair
than o' *ye,* wi' yer whirly-whas. Hech! but

---

* The affectionate diminutive very commonly, in speaking of
Burns, in use among the genuine Scotch populations.

it's thin, thin—a bit coloured wab, the like o'
whilk amaist ony speeder micht spin, gif ye
gie'd it vermeelion i' the guts o't. Nae claith
there to clead puir men's backs wi'!" Shelley
was "whiles bonny, bonny; but just clean daft,
puir fallow!—a' i' the air, like his ain laverock."*
Or again : " O' him ye ca' Wudsworth I hae jist
nae opeenion ava. He drank naething a' his life
but Lake.watter, they say; an' troth I weel be-
liev't; for little else e'er cam' oot o' him." For
Tennyson, his expressed contempt was extreme;
and once—the book being at hand—I remember
he effectively illustrated his position by a reading of " Airy, fairy Lilian." Working his *Scotch*
with vigour, and carefully emphasising any little
points of weakness—for which he had the keenest
eye—he produced with much ease a detestable
caricature, which nearly made us all expire
with laughter. Then, of course, he triumphed :
" Laugh awa', lads! Deed, ye may weel laugh
at him. O, but it's wersh, wersh,† that kin' o'

---

* The allusion is, of course, to Shelley's famous "Sky Lark;"
and generally, it is to be said, that *this* critic had, at least, been
at some pains to read the poets whom he professed to despise.

† *Wersh*, an exquisitely-expressive word, of which, as of most
of our exceptionally fine Scotch words, there is no exact English

B 2

thing, to put beside the like o' Rabbie! I tell't
ye he was nae poet." Finding himself in such
excellent company, when under the critical ban,
naturally Smith could not have his equanimity
much disturbed by Macdonald's abuse of his
" whirly-whas."

---

equivalent. Tasteless, flavourless, comes perhaps as near it as may
be ; but this is *itself*, by comparison, flavourless. *Wersh* is this,
and something more ; giving the negative, and, along with it,
some quaint sub-insinuation of scorn, half humorous, half dis-
gustful. And so of other words of the same kind, *e.g.*—

> " The *cantie* auld folks *crackin' crouse !*"

(from Burns' "Twa Dogs," of course). An exact *intellectual*
equivalent of each of these three words can readily be given in
English ; but a mere *caput mortuum* would thus be substituted
for a line, to beat which, in its own class of subject, you may
range the poetry of the world. What is *a crack* in English ? A
chat! The synonym is as perfect as possible ; yet the words
are subtly distinguished from each other by a whole hemisphere
of feeling. A *chat*, by comparison " wi' a *crack*," is a poor,
frivolous, shallow, altogether heartless business. A *crack* is,
indeed, only adequately to be defined as a *chat* with a good,
kindly, human heart in it ; whereas to chat is too probably to
chatter merely, as Mr Carlyle would say, " from the teeth outwards." It is in virtue of this shadow of home-grown emotion
over it, that Scotch is so exquisite a vehicle—this is, I suppose,
admitted—for the expression of the simpler forms of pathos, and
a particular type of humour—a humour which is deep in the
very genius of the language itself ; and seems always at least
as much indebted to *that* as to the talent of the particular
humorist.

Apart from the general charge of gross plagiarism—of which anon—afterwards preferred
against the " Life-Drama," I have seen it alleged
by here and there a depreciatory critic, that the
detail of nature in it seemed rather got up by
way of book than studied from the real thing.
I should suppose there might be something in
this ; inasmuch as Macdonald—by far the most
competent judge of such a matter I ever chanced
to come in contact with—used to tender the
same accusation. Botany he had studied at
once scientifically, and with the vivid interest of
delight proper to the poet ; and touching the
nature and habits of birds, beetles, butterflies,
every creeping or flying thing, he was a mine of
curious information.* Hence, as regarded the
minutiæ of nature, almost no poet was safe
from him ; and even " Rabbie " himself would
now and then be called in question   " The

---

* It will scarce ever, I believe, be found that a man of these
peculiar tastes is of other than essentially gentle nature ; and of
such Macdonald eminently was : a man of "impetuous blood,"
yet—as the phrase goes—who "would not have hurt a fly."
These odd brusqueries and outbursts in which, on occasion, he
indulged himself, were so *fused*—thus to speak—in the genial and
kindly nature of the man, that there could never be a shadow
of offence in them, but merely matter of amusement.

Posie" he could not abide, in its incongruous
conjunction of flowers which, as children of
different seasons, could never in nature co-
exist. Milton's "Lycidas" he abused on the
same ground—it is needless to say his point of
view was, in either case, quite wrong (though he
never could be got to see this), as confusing the
separate jurisdictions of the poet and the man
of science—and he wrote a song called " The
Flower Lovers" (really an exquisite piece), from
which, as done on exact principles, he plainly
considered both ".Rabbie" and Milton, had they
survived to hear him sing it, would have got
an important wrinkle or two. Smith's pretensions to any accurate knowledge of Nature he
treated with undisguised contempt ; and, in the
country walks they constantly took together, he
assiduously set himself to *coach him up* in these
neglected parts of knowledge. As frequently
present, I may certify, that seldom can the truths
of Natural Science have been communicated in
more original and amusing fashion. It was
commonly of a Sunday (the *Sawbith* they mostly
called it in these parts) that we sallied forth on
such excursions. How vividly I now remember
them ; and the figure of Macdonald, with its

oddity somewhat enhanced by a huge tin case slung round him, which he called, I rather think, a *Vasculum!* This implement was popularly supposed to receive and conserve botanical specimens; but I don't think I ever saw any in it. Not the less, on such occasions, Hugh never came abroad without it; and it was plain he considered it conferred on the expedition some savour of the dignity of Science. On this vasculum of Hugh's, Smith and I used to break at times a good deal of profane wit—or *wut,* as perhaps, it might be—but all to no purpose. And no doubt the thing had its uses; if it never brought back any specimens, at least it seldom failed to take out with it a fair supply of whisky and sandwiches. Our favourite walk was some five or six miles up Clyde from Glasgow, and included many reaches of river scenery so exquisite in beauty that I have scarce elsewhere seen them equalled. It had also the advantage of including (Forbes Mackenzie, as yet, was not) a certain modest hostelrie, a very pet "howf" of Macdonald's, kept by a fine, typical, old Scotch-woman, whose cakes and ale were excellent, and whose racy, old homely humours made you feel as if, in entering her hut, you had walked into a

Waverley novel.   These were delightful days;
and otherwise I consider it certain that Smith
well found his account in them.   With the truest
delight in Nature, which had in him the depth of
an instinct, his natural tendency was rather to
brood and expand in spirit over the wide glories
of the sky and earth, than to close and minute
observation in detail.   This, and the habit of
this, his association with Macdonald more and
more tended to educe in him.   Moreover, Hugh,
in his own person, was on these topics profuse
and inexhaustible, so as—*me judice*—nearly to
become a bore at times; and only to listen to
him thus a-field, was, for one with any care or
turn that way, to acquire a great deal of useful
and useless information.   It is scarcely too much
to say, that three-fourths of what, for Smith,
might be afterwards in this kind available, was
taught him by Hugh Macdonald.   Once, as we
were pacing quietly along a wooded stretch of
the river side, he broke out suddenly, " Od, but
he 's a queer fallow that ! " and catching on the
instant our surprise—no soul being visible in the
landscape to whom the remark could apply—
he added, " It 's that chiel Tennyson I 'm speakin'

o'. Hark ye baith, noo:" and in his very best English manner, he went on to quote,

> "Why lingers she to clothe her heart with love?
> Delaying, as *the tender ash delays,*
> To *clothe herself when all the woods are green.*"

"Ye mind it, Sandy! it's i' the 'Princess;' an' noo, look ye, *that's* an ash"—pointing with his staff —"maybe ye think it's an elm, Sandy! but it's *no* an elm, it's an ash; *an' deil a leaf on't*, see ye na? an' *a' the ither trees are oot!* I didna need ony o' yer Tennysons to tell *me* that; but neither o' *ye* kent it, I reckon. He's nae poet; I'll aye say that; but I'se alloo ye'll no aften find him wrang wi' his flooers, an' his trees, an' things; *he* kens them, Sandy! an' *ye* dinna. But ye're nae poets, neither tane nor t'ither o' ye. Damme if," etc., (the usual amen to the discourse). Another time, on a bright spring morning, the air all ringing round us with the keen, clear music of the larks, fluttering up and falling, he took occasion most learnedly to expound to us the meaning of the passage in the "Gardener's Daughter," in which the lark is said to

> "*Shake its song together* as it nears
> Its happy home, the ground"—

by both of us admitted somewhat obscure. I

am unable to reproduce his statement in the vernacular ; but, in effect, it was somewhat thus—that the note of the climbing lark is subtly distinguished from that of the descending one ; the effect in the one case being expansive, in the other, concentrative : the song of the creature as it soars seeming to fling itself rapturously abroad into the skyey spaces, and out of them as it descends, with equal rapture to collect itself, so to speak, converging on the home-nest beneath. To Macdonald's ear—if you believed him—this distinction in the notes was as perfect as any in music. On my venturing to say that to *mine*, after trying ever so, it remained quite inappreciable, a brusque " It 's weel seen *ye hae nae lugs*," was all the response vouchsafed me. Whether Smith had more success than I in the matter, I do not the least remember. With this sort of talk it was that Hugh was wont to regale us.*

Never since thus, with these men, have I walked up the Clyde from Glasgow. Should I ever

---

* It could not but at times occur as a question to one, whether, critically knowing Tennyson and the rest, as perhaps not most of their admirers do, Hugh's contempt was not more or less assumed. I was almost inclined to suspect in it, at times, an element of whimsical humour ; but if this was to any great extent really present, he kept his own counsel wonderfully.

again find myself treading the remembered path, which winds beside the shining river, it could scarcely be but that some ghost of the pleasant past would flit at times about the landscape, making sad for me its fairest sunshine.

I have, perhaps, a little unduly dwelt on this episodical topic of Hugh Macdonald; but somehow it pleased me to do so; and I allowed myself to take as my guide that idle instinct of pleasure, somewhat, it may be, to the detriment of my proper subject. Moreover, of Smith's life in Glasgow, Macdonald was really so large a part that, on looking back on these times, it is only by an effort of abstraction that I can disconnect the two men in imagination. Farther, his relations with Macdonald—who so loved him as a man, yet so consistently damned him, in good set terms, as a poet, the love being warmly reciprocated, and t'other thing good-humouredly set aside as of no importance whatever—give a curiously accurate, if slighty exaggerated, image of the easy terms on which, throughout, he lived with all who were so happy as to be intimate with him. Here, for once, was a Poet who did not, as a necessary condition of his friendship, insist you should admire his poetry;

who might be trusted not to like you any less if expressly you told him you disliked it, and would try to show him reason good.

In 1852, the " Life-Drama," in its completed form, was published by Mr Bogue of London, and its instant reception, by the critics alike and the public, might almost be called rapturous ; not since the morning on which Byron "woke and found himself famous," had such peals of applause been rung in honour of a youthful aspirant. The sins and shortcomings of the work were indeed on the face of it obvious, yet scarcely such as, in the eyes of a considerate critic, to weigh heavily against its merits. As Art, not much was to be said for it ; but it might well seem idle to criticise severely from this point of view a work so plainly announced as what it really was, a mere agglomeration to a great extent—as Heaven pleased, and the Poet could with pain contrive it—of certain masses of occasional poetry, independently conceived and executed. Admit, too—as even a kindly critic might not object to do, if asked—that beyond the Poet's aspiration after " Fame," and " divine despair," in contemplating it as unattainable ; the " first virgin passion of a soul com-

muning"* with so much of "the glorious universe" as opportunity had been given him to
observe ; the passion of love, for the most part as
passion *simpliciter*—a fierce confounding tumult
of soul and aching sense—rather than in its
tender mysteries, and those delicate gradations
of sentiment, in the subtle treatment of which
the poet attains a finer and more difficult success ; admit that, with exception of these things
and some crude occasional notions touching the
aims and functions of the art which he aspired
to practise, Mr Smith did not seem to have had
very much to write about when he set himself
to write the "Life-Drama." Admit this, and it
could not be held to amount to much, if admission had also to be made that, in treating of
these his inevitable subjects—no very bad ones
after all—the Poet exhibited true intellectual
mastery, a haunting sense of beauty as everywhere a "living presence ;" rare depth of emo-
tional tone, and such a rich full-flooding music,
as from these is naturally evolved. His special
predilection for the moon, stars, etc., it was
eminently easy to ridicule ; but, except for the
display of one's wit, it could scarcely seem

* Wordsworth.

worth while to do so, inasmuch as it is a sounder symptom in a poet to repeat frankly in his verse the things which he knows and loves than morbidly to seek for variety among things which he only imperfectly knows, and of which he cannot thus have the mastery which sincerity of emotion will imply. Of his fondness for figures and fine phrases, and tendency to accumulate them, like plums in a pudding, on the cook's principle that the more plums the better will be the pudding, clearly no sensible critic could feel called upon to speak very unkindly. A young poet shall as soon be got to sacrifice a flashy metaphor, as a wit to throttle his best *bon mot*, in sympathy with the feelings of a friend which the joke is certain to lacerate ; and the severer harmonies of style, when they come to a writer at all, are given him only as reward of a severe and persistent self-culture. In brief, such faults as those indicated might be recognised as incident, and indeed inevitable, to youth, and restrictions of opportunity and experience. Of a certain hankering after the charms of Cleopatra (afterwards by Aytoun so consummately quizzed), and tendency at times to some warmth of suggestive treatment, not much required to be said ; displeasing to some, it was rather refreshing to others (and these no mean judges), as a return to the robuster manner of the earlier day, and a relief from the over-squeamish refinements, which had somewhat tended, in purifying our poetry, to enfeeble it ; and, in any case, these *dulcia vitia* also—not in themselves excessive—as natural and proper to youth, might readily enough be forgiven to it.

Thus, for a while, it seemed ruled ; and the critics, with remarkable unanimity, merely hinting at faults which were obvious, concurred to celebrate the splendour of the poem in passages— the genuine power and passion displayed in it— the happy boldness of its abundant imagery—its frequent combination of strength and delicacy of expression, and the vein of real originality which was evident, underlying imitation as evident, now of this poet, now of the other. Glancing over a selection from these deliverances, which the publisher prefixed to his Second Edition, I find them highly curious reading, and not in their way uninstructive. The reflections they naturally suggest rather tend to take the form of a question as to what after all may be the worth of very much of our contemporary criticism. Did the critics and the public play the fool in these first raptures of delight; or was it *afterwards* they did so, in treating with depreciation and neglect by comparison, the distinctly better and more finished work which the Poet went on to give them? Or was it, perhaps, at *both* periods, and alike in their applause and their neglect, that they approved themselves incapable of a sane and discreet judgment? This last is the notion to which personally I am disposed to lean, as surmising that the truth in the matter is to be found, as usual, about half-way between the extremes of opinion indicated. The positive *furore* of applause and prophecy which greeted the poem on its appearance, was of the nature of irrational transport, some reaction from which might readily have been foreseen as inevitable.

> " These violent delights have violent ends,
> And in their triumph die."

And the reaction, when it came, was naturally as irrational and excessive as the first impulse of enthusiasm.

As to the "Life Drama,"—not to be ecstatic about it, as the critics were—it may very well at this date bear a reperusal. It is indeed

surprisingly *young* in parts, so as almost at
times to attain a fine, light, comic effect ; a good
deal of its showy imagery (which the critics
were so kind as to admire) an exact taste re-
jects as spurious ;* and a good deal more of
it, while striking and fairly to be admitted, is yet
not without some taint of the *bravura* business ;
much, however, remains which is thoroughly
genuine and noble, and, as such, will always,
I believe, be recognised by the competent in
such matters.   Over much of the book there is
clear impress of a passionate and peculiar mind ;
if oftentimes somewhat crude, the workmanship
is not seldom admirably finished and close in
texture ; and many passages might be indicated

---

* Take an instance, which has been admired, yet the artifice of
which becomes evident when we place beside it *the real thing:*—

> " More tremulous
> Than the soft star that in the azure east
> *Trembles with pity o'er bright bleeding day*
> Was his frail soul."

Compare Scott in "Rokeby," where *Bertram*—his mind over-
shadowed by prescience of violent doom—likens the exit he fore-
sees for himself to the setting of a tropic sun :

> "With disc, like battle-target, red
> He rushes to his burning bed ;
> Dyes the wild wave with *bloody* light,
> Then sinks at once, and all is night."

Or farther, Shakespeare—when by the same image he indicates

which, simply *as such*, may very well bear comparison with the best poetry of our time. Dismissing all questionable matter—the standard set up being as severe as you will—there remains from the book a not inconsiderable *residuum* of pure and beautiful poetry, some portion of which is perhaps even to be called *great*. (If some people who once thought it great, have now changed their minds about it, the poetry itself has not, I suppose, much changed). It might be held of good augury, that frequently, in condescending to be simple, the Poet attained his

---

the shudder of boding awe proper to the morn of Shrewsbury battle :—

> "How *bloodily* the sun begins to peer
> Above yon bosky hill ; *the day looks pale*
> At his distemperature."

In either case, more eminently in the last, there is grand imaginative suggestion ; emotion dominant brings together the disparates, and effects for them a true unity in the suggested emotion of the reader. In Smith's adaptation they are unified, if at all, only in a flash of barren surprise, instantly to fall asunder again. Moreover, such instant pleasure as there may be in the surprise, next instant the mind resents, as with a sense of having been—if only for the instant—*taken in.* And of this sort of thing, it is to be frankly admitted, there is somewhat too much in the "Life Drama." Nobody more frankly admitted this than Smith himself, when the book was scarce well out of his hands ; even then, it was curious and edifying to note how clearly in taste he had risen above it.

finest success. Here, for example, is a little piece, put into the lips of a dying girl, which I do not remember any where to have seen quoted, but which seems to me of rather superior merit:—

> " The callow young were huddling in the nests,
> The marigold was burning in the marsh,*
> Like a thing dipt in sunset, when he came.
>
> My blood went up to meet him on my face,
> Glad as a child that hears its father's step,
> And runs to meet him at the open porch.
>
> I gave him all my being, like a flower
> That flings its perfume on a vagrant breeze;
> A breeze that wanders on and heeds it not.
>
> His scorn is lying on my heart like snow,
> My eyes are weary, and I fain would sleep;
> The quietest sleep is underneath the ground.

* Of course, one very well knows whence this, in a sense, may have come :—

"The wild marsh marigold *shines like fire* in swamps and hollows grey."
        —*May Queen.*

"And at the root, through lush green grasses, *burned*
The red anemone."—*A Dream of Fair Women.*

But only think of a man wishing to perpetrate literary larceny, and hoping to escape detection, going for his plunder to Tennyson's "May Queen!" With the flower itself, the marsh marigold (or, Scottice, *lucken-gowan*), Smith, when he wrote this piece—about the last thing written of the "Life-Drama"—through Macdonald, if not otherwise—was nearly as familiar as he could be with the daisy or *gowan* proper.

C 2

Are ye around me, friends ? I cannot see—
I cannot hear the voices that I love,
I lift my hands to you from out the night!

Methought I felt a tear upon my cheek ;
Weep not, my mother! It is time to rest,
And I am very weary : so, good night !"

The point of view conceded which admits the thing as uttered—and almost no poetry is safe from a hard and literal criticism which would decline to concede it — surely this is highly successful. Exquisite is the art of contrast and just gradation with which the remembered flush of happy colour over the first verses, passing into chill and wintry bareness, subsides in the pale simplicities of death. Then the

" I lift my hands to you from out the night ! "

a line wonderful in its exceeding truth and mournfulness, its helpless pleading tenderness and depth of lonely doom! Farther, that "Weep not, my mother!" so touching, if its nice relations are caught with the previous,

"I cannot see—
I cannot hear the voices that I love ! "

The mists of death make dark the eyes ; already are the ears for ever shut from sound ; on the fading face there falls a tear, and the dim, sure instinct of love, outliving these decays of sense, recognises it as *a mother's;*—I should think it was not very unlikely to be. If there be not in this a particular subtle delicacy of simple and pathetic suggestion, worth a page or two of fine figures, my feeling in the matter is at fault. And throughout Smith's poetry, whoever does not find a good deal precisely of this class of merit, must simply be without the heart and the eye for it. But enough, and somewhat more than enough of criticism, at this time of day as good as idle, and, in any case, beside the present purpose.

How, meantime, did the youthful Poet comport himself with all this pother going on about him, and announcements reaching him from day to day that his "poems were in no respect inferior to those of the Laureate;" that he was "a finer poet than Keats in the very qualities in which Keats is finest;" "one whom we certainly believe to be the greatest poet Scotland has ever produced," etc., etc., etc. (some ten, or nearer twenty, pages of such matter might, if it seemed good, be quoted)? With a *sang froid* which might be held perfect; and so little like a man of Genius, one began to surmise that he might be so. Profoundly gratified, of course, he was; nor did he foolishly affect an indifference which, even had he really felt it, he would have been shrewd enough to be shy of expressing, as knowing it would not be believed in. Now, as always, his bearing was distinguished by a quiet and manly simplicity. Some little show of *elation* might here very well have been excused to him; but I should be surprised if any one could say he ever saw in him the smallest trace of such a thing. The theory of his conduct apart—to any one who knew him almost too absurd for even hypothetical statement—of a self-esteem so colossal, that it quietly absorbed, as no more than merely its due, the most extravagant incense that might be offered—there could be no better proof than it furnished of the essential strength, soundness, and solidity of his nature. The truth was—I before hinted as much—that already he stood considerably above his book, and the general ruck of its critics; at the more ecstatic flights of whom he did not the least object that you should pass on him a quiet jest or so. A perfect frankness in such matters he almost exacted from his friends—rather, in virtue of the beautiful candour, simplicity, and sweetness of the man's nature, such a frank way of treating him in such matters, for every one really his intimate became naturally the law of the case. Had I *thought*, as our admirable friend Hugh did, that he was " nae poet," it is, I fear, almost certain I would, some time or other, have *said* so to him ; and it is, at least, equally certain my criticism would have been received with much the same easy good humour with which he acquiesced in Macdonald's. Hence — as having often discussed it with him — in saying that nobody more sharply than its author could see the really vital defects of the " Life-Drama," even whilst the critics were clamouring their best and their worst applause over it, I say only what consists with my certain knowledge.

For the copyright of the book the Poet received from Mr Bogue £100, a sum which was afterwards supplemented according to the success of the work, as it ran through successive editions—to what precise extent I have forgotten, if ever I knew. £100! It is a small sum ; but to a young gentleman whose breeches' pocket thrills with it for the first time, it seems a considerable bit of money, with more good prospective spending in it than £1000 a year

or two after.   One's first £100 is somewhat like
one's first love, and is consecrated for ever in
memory, in connection with a good deal of folly
and rapture.   Of Smith's raptures with his first
£100, nobody could possibly know anything ; for
the reason that, except on paper to the public, he
never indicated rapture, or even the germ of a
capacity for it.   His folly, so far as I know of it,
amounted to this, that—a thing from the first
preordained and inevitable—he cut decisively
the pattern-designing concern—in which, to say
sooth, his forte did not greatly lie *—as surmising that literature, in one or the other form of
it, was marked out for him as his proper career ;
and farther, as second item, that his time being
thus at his own disposal, and the necessary funds
in hand, he considered a trip to London might
be allowable, taking the Lake or Wordsworth

---

* This I chance to know from a sure source, having had it
of one of his employers.   This gentleman, some time after,
along with another Glasgow friend of Smith's, I happened to
meet at an inn in the Highlands.   In the course of the evening
he fell into a state which I will tenderly call *communicative ;*
and my friend—well known in the West as a humorist—could
not resist the temptation to draw him out on the subject of
Smith and his poetry.   His *critique* of the "Life-Drama" was
exquisite, and curiously accordant with the opinion of some of
its later critics.   Of the Bard's designing talent (of which he

country on the way. On this little expedition he fared forth accordingly, accompanied by his friend, John Nichol (son of the then Professor Nichol, and now himself Professor of English Literature in Glasgow). Going by the Lakes, they visited Miss Martineau,* introduced by Nichol, senior—as naturally a little agog after anything in the shape of genius, were desirous,

---

might be admitted a better judge) he made so little, that he asserted the poetry had been written "*at my expense*, sir, every —— line of it." On the whole, it became pleasantly obvious that this worthy gentleman (he really was so, I believe, though, as I said, at the moment communicative) had for some years of his life been entertaining an Angel as entirely unawares as it is usual to entertain Angels. Of course, on the first opportunity, Smith was regaled with this little anecdote, and it seemed to delight him extremely.

* At Ambleside ; and here a rather ludicrous thing befell the Poet, who with much gusto retailed it. Miss Martineau, it is otherwise well known, is a little infirm of hearing. When the travellers arrived, several ladies were with her, and by the little circle of petticoats they were received with some *empressment*. Mr Nichol took up the running, and some little conversation proceeded, Smith, in the racing phrase, *waiting*. Presently he "came with a rush," and observed it "had been a very fine day"—an unimpeachable and excellent remark, which brought him instantly into "difficulties." Miss Martineau was at once on the *qui vive ;* the Poet had made a remark—probably instinct with fine genius, and worthy of the author of the "Life-Drama." "Would Mr Smith be so good as to repeat what he had said?" Mr Smith—looking, one need not doubt, uncommonly like an ass

through her, of making the acquaintance of
Charlotte Bronte, but found it could not be
done, the poor lady being in one of her dreadful
fits of hypochondriacal depression, so that no
intrusion on her could be ventured; *did* Festus
Bailey—to Smith an object of much interest—
somewhere in one or other of the Midland
Counties; and so to London, which they also
did, very much, I imagine, like any two other
young gentlemen of no particular genius *doing*
it for the first time. Naturally, on his return,
Smith had a good deal to speak about. St
Paul's he had seen, of course; the Abbey, with
its Poet's Corner, which, except for the deal of
good company in it, he thought an undesirable
place of residence; the theatres, Evans,' the Coal

—repeated it in somewhat a higher key. Alas! alas! in vain.
The old lady shook her head; "it was really *so* annoying, but
she did not quite catch it—would Mr Smith be *again* so good?"
and her hand was at her eager ear. The unhappy Bard, feeling,
as he said, in his distress, as if suicide might be the thing,
shrieked and again shrieked his little piece of information,
symptoms of ill-suppressed merriment becoming obvious around
him. Finally, the old lady's ear-trumpet was produced, and
proceeding to shriek through this instrument, of which the delicate use was unknown to him, the Bard nearly blew her head off.
She obtained, however, in this way, the piece of information she
wanted. Professor Nichol doubtless well remembers this; and
if in any little detail I err, I am liable to his correction.

Hole, and other such places of elegant evening recreation. Also, he had been thrown into the society of a good many interesting people. From Mr Lewes he had met with much kindness and attention ; of Mr Herbert Spencer, with whom he had come a good deal *en rapport*, he also spoke in terms of warm liking ; Mr Helps, with whom he spent a pleasant forenoon, wished to carry him off for a week or so to his place in some Shire forgotten, but he found himself unable to go. Various other such people he had met, and from his own very modest account, one surmised he had been made a little a Lion of. Mr Carlyle he had much wished to see—as then and always a very loyal admirer, though scarce at any time to be called a disciple—but somehow had failed to do so, and was not likely to think of violently intruding himself in the classic precincts at Chelsea. A Lion—as Mr Carlyle has frequently told us—is the most stupid of the beasts of the field, or more and more tends to become so ; but for one so quietly self-centred as Smith, the position was but little perilous. That on its one side, he found it unpleasant to be absurdly stared at, as if he were an animal in a cage, to be seen for the matter of sixpence, I

make no manner of doubt ; yet the thing had its
other and pleasant side ; it was plain that on the
whole he had thoroughly enjoyed his visit to the
great Babylon ; and more or less it could not
but be fruitful to him in various ways.

What may be held his chief exploit as a Lion
he executed soon after his return, in a visit of a
week or thereabout to Inverary Castle, as the
guest of the Duke of Argyle.   Burns, in his
earlier time, finding himself in company with an
amiable young nobleman, Lord Daer, felicitated
himself as on

> " A ne'er to be forgotten day—
> Sae far I sprachled up the brae
> I dinner'd wi' a Lord."

It seemed then for Burns a great honour doubtless ; to day it almost seems as if for Lord Daer,
of the two, the honour was distinctly the greater.
Whether or no Smith considered that the Duke*
did him great honour in inviting him to Inverary Castle, I could not undertake to say ; if

---

* It is a pity to spoil a point for a critic who may chance to
be in want of one; but I am really not here implying that Smith
was as great a genius as Burns, any more than that Lord Daer—
an amiable person, but never specially considered bright—had
he lived into this age of Science, could have written the " Reign
of Law."

so, it did not, at least, any way discompose him. In so far as he might really be a man of Genius— as to which there did not at that time seem to be any question—the only honour very obvious to myself in the matter, is that which the Duke did himself, in the exercise of his graceful courtesy.

With a very nice eye for the humorous side of things, here a little sharpened by contrast, the Poet, when he returned, was able to amuse us considerably ; but should I seek to amuse the reader with his notes of the Ducal *menage*, the proceeding would perhaps be reckoned somewhat too American. Not that there was anything whatever in them which might not quite frankly be printed. It is almost needless to say that, as guest of the Duke, he was treated with every courtesy, kindness, and attention. It is not from the *haute noblesse*, as a rule, that one need look for that species of more or less refined brutality, which, with so many of the uneasy class below, seems all they can ever know of good manners. On the whole, he had passed his time pleasantly. With Lord Dufferin—also a guest—as much about his own age, he was a good deal thrown together, and found him an affable and pleasant gentleman. That some time after this, Smith visited him at his seat in Ireland, might be held to indicate that the appreciation was more or less mutual.

Though "Fame" seemed thus in a manner to have come to him, beyond the bliss of his dreams, the immediate outlooks of the Poet were not now particulary brilliant. A man cannot live by bread alone ; and if he could, poetry of itself—even if rather successful—is not likely to procure him a sufficiency of it. To hack literature, if only it be honestly done, is a perfectly honourable occupation. So is the hacking of wood ; perhaps of the two the more to be desired for a person well thewed and sinewed. The former kind of labour seemed that predestined for Smith ; and, if I rightly remember, he was now for some little time engaged in editing a weekly literary Serial, under the auspices of Mr R. Buchanan, proprietor of the *Glasgow Sentinel,* and father of Mr Robert Buchanan, of whom the literary world has cognisance as a Poet, and otherwise. There did not seem any great life in the thing; and, indeed, an Archangel as its Editor, instead of the "Author of the 'Life-Drama,'" would scarcely in Glasgow have ensured for such a thing success. Consequently when, in 1854, the post of Secretary to the Edinburgh University became vacant, and it was suggested from that quarter that it might very well suit Smith, the suggestion seemed a highly sensible one, and he became, accordingly, a candidate. For any little place of the kind, the competitors in these days are numerous; even in regard of Literature, more than one of those pitted against him had very considerable claims; and the contest was somewhat a keen one. It was, however, decided in his favour, a good deal—it is only proper to say—through the influence of the then Lord Provost of Edinburgh, Mr Duncan M'Laren, now M.P. for the City. Of all men I have ever known, Smith was, perhaps, the stillest in external procedure; and he took his-success very coolly. To myself, as to his other Glasgow friends, the matter was occasion of some anxiety; as to himself, without doubt it must have been. On the afternoon of the day of election, I called on him, saying, as I entered, "Well, have you heard? —how is it?" "All right!" he answered, looking up, with an air of impassivity as entire as if the matter were of no personal concernment to him— "I heard about half an hour ago; suppose we go

and do a quiet pipe over it!" This we proceeded
to *do;* and such little details as had reached him
were, through that easy medium, communicated.

In leaving Glasgow for Edinburgh, Smith undoubtedly made a change for the better, as
regarded the influences bearing on his mental
culture and development. Not that Glasgow
was by any means the intellectual Bœotia some
people are disposed to suspect it. Cotton bags
indeed abounded; but even your cotton bag, if
you moisten it to the due pitch, will surprise
you, from time to time, by developing some
gleam of human intelligence; and there were
others by no means cotton bags, if a little immersed in the article. The mildly Bohemian
circle, which the reader had a little peep into,
in making the acquaintance of Macdonald,
included men of sound and cultivated intelligence, with keen literary interests; humorists
of a somewhat rare quality; and two really profound metaphysicians, whose conversation would
have been most instructive, if one could only
have understood a word of it. But so *deep* were
these good fellows, that, for my own poor part,
I never could. This naturally made their conversation for a time amusing, though it was

possible to have too much of it. Of men more formally accredited in the intellectual way, Smith also knew several; notably, Professor Nichol, from whom he met with much kindness, and in whom he had a specimen of an unusually fine and finished talker, somewhat different in type from Macdonald. Some of the other professors, I rather think, he also knew. At least, I remember his dining with one or other of them at College, to meet Mr Ruskin, then in Glagow.*

Still, though Glasgow was thus not wholly a

---

* Of a certain passage at this learned feast, Smith—as his way was—gave a rather amusing account. To do honour to the great Art-critic, as much as the City could furnish of ponderous erudition, and stupidity of the finished intellectual kind, had carefully been got together. The concourse of Wigs was formidable. Later in life, Smith for a wig *per se* had as little reverence as most men—as aware that, not seldom, precisely proportioned to the bigness and fuzziness of the wig, is the depth of the vacuity behind it ; but as yet he was raw and inexperienced ; had not seen many Wigs of the Academic kind, and only dimly began to guess at that invaluable point of knowledge. If a man was a professor of Hebrew, his innocent notion was, he' was to be looked at with religious awe, as knowing a supernatural deal of the Old Testament, and of nearly everything else. Such is the ingenuous credulity of youth. As the least thing afraid of his company, he kept himself pretty quiet ; but a Lion cannot with decency sit for hours, and be only stared at ; it is tacitly a part of the bargain that, for his victual and liquor consumed, he is to *roar*, if only a little. The conversation turning on Art, and

desert for him, Edinburgh was unquestionably
the fitter place ; and shortly he migrated thither.
His situation as College Secretary might also
be held fairly suitable ; and his getting it just
when he did, a clear hit of good luck for him.
In a money point of view the thing could not be
held great, the salary amounting to £150. It is
a modest sum ; but one has to scribble a good
deal at per page before netting it ; and for
Smith's very simple needs, so long as he remained
unmarried, it might be reckoned reasonably suf-

---

particularly on Mr Millais' "Order of Release," he remarked to
the Philosopher next him, that the face of the woman in it
seemed to him a triumph of complex expression, in the inter-
blending of at least *three* distinct emotions. Mr Ruskin, who
sat opposite, snapped him up on the instant—".Would you
be good enough to let us know *distinctly*, Mr Smith, *what* are
these three emotions you speak of ?" Mr Smith did not in the
least *distinctly* know *what* they were ; and here, much to his
disgust, he found himself committed to a formal and elaborate
exposition of them before this very learned audience, who hushed
themselves duly to listen. "An' what did ye mak' o't, Sandy ?"
asked Macdonald. "Mak' o't !" he answered—the irritation of
remembered discomfiture dissolved in his own amusement at it.
"I made an ass of myself, of course." "I doot na that,
Sandy !" observed his friend. "But what just was't ye *said*,
man !" Of what he *said* Smith could give but poor account ;
but he was clear as to what he *thought*, as he went on with his
broken-kneed deliverance ; and it amounted pretty frankly to
this, that he wished Mr Ruskin at the devil.

ficient. Such as it was, it gave him just what was
desirable—a sound basis for his farther literary
procedure, making him free to write genially
the thing he *would*, not painfully the thing he
must. The duties could not be held excessive.
Personal presence at the College was required
from ten till four; and given throughout, with
what certain of his friends were even disposed to
quiz at times, as a too nice, scrupulous, and essentially *unpoetical* regularity. What—it would
be urged—could in reason be expected of his
next book, if, in the process of writing it, he
did not neglect his duties a little? At certain
seasons—the beginning and end of the Session
more particularly—there was really hard work
of somewhat a harassing character; and at other
times, when the work was in itself not much,
there was constant liability to interruption, so
that the time not employed in work was yet
murdered as leisure available for any serious
work of his own. And in fact, at the College,
he found that little such work could be done,
his evenings only being thus disposable to any
good literary purpose. But, on the whole, the
position was a fairly fortunate one; and as such,
on the whole, he considered it.

D 2

In visiting Edinburgh—as one frequently did—I found him, as it seemed to me, very happily situated, and the centre of a most pleasant circle of friends, chiefly men of somewhat the same age, whose aspirations were like his own, towards Literature, and some of whom have since done considerable things in it; with an Advocate or two, and a sprinkling of Artists, the society of whom he always rather specially affected. Once or twice I went with him to the "Raleigh Club" (so called in honour of Sir Walter, the introducer of the fragrant weed), a weekly meeting of such his intimates, with some pretext of an intellectual aim, in the reading of an occasional paper or so, but obviously convened in the main for good, honest, social purposes of the pipe and the modest tumbler. Of this exceedingly agreeable *reunion*, I rather think, he was in some sort to be reckoned the founder. With every one—as indeed it could scarce be otherwise—he was plainly an immense favourite; and on this side of his society—his "little Bohemia," as we may call it,—he could nowhere have been more fortunate. As to his relations at this time with Society, in the more formal and accepted sense, I really do not know anything. I should think it not very improbable that, on his first coming to the place, people asked him a good deal to dinner to look at him as the " Author of the ' Life-Drama.' "

During the winter of 1854, Mr Sydney Dobell, author of " The Roman," and " Balder," came to reside in Edinburgh. Naturally the two Poets were drawn together ; and whilst Dobell remained, they were united in a very close and affectionate friendship, one fruit of which next year came before the world in their little joint issue of Sonnets on the Crimean War. It is throughout—if I rightly remember—a little infested with the really very dreadful heresy that any rhymed thing in fourteen lines is entitled to call itself a " Sonnet ;" but otherwise, might be held to fairly maintain, if it could not greatly add to, the reputation of the two writers. In connection with this work, a little anecdote may be here inserted, not much in itself, yet with some slight savour of amusement in it. Simultaneous with the appearance of these " Sonnets on the War," was that of certain War-vessels in the Firth ; and the whole population of Edinburgh rushed to see them ; a visit to the Men-of-war was in fact the fashionable order of the day. Smith, chancing to be at an evening party at the house of an eminent Publisher, found himself standing beside this gentleman. Some sort of strumming of a piano, or squall of song, was in progress, making conversation, as a relief from it, at once imperative and difficult; and it occurred to him to ask his friend: "Had he yet paid a visit to the War-ships?" The Publisher looked at him for an instant with somewhat a puzzled eye; then answered, with grave *empressment*, "Yes; *and I think they'll add greatly to your Fame!*" The play of cross purposes tickled the poor bard extremely; he had not the heart to annoy his host by a protest against his absurd, though innocent, blunder; but was content to remain under the imputation of being, as he phrased it, "a fool who was fishing for a compliment."

In the Spring of 1857 occurred what was properly the one event of his necessarily somewhat monotonous life, after he went to Edinburgh—his marriage, which was altogether a happy one, as that of some poets has not been. The lady he married was a Miss Flora Macdonald, from Skye, eldest daughter of Mr Macdonald of Ord, and nearly akin by blood to the historic heroine of that name. Within some year or two after, he moved to a pleasant villa at Wardie, near Granton. There he thenceforth lived ; there he died ; and there it is that his friends best love to remember him. Not one of his pretty wide circle of allies but had always hearty welcome of an evening there, even if, as it might chance—by reason of some stress of work—his coming was a little inopportune. For his literary work he had a true love on its own account ; and when, in his later years, the call of duty was superadded, it became " stuff o' the conscience" with him. But scrupulous as his conscience was as to dereliction in that kind, it would have pinched him still more dreadfully had he told a poor fellow to be off, who had quietly dropped in to have a comfortable talk and a pipe with him. Of this form of hideous social barbarity he was never once known to be guilty, sorely as he must at times have been tempted to it. That most savoury of all viands, known as Pot-luck, was always kept warm on the premises ; and in some more regular, though pleasantly informal fashion, he dearly delighted, as occasion served, to dispense his modest hospitalities. Three or four of the select—not any

larger number—a cosy bit of supper, or of
dinner, if the whole evening could be spared—
for we seldom went off very early from that
establishment — this was, I think, his very
choicest form of rest from a little spell of over-
exertion. The solids despatched, and such
little interval elapsed as courtesy to the lady
or ladies—if there chanced to be a plurality—
seemed inevitably to suggest, a move would be
made to the Poet's little study. Pipes would be
lit ; the spirit-case being on the table, and a
kettle singing its syren suggestions close by,
the inference of toddy is obvious; and the
tumbler being duly mixed, the business of the
evening would commence, which was good,
hearty, careless talk, frequently of a dreadfully
unintellectual character. As a man of strong
sense, Smith had but slight relish for what is
called intellectual conversation ; in fact, the one
kind of person to whom he had serious objection was the blockhead, who, at great length,
insisted on devolving wisdom upon him. Moreover, *this* was strictly to be held *A*-musement—
away as far as possible from the Muses, of
whose delightful society he had got for the time
a little sick or so. Sunk in his easy chair, the

Poet would placidly sit, beaming on his friends
a quiet kindliness, and vomiting volumes of
smoke upon them—not for the most part himself very greatly caring to talk, but simply
dropping into the conversation from time to time
some pertinence of sense or humour, and plainly
with his whole soul lapped in easy, indolent
delight. Thus pleasantly the hours would fleet,
and unawares the evening would be over. It is
almost needless to say that in these, as in other
matters, his excellent wife (though necessarily
excluded from the smoking) always went heartily
with him. I have said she came from Skye.
To the bagpipe the over-refined ear may object ;
a nice taste may decry the kilt, if it will, as a
somewhat too airy costume ; but when any
shock of steel might be in question, it has never
yet been known to decline it, and the name of
Highlander is almost a synonym for a warm
and exuberant hospitality.

These are pleasant memories, if also now necessarily sad ones, inasmuch as over the remembered blameless satisfactions, the stern *fuerunt*
must be written. They *were;* and whilst Time
may roll for us its idle round, they cannot any
more be. It would be very pleasant if they

could renew themselves like the floral year ; but, in point of fact, they cannot, and there an end. To the most obstinate *Encore* of the heart, in such a matter, the Destinies, unhappily or happily—who can ever know which?—are as deaf as the dead we would fain recall.

From this time forward Smith's Biography resolves itself pretty much into this—the appearance of his books before the public ; the emergence in his pleasant home at Wardie of a series of little baby faces, dearly welcomed, as the reader may suppose. Daily, with dreadful regularity, he paced his way up to College ; despatched what might chance to be his work there ; and, with a regularity perhaps a little less positively dreadful, paced his meditative way home again. In the evening, what literary work might be on hand would be gone in upon, subject always, as hinted, to interruptions of the social good-fellow or fiend, who, dropping idly in to kill his own evening, might now and then kill the Poet's. In August, he had a clear month of holiday ; and almost always he passed it in Skye, with his wife's relations—the whole household making joyous migration thither. His love for the misty Island was intense. Its grand scenery profoundly impressed his imagination. The primitive modes of life, and the lingering of the old patriarchal relations—nearly everywhere else now as good as extinct—were matter to him of unfailing interest and amusement. Dearly loving Skye as he did, there, as elsewhere, he was much beloved; and, I doubt not, many an honest Celtic heart was sad—of shepherds and fellows about the hills—when they heard that their "fery coot friend Mr Smuth" was never more to appear among them. It may interest his admirers to know that once at Broadford fair—which he always made a point of attending, though not wanting to purchase any sheep there —he did battle with an obnoxious drover, and, so far as I could ever learn, acquitted himself so as to impress on the countenance of his antagonist, and on the Celtic mind generally, a fair notion of the prowess of the "Sassenach." Of this exceptional exploit he was not so proud as he ought to have been; but surely it does him nothing but honour. Eminently a man of peace as he was, it always seemed to me to indicate a particular versatility of genius I should scarcely have been disposed to expect in him. A squeamish biographer would suppress a little trait of this kind; but *why*, in the name of common sense? Smith's life, as every man who knew him knew, was one of quite *exceptional* discretion and correctness, challenging the severest rigour of scrutiny. If *once*, and probably under provocation—

> "Yet surely Cassio, I believe, received
> From him that fled some strange indignity
> Which patience could not pass,"—

he showed a pugnacity strange to him, where is the mighty harm? Moreover, he had good Academic precedent for it. On two occasions—once at Hawick, and again at Tomintoul in the north—it stands recorded that Professor Wilson, in his practical capacity as teacher of the Moral Sciences, taking off his coat in the market place, proceeded to admonish a miscreant, some point of whose conduct seemed, to his nicer sense, to outrage the Immutable Fitness of Things. And surely what is permitted to a Professor of a University may be excused to its emulous Secretary.

In 1857 the "City Poems" were issued by Messrs Macmillan & Co., of Cambridge; and though eminently deserving success, they failed to find it with the public. For this there might be reasons not proper to the book itself, at which it may be well to glance. Though for a while nothing was heard but loud-mouthed applause of the "Life-Drama," the very excess of the eulogy made certain some little protest against it, and presently the work was subjected in one or two quarters to a tolerably trenchant criticism. Certain other attacks followed from time to time, which, so far as they dealt fairly —no matter how severely—with the real defects of the book, was really quite as it should be ; and we very soon found that the Poet took his pain with much the same easy equanimity he displayed in relation to the sweet of the business. Not that he dissembled his pain, or professed it a form of pleasure ; he was incapable of these stupid affectations ; and as regarded praise and censure, always very frankly confessed that, of the two, he found the first the more agreeable. But as the first could not idly elevate, neither could the other depress him—disturb his serene good humour, or for a single instant betray him into exhibition of anything like small irritation. This admirable balance and serenity in such matters was one of his most curious traits ; nor could I ever quite make out how he came by it, being, as he was, a man profoundly humane, to whom the judgments of his fellow men could never be matter of indifference, and withal—his still ways notwithstanding—of exquisitely sensitive fibre. A stern and haughty self-opinion, and—as holding of this in a measure—a certain cynical depth of world-embracing scorn, might no doubt effect something of the same result; but an inhuman attitude of this kind was not in the least in Smith's way.

From such criticism as that spoken of—intelligent as well as severe—nobody could be more capable of profiting than Smith; and seeing it could not irritate him, I should suppose it may have done him good, in so far as in way of corrective he *needed* it, which he never seemed at all to do. And neither in amount, nor in vigour of virulence, was it such as to harm him with the general public. The case was, however, somewhat otherwise, when, first in "Blackwood," and afterwards in the finished "Firmilian," Professor Aytoun perpetrated his consummate quiz of what he called "The Spasmodic School" of Poetry, whereof Smith and Dobell were gibbeted as the chiefs. "Firmilian" is a work in which Parody attains the positive rank of genius; and, tickling the public extremely, it really proved

for its victims, in some sort, a shot between wind
and water, so to speak. It turned the laugh
against them ; and though ridicule is no more
the test of Poetry than of Truth, it is always an
effective weapon with a public which, above
everything, desires to be amused, and commonly
for its likings and dislikings, has no more basis
of reason than if it were a huge Quadruped.
Moreover, the nickname "Spasmodic" prospered
in the world ; it *stuck;* and a patch upon one's
nose of this kind is always a point of peril in
addressing serious remarks to an audience. The
epithet did not originate with Aytoun, who
merely "conveyed" it from Carlyle, who had
used it with his wonted felicity to characterise
the Byronic *œstros.* The critics and the public
caught eagerly at the phrase ; it passed into
current use ; and, in fact, it is, at this very day,
going about alive and well. But, as used by
nine in ten people, it had never very much more
intelligence behind it than the "Pretty Poll" of
the parrot.

By a true master in the art critical, this phrase,
as I said, was first applied to Byron. Like most
phrases from that mint, *as* so applied, it has
felicity and close pertinence ; yet, when every

just deduction is made, Byron does not the less survive as one of our "prevailing Poets;" a spiritual potentate, whose power is nowhere expressed in adequate or perfect forms, but precisely for this very reason, remains a portent and a marvel. This, of itself, might suggest that the true question can never be, whether or no a particular Poetry is "Spasmodic;" but solely whether or no it is *good* "Spasmodic Poetry." Poetry may be as Spasmodic as you will, yet not the less include, like that of Byron, very genuine and noble elements. What, as exactly defined, really *is* "Spasmodic Poetry?"—the Poetry of unrest and despair; of irregular struggle; of baffled effort, wild, bewildered, and mistaken—the Poetry, in one word, of *Scepticism*, not cool in the intellect, as Hume's, but raging, like mutiny of passion in the blood, with the whole perverted might of the heart and the moral emotions. As such, who will may denounce it; but it will be best not to do so without being fully aware that, in so doing, you *expunge* very much of the noblest Poetry of the world. It would be almost stupid to cite an array of instances; Goethe's "Faust" is by nearly common consent the grandest of modern Poems; and precisely because it vibrates

and thrills throughout with very passion of
spasmodic agony. Hamlet, again—to.take an
older instance—is, for any one who can trace in
the least the workings of the Hero's mind—his
doubt, his hesitancy, and delay; the fierce, im-
patient spurts of passionate resolve with which he
compensates his conscience for them ; the abor-
tiveness of these as quenched in the dull miasma
of inevitably recurring doubt—may stand as the
very type of that decried thing, a "Spasmodic
Poem." Scepticism does not indeed, as yet,
appear in it, in fierce modern guise, as active
mutiny; it could not then possibly do so ; but
whoso does not see in it distinct premonition of
this—the first slow drops of the thunder-shower
which since has so deluged the world—has really
not read the Poem, and may just as well shut up
his Shakespeare, and never again open it. It is
not to be denied that a certain class of readers
shrink from Poetry of this class with a very
strong distaste.* The amusing thing is—there is
almost, a comic element in it—they seem to

---

* See the amusing remarks of Sir James Mackintosh on the
"Faust." Shudders are his only criticism. His emotions of
terror seem much as if some day, in the street, .he had found
himself charged by a mad dog.

consider their attitude in so doing a pious one ; whereas it is essentially, as often as not, one of Fear, and not of Faith. To readers, again, of another class, it is the Poetry, of all others, which has profound and enthralling interest.

As to the license permitted to the Poet in his choice and treatment of this class of subject— dark disorder of the heart and brain, and of the issues of life which are out of these—this is greatly too big a subject to be here at all touched with effect. But suppose his wild material granted him to work in—what then ? Poetry is in strictness to be defined as a form of *life*, in which, as in other forms of it, the inner spirit, and the matter in which it is revealed, are properly to be considered as one. By the same law which makes the human face significant of emotion, and, if we had only wit to read it, a manual of character, and severely expressive record of every lightest shade of feeling which has ever flitted over it, the varying music of the Poet is, in every least capricious turn of it, expressive of some determining peculiarity in the shaping ideas and emotion. If, therefore, here, as elsewhere, " Soul is form, and doth the body make,"* and the peculiarities of poetical execution are determined by a peculiarity presupposed in the subject and conception itself, it will follow, of course, that if a Poem be boldly Spasmodic in its main motives, it will scarce be much worth as a Poem if it does not, in the technic of detail, afford some significant reflex of *spasm.* In delineating the blind strivings of a great soul, wildly disordered and at war with itself, shall the Poet discourse you such dulcet strains as might be proper to a shepherd of Arcady piping to his shepherdess on a flowery hill? There be they who would perhaps exact this; yet, contrariwise, it might rather seem that, in the detail of the poetical execution of a work, Spasmodic by its very conception, as dealing with lawless and ungoverned moods of mind, some sub-insinuation of excess and misrule is not only to be excused, but demanded, as the fit and necessary reflex of the originating ideas and emotions. And only when excess itself becomes, as such, excessive, refusing to be rounded in, and subordinated by the poetical form and the larger harmonies of Art, is the

---

* Spenser—" Hymn to Beauty."

E 2

work to be rightly censured, as, in the *baser*
sense, Spasmodic, and ceasing, in fact, to be
Poetry. The question is thus always to be
asked in regard of such a piece as the "Life-
Drama," Mr Dobell's " Balder," and other justly
so-called "Spasmodic Poems," how much that
seems violent and excessive in them is yet to
be justified as simple and proper reflex of
Spasmodic subject, at once truly expressive of
mental state, and subtly commended to feeling
by the reconcilement of the musical form—how
much is to be stigmatised as excessive under
conditions of excess — what in the book is
Poetry, in fact, as result of a truly *imaginative*
mastery of the wild mood—what sheer violence
of failure, betokening want of such mastery, and
wilful, irregular action in the mind of the writer
himself, as under tyranny of the mood, and thus
incapable of translating it for us into forms of
clear art? And it is simply mere ignorance to
pooh-pooh such Poetry as "Spasmodic," and
there an end ; seeing it may very well be Spasmodic, and yet justly and nobly so, as much in
the "Life-Drama" *is ;* much also in the Poem
of Mr Dobell ; while in both there may be
something to be set aside as Spasmodic in the

wilful and bad sense. Such considerations did not, however, disturb the public in the new turn that things had taken ; the word had no meaning for it except as associated with Aytoun's delightfully ludicrous Parodies ; and to call a writer "Spasmodic" was to dispose of his claim as Poet, and simply laugh him out of court. I do not think any one more heartily than Smith himself—with his abundant sense of humour—joined in Aytoun's laugh at his expense, and that of his friends ; and accordingly, when he and the Professor came together— as Mr Martin in his "Life" has noted—it was into terms of very cordial kindness on both sides that their intercourse speedily resolved itself.

In aid of this little reaction which had thus set in,—just before the publication of the "City Poems," came a serious impeachment of him, as throughout no more than the merest Plagiary, in a very ably-conducted and influential Literary Journal ; and when his new Book appeared, the charge was, in regard of it, renewed. The attack upon the "Life-Drama" Smith took, to all appearance, with his usual imperturbable good-humour. It brought him, I remember, a very

kind and beautiful letter from his friend Mr
Helps, not of condolence, but encouragement,
in case such a thing might be needed; written
pretty much as an elder brother might have
written it; and the receipt of which seemed to
give him more pleasure than the wound could
cause him pain, as salve of which it was intended. One phrase of it clings to my memory,
to effect, that "really, if people at all were
critics, they should be able to distinguish between the man who *conquers*, and the man who
steals." When, however, the attack was renewed upon the "City Poems," and re-renewed,
for the first and only time I ever knew, or
could surmise it in him, he *did* indicate serious
irritation. It was not that for the thing in itself,
as before his peers, he greatly cared; but he
very sharply saw that such a charge—if at all
held substantiated—tended to damage him with
the general public, and, prospectively, to touch
his pocket.   .

> "Who steals my purse steals trash, etc.,
> But he who filches from me my good name," etc.

It is the peculiarity of literary "good name,"
more than of other kinds of it, that to filch from

a man any of it is directly to operate upon his purse ; and as to the purse being " trash," which whoso will may steal, and welcome, this was a height of philosophic elevation to which, if Smith—as a man of narrow income, just married —found himself unable to soar, I hope it may not be accounted sin to him. His annoyance was, however, transient ; and throughout he had the comfort of finding himself tolerably well defended. A little paper on the subject by the facetious *Mr Punch*—for which I should suppose him indebted to Mr Shirley Brooks—was really a complete *reductio ad absurdum* of the charge, as made. Mr Lewes, then editing the *Leader*, from the more serious point of view, very generously and ably defended him ; and, no doubt, there were others who drew the quill effectively in his behalf. Still, beyond question, a very considerable effect to his disfavour was produced ; with results more or less feelingly known to Mr Macmillan, who had given £200 for the Book. Nor at this need one be much surprised ; for the evidence produced against him—however little, when analysed, it could weigh with any competent person—was really in *mass*, at first sight, formidable and startling. And the first effect is everything for many readers ; not caring to examine farther, and if they did, disqualified by ignorance from arriving, without assistance, at true views of any such matter. The truth was, that not a few of the passages cited were *really reminiscent* of things in the Poet's reading, lingering in some blind corner of the brain, and reproduced *bona fide* as his own, in virtue of a memory at once tenacious and treacherous ; and there is simply no poet whatever in whom instances of the like may not be found. The great mass of the things produced were in themselves quite too frivolous ; but at times, in order to see *how* frivolous, a little care was needed ; and if this was not given, the whole being indolently glanced over in the light of these *undeniable* cases of obligation, the effect, as regarded Smith, might very well be somewhat damaging. But while there seemed no reason to question the perfect *bona fides* of the writer, his laboured demonstration was, for any reader of care and competence, even curiously without result. Though quite without desire to resuscitate extinct literary squabbles, I may as well try, in some more formal way, to show this ; the subject being in itself a somewhat curious one, and not without interest.* Here, meantime, it is enough to say, that though the work was in many quarters very favourably noticed, it could scarcely be said to *succeed;* the enthusiasm excited by the "Life-Drama" was gone, and not to be recalled.

Whatever the causes of this, they could scarcely be said to lie in the Book itself, which indicates, as compared with the first work, a clear advance in the writer. For one thing, if "Spasmodic Poetry" be objectionable, *here*, at least, there was little, if anything, to be termed, without the merest absurdity, Spasmodic. The youthful heat and unrest are allayed ; the whole tone of the book is milder, calmer, wiser ; only in an occasional tone of meditative melancholy is there the least reminiscence of the old fever of discontent. As holding of this mellowed feeling, there is a riper and purer finish ; the clear type of individual style, with still some occasional trace of imitation, is much more consistently maintained ; there is greater refinement of thoughtful analysis, a subtler interpretation of nature, together with extended observation of

---

* See Appendix.

it, as also of the facts of life. In particular, the
fine lyric, "Glasgow," marked the point of improvement reached, and compelled the praise of
critics not otherwise specially disposed to praise.
But the public, it appeared, would not *buy* as
before ; the tide which came in so sweepingly
had turned, and was now running out ; with just
about as much reason in the phenomenon as
may go to the ebbing of waters. That "mis-
cellaneous rabble" (the phrase is Milton's) called
the "people," or public, is little at any time but
a rush of uncomprehending sheep—

> " They praise, and they admire, they know not what,
>   And know not whom, *but as one leads the other.*" *

Their ignorance on all matters relating to finer
culture is so total, that they are not even aware
of it. Hence their giddy judgments ; their helpless instability in opinions come at by hap-
hazard ; the absurd way in which they go a-
gadding after a new thing, and then go a-gad-
ding away from it ; so that their praise and their
censure are alike worthless, and they are never
in the right but by accident.

My reference to Mr Helps' letter may have

---

* " Paradise Regained."

suggested that common source of interest in a literary biography supplied by the author's correspondence. In this case it is necessarily absent. A diligent search in the Poet's repositories has been rewarded by only *one* letter. It is from Mr Rarey, the American horse-tamer, enclosing tickets to admit to the subjugation of some local " Cruiser," and begging, "in the name of the Great American People " (among whom, by the way, Smith's works were always more widely circulated than at home), to express his gratitude, admiration, etc. Something, I suppose, in the slight magniloquence of its terms must have tickled the Poet a little, and led to its preservation, in the disappearance of more important, if perhaps less amusing, documents— as notably this letter of Mr Helps ; one which he had from Mr Tennyson, of a very pleasant and cordial character ; the like from Mr Aubrey de Vere—and what others such I know not, though doubtless various such others there must have been. Recognition of this clearly *a laudato* kind always much gratified him, as no anonymous notice could ; and with frank pleasure he would show the things to such of his friends as he thought they would be likely to interest.

That he should not have thought of preserving them may be noted as a point of idiosyncrasy in him, befitting his simple character. Another point of idiosyncrasy must, however, be noted of him, in regard of such things, of a much more dreadful nature. He was almost sure *never to answer them.* In *two* of the three cases above, to my certain knowledge, no answer was returned ; and it would almost surprise me to learn that compliment had been vouchsafed in the third. Savage incivility, the reader, of course, thinks to himself—and yet in his tenderness and just nicety of feeling, the man of anything like wilful discourtesy was as incapable as of wilful murder. That being of this strain, he should have received such courteous, volunteered communications ; been truly gratified by receipt of them, showing them to a friend, mayhap, with undissembled satisfaction ; yet habitually (I am dreadfully afraid it was so) have neglected even simple acknowledgment, does seem really strange —one of those odd incongruities which so often puzzle us in character. From my knowledge of him, I partly to myself account for the oddity thus : As a matter of course, intending immediate answer, he yet did not quite know how to set about it—disliked the complimentary *phrase-making*, and suspicion of the *claw me, claw thee*, which tends a little to beset correspondence of this particular kind—consequently, put it off to be done "to-morrow," oblivious of the obvious wisdom that duties to be done to-morrow are not unlikely to impeach us at the day of judgment as duties not at all done. The document would thus be allowed to crumble indefinitely about his pockets, his intentions being all the while most virtuous; finally, with a certain *insouciance* natural to him, he would some day light his pipe with it, in defect of non-literary material, and the *corpus delicti*—so to call it—being thus vanished, all hope in the matter was over. His dereliction would continue, however, to distress him not a little, so that he especially detested reference to it by any friend aware of the facts, and disposed, for his good, to rally him on the subject. So much for whom it may concern: it has seemed to me a point to be explained.

As naturally suggested by this matter, admission may also be made in him of a certain carelessness, indifference—or what might very well seem such—in the conduct of his social relations otherwise. He was by no means very careful to *cultivate* people, and would drop somewhat too readily out of the acquaintance even of those—not chancing to come actually in contact with him—who had been at express pains to show him goodwill and kindness. Not that his memory was ever liable to fail him on that side; but the past he did not seek, as he might have done, to reproduce in the present. Neither should I suppose him ever to have been specially eager to rush with his acknowledgments to admirers, for their kindness in expressing admiration of him. As to all this he somewhat failed; he failed, that is, precisely where the courtesies of life are terribly apt to corrupt themselves into the questionable arts of the provident literary gentleman. These are sufficiently understood; any poor blockhead who will may practise them; and doing so with sufficient diligence and astuteness, he may hold himself an ill-used man, if some time, and for some ten days of his life, he is not recognised as a Genius. Of all this sort of thing Smith had an honourable scorn; and as deep in his quiet nature there was a vein of impracticable pride, he held himself utterly aloof from it. That in doing so he drew his line accurately—it is a very fine line to draw—in common with others of his friends, I do not quite think. Gratitude has been defined an " acute sense of favours to come." A good deal of what passes for gratitude, of course, is so; yet the genuine article , exists, and may now and then be expressed, without any compromise of character. So of the other virtues; each of them has some vile impostor at its heels, in their deadly dislike of which honest people have been known, at times, to forget their fealty to the real thing.

A little disappointed perhaps—but not disheartened, or moved any jot from the cheerful tenor of his way — by the reception of the " City Poems," Smith was now quietly at work on his " Edwin of Deira." He chose the subject thoughtfully, as knowing that his besetting sin was a certain unstrictness and vagrancy—so call it—a want of severity in the outline of substantial forms—and seeking without in the defined Historic framework some supplement of the deficiency within. (In this I simply in effect repeat what I remember to have heard him say.) In 1861 the Book was published, again by Messrs Macmillan & Co.; and on the whole it

may be said to have been tolerably well received, a second edition being within a reasonable time called for.   But it failed to reinstate
the Poet in his old place with either critics or
public.   In one respect it must be held to have
been one of the most unfortunate of books.
Written in great part *before* Tennyson's " Idyls
of the King " (I myself had seen at least half of
it in MS., if not absolutely before Tennyson's
work was talked of, certainly before any hint of
its precise nature had reached the public, and
there are perhaps some three or four people in
Edinburgh who could in this corroborate me), it
was published some time *after* it.   Not only did
it thus challenge a comparison with that masterpiece, but the inference was obvious and *fair*, of
direct *imitation ;* and the hands of the detrac-
tors were strengthened who had more lately
been saying he could do nothing distinctively
his own, but only more or less cleverly follow
where cleverer fellows had led.   This was simply
of the nature of *misfortune* for him ; and as
such, providentially sent him, he accepted it with
his admirable quietude, not needlessly kicking
against the pricks, yet not the less, doubtless,
in his soul, cursing it a little as true misfortune.

With Tennyson's consummate work, only an injudicious admirer will think of comparing "Edwin;" but Smith runs him perhaps a fair second; and I do not doubt the book would have done better, had the public got it, as in much written, *before* Tennyson's, not *after*. To say sooth, the material seems, in parts, but imperfectly mastered; yet the effect is on the whole fine, and the book abounds in passages of beautiful, and sometimes noble, poetry. Moreover, apart from substantive success, the truth and height of aim are, by comparison, to be recognised; and on the whole perhaps *advance* is again to be noted. But the Poet's victory—if such to be held—was like one of Napoleon's *later* victories—as at Bautzen, where the great Captain, having driven his foes from the field, had to cry, in passionate disgust, "What! no prisoners! no guns! no *results!*" The *net* result here to Smith on the system of half profits — now adopted —as given in a tragical Publisher's document before me — was, for his really stiff spell of anxious and careful work, precisely £15, 5s. 3d. —absolutely only 5s. 3d. more than Milton, first and last, had for his "Paradise Lost." For Smith *this* was a "Paradise Lost"—the Paradise,

to wit, of Poetry, not farther on these bare terms
to be prosecuted by a gentleman of small income
unfortunately *fixed;** of family only fixed in this
sense, that it was fixed by fate as always steadily
on the increase.   Some " Paradise Regained " of
Prose was thus now the thing to be aimed at.
With Prose he had, ere this, somewhat begun to
concern himself.   And now, he very steadily
betook himself to it ; writing of the other and
always dearer thing, only such an occasional
lyric or the like as " came to him," and coming,
could in no wise be cast out.   If a Poet—one of
the born breed, who " sings but as the linnet
sings "—could subsist himself as the linnet does
by pecking easily about the hedge-rows, the
arrangement might have its advantages ; but it
has not been so ordered.   Not even Mr Tenny-

---

* Let me be exact as to this.   Originally, as said, his income
was £150.   More lately, by increase which accrued to him as
Registrar and Secretary to the University Council, it amounted
to £200.   As economics are in question, it may farther be explained, as illustrating the necessity under which he latterly
found himself of drudging pretty hard with his pen, that his own
immediate and increasing family expenses were by no means the
sole claim upon him.   To others he was fairly liable ; and once,
in particular, had to fit out and send to India one of his younger
brothers, in itself a somewhat serious pull upon a purse no better
furnished than his.

son, I expect, finds that he can pay his butcher with an autograph, unless it be written on the duly stamped cheque of some Bank, in which he has a deposit. So with Smith and *his* butcher; and as poetry would not pay the butcher, prose now *must.* In prose he had a graceful and facile gift; and he speedily found that for what he might write there was always ready market, and gratifying acceptance with the public. His books may rapidly be chronicled—which, however, give only the faintest notion of the quantity of work produced; what might, by comparison, be termed the *spray* of his mind being thrown off besides constantly and in various directions. In 1863 appeared "Dreamthorp" (published by Messrs Strahan) a volume of delightful "Essays," embodying in parts a great deal of really fine and subtle thinking, and written throughout in a style of much grace and sweetness, delicately shimmering from time to time with the lights of essential poetry. It seems to me that, of all his books, this has most of *himself* in it; gives the most express image of the man as he was to those who best knew him; of his quiet, hearty ways, his lurking humour, the general effect of geniality he produced; geniality sweetly acidulated—were

F 2

such a phrase to be permitted—with a cynicism never untender. So long as the world may chance to want reading of this particular kind, it might do worse than remember " Dreamthorp." Meantime, it was a highly successful book, and achieved a wide circulation. " The Summer in Skye" (also by Messrs Strahan) followed in 1865 ; and as written thoroughly *con amore*, as it could not fail to be, on a subject very near his heart, it had at least equal success. No one should visit the island without scanning its vivid and charming pages. Written originally, however, in two volumes, and not as at first he had himself proposed, in one, it contains at the beginning and the end a good deal of extraneous matter, not in itself to be wished away, yet which has not always delighted purchasers careless of Literature, who bought it on trust of its title page, for severe business purpose of a Guide Book. Neither as such, in its Skye portion, will it quite bear to be regarded with strictly a business eye. In this same year was produced by Messrs Macmillan an edition of Burns edited by him, to which was prefixed an extended and elaborate Memoir, which, after all that has been written on its

subject by men very famous indeed, bears exceedingly well perusal. To the whole there was
added a Glossary on some new and complex
principle, which cost him a deal of pains; in fact, it
bored him dreadfully, and he growled a good deal
over it, while admitting that in strictness he ought
not to growl, as having for the total performance
very liberal *solatium* from the publisher.

Meantime, from month to month, in the pages
of " Good Words," was appearing his little story,
" Alfred Hagart's Household." This, too, he had
planned as one volume ; but the publisher, finding it a highly popular item of the Magazine,
prevailed on him to extend it into two, very
obviously to its detriment, the later portions—in
themselves inferior—but indifferently coalescing
with the first. This work he undertook as simply
a tentative of what he might be able to do in
fiction. There is in it a great deal of tender,
quiet sketching, both pathetic and humorous,
with nice *aperçus* of character ; and especially
it seems to succeed in its renderings of child-
nature, than success in which there is perhaps no
more decisive guarantee of the true gift of a
subtle humane insight. With the reception ac-
corded to the book, he had every reason to be

gratified ; and it was in this field that his next, and more serious effort would have been made—there seems every reason to believe, with good and effective result. Whilst death was unawares busy with him, he was maturing the scheme of a Novel on the understood scale. As knowing himself a little shaky on the constructive side, he said he did not mean to write a word till he had got the whole thing, to some distinct and satisfactory extent, imaginatively made compact within him. Thus, so far as is known, nothing of it was ever written. All I know of it is, that it would have included a *Scotch* element. About the very last time I dined with him, I remember retailing a highly ludicrous scene I had just chanced to be witness of, illustrating the fierce theological proclivities of the Scottish carter; and the little amusement it caused being over, I generously said, "I don't mind making you a present of that for your novel, Smith !" "Thank you for nothing, old fellow !" with base ingratitude he answered, "I *spotted* it as it left your lips ; and one or other of these fine days, perhaps you'll see it in print." This was, however, not to be.

Within the space of time indicated, there is

given in the above, a fair modicum of work ; and as before said, it was only a tithe of that really done. Of this other desultory business no account need be attempted. From the time of his decisively taking to prose, as, after all, the thing to boil the pot by, his irons in the fire were always numerous. For three Encyclopedias, in succession, he did a good deal of work—*Mackenzie's Biographical*, the *Britannica*, and *Chambers's*—the Editor of the last of which, the excellent and accomplished Dr Findlater—from the old Raleigh Club time, one of his fastest friends—used to say that, for neat, felicitous, carefully-condensed work on the prescribed conditions—by comparison, of some brevity—he had no such literary contributor. Of Magazines, Newspapers, and so forth, it need only be said they were numerous.

One newspaper only need be particularised— the *Caledonian Mercury*—an otherwise unnoticeable organ, now defunct—to which, in mere love of the thing (though paid, of course), he from year to year contributed notices of the Royal Academy Pictures—bright, easy, lively sketching and criticism, such as not many newspapers favour their readers with on that particular topic.

Of Art, in the technical sense, he made small profession of knowledge, eschewing the wretched jargon supposed to indicate knowledge ; but from their intellectual side as *Poetry* he *read* pictures with a subtlety somewhat rare ; and even of the technical business, *en amateur*, knew probably a good deal. Almost all the artists he knew, so as to drop in at their studios ; with not a few of them he was intimate ; and Horatio Macculloch, not improbably the greatest master of landscape who ever touched a brush in Scotland, was, as it were, a sort of elder brother to him. They lived only some quarter of a mile apart ; and when not found at home of a Saturday or Sunday afternoon, he was nearly sure to be found smoking in Macculloch's studio, exchanging easy talk with the artist, as, under the deft hand, the landscape grew upon the canvas. For artists, as a class, as I before said, he had always rather a liking ; their careless, pleasantly-Bohemian ways suited him somewhat better than those of men of business.

Properly, his love of Art was one with his deep instinctive feeling for Nature ; as indeed in a man of any culture, the presence of the last, in any force, will more or less imply the other. Mr

James Hannay, in a tender and graceful reminiscence of him, contributed to "Cassells'
Magazine," has said that his was "a life of
which enjoyment of Nature formed a great part."
Nothing can be more true; if at all you knew
him, you *knew* this; though it was not quite
easy to say how you could come by your knowledge, as of anything like expressed rapture and
rhapsody on this, as on the other understood
topics for such, he was always entirely innocent.
He was one of those invaluable men, with
whom it was possible to walk for an hour or so
through a beautiful stretch of landscape, and be
bored with no single exclamation about it.   For
which precise reason you *knew*, as I said, that
in soul he exulted and expatiated.   As in fact it
might be gathered from his books, it was somewhat less in the severer beauty of form than in
the festal glory of colour superinduced, that by
instinct he took delight—a fact perhaps to be
noted as not wholly without pertinence to his
writings, as giving — by analogy—the key to
somewhat of their beauty, if also to somewhat
of their defect.   A silence utter and total on
such subjects he did not enforce upon himself;
and now and then one admired the watchful

exactitude of his eye for nice minutiæ of this kind. Thus—merely as an instance—once in late autumn, as we lay, smoking and silent, on the hill above Bonaly — the noble landscape stretched beneath, with the fretted outline of the city bounding it, and beyond, far reaches of shining sea, in dim distance wedded with the sky—he said suddenly: " Oh ! look at these sprays of birch there between us and the tints of far sky ; don't they look as if they would *drip purple wine to us ?*"—adding, with one of the whimsical turns familiar to those who knew him, " I wish to heaven they *would !*" Very cordially echoing the wish, I looked, and saw that he had photographed the effect in words, as probably his friend Macculloch would have given £100 to be able to put it on canvas.

For something more. than a year before his death, it was known to his friends that all was not strictly right with him. While looking well and rosy—of which he would humorously complain as a great aggravation of his distress—he had strange nervous distemperatures — unaccountable panic would beset him at times ; at other times he would suddenly feel as if the solid earth had gone from beneath his feet, and he was insecurely walking on clouds—*so* insecurely, indeed, that he had hastily to throw himself into a cab, etc., etc. One sees it all now with doleful clearness. His brain had been overworked ; had in some sense given way, and needed entire rest. And if his brain would decisively have *given way*, thus making rest *imperative*, he might now have been alive and with us. But the unhappy brain would not do this ; and so long as it did not fail him, his sense of duty would insist on *working* it. And all the time he looked so *well* that, thinking his complaint some form of mere hypochondria, in one's wisdom, as thinking this the scientific treatment of the disorder, one rather fleered at than sympathised with him. These points of supposed wit at the time are not now very amusing, and need not be here commemorated.

In August 1866, he took his last holiday, which, it was hoped, might do him good ; but, alas ! even in the wilds, his inevitable Devil (the Printer's) more or less continued to haunt him ; and he returned not much renovated. There is evidence he had become seriously uneasy about himself. It has often been noted how frequently in his writings there appears a melancholy brood-

ing over death ; and in the " Spring Chanson,"
at the close of the Book, written in May of the
year, this recurs so strangely as to suggest distinct prescience of the coming doom. Very
touching is it now to note, how the cheery tone
of Spring, with which it opens, as a forced and
artificial gaiety, imperceptibly, as quite unwilfully,
slides into the autumn sombreness, and suggestions of decay and death. Some little time
before he was taken ill, he called on his friend
Mr J. F. M'Lennan, Advocate, very well known
to Anthropologists as author of a work on " Primitive Marriage," and otherwise as writer of the
" Life of Henry Drummond," and asked instructions as to the making of his will, saying that he
" felt death in him." The instructions, as a matter
of course, he got ; and almost equally, as matter
of course, proceeded *not* to make the will. This
was about the opening of the winter session in
November, which always involved for him hard,
continuous, and somewhat harassing work. He
was looking as fresh and well as ever in his life ;
and to no soul could it be evident that he should
not undertake it as usual—as accordingly he did.
But it might seem to have been too much for
him. Shortly after we heard he was laid up ill ;

then that his illness was serious; then that it had determined itself into typhoid fever, complicated with diphtheria. One of these might have been enough for him to struggle with; both of them proved too much. He was laid up on the 20th November; on the morning of 5th January 1867 he quite peacefully died, with those he loved watching round him. It is needless to say that, throughout his illness, he had the best medical advice which Edinburgh could bestow (and in the world there is perhaps no better), the best tendance which could be furnished by the solicitudes of those who loved him. But all would not avail; he died, as above said.

How does one feel on such an occasion? Taking a survey of the survivors, a little bewildered, like *Lear*, and not quite able to grasp the "dispensation:"

> "Why should a dog, a horse, a rat have life,
> And *thou* no breath at all?"

Of the blank which was left by his death in the very wide circle of his friends, I do not in the least care to write. Of the blank yet deeper and sadder in the circle of those to whom he was endeared by ties yet closer and dearer, no sensible person will ever in any such case even dream of trying to write. Where, in truth, can ever be the sense or the use of such a thing? The love which is true, deep, and unselfish, is in secret its own best comforter; and, in subtle and unsuspected ways, ministers to itself a finer and softer solace than sympathy, so called, can ever do, imperfect when most sincere. In the memory of the loved and lost—when the agony of the *wrench* is overpast—a "tender grace" and charm abides, making sadness, and sorrow itself, as precious as the living joy. The music is, indeed, for ever dead upon the strings; but they cannot cease to vibrate strangely to echoes of it, lingering and far prolonged, and infinitely tender and sweet.

Yet if sympathy, idle as in much it always is, may now and then be held appropriate, here it was surely due. Within two days of Smith's death, news from Skye arrived that good old Ord—Mrs Smith's father—was also suddenly dead. Her mother she had lost only three months before. Only some two months later, beside poor Smith, where he sleeps, was laid his eldest born; his first little pet daughter Flora, whose arrival is so sweetly alluded to in his beautiful lyric " Blaavin." Seldom to any household comes so sore a complication of bereavement. Except as it is mercifully appointed that great sorrows coming together in some strange way absorb and neutralise one another, people in such wretched conjunctions as this would have either to go mad or die.

Of Shakespeare as a *man* we know but little ; and those of us who make a point of never writing of him, except as always and in everything " Divine," do not know much more of him as a Poet. What is known of Shakespeare as a man amounts to little more than this—that nearly every one who knew him *loved* him. As to *this* the consensus of testimony is complete. The greatest Genius of all time was not, *as such*, at all known or cared for at " the Mermaid." Had you under that title asked for him at the door there, it is quietly my own notion Ben Jonson would have probably come reeling out upon you. He was known there as " *sweet* Will Shakespeare," "*gentle* Will ;" or, as Spenser, in his " Tears of the Muses," calls him, " Our *pleasant* Willy."* How sweetly seems the phrase

---

* It has been maintained that Spenser's reference here is to Sydney as " Willy," a supposed shepherd in a pastoral ; and

to fondle him!—"*our* Willy!" What nice insinuation of heart in that!—yours and mine; our own true friend and brother. So, most emphatically, also of Alexander Smith. It was never alleged, even by the most ecstatic of his earlier critics, that, in point of Genius, Smith was quite equal to Shakespeare; but if I am willing to suppose that Shakespeare— as "sweet" and "gentle" I do not greatly doubt as he — was also as true, and honest, and good, I consider I pay Shakespeare a very high compliment indeed. None of Smith's friends that I know of ever made much of his Genius; nor is it worth while at all to speak of it here. That he *was*, in some very distinct sense, a man of Genius, I myself do not doubt, nor would I care to argue the matter with a critic who should dispute the claim for him. As to the precise nature and limits of his Genius— how far he effectively utilised it—and the substantive value of the results as they lie before

it is alleged, in proof of this, that Sydney *elsewhere* undeniably *is* so alluded to. The context looked to, the thing will not bear two minutes' discussion. That Shakespeare is *here* intended, is as unquestionable as if it had never been questioned, or could be so.

us, there may quite reasonably be room for considerable differences of opinion. But about his Genius, as I said, his friends never greatly cared : it was seldom made subject of conversation to him ; and when I said that the *one* man he rather eschewed was the prolix and wise bore and blockhead, I forgot that there was *another*— the fool who might be feared, as likely to vociferate applause upon him. This kind of person, I rather think, if sufficiently diligent in his operations, could have caused him rather sharp annoyance. It is almost needless to say, the circle of his friends—properly so called—included no such nuisance. It included, on the other hand, several Aristarchs, whose cool insolence to him, in such matters, nearly rivalled that of his early friend Macdonald ; and with whom he was always delighted to discuss the points of criticism, perfectly resolute where he felt himself to be in the right—candid as the day in admission of any little flaw, which, as really such, he would recognise with curiously exceptional readiness.

The best thing ever likely to be said of Smith's genius is, that those—and there were many such—who, because of it, were led to make his acquaintance, so soon as they suc-

ceeded in doing so, found that they forgot all
about it ; that the "Author of the 'Life-Drama'"
presently came to seem to them a comparatively
poor creature, and, indeed, disappeared entirely,
leaving behind him, as substitute, "the human-
hearted man we loved." It would not, I think,
have been possible to find a man more entirely
simple and amiable. Great warmth of affection ;
great truth of it (the two are unhappily not
always conjoined) ; and, as holding of truth,
steadfastness—this was the man's deepest and
most distinctive peculiarity. He could as little
have been untrue to a friend, as unworthily have
befouled an enemy (supposing him to have had
one, of which I am not aware). Friendship may
in two ways be compromised. You may have
done something so dreadful — swindled your
creditors, let us say—as to make all discreet
Christians shy of you. Even had he chanced
to be a creditor, I don't think that with Smith a
little peccadillo of this kind would have made
any very great difference. He was no very
rigorous *censor morum ;* of any *mores*, that is,
except his own, of which he always made excellent censorship. On *that* side you might consider yourself pretty safe with him. On the

other side, of small touchiness in *himself;* suspicions; uneasy broodings and hatchings over questionable points of conduct which might seem to require explanation, you might hold yourself equally safe. There was a certain largeness of nature in the man—a magnanimity,* I will say—it is a dreadfully big word to use, yet the right one—which made him free of all that sort of thing—the poison of noble intercourse. Consequently, admitted to his friendship, you might consider you were in for a spell of it; in fact, there did not seem any way in

---

* In the excellent Memoir of Smith—of which I have everywhere freely made use—contributed to *Good Words* by his friend Mr Alexander Nicholson, Skye-man and Advocate, this word "magnanimous" is used of him. I quite remember, in reading it, recognising its fine pertinence—though surely never among men can so grand a virtue have exhibited itself in more still and simple guise. Magnanimity! largeness of soul and nature; that elevated cast of mind, to which, precisely because great things are great, little things are little! It is not a British virtue—our whole Society being obviously ruled on the principle, that little things being accounted great, great things are to be held little. Oddly enough, Smith had it; and it is really so much a virtue, that almost a Vice *with* it is better than a Virtue *without.* The things which were great to him were Poetry, and generally the intellectual business, prosecuted simply and for itself; this, and what with *him* was fundamental to this, duty and the quick life of the affections. So far as I could ever read the man, nothing else was of any really vital concernment to him.

which, had you even wished it so, the relation could ever, as the lawyers say, "cease and determine." It would not have been quite easy so to offend Smith as to lead him to perpetrate rupture with one whom he held his friend. Some sort of obviously studied and deliberate *insult* to him, would, in fact, have been your only way out of the entanglement. In years of close intercourse with him, I cannot remember that ever there came between us so much as a start or flaw of uneasiness—no mighty inference of virtue, I admit, on the one side, but more or less, I should really fear, on the other. And I am nearly positive, every other friend he had of tried standing would say precisely the same thing.*

* As instance of his tolerance in such a relation, I remember that once in a skittish mood, I expressly satirized him in the columns of the *Scotsman*—which in Edinburgh is somewhat as if in London you found, on going to your Club, all the readers of the *Times* on the giggle at you. It was *a propos* of some poor American Poet who had plainly gone mad over the "Life-Drama;" and I said that, as the unhappy creature was no doubt ere this in a strait-waistcoat, with his mother weeping over him, Mr Smith had really a great deal to answer for; moreover, that if Mr Smith would glance into the work, perhaps it might be of use to him, as seeing in it—pretty much as one's fine features are given back to one in a silver spoon—something much more likely to do him good than anything he ever saw in his mirror of a morning—some wretched ribaldry of that kind. This he did

And in this, his extreme amiability, he was really entitled to some credit; for, as one of the "*genus irritable*," there was in 'him a thrill of irritable fibre, making him one with others of the race, wretched themselves by reason of it—combined with a small self-seeking vanity—and ministers of wretchedness to others. But as having in him no taint of the last, the other was in Smith so neutralised, that it would not surprise me to learn I am held to do him wrong, in hinting here that he had any of it. Neither was his almost unfailing mildness that of a weak and negative nature incapable of a manly self-asser-

---

not quite relish. "O, hang it!" he said to a friend, "this is going a little too far. Hang me, if I stand this kind of thing. I must really pull the fellow up." When I met him, and asked if he had seen the compliment I had paid him, he said—trying to pinch his bland face into a just severity, and almost ludicrously failing: "O yes—I've seen it—and it's all very funny, no doubt" (a fine broad grin of forgiveness expanding over his features;) very clever, I dare say, you think it; but just don't do it *again*, old fellow! *that's all.* If you do—" the dreadful threat was never uttered; he knew it would only be laughed at; farther, he knew as well as I did, that if the thing were next week repeated, it could lead to nothing but a repetition of the easy transaction in progress. It was not by a little offence of this kind, repeated as often as you pleased, that you could have forfeited the good-will of Alexander Smith, or stirred into any kind of gall against you that sweetness which was born in the blood.

tion. He could assert himself pretty promptly on occasion ; and more than once I have known him do so, manifestly much to the surprise of the person—and it did not greatly matter who he was —who found himself—metaphorically, of course, —so sharply taken by the throat. Insult he would have brooked from no man ; but he must have been almost a brute who would have offered offence in this kind to one himself so inoffensive.

Yet, if I should suspect a fault in him, it was here, in a certain deficiency in the acrid and evil emotions. He did not make any enemies. I wish he had made a *few;* only one or two to go about expressing an active detestation of him, would a little, in my mind, have contributed a finishing grace to his character. I could never quite catch his secret ; or see how it was he contrived to go about and never make himself disagreeable to anybody—in a world, too, abounding with malefactors, to whom it is almost one's duty to be disagreeable. Partly, perhaps, *this* helped him to it : he was a man not heavily weighted with *convictions.* In politics, for instance—the great Whig and Tory wrangle—his interest was precisely—*nil.* I don't think he ever even read

these "Speeches" other people make so much of;
and perhaps, in his intellectual developments, he
did not by this greatly suffer. With Religion, as
a topic of social discussion, he quite declined to
meddle; indeed, as such, he plainly disliked the
subject, and, keeping himself carefully away
from it, naturally avoided all risk of incurring
the savage ill-will of those with whom he might
have chanced to differ on some trivial point of
dogma or other. Elsewhere it was the same.
The proposition that Man is a developed Mollusc,
when laid down over the wine and walnuts,
stirred in him no vehemence of angry antipathy.
Badgered into saying something of it, he would
probably say he knew that Man was Man, and did
not care to know any more, *that* being the really
important article of belief;—farther, perhaps, that,
so far as he could see, nobody *ever would* know any
more. On all such questions of the Mollusc, he
himself was so perfectly a molluscous animal, he
almost went some way to prove the theory. As
to the claims of the Nigger again, his indifference
was entire and contemptuous; but he would
allow the fiery Abolitionist to rage along upon
his sable hobby perfectly unchecked—not caring
enough about the matter, one way or the other,

to lead him at all to interfere in it. And the
" Nigger" may stand as representative of all the
other great "Causes" which set men together by
the ears. I fear he was but a cool philanthropist
in anything of the large and sublime sense ;
and I can suppose him giving now and then a
penny to a poor starving child in the street,
who reminded him of his little ones at home,
though doubtless theoretically aware that in so
doing, precisely to the extent of the penny's
worth, he was sacrificing "the happiness of the
greatest number." Nothing of all this am I
alleging as if in his honour ; something is perhaps to be said for it, and, undoubtedly, a good
deal against. I am simply noting that this was
the kind of man he was, and explaining to myself how it was that—as with no outfit of fanatical convictions of his own—he could go on
so quietly as he did, not treading upon other
people's gouty toes of conviction, and thus singularly without offence to any one. Of all good
Scotchmen born, surely Alexander Smith was the
very least of a *Fanatic*, either in the good or the
bad sense ; and verily he had his reward, in the
cloudless and beautiful serenity throughout, of
his relations with his fellow-men.

In his way of life, by testimony of all who ever knew him, Smith was throughout a man of unusual discretion and correctness, tried by the strictest conventional standard; and here also he had some credit, inasmuch as his correctness was wisdom of strong self-rule, and by no means the merely negative virtue, bred of thinness and meagreness of nature, and lack of all exuberance of impulse. There was in him no taint of the Puritan; and of "the gifts the gods provide" he had a genial and manly enjoyment; but he used them as not abusing, and seldom, indeed, in anything, was known to transgress the rule of the *ne quid nimis*. That now and then, and as merely in the round of human experience, he may have "heard the chimes at midnight," is assumed in this, as matter of course. So sedate a man, in fact, was he that, on this ground, his title to rank as a Genius has seriously been called in question. Only the other evening, I heard one of his oldest friends—a Genius somewhat eccentric — depreciate his Poetry from this point of view. His notion was, that Genius in general, and Poetical power in particular, are of needs allied with the more desperate forms of blackguardism; and this he went on to illustrate copiously from the records left us of the Gifted. Consequently—such was his line of reasoning— as Smith's dearest friend could not make out any case for a moment to be listened to, entitling him to rank as a scoundrel, the inference was clear—the critics must have made a mistake in supposing he could possibly be a Poet. The syllogism seems to be perfect; and certainly, if its Major be admitted, the Minor being quite indisputable, the conclusion was, by rigour of logic, arrived at. On the other hand, Smith's Genius being admitted to start with, his friend's Major premiss of Theory might be held, by equal rigour of logic, demolished. And whatever we make of this Theory of Genius being a mode of blackguardism—there seems to be a good deal in it, if we do not push it too far—it received no countenance whatever from the practice of Alexander Smith. If it be critically ruled, that on that account he cannot have been a man of Genius, be it so. He did not leave behind him a friend who, from this point of view, however anxious to do so, can find a word to say for his Poetry.

Having said so much of him, it is almost needless I should say farther, that Smith was one of the most delightful of companions. In anything like formal company—for which he did not greatly care—he was not rightly to be relished, though he can scarce anywhere have been held to be otherwise than a pleasant and agreeable man. But in any little circle of his intimates, he radiated round him warmth and easy satisfaction. When I knew him in his early days, an occasional mood of gloom and abstraction might be noted in him; and half suspecting him at times of *doing* the "Author of the Life-Drama" upon us, I took the liberty to quiz him accordingly, when we had become sufficiently intimate. (I need not say how completely, on farther acquaintance, I acquitted him of any such affectation.) In his later time, these moods —slight and transient as they were—had quite disappeared, and his was eminently, and at all times, a *cheery* presence—though, by nature *au fond*, I should suppose him to have been always a somewhat brooding, meditative, and sad man. This only revealed itself, however, in the pleasant reaction and protest of *humour*, which was one of the ruling qualities of his mind, and, had he lived, would probably more and more have announced itself dominant. As it is, in anything he wrote,

there is only some hint or suggestion of his
really fine gift in that direction. Characteristi-
cally, his humour was of the quiet and not of the
explosive sort ; anything ludicrous—and in this
kind he missed nothing—you could see he was
rolling quietly under his tongue, as it were ;
nursing it as a nice morsel, till he had sucked
its inmost sweet. It was rather by sympathy
with this in him, than in anything he would
actively produce to make you "roar and laugh,"
as they say, that his humour became enjoyable ;
and *how* enjoyable it was, how pleasantly it
flavoured the man, so to speak, interfused as a
genial element throughout his whole speech and
ways, all his really close friends must forget him
—if that in the least were possible—before they
cease to remember. Of his conversation a word
or two may suffice. On his return from London,
on my asking him about that of Mr Helps, he
answered as nearly as possible thus : "Pretty
much what his books would have led me expect
of him—not specially remarkable, as not at all
caring to be so—just the careless, easy, intelligent talk of a cultivated English gentleman,
with now and then a noticeably good and happy
thing dropped lightly into it unawares, and as if

he himself did not know;" and some instances
of these he gave, which I don't remember, and
ought not to repeat if I did. This seems pretty
narrowly to hit his own perfectly unstudied,
unsolicitous, carelessly-articulated talk. In its
way it was very pleasant; most so, perhaps,
when by himself you could get him to flow forth
to any extent on matters literary. On Poetry
in particular, it might well be supposed preg-
nant, as, with a very nice critical eye, he had
read widely and exactly. I should suppose him
to have been in this branch one of the very best
read men in Scotland. And in the other literary
branches, if not so supremely, he was yet unusually well informed. One only he eschewed,
somewhat as by instinct an animal declines a
food unsuited to it—Metaphysics and Mental
Philosophy. Of these he declined to talk, except in terms of obstinate distaste .and contempt. As to *reading* anything of the kind, not
even a strong call of duty and friendship—as
when possibly one or other of his allies, casually
immersed in these bewilderments, would present
him with a poor little volume—could prevail with
him to seriously attempt such a thing. He would
profess to have *tried* to read; and his criticism

would, on such an occasion, be thus compendi-
ously conveyed: "Do you really suppose, my
good fellow, that I'm going to bother my brain
with *stuff of that kind?*"—this with a certain
vice, as if he really resented the waste of time
incurred in his abortive attempt. This obstinate
antipathy always struck me as curious; inasmuch as readers who know such a thing when
they see it, will frequently ˙take note in his
writings of a nice philosophic intuition. But of
anything like exact logical process he was intolerant. Consequently, he hated *argument* on
all subjects; on religious topics more particularly; and, indeed, about religion he almost
utterly declined, in any form whatever, to talk.
He has been styled a "reticent" man; this, I
think, he only otherwise was, as not insisting
on boring his friends with matters which were
strictly his own concern: but on *this* subject he
was reticent to a degree. It showed his strong
good sense, I think; as not likely to throw any
new lights upon the subject, it was as well for
him to hold his peace about it. Doubtless he
thought much of it, saying, as he did, so little.
That his mode of thought was entirely *reverent;*
that of *ir*reverence you heard from himself no

word ; that he disliked it in others, and actively *detested* it when so expressed as to take any form of social outrage ; that, finally, he was no very positive Philosopher, or " intellectual all-in-all," and considered the Ignotum, with its grand possibilities, rather more entitled to respect than the devoloped 2 + 2 = 4, which is the sum of all of our Science ; farther, that unless in some distinct sense, he had held to the faith of the Christian, he would scarcely—so sincere a man as he was—have written as he did in the " Christmas " Essay in " Dream-thorp"—this is, I should say, about all that any one ever knew of the religion of Alexander Smith. As I said, he could scarcely be got to talk at all on the subject. In his steady avoidance of every theological topic, his obstinate indisposition to " Metapheesics," and eschewing of every form of pertinacious and wrangling dialectic, he was a positive disgrace to his country. And in truth, taken all over, there was a good deal in him that almost might be held to approximate to the English rather than the Scotch type of understood character. He was, it may be hoped, however, Scotch enough to have considered that, in say-

ing this, you paid him no very astonishing compliment

With considerable distress throughout, I have
found myself elaborating a sketch, with a dreadful suspicion of the " Ideal " about it ; of "the
self-less man and stainless gentleman" who
figures in Mr Tennyson's Poem, and is not often
to be met with out of it. And I have anxiously
considered and cast about, as wishing a good
strong shadow or two to dash into the picture,
were it only to make it something rather more like
a work of Art. But, almost to my grief, I found
they were not to be had in nature, and not even in
the interests of art could I think myself entitled
to *invent* them. I am not, however, in the least
alarmed lest my sketch should be held idealised
by those who personally and intimately knew
the simple and homely reality from which it is
studied. Faint and inadequate it must needs
be—on that side I willingly admit deficiency ;
but to all such I confidently appeal against
suspicion of having traced in it a single line of
exaggeration, or exercised the smallest art of
either suppression or extenuation. In fact,
there was nothing to extenuate or suppress.
As Art, my performance may be wretched ; but

it does not profess to be Art, but only simplicity of Nature and truth; and as such, except on some ground of inadequacy in execution, I know it quite safe from impeachment.

As regards Smith's relations with the University, remarks have been made before the public from which there seemed to be inference of his feeling himself uncomfortable there, as not quite treated as he should be. I am bound to say that for these I am aware of no just foundation in anything I ever heard from himself. Yet, inasmuch as there was really a ground from which misconception might arise, a brief word or two seems almost to be called for on the subject Frankly, then, latterly the College business had got to *bore* him somewhat more than it did in his earlier time. (This phenomenon of growing boredom with strangling monotonies of life is not, I should suppose, peculiar to the duties of the Secretary of the Edinburgh University.) The situation, always, it seems to me, fairly suitable for him, as giving him a basis to proceed upon, did not in this sense now quite so approve itself to him as it *had* done. The duties had gradually been getting heavier; and, latterly, had come to include little points of duty, for discharge of which a just taste would, perhaps, have ruled that the Porter at the gate was, on the whole, the more proper person. Farther, as I said, for the last year or two of his life he was working under morbid conditions, which precluded him from quite enjoying, as before, the element of humour in such things. In a word, he had got just a little weary and sick of the whole concern. I surmise so, as supplementing *or producing*, so to phrase it, the casually-dropped remarks of a man so entirely unqueru- lous, so little given to complaint as he. He had some dream of a sheep-farm in Skye ; and to the obvious objection that his knowledge of sheep was *nil*, except in the form of mutton, he did not seem disposed to give due weight. This scheme ran much in his mind, and, had he lived a year or two longer, would almost certainly have been carried out, with results Arcadian or otherwise. Probably, I should say, otherwise. In his taking up with this project I seemed to apprehend the Poet rather than the practician, and man of calm, strong sense he on all other matters exhibited himself. It gives us,

however, pretty accurately the measure of the
distaste he had got to feel for the University.
But that, in his personal relations in that quarter,
there was ever anything unpleasant, not positively
inevitable to the position, very strong evidence
indeed would be needed to make me believe.
And of such evidence, I venture to say, none will
ever be produced. Of his relations with the
general body of the Professors, I know not very
much. Of a good many of them I have heard
him speak in terms of true liking and kindliness.
Of no one of them did I ever hear him speak
*un*kindly. His relations with Aytoun have already been alluded to; and with Aytoun he had
much pleasant intercourse.* Even if not specially
alluding to the University, I could scarce have

---

* An instance being known to me in which Aytoun's kind
feeling towards Smith took a very practical and business form,
it may not be amiss to commemorate it. Some little time after
Smith's marriage, the Professor came to him one morning in his
room at College, and addressed him in effect somewhat thus—
"You're now married, Smith, and have got a household and
family to care for. What we give you here is, sooth to say, no
very fat provision. Poetry is well; but it don't *pay* for the
most part. Why not try a little Prose?" (This was before
Smith had to any extent taken into that line, or cultivated a
Magazine connection.) "Suppose you write something for
Blackwood; try; write the stuff, and let me know when you

avoided allusion to the terms of really frank, easy, and cordial *friendship*, on which, from the first and throughout, he stood with Professor Blackie ; and with more of the body I should suppose him to have been pretty intimate. If others of them did not greatly heed him, this might seem to be pretty much in the nature of the case ; and it may be held to be equally in the nature of it, that quite as little did he them—which seems all that need be said on the subject. As to the other subject—in regard of which unnecessary remarks have also been laid before the public—as to how far from Edinburgh " Society" he met with the " recognition" to which he was entitled, a few brief words may dispose of it. Of *such* recognition he had always quite as much as he cared

---

send it in. I'll do what I can for you in that quarter, and I don't much doubt I'll be able to get it admitted. Thereafter as may be. An occasional cheque coming in, of fifteen or twenty guineas, under these new conditions, might not perhaps inconvenience you." The paper was written accordingly, sent in, admitted, and followed by one or two more ; and though the relation with *Blackwood* did not take a form of permanence, this was not Aytoun's fault—nor did I ever hear of fault anywhere—and can no way affect our estimate of his thoughtful kindness. So much for the hearty relation which subsisted between Smith and his literary foe of " Firmilian." The trait is to Aytoun so honourable, that it seems as well here to set it down.

for, or could quite conveniently manage; and supposing he had had none at all, what then? With
matters so entirely despicable, that in life the
man could never possibly have "filed his mind"*
with them, it would be foolish to defile his grave.
I have written to little purpose, if it has not become plain to the reader, that of necessity the
man's life must have been lived some considerable
way *above* that not very elevated atmosphere
which is breathed by Edinburgh Society.

Smith's grave, above alluded to, is in Warris-
ton Cemetery, about half way between the city
and the sea. Over it, by the tender care of a
circle of his friends, has been erected a Runic
cross, distinguished by its singular beauty and
the grace of its appropriate decorations. It
was executed under the superintendence of his
friends, Sir J. Noel Paton and Mr James Drummond, R.S.A., by the latter of whom, as a tribute
of affection to the Poet, the beautiful design was
furnished. The medallion likeness in bronze
is from the hand of his friend Mr William

---

* " For *Banquo's* issue have I filed my mind."—*Macbeth.*
One of the constantly recurring instances in which Shakespeare
writes excellent *Scotch. Filed*—dirtied, or, as we say in English,
de-filed.

Brodie, R.S.A., sculptor. "Alexander Smith, Poet and Essayist. Erected by some of his personal friends." Such is the simple inscription. There is on it besides nothing of text or epigraph; and it struck me, in noting the deficiency, that had such a thing been wanted, a good one might readily have been found. It is not to Scripture I should have gone for it, but to one of the grand old Ballads which he himself so loved. I almost wish the stone, to those who might chance to look on it, had chanted this little burden—

"A kindly Scot lies here."*

A *kindly* Scot—thus it was that in the noble pathos of the old minstrel, the Douglas who died at Otterbourne had last thought of himself, as the brave blood and life ebbed together; the spirit, tender as heroic, exhaling itself in that sweet, sad farewell sigh of brotherhood to those he left. Thus it was that Alexander Smith would have wished, above all, by his fellow-men to be remembered. "A kindly Scot!" A Scot

---

* "O! bury me by the bracken bush,
      Beneath the bloomin' brier;
   Let never livin' mortal ken
      That a kindly Scot lies here."

with all the best virtue of the race in him, and as little as might be of its defect—withal, of such a depth of honest quiet heart and kindliness, as must be rare among men of any race. Most essentially the *Man* is given in that ; excepting only his Genius, which is not, by comparison, important, and would never to himself have seemed so.

In concluding a sketch which has strayed much beyond the limits intended, so as seriously to sin against the law of proportion in the book, I have simply to say some word or two of its contents. The Essay on "Scottish Ballad Poetry" was contributed in 1857 to a volume of "Edinburgh University Essays," and might be said to be the writer's first serious attempt in Prose. As it stands, he himself would certainly not have reprinted it ; in fact, I have heard him pooh-pooh it not a little, saying he should like to have it to do over again, as confident he could make a very much better thing of it. For kind permission to make use of it, the Publisher has to thank Messrs A. & C. Black, with whom is the copyright of the volume. To Messrs T. & T. Clark his thanks are also due for the paper on "Essayists Old and New," which is taken with permission from the *North British Review.* The shorter papers appeared in *Good Words* and *The Argosy,* and were thus the property of Messrs Strahan and Co., who with ready kindness have allowed them to be here reproduced. They have been selected on no principle save that of simply giving in series the last things of the kind produced by the writer. The paper on "Sydney Dobell" is, in this way, the very last thing he wrote. During the summer, Dobell had again visited Edinburgh, and after a separation of years, the two Poets had renewed their intimacy on the old affectionate terms. This must have suggested the paper. Some of the pieces are slight, and that on "Literary Work" is not only slight, but, as I think, so one-sided, if not entirely erroneous in doctrine, that I had some thought of excluding it. But on second thoughts I allowed it to remain, if only to mark more distinctly the point of view from which it is meant that the volume should be regarded. While criticism is not of course deprecated, in no sense is it intended as a document on which to found an estimate of Smith as a Prose writer. As such let him be judged by the books which he himself gave to the world. For the issue of the present one, a good deal of which is obviously no more than what I have called the *spray* of the writer's mind, I only am responsible; and if in issuing it I have judged amiss, the Virgilian *in me convertite ferrum,* seems naturally enough to suggest itself. Smith himself, sleeping very quietly about half-a-mile from where I now write, will not the least be distressed by anything ill-natured said of him ; that sort of thing did not much pain him while he lived, and now it cannot at all pain him ; on which ground it will probably be obvious to the critics, that good wit need not be wasted on him. It is my hope that to a sufficient circle of readers, interested in the writer, as aforetime having drawn delight from the products of his graceful pen, these Essays, as they now re-appear, will need no justification.

P. P. A.

SCOTTISH BALLADS.

A GREEK girl traced the shadow of her lover's face on a sunny wall. That, says the legend, was the birth of painting. The death of one of the lions of the early world may have given birth to the twin arts of poetry and music. The barbarian returning to his village laden with the spoils of the chase, or driving before him a crowd of captives, must have a poet to rehearse his triumphs, to celebrate the strength of his arm and the terrors of his unconquerable spear. To some such rude source we may trace back the sacred streams of poetry and music which have flowed down to us out of unknown time. From his power of conferring a new distinction on warlike achievements, the bard or singer has ever been

A

held in respect. His songs are a kind of rude
fame. He is the depositary of the traditions of
his tribe. His memory is the archives of his
people, and therein are preserved their rolls of
glory. We find the singer in every ancient
nation, by the rainy shores of the Baltic, in the
vast Germanic forests; and everywhere he is
regarded as one possessing surpassing knowledge, who has mysterious kindred with the
elements, and who, in solitary places, hears the
messages of the gods. He passes from land to
land, walks into the heart of hostile camps, and
sits down at the very carousals of his foes. He
finds a welcome in the den of the robber, and in
the rush-strewn hall of the prince. When at
rich and solemn feast the monarch is seated on
the dais surrounded by his earls, there is also the
minstrel with his harp. What were a banquet
without song and the recital of the deeds of
heroes? The wild boar's flesh is tasteless, the
mead is ditch-water; it cannot fire the blood, nor
tingle to the brain. In course of time chivalry
brought the Troubadour, a more courtly and
splendid personage than his predecessor, who
knew another god than Odin, believed in quite
a different Valhalla, and relished softer pleasures

than drinking ale out of the skulls of departed warriors. Some of these men were soldiers as well as minstrels, and were cunning with the sword as with the harp-string. On the morning of Hastings, Taillefer asked and obtained permission from William to lead the onset. He sang in a loud voice the "Song of Roland" in the front of the Norman army; then, striking spurs into his horse, he rode forward still singing, and dashed his life out in an ecstasy on the Saxon spears. After the Conquest, the English kings were great patrons of poets and minstrels, and some of them were no mean brethren of the craft, and could touch the harp themselves. Richard I. was an accomplished musician, and composed verses. The story how one of the king's minstrels, Blondell by name, rescued his master from captivity, is familiar to most readers. It was known in England that Richard had returned from Palestine, but no one could tell in what country he was detained. Blondell travelled through many lands in search of the king, till his wanderings led him one day to a strong castle. On inquiry he learned that the fortress belonged to the Duke of Austria, and that it contained a single prisoner; but no one could tell him his name. The minstrel took up his place beneath one of the grated windows, and began to sing a song in French, which he and the king had at one time composed together. Richard started when the familiar tones fell upon his ear, and recognised Blondell's voice. He immediately took up the strain, and sang the remaining half. By that token Blondell knew it was the king, and, returning to England, discovered to the barons where their master was imprisoned. In the reign of Richard II. a court of minstrels was established, which obtained a charter, had power to enact laws, and every year elected a king to preside over them. By the time of Elizabeth the craft had fallen into disrepute, the minstrel was profanely classed with " rogues, vagabonds, and sturdy beggars," and seems to have been better acquainted with the staff of the constable than with the tables of the rich or the favour of princes. Although more emphatically the home of minstrelsy than England, we have but little information relative to the worldly prosperity of the minstrels in Scotland. Celtic bards, we know, frequently left their mountains and wandered through the Lowlands singing their wild songs, and the inhabitants of the Borders were passionately fond of listening to strains in which the struggles of clans and the forays into England were celebrated. Some provision appears to have been made for poets or musicians among the Celtic tribes; a piper seems to have been as indispensable to a Highland chieftain as a claymore or eagle's feather; and a portion of the land of the tribe, called the " piper's croft," was set apart for the support of that important individual. In the Lowlands the poets seem to have found few royal favours. Dunbar and Sir David Lindsay resided at court, and although the first was sometimes attached to the train of a noble when he visited France on an embassy of state, and the second was honoured by bearing a young prince on his back, he meanwhile romping about on all-fours, they do not seem to have lived in the most flourishing condition. A considerable portion of their poetry is of the begging-letter species. If wit and eloquence had had power to charm coin from the pocket of the king, theirs had been better supplied. . It is to be hoped that the poets were the most troublesome duns of the Jameses, else the unfortunate monarchs must have frequently been at the end of their royal wits. It is hardly to be expected, however, that a line of kings, of lineage unexceptionable and most irreproachable blood, some of whom were occasionally hard-pushed in the matter of silk stockings, could afford to be generous to singing men and singing women—to poets, jesters, and buffoons.

But it was not from the court poets that the Ballads sprung. They grew up over the country like wildflowers. Their authors were most probably part minstrels, part gaberlunzies, who wandered about the kingdom, dwelling often "under the canopy with the choughs and crows," haunting fairs, markets, and all assemblies of people, and when fortunate enough to procure a supper and a couch of straw, paying their lawing with a song, and then forward on the morrow; and often, doubtless, we should find the minstrel equipped iu the steel jacket of the moss-trooper, urging a drove of floundering and terrified cattle before him from Cumberland on a moonless night, with many a prick of lance and a great superfluity of curses. Many of the Border Ballads are so reál and life-like, so full of character and humour, that we feel as if the singer had himself wielded a sword in the combat, or ridden into

England to lift a prey. The form of this kind
of poetry is of course necessitated by the circumstances of the minstrel and his audience.
It was meant to be sung on public occasions
to the harp or some other musical instrument,
and in order to produce effect and sustain interest, the theme must be some exploit which
flashed out far above common raid and the
skirmish of rival clans—some surpassing tragedy
which steeped a whole country-side in tears.
The story claimed, too, to be told in the most
direct and natural manner, and the lighter poetic
graces—ornaments and efflorescences, precious
and delightful enough in a calmer hour—were
scared away by the fury of the minstrel's hand
and voice. These compositions—and some of
them are very ancient—were not, till a comparatively recent period, preserved by printing;
living, therefore, on the lips and in the memories
of several generations, and sung extensively over
a country where, even at the present day, every
twenty or thirty miles you come upon a dialect
locally peculiar, it is not surprising that in process of time they underwent considerable modi-
fications; that we frequently find half-a-dozen
versions of the same story, and several stanzas

of one ballad imbedded in the very heart of another. When a minstrel met a brother of the craft, they would in all probability exhibit their stock-in-trade, and both thereby acquire fresh materials. The meeting over, and reciting his novelties in distant parts of the country, if memory failed, the singer who could not afford to pause in his strain would hardly hesitate to thrust into the hiatus any set of stanzas which, without outrage to the proprieties of the story, carried along with it the feelings of his audience. In these compositions there are great similarities of incident and feeling. One thing at least never fails the reader : when two lovers die they are of course buried together ; and out of the grave of one there springs a rose, and out of the grave of the other a briar, which, rapidly growing, contrive, as a sort of poetical justice and compensation for their cruel fate, to interlace and marry their branches above the spire of the church— a spectacle which, however it might astonish people now-a-days, seems to have had the most touching associations for the grim moss-trooper and the lawless reiver of the marches. None of these Ballads can be looked upon as the work of a single author. Their present form is the work of generations. For centuries the floating legendary material was reshaped, added to, and altered, by the changing spirit and emotion of man. Rude and formless, they are touching and venerable as some ruin on the waste, the names of whose builders are unknown; whose towers and walls, although not erected in accordance with the lights of modern architecture, affect the spirit and fire the imagination far more than nobler and more recent piles; for its chambers, now roofless to the day, were ages ago tenanted by life and death, joy and sorrow; for its walls have been worn and rounded by time, its stones channelled and fretted by the fierce tears of winter rains; on broken arch and battlement every April for centuries has kindled a light of desert flowers, and it stands muffled in ivy, bearded with moss, and stained with lichens, crimson, golden, and green by the suns of forgotten summers. We are told to imitate this; but who can recall the strong arms and rude hearts that piled huge stone on stone? Who can simulate the hallowing of time? Who can create us a ruin *to-day* with the weather-wear and lichens of five centuries upon it?

The Scottish Ballads may be divided into two

classes : 1. Those poems founded on historical
events, private tragedies, and the fairy myth-
ology.   2. Those which more specially pertain
to the Borders, and relate the sturt and strife,
the wild revenges, the exploits, skirmishes, and
cattle-lifting expeditions of the marchmen.   The
first contains much of the finest poetry and the
deepest pathos.   Those of the second attend
closely to the business in hand, are rude and bust-
ling, and are frequently enlivened by flashes of
savage humour.   In every stanza you seem to hear
the clatter of hoofs and the rattle of steel jackets.
Both are valuable, as throwing light on a condition
of man which can never recur in these islands ;
as exhibiting in a mighty mirror pictures of a
strong, passionate, turbulent time.   Nowhere is
the reader more impressed, not even on the page
of Shakespeare himself, with the reality of the
scenes and the men and women.   Yet with all
this naturalness, it is difficult for the reader of
to-day, with his complex environments and
difference of training, to imagine himself so
actuated, so subdued by fears, so stormed along
by passion.   In reading these compositions, we
see what we have gained and lost in the course
of a few centuries, what new elements have

entered into human life, what more of awfulness
or frivolity, of truth or falsehood; we discover
the old sea-margins of right and wrong, and
compare with them the point the tide reaches
to-day. All that far-off, lawless, and generous
life is unroofed to us in these Ballads; we
wander amongst the relics of a past society as
we would amongst the ruins of Pompeii. We
see the domestic economy of the houses of our
ancestors; everything is left there for our inspection. We can take up a household implement and examine its material and shape. The
first thing which strikes the reader of the Ballads
is their direct and impulsive life. There is nothing cloaked or concealed. You look through
the iron corslet of the marauder, and see the
fierce heart heave beneath. None of the heroes
ever seems to feel that hesitancy and palsy of
action which arises from the clash of complex
and opposing motives. At once the mailed hand
executes the impulse of the hot heart. There
seem to have been no dissimulators in those
days. If a man is a scoundrel, he speaks and
acts as if he were perfectly aware of the fact,
and aware, too, that the whole world knew it as
well as himself. If a man is wronged by an-

other, he runs him through the body with his sword, or cleaves him to the chin with his pole-axe, and then flees, pursued day and night, awake and asleep, in town and wilderness, by a bloody ghost. If two lovers meet in the green-wood, they forget church and holy priest, and in course of time the heron is startled from his solitary haunt, and shame and despair are at rest beneath the long weeds of the pool, and a ghost with dripping hair glides into the chamber, and with hand of ice awakes the horrified be-trayer from his first sleep on his bridal night. And these men had their rude reverences and devotions, terrors of the solitary mountain-top and the moonless waste, wandering fires of the morass, spirits of the swollen stream: Edom o' Gordon, who burned a mother and her children in their own tower, with laughter and mockery, as if agony were a jest, would ere night mutter an Ave to Mary Mother, and cross himself as devoutly as ever a saint in the calendar; and the moss-trooper who could impale an infant on his spear-point, would shiver at an omen which a schoolboy laughs at. These people were not afflicted with the maladies of hair-splitting and nice distinctions. A character like Hamlet's, where doubt balances resolve, and thought action, was impossible in those straight-forward days ; perhaps quite as well for Hamlet. Before he could have made up his mind how to act under the circumstances, the sweep of a sword-blade would have solved that and every other problem for him for ever. Public opinion had not come into their world to make men walk gingerly as if upon knives, to add hypocrisy to vice, to rub the fine bloom off goodness, and to make a *faux pas* worse than a crime. The wild eyes of passion, on whatever message she is bent, whether to kill or save, are seldom turned in the direction of the Decalogue. The full heart is its own law, its fluctuations its only creed ; and, describing these men and women, singing their tragedies, the ballad-monger frequently, in utter innocence and unconsciousness, and in words simple as the babble of childhood, goes to the inmost core of the matter like the inevitable arrow of a William Tell, and the tears are on our cheeks before we are aware. This is an art which the world has lost, and which cannot be recovered until centuries are cancelled, and knights are again pricking through the greenwood, ladies sitting among the roses of their bower-windows, and minstrels wandering through the country harp in hand. Society is migratory, settling age after age in different districts, with changing abodes and occupations ; and wherever she dwells, whether in the hut of the trapper, or in the glittering capitals of civilisation, Poetry must attend, and take delight in representing the life which lies around the loghouse or the palace.

The literary merit of many of these Ballads is great ; in the majority, the singer is in utter abeyance, and the subject is all in all. There is no straining or effort ; no artifices are employed to fillip the dull spirit of the reader ; no impertinent ornaments distract the attention from the agony or the woe. Their authors were not literary men, and there was no existing literature by which their efforts were measured. Originality was not expected of them, and they were consequently never tempted to call grass *purple*, to avoid the imputation of plagiarism, some former writer having called it *green*. There were no critics to show up their failings and shortcomings, or to parade their good things— perhaps a line and a half in length—in italics, as the manner of some is. It may fairly be

doubted whether the present time is favourable
to the production of poetry of a high class; not,
as is commonly supposed, that there is anything
necessarily unpoetical in the artificial state of
society, in the eternal struggle and roar of
labour, in the shifting of the points of interest
from green fields and meadows, and the sweet
goings on of pastoral life, to the joys, crimes,
and tragedies of men congregated in thousands
beneath the smoke of mighty towns; but mainly
from the greatness of existing literature, the pre-
valence of criticism, and its immediate applica-
tion to literary productions. In 1824 we find
Goethe expressing himself in the following terms
to Eckermann :—" And how could one get courage only to put pen to paper, if one were conscious, in an earnest appreciating spirit, that such
unfathomable and unattainable excellences (as
Shakespeare's writings) were already in existence! . . . It fared better with me fifty
years ago in my own dear Germany. I could
soon come to an end with all that then existed;
it could not long awe me, or occupy my attention. I soon left behind me German literature
and the study of it, and turned my thoughts to
life and to production. So on and on I went in

my own natural development, and on and on I
fashioned the productions of epoch after epoch.
And at every step of life and development my
standard of excellence was not much higher
than what at such step I was able to attain.
But had I been born an Englishman, and had
all those numerous masterpieces been brought
before me in all their power, at my first dawn of
youthful consciousness, they would have over-
powered me, and I should not have known
what to do. I could not have gone on with
such fresh light-heartedness, but should have
had to bethink myself, and look about for a
long time to find some new outlet." It is this
seeking a "new outlet for oneself" which is
the cause of nearly all the vices of contemporary literature—of poetry especially. On it
may be charged the strain and glitter, the
forced and perverse originality, and the extra-
ordinary innovations, in rythm and measure, of
which so much is heard both in the way of applause and condemnation. The primal emotions
of humanity have been so fully sung in England
during the last two hundred years, that a poet
of the present period, unless he is swept away
by the torrent of feeling, or is bold enough—

which he is perfectly justified in being—to look upon every situation of life, whether expressed before or not, as merely poetic material, and to use it for his own purposes, colour it by his own mind, shape it by his own emotion,—is tempted, when he remembers in a former writer some consummate expression of an idea, indispensable to the sequence and stream of emotion, to diverge from the direct path, and attest his originality by becoming unintelligible or unnatural. It is required of every builder that he should erect a house new and well-proportioned; it is *not* required that he should, with his own hands, have baked every brick employed in the edifice. The existing system of criticism, and the greatness and fulness of literature, are in many respects injurious to poetical writers. An author's first book is generally written *con amore* and for himself; critic and reader are forgotten in the heat and delight of the task; but after he has run the gantlet of dailies, weeklies, monthlies, and quarterlies, he becomes more conscious and less single-hearted. He writes with one eye to his subject, and the other to what the reviewers will say of him. He is more careful of the expression than of the thought.

B

He desires to dazzle and astonish. He is no longer an inspired singer uttering words of fire ; he is a lapidary coldly polishing a gem. The condition of the modern author resembles that of the flying-fish : if it seeks the air to escape its water foes, pounce come the gulls upon it. If he writes quietly, he is commonplace ; if strikingly, he is a sky-rocket with a noisy rush to heaven, a brilliant burst and shower of falling splendours, and then utter darkness and oblivion. He must either be crazy or dull. Under which king, Bezonian ? speak or die ! Most men prefer the former. The ballad-writers, living under different circumstances, were of course untouched by these peculiar temptations, nor had they to face the spectres and questions which centuries of life and speculation have since started. They had simpler hearts and lived in simpler times. They sang to rude and uncultured men ; their task was to touch their spirits and evoke their sympathies; and from their peculiar environment and training, they exhibit an artlessness and simplicity which become at times the very perfection of style, and which—whatever other merits modern singers may possess—cannot be expected to appear in anything like the same degree in an artificial and fastidious age. In pathos they are supreme. Nothing can be placed beside them. The feeling is so direct and simple, and goes so to the heart. There is an element of helplessness in it which is overpowering. It is piteous as the complaint of a little child.

Sir Philip Sidney said long ago that the ballad of Chevy-Chase, although "sung but by some blinde crowder," stirred his blood "more than a trumpet." The publication of Bishop Percy's "Reliques," at the close of the last century, was the salvation of English poetry. The world was weary of the museums of Darwin and Hayley, with their wax figures arrayed in dresses stiff with embroidery and gold ;—pretty enough to look on as curiosities in their gorgeous apparel, but with never a flash in their glassy eyes, never a throb beneath their costly clothes. In the "Reliques" had returned tenderness, and nature, and passion. The voices of men and women were again heard in gladness and grief, the globed dews were lying thick on the purple moors, the wind was blowing strong and fresh, curling the faces of the streams, and bringing odours from the forests. The rivers of poetry had been frozen up, but the spring had come and loosened their icy chains, and they flowed forth again exulting and abounding.

Coleridge has praised the "grand old ballad of Sir Patrick Spens." Being familiar to most readers, it need not now be quoted at length. Passing, however, such graphic touches of description as—

> I saw the new moon late yestreen,
> Wi' the auld moon in her arm ;

or—

> He hadna sailed a league, a league,
> A league, but barely three ;
> When the lift grew dark, and the wind blew loud,
> And gurly grew the sea,

attention may be drawn to its magnificent close—

> O lang, lang may the ladyes sit
> Wi' their fans into their hand ;
> Before they see Sir Patrick Spens,
> Come sailing to the strand.
>
> And lang, lang may the maidens sit
> Wi' their gowd kames in their hair ;
> A' waiting for their ain dear loves,
> For them they'll see nae mair.
>
> O forty miles off Aberdour,
> 'Tis fifty fathom deep ;
> And there lies gude Sir Patrick Spens,
> Wi' the Scots lords at his feet.

Whoever he was, the nameless and forgotten author of this old song was a poet, and a great one too.

The ballad of Fair Helen is well known, and the story is simple. Helen, a lady of great beauty, had two lovers, one of whom was preferred; but their passion being displeasing to her family, they were obliged to meet in secret. During one of these interviews the discarded suitor appeared on the opposite bank of the stream, and in a fit of jealous rage, levelled his carabine at his rival. Helen sprang before her lover to shield him, and received the bullet. The following song is supposed to be sung by the bereaved man over her grave :—

I wish I were where Helen lies,
Night and day on me she cries ;
O that I were where Helen lies,
    On fair Kirkconnell Lee !

Curst be the heart that thought the thought,
And curst the hand that fired the shot,
When in my arms burd Helen dropt,
    And died to succour me !

O think na ye my heart was sair
When my love dropt doon and spak nae mair !
Then did she swoon wi' meikle care
    On fair Kirkconnell Lee.

As I went doun the water side,
None but my foe to be my guide,
None but my foe to be my guide,
  On fair Kirkconnell Lee :

I lighted doun my sword to draw,
I hackit him in pieces sma',
I hackit him in pieces sma',
  For her sake that died for me.

I wish my grave were growing green,
A winding-sheet drawn ower my een,
And I in Helen's arms lying
  On fair Kirkconnell Lee.

The reader will note the curiously intermingled ferocity and pathos of these verses ; the lament with which they open ; the grim satisfaction with which he recounts his progress down the river, his foe being his "guide," repeated as if *that* gave an additional zest and flavour to his revenge ; the terrible reduplication,—

I hackit him in pieces sma',
I hackit him in pieces sma'—

in which he lingers over, and is loath to leave the savage sweetness of the memory, killing the wretch again and again in imagination. That done, he is weak as tears. How desolate and hopeless is the music,—

> I wish my grave were growing green,
> A winding-sheet drawn ower my een.

His vengeance is sated. The fiery thirst which kept him alive, and all too eager for sleep, is abundantly slaked. There is nothing now to live for on earth. Blind him, therefore, with a winding-sheet, shut out the world from him with its peaceful folds, and lay him side by side with Helen in the grave.

A dreadful scene is described in the ballad entitled " Edom o' Gordon." This marauder clatters up to the house of Rodes with a band of ruffians at his heels, and in the absence of the lord demands that the lady should deliver up to him the keys of the castle. She refuses, and the freebooter orders the house to be burned. The poor mother is standing at one of the windows with her children, girt with climbing and quivering fires, and rolled in volumes of choking smoke, and reproaches one of her servants whom she discovers busy among the yelling fiends outside.

> " Wae worth, wae worth ye, Jock, my man,
> I paid ye weel your fee;
> Why pu' ye out the ground-wa stane
> Lets in the reek to me ?

" And ein wae worth ye, Jock, my man,
   I paid ye weel your hire ;
Why pu' ye out the ground-wa stane
   To me lets in the fire ?"

" Ye paid me weel my hire, lady,
   Ye paid me weel my fee,
But now I'm Edom o' Gordon's man,
   Maun either do or dee."

O then bespaik her little son,
   Sate on the nurse's knee :
Says, " Mither dear, gi' ower this house
   For the reek it smithers me."

" I wad gie a' my gowd, my child,
   Sae wad I a' my fee,
For ane blast o' the western wind
   To blaw the reek from thee."

O then bespaik her dochter dear,
   She was baith jimp and sma',
" O, row me in a pair o' sheets,
   And tow me ower the wa'."

They row'd her in a pair o' sheets,
   They tow'd her ower the wa' ;
But on the point o' Gordon's spear
   She got a deadly fa'.

O bonnie bonnie was her mouth,
   And cherry were her cheeks ;
And clear clear was her yellow hair,
   From which the red bluid dreeps.

Then wi' his spear he turned her ower,
   O gin her face was wan !
He said, " Ye are the first that eir
   I wished alive again."

He turned her ower and ower again,
　　O gin her skin was white !
"I might hae spared that bonnie face
　　To hae been some man's delight.

"Busk and boun, my merry men a',
　　For ill dooms I do guess ;
I canna luik on that bonnie face
　　As it lies on the grass."

The writer of " Edom o' Gordon " had no theories of art. He uttered only what he saw and felt ; but what words could add to that picture of the burning tower, the unutterable sigh of the mother for " ane blast o' the western wind," and the mute reproach of the face on the grass, more terrible to the marauder than the gleam of hostile spears ?

There is an expression of misery in these Ballads which appears frequently in Scottish song, and is in some degree peculiar to the compositions of the nation. It is a ghost which rises out of the ashes of passion ; the despair— caused by stroke of death or heartlessness of man—of that love which knew neither pride of birth, nor riches, nor shame, nor death ; which was conscious only of itself, blind to everything save its own rapture and its own joy ; a mental state, not grief, not pain, but rather a dull stupor

of misery, which would welcome sharp pain
itself as a relief from its own bewilderment,
which turns passionately to death, and hugs
oblivion like a lover.   The heart has crowded
all on one throw of the dice: that lost, the forgetfulness of the grave, and a quiet coverlet of
waving grass, are all that even Hope desires.

In 1529 James V. made an expedition to the
Borders, and executed many of the freebooters.
One of those who suffered was Cockburn of
Henderland.   He was hanged by command of
the king over the gateway of his own tower.
The following verses seem to have been com-
posed by his wife :—

> He slew my knight to me sae dear,
> He slew my knight and poin'd his gear :
> My servants all for life did flee,
> And left me in extremitie.
>
> I sewed his sheet, making my mane :
> I watched the corpse myself alane ;
> I watched his body night and day,
> No living creature came that way.
>
> I took his body on my back,
> And whiles I gaed and whiles I sat ;
> I digg'd a grave and laid him in,
> And happed* him with the sod so green.

* Can the English reader catch the strange tenderness and
pathos of the word *happed?* It is one of the dearest to a

But think na ye my heart was sair,
When I laid the moul' on his yellow hair;
O think na ye my heart was wae,
When I turned about away to gae.

Does the reader remember anything half so touching as that woman's lonely vigil by the dead, in a solitude where no creature came, or her progress to some secret place, carrying the body of her lord, sitting down weary with the burden, and then up and struggling on again? There is in the verses no tumult, no complaint, no wild wringing of sorrowful hands, no frenzied appeal to the pitiless Heaven that saw the deed and made no sign. A broken heart indulges in neither trope nor metaphor; the language is simple as a child's, the circumstances are related without any passion or excitement. All lesser feelings are lost and swallowed up in utter desolation and woe.

Scottish ear, recalling infancy and the thousand instances of the love of a mother's heart, and the unwearied care of a mother's hand. The red-breast *happed* the dead bodies of the Babes in the Wood with leaves. Happed is the nursery word in Scotland, expressing the care with which the bed-clothes are laid upon the little forms, and carefully tucked in about the round sleeping cheeks. What an expression it gives in the verses quoted above to the burden and agony of fondness, all wasted and lavished on unheeding clay!

There is an old song, published by Dr Percy
in his "Reliques," which illustrates the hopeless pathos to which allusion has been made.
The circumstances of the tragedy are unknown.
All that has come down to us is the following
strain of mournful music :—

> O waly waly up the bank,
>   And waly waly down the brae,
> And waly waly yon burn side,
>   Where I and my love were wont to gae.
> I lent my back unto an aik,
>   I thought it was a trusty tree,
> But first it bowed and syne it brak,
>   Sae my true love did lichtly me.
>
> O waly waly gin love be bonny
>   A little time while it is new ;
> But when it's auld it waxeth cauld,
>   And fades away like morning dew.
> O wherefore should I busk my head ?
>   Or wherefore should I kame my hair ?
> For my true love has me forsook,
>   And says he 'll never loe. me mair.
>
> Now Arthur Seat shall be my bed,
>   The sheets shall ne'er be fyled by me ;
> Saint Anton's well shall be my drink,
>   Since my true love has forsaken me.
> Marti'mas wind, when wilt thou blaw,
>   And shake the green leaves aff the tree ?
> O gentle death, when wilt thou cum ?
>   For of my life I am wearie.

'Tis not the frost that freezes fell,
  Nor blawing snaw's inclemencie :
'Tis not sic cauld that makes my cry,
  But my love's heart grown cauld to me.
Whan we came in by Glasgowe town,
  We were a comely sight to see ;
My love was cled in black velvet,
  And I mysell in cramasie.

But had I wist before I kist,
  That love had been sae ill to win,
I had lockt my heart in a case o' gowd,
  And pinned it with a siller pin.
And oh ! if my young babe were born,
  And set upon the nurse's knee,
And I mysell were dead and gane,
  For a maid again I'se never be.

Burns, in one of his letters, quotes the following stanzas from an old ballad he had picked up among the country people. It breathes the same hopeless misery as those already quoted, and pines like them for the rest of the grave :—

O that my father had ne'er on me smiled !
  O that my mother had ne'er to me sung !
O that my cradle had never been rocked,
  But that I had died when I was young !

O that the grave it were my bed !
  My blankets were my winding-sheet !

The clocks and the worms my bed-fellows a',
And, O, sae sound as I should sleep !

"What a sigh was there!" Burns adds; "I do
not remember, in all my reading, to have met
with anything more truly the language of
misery than the exclamation in the last line.
Misery is like love; to speak its language truly
the author must have felt it."

The Ballads relating to sprites, fairies, and
other supernatural creatures, are not many in
number, but are mostly of great poetic beauty.
From these compositions we gain considerable
information regarding the spiritual agents in
which the mounted robber of the marches believed, and at the mention of whose name, or
on approach to the district in which they were
supposed to reside, he piously crossed himself,
and murmured a prayer to Mary Mother. Perhaps, owing to the desolate aspect of the scenery
and the sterner character of the people, the
superstitions of Scotland are of a more terrific
nature than those of the sister kingdom. The
Scotch have no Puck or Robin Goodfellow.
The taciturn Brownie who sets the house to
rights, who threshes as much corn in a single
night as six husbandmen could accomplish in a

summer day, and forsakes the family when he is
insulted by any offer of gift or reward, is the most
kindly disposed to human beings. The greater
proportion, however, of the creatures of popular
superstition are of an uncanny and vindictive disposition. There is the restless Will-o'-the-Wisp,
who betrays the traveller into the treacherous bog and deep morass; the Water-Kelpie,
who haunts at midnight the fords of swollen
streams, and raises shrieks of eldritch laughter,
when horse and man are swept away by the
current; and there are the Fairies, whose mossy
rings are still to be seen on the hill-side; and
when the peasant is overtaken on the lonely
moor by these phantom riders in chase of a
phantom stag, although he sees nothing, a sound
of horns and dogs sweeps past him on the wind;
and on Hallowmas Eve, when they ride forth
in courtly and measured procession, dim shapes
are visible in the moonbeam, and he hears the
trampling of innumerable tiny hoofs and the
music of their bridle bells. The Fairies are a
kidnapping people, and have acquired great
dexterity in their art. They carry off young
children, and leave a peevish and misshapen elf
in its place; and persons of maturer age, if they

happen to sleep within the rings after sunset, are pretty certain to awake in Fairyland. Many a child who wandered out to gather berries in the wood, and who was sought in the evening with tears and a broken heart, and so the next day and the next, is now a happy page to the Fairy Queen. Many a man who never returned from his distant journey, and for whose soul mass has been sung and prayers offered, and whose wife, who thought she never could have forgotten him, sleeps in the bosom of another husband, is at this moment stretched in one of the sweet-smelling valleys, and basking in the everlasting sunshine of that Land of Dream, wondering, perhaps, what his old companions are about on the earth, and if they ever think of him now. Seek not to return, O lost one! However unpleasant to believe, the world wags just as comfortably as when you were one of its denizens. The chair you sat upon is filled. The heart that loved you once has changed its allegiance, and loves another quite as fondly and devotedly. The guests have sat down; every seat is occupied; there is no room for you at the feast. When one of these lost ones wishes to return to earth, he informs some friend, by dream that he has been carried away by the "good people," and points out the method in which his release can be accomplished. The friend thus commissioned takes his station on Hallowmas Eve on the highway along which the Fairies are to pass. Soon the cavalcade is heard approaching. He stands forward and seizes a rider by the mantle, and claims him by name. After some altercation and fierce struggles, the procession sweeps on with murmurs of discontent; a hurried trample of innumerable hoofs and clash of angry bells, and *two* human beings are standing on the midnight road. In the ballad of "Young Tamlane," we are told how a lady rescued her lover in this manner from the Fairies, and we are also admitted behind the scenes, and learn *why* the "good people" have a *penchant* for the children of human parents. Elf-land, it seems, like every other land, has its secret history and its own annoyances. It appears, then, that the land of Fairy must pay tribute to Hell once every seven years, that tribute being its fattest inhabitant. The Fairies naturally prefer handing over to the tender mercies of the Fiend one of the human mortals whom they have ensnared, rather than

C

one of their own race. Young Tamlane is unhappily inclined to obesity; in fact, he is the
Jack Falstaff of Fairyland; and as the seven
years are well-nigh expired, and the time draws
near when Hell must receive its due, his sleek
and well-to-do condition throws him into a
state of considerable trepidation. He therefore
appears to his lady-love, and tells her that he
enjoys exceedingly the pleasures of Elf-land;
indeed, he would not think of changing his
residence but for the weighty considerations
already mentioned, which he describes with considerable *naïveté* and pathos :—

> Then I would never tire, Janet,
>   In Elfish land to dwell,
> But aye, at every seven years,
> They pay the teind to hell;
> And I am sae fat and fair of flesh,
>   I fear 't will be mysel'.

He adds that that evening is Halloween, the
evening when the Fairies would ride abroad,
and that if she would save him, she must act
to-night or never. She asks how she should
recognise him among the passing troops of
ghostly knights and unearthly cavaliers. He
replies :—

The first company that passes by,
    Say na, and let them gae ;
The next company that passes by,
    Sae na, and do right sae ;
The third company that passes by,
    Then I'll be ane o' thae.

First let pass the black, Janet,
    And syne let pass the brown ;
But grip ye to the milk-white steed,
    And pu' the rider doun.

For I ride on the milk-white steed,
    And aye nearest the toun ;
Because I was a christened knight,
    They gave me that renown.

My right hand will be gloved, Janet,
    My left hand will be bare ;
And these the tokens I gie thee,
    Nae doubt I will be there.

They'll turn me in your arms, Janet,
    An adder and a snake ;
But haud me fast, let me not pass,
    Gin ye wad buy me maik.

They'll turn me in your arms, Janet,
    An adder and an ask ;
They'll turn me in your arms, Janet,
    A bale that burns fast.

They'll turn me in your arms, Janet,
    A red-hot gad o' airn ;
But haud me fast, let me not pass,
    For I'll do you no harm.

They'll shape me in your arms, Janet,
    A tod, but, and an eel ;
But haud me fast, nor let me gang,
    As you do love me weel.

They'll shape me in your arms, Janet,
    A dove, but, and a swan,
And last they'll shape me in your arms
    A mother-naked man :
Cast your green mantle over me,
    I'll be myself again.

Janet takes her station at the Miles Cross, pulls down the rider on the milk-white steed, and holds her lover fast through all his changing shapes. After her green mantle is thrown over him, the wrathful voice of the Fairy Queen is heard—

Up then spake the Queen of Fairies,
    Out o' a bush o' rye,
" She's taen awa' the bonniest knight
    In a' my companie.

" But had I kenned Tamlane," she says,
    "I lady had borrowed thee—
I wad ta'en out thy twa grey een,
    Put in twa een o' tree.

" Had I but kenned Tamlane," she says,
    " Before ye cam frae hame—
I wad ta'en out your heart o' flesh,
    Put in a heart o' stane.

" Had I but had the wit yestreen
   That I hae coft the day—
I paid my kane seven times to Hell,
   Ere you'd been won away."

But the most famous earthly inhabitant of
Fairy-land was Thomas Learmont of Ercel-
doune, better known by his traditionary name
of Thomas the Rhymer, poet, prophet, and the
beloved of the Queen of Elf-land, who alone of
mortal men dared to kiss her lips, and whose
grey tower nods over the Leader, still regarded
with superstitious awe by the natives of that
district. This apparition True Thomas saw as
he lay stretched on the Huntly Bank on a
summer's day :—

True Thomas lay on the Huntlie Bank ;
   A ferlie he spied wi' his ee :
And there he saw a ladye bright,
   Come riding doun by the Eildon tree.

Her shirt was o' the grass green silk,
   Her mantle o' the velvet fyne :
At ilka tett of her horse's mane,
   Hung fifty siller bells and nine.

True Thomas he pulled aff his cap,
   And louted low down to his knee,
" All hail, thou mighty Queen of Heaven !
   For thy peer on earth I never did see."

"O no, O no, Thomas," she said,
   "That name does not belong to me ;
I am but the Queen of fair Elf-land,
   That am hither come to visit thee.

"Harp and carp, Thomas," she said,
   "Harp and carp along wi' me ;
And if ye dare to kiss my lips,
   Sure of your bodie I will be."

"Betide me weal, betide me woe,
   That weird shall never daunton me."
Syne he has kissed her rosy lips,
   All underneath the Eildon tree.

From that day for seven years Thomas was
seen no more among men. After that period
he returned and scattered abroad prophecies of
days of dool and woe to Scotland, when the
fields should be harvestless, and the hare bring
forth her young on the hearthstone of the castle ;
of storms raging from sea to sea, of disastrous
battle-fields, of the strange overflow of rivers,
and the final union of the crowns. When he left
Elf-land, he was bound to return at the pleasure
of its Queen. One day Thomas was feasting in
his own tower, when a messenger burst into the
apartment, and told that a doe and fawn of
wonderful beauty were pacing, without fear, and
silently as a dream, the streets of the little

village. Thomas knew the signal, and immediately arose, followed the creatures into the forest, and was never again seen on earth. Had the Queen pined for her favourite? To what glory was he marshalled? What weird had he to dree? His countrymen for centuries believed that he was still alive in Fairy-land, and looked for his return.

The district of country which produced the Border Ballads—stretching from the cataract of the Grey Mare's Tail, along the green valley of the Yarrow, onward to where the castle-keep of Norham blackens against the sinking sun, and embracing, amongst other streams, the Tweed and the waters of the Teviot and the Ettrick—is, although somewhat limited in extent, by far the most interesting in Scotland. It is a region for the most part pastoral, with round swelling hills of no great altitude, and valleys through which run waters whose names are familiar to every Scottish ear. The traveller passes in a day's journey over fifty battle-fields, some famous, some forgotten, descrying every few miles as he goes, on the hill-side or up the retreating glen, the grey peel of a border laird, roofless and open to the sky, the walls crowned with

long withered grasses, which sigh in the passing
wind, and half a dozen sheep feeding around its
base, with bits of straggling brambles sticking in
their wool ; or perhaps, as the day draws to a
close, the mightier ruin of the castle of some
feudal lord looms upon him through the fast
fading light.   The whole district is full of associations.   Every stream has its tradition, every
glen is peopled by legends, every ruin is consecrated by a story of love or revenge.   Genius
has thrown an additional charm over the country.
As you pace beside the crystal mirror of St Mary's
Loch, or visit the farm-house of Altrive, you
remember Hogg.   The shade of Wordsworth
wanders along the silver course of the Yarrow ;
and when the swollen Tweed raves as it sweeps,
red and broad, round the ruins of Dryburgh,
you think of him who rests there—the magician
asleep in the lap of legends old, the sorcerer
buried in the heart of the land he has made
enchanted.   This region, so peaceful now, quietly
growing its harvests and fattening its flocks, was
in the olden time one great theatre of strife
and bloodshed.   It was the battle-field of the
Percy and the Douglas ; and, to quote the old
chronicle—

There was never a time on the March partes,
    Sen the Douglas and the Percy met,
But yt was marvell an the redde blude roune not
    As the rane does in the stret.

The Kers, Scotts, Armstrongs, and other
Border clans, dwelt on the waters of the Ettrick,
the Whitadder, and the Teviot, and preyed on
England, Scotland, and on one another, with
great impartiality. Though the cloud of English
war first burst on the Border, and midnight was
reddened by flames from peel and farm-stead-
ing, and rendered hideous by the shouts of the
plunderers and the lowing of cattle driven off
with a tumult and rapidity utterly repugnant
to their meditative and decorous mode of life ;
—though the Jameses, in moments of unusual
vigour, suddenly appeared on the marches with
an army, and left dozens of the robbers wavering in the wind over the gateways of their own
towers,—still Ishmael was untamed; in a week
Cumberland was swept, or the flocks of the
Lothian farmer driven off by the light of his
burning house. Crushed and broken, the spirit
of the Borderer was never subdued ; his hand
was against every man, and every man's hand
against him. " Forgive your enemies " was never

a part of his creed; and revenge, prompt and terrible, was elevated into a chief place among the virtues. He never forgot an injury; and although the insult was given in hot youth, and years had elapsed, the avenger was silently upon the track, and in grey hairs blood was exacted for blood, and groan for groan. On one occasion, Sir Robert Ker, the Warden of the Scottish March, was murdered by three Englishmen, two of whom made their escape. After some time they began to appear in public, and one of them fixed his residence at a considerable distance from the Scottish Border. On this becoming known, two servants of the murdered man's son passed into England during the night, slew him in his own house, and brought the head to their master in Edinburgh, who exposed it on a pole in one of the public streets, and left it there to wither in the sun like a gourd. In the reign of James V., Albany, then Regent of the kingdom, thirsting for an opportunity to gratify his private revenge, invited Lord Home to a solemn council to be held on State affairs at Edinburgh. When the hapless chieftain arrived, he was seized, condemned on a charge of treason, and executed along with his brother. Before sailing for

France, Albany appointed Sir Antony Darcy, a French knight of great ability, to be Warden of the East March in his absence. This Frenchman was an object of intense hatred to the whole clan whose leader had been slain. On the occasion of a border riot, he encountered Sir David Home, who reproached him with the death of his chief. A scuffle ensued, and Darcy sought refuge in flight. He was pursued for miles; at last his horse sank up to the haunches in a morass. His enemies coming up, struck off his head, and Sir David Home, shearing off his long flowing hair, plaited it into a wreath, and wore it as a trophy at his saddle-bow. From a passage in the Memoirs of Beaugué, a French officer who served in Scotland (quoted by Sir Walter Scott in his " Minstrelsy "), we learn the dreadful nature of the animosity which flamed between the English and the marchmen. The Castle of Fairnihirst being besieged by the Borderers, and reduced to extremities, the commandant crept through the breach made in the wall, and surrendered himself to a French officer. A Borderer immediately stept forward, and at one blow struck the Englishman's head four paces from his trunk. A hundred Scots rushed

forward to wash their hands in his blood. After
the Scots had slain all their own prisoners, they
bought up those of the French, and their hatred
may be imagined, when it is not mentioned that
in a single instance they attempted to cheapen
the price. Beaugué mentions that he himself sold
a prisoner for a small horse to a Scot, who
doubtless conceived that he had secured the
luxury of killing an Englishman in the manner
after his own heart at a decided bargain. There
are some anecdotes preserved of Walter Scott of
Harden, which give a curious enough peep into
the domestic manners of a Border chief. Harden
married the Flower of Yarrow, who bore him
six stalwart sons, and it sometimes happened,
when the giants strode in to dinner with appal-
ling appetites, whetted by the chase and the
mountain breeze, they found, on uncovering the
dishes, a pair of clean spurs in each, placed
there by the fair hands of the Flower herself.
That night an English farmer would mourn over
empty stalls. A prompt grim old man was the
Laird of Harden,—no danger of his armour
rusting, or grass growing beneath his horse's
hoofs. On one occasion his youngest son was
slain in a fray with the Scotts of Gilmanscleugh,

but the old warrior had no tears to shed over his youngest born. The Flower of Yarrow might throw herself on the body of her dead son in clamorous grief. That was what women were fit, for. He had other work to do. His sons flew to arms, and were eager for revenge. Harden quietly locked them up in their own tower, and put the keys in his pocket, letting their fierce hearts fret themselves out there. He then mounted his horse and rode to Edinburgh, where he proclaimed the crime, and gained from the Crown the gift of his enemies' lands. He rode back as rapidly as he had come, the charter in his hands. Releasing his sons, he cried, with a gleam in his grey eye, " To horse, lads, and let us take possession. The lands of Gilmanscleugh are well worth a dead son!" Educated in the belief that plunder was the whole duty of man, and revenge the most exalted virtue, the Borderer when brought to suffer, whether by royal authority or at the hands of an opposing clan, met his fate with an unfaltering heart. It was a misfortune, of course, to be hanged, a thing to be avoided if possible; but he could not feel that he was a criminal, and for him the gallows had no ignominy. He knew that his execu-

tioners merited the same fate as himself, and his
last thought on earth was the comforting one,
that in all probability they would meet it one
of these days—consolation dashed next moment
by the thought that he could not be there to
see. Pity that! So a curse to his foes, to his
friends the stern'st goodnight, and now ——.
Yet these boisterous men had their virtues.
They were possessed of a rude generosity, and
would go through fire and water and dare captivity to save a friend. They were civilised
enough to abhor wanton bloodshed ; they were
savage enough to hate like death all lying
and deceit. When a prisoner was dismissed on
parole, he transmitted his ransom, or, failing that,
returned into the hands of his captor. They
sacredly observed their word, and a bargain
sealed by a clash of their iron palms was in-
violable as a usurer's bond. Deep down in their
grim hearts dwelt tears and woman's tenderness, fountains which, if they seldom overflowed, .
never entirely dried up. One of the Armstrongs,
before he was executed in Edinburgh for the
murder of Sir John Carmichael, sang the following lament :—

This night is my departing night,
  For here nae langer must I stay;
There's neither friend nor foe o' mine
  But wishes me away.

What I hae done thro' lack o' wit
  I never never can recall;
I hope ye're a' my friends as yet,
  Goodnight, and joy be with you all.

And a strain is put into the mouth of Lord Maxwell, on his leaving Scotland for France a banished man, which suggested "Childe Harold's Goodnight;" but the Border lord's lament to "Dumfries, his proper place," and "Carlaverock Fair," surpasses in tenderness and pathos the modern poet singing as he gazed on England like a cloud on the horizon, the sun setting behind him in the splendid sea.

In the Border Ballads, this savage state of society, with its strife and turmoil, its rude nobleness and generosity, is faithfully represented. We open their pages, and find ourselves in a new world. The Scotch moss-troopers have been across the Borders with the dawn, and are now pushing rapidly homeward with flocks of sheep and a hundred head of cattle. The alarm has spread for miles, and Cumberland is mounting in haste with spear and lance. Across barren waste and up steep ravine a bloodhound is already baying on the robbers' track. Men are posted on every ford on the Liddel; and afar on the Souter Moor, Will, stalwart Wat, and long Aicky are sitting, with a sleut-dog on the watch. We have fairly trapped the Scots to-day; and before night there will be many an empty saddle in their troop. Here is part of the rude song of one of the sufferers in the raid :—

Sleep'ry Sim of the Lamb-hill,
And snoring Jock of Suport-mill,
Ye are baith right het and fou ;
But my wae wakens na you.
Last night I saw a sorry sight—
Nought left me o' four-and-twenty guide ousen and ky,
My weel-ridden gelding and a white quey,
But a toom byre and a wide,
And the twelve nogs on ilka side.
　　Fy lads ! shout a' a' a' a' a'
　　My gear's a' gane.

Weel may ye ken
Last night I was right scarce o' men ;
But Toppet Hob o' the Mains had guestened in my house by
　　chance.
I set him to wear the fore-door wi' a spear, while I kept the
　　back-door wi' a lance ;
But they hae run him thro' the thick o' the thie, and broke
　　his knee-pan,

And the mergh o' his shin-bane has run down on his spur-
leather whang ;
He's lame while he lives and where're he may gang.
Fy, lads ! shout a' a' a' a' a'
My gear's a' gane.

Battle is an everyday occurrence, and wounds
and dislocations are matters of course. Tush,
man, don't look so white, tie up the ugly thing
with a napkin ; it is your turn to-day, it may be
mine to-morrow. Death, too, is always walking
about on the Borders ; even the little children
have seen him, and know his face. The older
troopers when they meet him give him good
day, like a common acquaintance, and some of
the more familiar stay for a moment to bandy a
grim jest or two with him.

Ane gat a twist o' the craig,
Ane gat a punch o' the wame ;
Symy Haw gat lamed of a leg,
And syne ran bellowing hame.
Hoot, hoot, the auld man's slain outright !
Lay him now wi' his face doun—he's a sorrowful sight.
Janet, thou donet,
I'll lay my best bonnet,
Thou gets a new gudeman afore it be night.

A fit place, truly, to jest about a new husband ;
the old one lying so still there, face downward,
on the trampled grass.

D

In the ballad entitled "Jamie Telfer," we
have a spirited description of a foray, and the
subsequent pursuit and rescue of the prey. The
Captain of Bewcastle had carried off Jamie's
cattle, and the ruined man starts up, "leaving a
greeting wife and bairnies three," and runs ten
miles afoot over the new fallen snow to summon
aid. He alarms peel after peel, and the awaked
inmates hurry on jack, and grasp lance, and
push on in hot haste to Branksome Ha', where
Buccleuch dwelt in a sort of feudal state. "Wha
brings the fray to me?" cried the old lord, as
the riders clattered up to his gates—

> "It's I, Jamie Telfer o' the fair Dodhead,
>   And a harried man I think I be !
> There's nought left in the fair Dodhead
>   But a greeting wife and bairnies three."
>
> "Alack for wae !" quoth the guid auld lord,
>   "And ever my heart is wae for thee !
> But fye, gar cry on Willie, my son,
>   To see that he come to me speedilie.
>
> "Gar warn the water braid and wide,
>   Gar warn it sune and hastilie ;
> They that winna ride for Telfer's kye,
>   Let them never look in the face o' me.
>
> "Warn Wat o' Harden and his sons,
>   Wi' them will Borthwick water ride ;

Warn Gandilands and Allan-haugh,
 And Gilmanscleugh and Commonside."

The Scotts they rade, the Scotts they ran,
 Sae starkly and sae steadilie ;
And aye the ower-word o' the thrang
 Was—"Rise for Branksome readilie !"

With their number augmented, they ride forward, and in a short time come in sight of the Captain of Bewcastle and his men driving the booty straight for England. As was to be expected, little time is wasted in words:

Then tilt they gaed wi' heart and hand,
 The blows fell thick as bickering hail ;
And mony a horse ran masterless,
 And mony a comely cheek was pale.

But Willie was stricken ower the head,
 And thro' the knapscap the sword has gane,
And Harden grat for very rage,
 When Willie on the grund lay slain.

But he's ta'en aff his gude steel cap,
 And thrice he's waved it in the air ;
The Dinlay snaw was ne'er mair white
 Nor the lyart locks of Harden's hair.

"Revenge ! revenge !" auld Wat gan cry ;
 "Fye, lads, lay on them cruellie,
We'll ne'er see Teviotside again,
 Or Willie's death revenged shall be."

O many a horse ran masterless,
  The splintered lances flew on hie ;
But or they war to the Kershope ford,
  The Scotts had gotten the victory.

Having now secured Jamie's cattle, the idea suggests itself to one of the party that they might improve the occasion by robbing the Captain's house :

There was a wild gallant among us a',
  His name was Watty wi' the Wudspurs,
Cried—" On for his house in Stanegirthside,
  If ony man will ride with us ! "

When they cam to the Stanegirthside,
  They dang wi' trees and burst the door,
They loosed out a' the Captain's kye,
  And set them forth our lads before.

There was an auld wyfe ayont the fire,
  A wee bit o' the Captain's kin :
" Whae dar loose out the Captain's kye,
  Or answer to him and his men ?"

"It's I, Watty Wudspurs, loose the kye,
  I winna layne my name frae thee !
And I will loose out the Captain's kye
  In scorn of a' his men and he."

When they cam to the fair Dodhead,
  They were a wellcum sight to see !
For instead of his ain ten milk kye,
  Jamie Telfer has gotten thirty and three.

And he has paid the rescue shot,
    Baith wi' goud and white monie ;
And at the burial o' Willie Scott
    I wat was mony a weeping ee.

But "Kinmont Willie" is the finest of all these Ballads ; remarkable for the daring deed it celebrates, and the light and laughing scorn of danger which it exhibits. The moss-trooper encounters peril with as gay a heart as he opens a dance with a rustic beauty at a Border fair. Lord Scroope and Sheriff Salkelde have succeeded in capturing Kinmont Willie, a robber whose exploits were well known on the marches :

They band his legs beneath the steed,
    They tied his hands behind his back ;
They guarded him five-some on each side,
    And they brought him ower the Liddel-rack.

They led him thro' the Liddel-rack,
    And also thro' the Carlisle sands ;
They brought him to Carlisle castel,
    To be at my Lord Scroope's commands.

"My hands are tied, but my tongue is free,
    And whae will dare this deed avow,
Or answer by the Border law,
    Or answer to the bauld Buccleuch ?"

"Now haud thy tongue, thou rank riever !
    There's never a Scot shall set thee free ;
Before ye cross my castle yate,
    I trow ye shall take farewell o' me."

"Fear ye na that, my lord," quo' Willie ;
  "By the faith o' my body, Lord Scroope," he said,
"I never yet lodged in a hostelrie
  But I paid my lawing before I gaed."

So while Willie lies in the central dungeon under a load of clanking chains, thinking on his sins, and the cheerless hours creep on that bring his death on Haribee, intelligence of the capture reaches Buccleuch in Branksome Hall.   How the blood of the Border chieftain boils up—

He has ta'en the table wi' his hand,
  He garr'd the red wine spring on hie ;
"Now Christ's curse on my head," he said,
  "But avenged of Lord Scroope I'll be.

"O is my basnet a widow's curtch,
  Or my lance a wand o' the willow tree,
Or my arm a ladye's lilye hand,
  That an English lord should lightly me ?

"And have they ta'en him, Kinmont Willie,
  Against the truce of Border tide ?
And forgotten that the bauld Buccleuch
  Is Keeper here on the Scottish side ?

"And have they ta'en him, Kinmont Willie,
  Withouten either dread or fear ?
And forgotten that the bauld Buccleuch
  Can back a steed and shake a spear ?"

Kinmont is to be delivered, and the rescuing party is described. Note the characteristic touch

of Border humour at the close.   It is quite an
exquisite jest to run a man through the body,
and the want of appreciation of the joke on the
part of the skewered makes it all the more delightful :

> He has called him forty marchmen bauld,
>   Were kinsmen to the bauld Buccleuch ;
> With spur on heel, and splent on spauld,
>   And gleuves of green and feathers blue.
>
> There were five and five before them a',
>   Wi' hunting-horns and bugles bright ;
> And five and five came wi' Buccleuch,
>   Like warden's men arrayed for fight.
>
> And five and five, like a mason gang,
>   That carried the ladders lang and hie ;
> And five and five, like broken men,
>   And so they reached the Woodhouselee.
>
> And as we crossed the Bateable land,
>   When to the English side we held,
> The first o' men that we met wi',
>   Whae sould it be but the fause Sakelde ?
>
> " Where be ye gaun, ye hunters keen ?"
>   Quo' fause Sakelde ; " come tell to me ?"
> " We go to hunt an English stag
>   Has trespassed on the Scots countrie."
>
> " Where be ye gaun, ye marshal men ?"
>   Quo' fause Sakelde ; " come tell me true ?"
> " We go to catch a rank riever
>   Has broken faith wi' the bauld Buccleuch."

" Where are ye gaun, ye mason lads ?"
    Quo' fause Sakelde ; " come tell to me ?"
" We gang to harry a corbie's nest
    That wons not far frae Woodhouselee."

" Where be ye gaun, ye broken men ?"
    Quo' fause Sakelde ; " come tell to me ?"
Now Dickie of Dryhope led that band,
    And the nevir a word of lear had he.

" Why trespass ye on the English side ?
    Row-footed outlaws, stand !" quo' he.
The nevir a word had Dickie to say,
    Sae he thrust the lance through his fause bodie.

Here is the rescue and conclusion :—

Wi' coulters and wi' forehammers,
    We garred the bars bang merrilie,
Until we came to the inner prison,
    Where Willie o' Kinmont he did lie.

And when we cam to the inner prison,
    Where Willie o' Kinmont he did lie—
" O sleep ye, wake ye, Kinmont Willie,
    Upon the day that thou's to die ?"

" O I sleep saft, and I wake aft ;
    It's lang since sleeping was fleyed frae me !
Gie my service back to my wife and bairns,
    And a' gude fellows that speir for me."

Then Red Rowan has hente him up,
    The starkest man in Teviotdale—
" Abide, abide, now, Red Rowan,
    Till of my Lord Scroope I take farewell.

" Farewell, farewell, my gude Lord Scroope,
   My gude Lord Scroope, farewell," he cried ;
" I'll pay you for my lodging maill,
   When first we meet on the Border side."

Then shoulder high, with shout and cry,
   We bore him down the ladder lang ;
At every stride Red Rowan made,
   I wot the Kinmont's airns played clang !

" O mony a time," quo' Kinmont Willie,
   " I have ridden a horse baith wild and wood,
But a rougher beast than Red Rowan,
   I ween my legs have ne'er bestrode."

" And mony a time," quo' Kinmont Willie,
   " I've pricked a horse out once the furs ;
But since the day I backed a steed,
   I never wore sic cumbrous spurs."

We scarce had won the Staneshaw-bank,
   When a' the Carlisle bells were rung,
And a thousand men on horse and foot
   Cam wi' the keen Lord Scroope along.

Buccleuch has turned to Eden Water,
   Even where it flowed frae bank to brim ;
And he has plunged in wi' a' his band,
   And safely swam them through the stream.

He turned him to the other side,
   And at Lord Scroope his glove flung he—
" If ye like na my visit in merry England,
   In fair Scotland come visit me."

All sore astonished stood Lord Scroope,
   He stood as still as rock of stane;
He scarcely dared to trew his eyes,
   When thro' the water they had gane.

"He's either himsel' a devil frae hell,
   Or else his mother a witch maun be;
I wadna hae ridden that wan water
   For a' the gowd in Christentie."

So all those fierce spirits have stormed themselves out, and we learn the stories of their
strifes and hatreds, their generosities and revenges, their burnings and plunderings, from
the strains of a few wandering and forgotten
minstrels. . They were brave men, who did what
work they had to do with promptitude and
vigour, dandled children proudly enough on their
knees, and when it came to that at last, they
clashed down in harness, and death and pain
got as few groans out of them as out of most.
Times are changed now, however. Their sons
have the same bold hearts and strong arms, but
they are turned to other uses, and worn out in
other tasks. The stream which of yore rushed
wastefully from fount to sea, is banked and
bridged; it turns the wheels of innumerable mills,
carries on its bosom barge and stately ship,
sweeps through mighty towns where thousands

live and die beneath an ever-brooding canopy of
smoke, and melts at last into peaceful ocean-
rest, a labourer, grimed and worn ; but its cradle
is still, as of old, on the mountain-top among the
sacred splendours of the dawn, its companions
the flying sunbeams and the troops of stars, its
nurses the dews of heaven and the weeping
clouds.

There are modern writers who conceive that
man is only poetical when he clanks about in
mail and swears by St Bridget ; when he in-
habits an immense castle turreted and moated,
with a background of savage pines, amongst
which the winds make a great roaring of winter
nights ; spends his forenoons amongst his dogs,
or amuses himself with flying his falcon at
the blue-legged heron that rises screaming from
the weedy pool ; and they are careful to inform
the world that the ballad is the most natural
form of poetry, and ought to be the model of
all future compositions. The wisdom of this
seems very questionable. The most profitless
work on this planet is the simulation of ancient
ballads ; to hold water in a sieve is the merest
joke to it. A man may as well try to recall
yesterday, or to manufacture tradition or anti-

quity, with the moss of ages on them. It has been attempted by men of the highest genius, but in no case with encouraging success. If ever a man was qualified for the task, it was Sir Walter Scott. No one lived more in the past than he. He was more familiar with the men of the Middle Ages than with the men who brushed past him in Princes Street; and yet his efforts in the ballad form—beautiful and spirited poems as they all are—are devoid of the homely garrulousness, the simple-heartedness, the carelessness and unconsciousness which give such a charm to the productions of the old minstrels. There is no modern attempt which could by any chance or possibility be mistaken for an original. You read the date upon it as legibly as upon the letter you received yesterday. However dexterous the workman, he is discovered—a word blabs, the turn of a phrase betrays him. Simplicity, which is seen at a glance to be affected, carelessness elaborately feigned, and modes of thought and expression which have no correspondence with the feelings or the language of living men, are not ornamental to any form of composition. Why should we go to steel-clad barons and rough-riding moss-troopers; is there not sufficient poetry in the life which environs us to-day? It is, of course, the merest truism, that in every age and under every disguise—beating beneath the mail of the Crusader or the vest of the English gentleman—the same human heart sorrows and rejoices, and that all poetry resides in *it*, and not in its encasement of Yorkshire broadcloth or Spanish steel; but it is astonishing how frequently a truism which has passed for generations among men like current coin, would startle them if they only took the trouble to examine it. The more generally a thing is supposed to be believed by mankind, the less real faith there is in it. Handle your truism, and it explodes beneath your unsuspecting nose like a bombshell. Carlyle utters the merest truisms, and what a strange sound that is;—there is again a prophet amongst men! Our ballad poetry is valuable; for certain special merits of genuineness and nature, second only to the Shakespearian drama; but why it should be chosen as a model, and sedulously imitated, is not altogether evident. Let genius have free range and scope; it has its own laws which it must obey, and no others; and, although ever new, its developments are ever beautiful and harmonious. Poetry has a value in right of its truth and beauty; it has also a value of an historical and illustrative nature; the first may decrease, and be less regarded from the changing habits and feelings of society; the second increases necessarily as the ages roll.   Every bygone period of the world has reflected itself in its contemporary poetry. History storms on with siege and battle and political crisis, but Poetry runs alongside supplementing History, smoothing its austerities, filling up its chasms and interstices with music, catching up the life of the streets and the current talk and humours of men, chronicling the emotions, the desires that inflame, the fears and spectres that daunt the heart.   The Ballads are full of the turbulent times which environed their authors.   When we wish to know something of the fourteenth century, we derive our knowledge, not so much from formal history, as from Chaucer's picture of the pilgrims in the room at the Tabard, or his description of their ride to Canterbury on the following morning. Though so long ago, we can see the flutter of their dresses and hear them laughing yet.   The reader of Pope values him, not so much for his

splendid antitheses and his glittering wit, but
because in his pages he comes face to face with
the century, breathes its very air, walks into
its saloons, sits among beruffed and rapiered
dandies and beauties with patches on their
cheeks, hears all their delicious scandals, and
the good things of the wits; and whether in-
tentionally or unintentionally—perhaps all the
better and completer that it is done without
special purpose or design—the day which is now
passing will be preserved for future men in its
poetry.   And while history shall repeat the
names of Alma and Sebastopol, and the story
of the silent Emperor across the water, Tennyson and the Brownings will open the doors of our
houses, so that readers may see the faces, hear
the voices, and note, if they choose, the very
furniture of the rooms, with the spaniel asleep
on the rug, of the men who are living now.

AN ESSAY ON AN OLD SUBJECT.

THE discovery of a grey hair when you are brushing out your whiskers of a morning—first fallen flake of the coming snows of age—is a disagreeable thing; so is the intimation from your old friend and comrade that his eldest daughter is about to be married; so are flying twinges of gout, shortness of breath on the hill-side, the fact that even the moderate use of your friend's wines at dinner upsets you. These things are disagreeable, because they tell you that you are no longer young—that you have passed through youth, are now in middle age, and faring onward to the shadows in which somewhere a grave is hid.

Thirty is the age of the gods; and the first grey hair informs you that you art at least ten or twelve years older than that. Apollo is never middle-aged, but you are. Olympus lies several years behind you; you have lived for more than half your natural term; and you know the road

which lies before you is very different from that
which lies behind. You have yourself changed.
In the present man of forty-two you can barely
recognise the boy of nineteen that once was.
Hope sang on the sunny slope of life's hill as
you ascended; she is busily singing the old
song in the ears of a new generation, but you
have passed out of the reach of her voice. You
have tried your strength; you have learned precisely what you can do; you have thrown the
hammer so often that you know to an inch how
far you *can* throw it—at least you are a great
fool if you do not. The world, too, has been
looking on, and has made up its mind about
you. It has appraised you as an auctioneer
appraises an estate or the furniture of a house.
"Once you served Prince Florizel and wore
three pile," but the brave days of campaign-
ing are over. What to you are canzonets
and love-songs? The mighty passion is vapid
and second-hand. Cupid will never more
flutter rosily over your head; at most he will
only flutter in an uninspired fashion above
the head of your daughter-in-law. You have
sailed round the world, seen all its wonders, and
come home again, and must adorn your dwell-

E

ing, as best you can, with the rare things you have picked up on the way. At life's table you have tasted of every dish except the Covered One, and of that you will have your share by and by. The road over which you are fated to march is more than half traversed, and at every onward stage the scenery is certain to become more sombre, and in due time the twilight will fall. To you, on your onward journey, there will be little to astonish, little to delight. The Interpreter's House is behind where you first read the poets; so is also the House Beautiful with the Three Damsels, where you first learned to love. As you pass onward you are attended by your henchman Memory, who may be either the cheerfullest or gloomiest of companions. You have come up out of the sweet-smelling valley flowers; you are now on the broken granite, seamed and wrinkled with dried up water-courses; and before you, striking you full in the face, is the broad disc of the solitary setting sun.

One does not like to be an old fogy, and still less perhaps does one like to own to being one. You may remember when you were the youngest person in every company into which you entered, and how it pleased you to think how precociously clever you were, and how opulent in Time. You were introduced to the great Mr Blank—at least twenty years older than yourself—and could not help thinking how much greater you would be than Mr Blank by the time you reached his age. But pleasant as it is to be the youngest member of every company, that pleasure does not last for ever. As years pass on you do not quite develop into the genius you expected; and the new generation makes its appearance and pushes you from your stool. You make the disagreeable discovery that there is a younger man of promise in the world than even you; then the one younger man becomes a dozen younger men; then younger men come flowing in like waves; and before you know where you are, by this impertinent younger generation—fellows who were barely breeched when you won your first fame —you are shouldered into Old Fogydom, and your staid ways are laughed at, perhaps, by the irreverent scoundrels into the bargain. There is nothing more wonderful in youth than this wealth in Time. It is only a Rothschild who can indulge in the amusement of tossing a sovereign to a beggar. It is only a young man who can dream and build castles in the air. What are twenty years to a young fellow of twenty? An ample air-built stage for his pomps and triumphal processions. What are twenty years to a middle-aged man of forty-five? The falling of the curtain, the covering up of the empty boxes, the screwing out of the gas, and the counting of the money taken at the doors, with the notion, perhaps, that the performance was rather a poor thing. It is with a feeling curiously compounded of pity and envy that one listens to young men talking of what they are going to do. They will light their torches at the sun! They will regenerate the world! They will abolish war, and hand in the Millennium! What pictures they will paint! What poems they will write! One knows while one listens how it will all end. But it is Nature's way; she is always sending on her young generations full of hope. The Atlantic roller bursts in harmless foam among the shingle and driftwood at your feet, but the next, nothing daunted by the fate of its predecessor, comes on with threatening crest, as if to carry everything before it. And so it will be for ever and ever. The world could not get on else. My experience is of use only to myself. I cannot bequeath it to my son as I can my cash. Every human being must start untrammelled and work out the problem for himself. For a couple of thousand years now the preacher has been crying out *Vanitas vanitatum*, but no young man takes him at his word. The blooming apple must grate in the young man's teeth before he owns that it is dust and ashes. Young people will take nothing on hearsay. I remember, when a lad, of Todd's *Student's Manual* falling into my hands. I perused therein a solemn warning against novel reading. Nor did the reverend compiler speak without authority. He stated that he had read the works of Fielding, Smollett, Sir Walter Scott, American Cooper, James, and the rest, and he laid his hand on his heart and assured his young friends that in each of these works, even the best of them, were subtle snares and gilded baits for the soul. These books they were adjured to avoid, as they would a pestilence or a raging fire. It was this alarming passage in the transatlantic Divine's treatise that first made a novel reader of me. I was not content to accept his experience: I must see for myself. Every one

must begin at the beginning ; and it is just as
well. If a new generation were starting with
the wisdom 'of its elders, what would be the
consequence ? Would there be any love-making
twenty years after ? Would there be any fine
extravagance ? Would there be any lending
of money ? Would there be any noble friend-
ships such as that of Damon and Pythias,
or of David and Jonathan, or even of our
own Beaumont and Fletcher, who had purse,
wardrobe, and genius in common ? It is extremely doubtful. *Vanitas vanitatum* is a bad
doctrine to begin life with. For the plant
Experience to be of any worth, a man must
grow it for himself.

The man of forty-five or thereby is compelled
to own, if he sits down to think about it, that
existence is very different from what it was
twenty years previously. His life is more than
half spent, to begin with. He is like one who
has spent seven hundred and fifty pounds of his
original patrimony of a thousand. Then from
his life there has departed that "wild freshness
of morning" which Tom Moore sang about. In
his onward journey he is not likely to encounter
anything absolutely new. He has already con-

jugated every tense of the verb To Be. He has been in love twice or thrice. He has been married—only once, let us trust. In all probability he is the father of a fine family of children. He has been ill, and he has recovered; he has experienced triumph and failure; he has known what it is to have money in his purse, and what it is to want money in his purse. Sometimes he has been a debtor, sometimes he has been a creditor. He has stood by the brink of half a dozen graves, and heard the clod falling on the coffin-lid. All this he has experienced; the only new thing before him is death, and even to that he has at various times approximated. Life has lost most of its unexpectedness, its zest, its novelty, and has become like a worn shoe or a thread-bare doublet. To him there is no new thing under the sun. But then this growing old is a gradual process; and zest, sparkle, and novelty are not essential to happiness. The man who has reached five-and-forty has learned what a pleasure there is in customariness and use and wont—in having everything around him familiar, tried, confidential. Life may have become humdrum, but his tastes have become humdrum too. Novelty annoys him, the intrusion of an unfamiliar object puts him out. A pair of newly embroidered slippers would be much more ornamental than the well-worn articles which lie warming for him before the library fire ; but then he cannot get his feet into them so easily. He is contented with his old friends — a new friend would break the charm of the old familiar faces. He loves the hedgerows, and the fields, and the brook, and the bridge which he sees every day, and he would not exchange them for Alps and glaciers. By the time a man has reached forty-five he lies as comfortably in his habits as the silk-worm in its cocoon. On the whole, I take it that middle age is a happier period than youth. In the entire circle of the year there are no days so delightful as those of a fine October, when the trees are bare to the mild heavens, and the red leaves bestrew the road, and you can feel the breath of winter, morning and evening—no days so calm, so tenderly solemn, and with such a reverent meekness in the air. The lyrical up-burst of the lark at such a time would be incon-gruous. The only sounds suitable to the season are the rusty caw of the homeward-sliding rook —the creaking of the wain returning empty from the farm-yard. There is an "unrest, which men miscall delight," and of that "unrest" youth is, for the most part, composed. From this middle age is free. The setting suns of youth are crimson and gold ; the setting suns of middle age

> Do take a sober colouring from an eye
> That hath kept watch o'er man's mortality.

Youth is the slave of beautiful faces, and fine eyes, and silver-sweet voices—they distract, madden, alarm. To middle age women are but the gracefullest statues, the loveliest poems. They delight but hurt not ; they awake no passion, they heighten no pulse. And the imaginative man of middle age possesses after a fashion all the passionate turbulence, all the keen delights, of his earlier days. They are not dead—they are dwelling in the antechamber of Memory, awaiting his call ; and when they *are* called they wear an ethereal something which is not their own. The Muses are the daughters of Memory : youth is the time to love, but middle age the period at which the best love-poetry is written. And middle age too—the early period of it, when a man is master of his instruments, and knows what he can do—is the best season of intellectual activity. The playful capering flames of a newly kindled fire is a pretty sight, but not nearly so effective—any housewife will tell you—as when the flames are gone, and the whole mass of fuel has become caked into a sober redness that emits a steady glow. There is nothing good in this world which time does not improve. A silver wedding is better than the voice of the Epithalamium ; and the most beautiful face that ever was, is made yet more beautiful when there is laid upon it the reverence of silver hairs.

There is a certain even-handed justice in Time ; and for what he takes away he gives us something in return. He robs us of elasticity of limb and spirit, and in its place he brings tranquillity and repose—the mild autumnal weather of the soul. He takes away Hope, but he gives us Memory. And the settled, unfluctuating atmosphere of middle age is no bad exchange for the stormful emotions, the passionate crises and suspenses of the earlier day. The constitutional melancholy of the middle-aged man is a dim background on which the pale flowers of life are brought out in the tenderest relief. Youth is the time for action, middle age for thought. In youth we hurriedly crop the herbage; in middle age, in a sheltered place, we chew the ruminative cud. In youth, red-handed, red-ankled, with songs and shoutings, we gather in the grapes; in middle age, under our own fig-tree, or in quiet gossip with a friend, we drink the wine free of all turbid lees. Youth is a lyrical poet, middle age a quiet essayist, fond of recounting experiences, and of appending a moral to every incident. In youth the world is strange and unfamiliar, novel and exciting, everything wears the face and garb of a stranger; in middle age the world is covered over with reminiscence as with a garment: it is made homely with usage, it is made sacred with graves. The middle-aged man can go nowhere without treading the mark of his own footsteps; and in middle age, too, provided the man has been a good and an ordinarily happy one, along with this mental tranquillity there comes a corresponding sweetness of the moral atmosphere. He has seen the good and the evil that are in the world, the ups and the downs, the almost general desire of the men and the women therein to do the right thing if they could but see how; and he has learned to be uncensorious, humane,

—to attribute the best motives to every action, and to be chary of imputing a sweeping and cruel blame.   He has a quiet smile for the vain-glorious boast, a feeling of respect for shabby-genteel virtues, a pity for the thread-bare garments proudly worn, and for the napless hat glazed into more than pristine brilliancy from frequent brushing after rain.   He would not be satirical for the world.   He has no finger of scorn to point at anything under the sun.   He has a hearty " Amen " for every good wish, and in the worst cases he leans to a verdict of Not Proven.   And along with this pleasant bland-ness and charity, a certain grave, serious humour, "a smile on the lip and a tear on the eye," is noticeable frequently in middle-aged persons —a phase of humour peculiar to that period of. life, as the chrysanthemum to December.   Pity lies at the bottom of it, just as pity lies, unsus-pected, at the bottom of love.   Perhaps this special quality of humour—with its sadness of tenderness, its mirth with the heart-ache, its gaiety growing out of deepest seriousness, like a crocus on a child's grave—never approaches more closely to perfection than in some passages of Mr Hawthorne's writings, who was a middle-aged man from earliest boyhood. And although middle-aged persons have lost the actual possession of youth, yet in virtue of this humour they can comprehend it, see all round it, enter imaginatively into every sweet and bitter of it. They wear the key Memory at their girdles, and they can open every door in the chamber of youth. And it is also in virtue of this peculiar humour that—Mr Dickens's *Little Nell* to the contrary—it is only middle-aged persons who can, either as poets or artists, create for us a child. There is no more beautiful thing on earth than an old man's love for his granddaughter; more beautiful even—from the absence of all suspicion of direct personal bias or interest— than his love for his own daughter; and it is only the meditative, sad-hearted, middle-aged man who can creep into the heart of a child and interpret it, and show forth the new nature to us in the subtle cross-lights of contrast and suggestion. Imaginatively thus, the wrinkles of age become the dimples of infancy. Wordsworth was not a very young man when he held the colloquy with the little maid who insisted, in her childish logic, that she was one of seven. Mr Hawthorne was not a young man when he

painted "Pearl" by the side of the brook in the
forest; and he was middle-aged and more when
he drew "Pansie," the most exquisite child that
lives in English words. And when speaking
of middle age, of its peculiar tranquillity and
humour, why not tell of its peculiar beauty as
well? Men and women make their own beauty
or their own ugliness. Sir Edward Bulwer
Lytton speaks in one of his novels of a man
"who was uglier than he had any business to
be;" and, if we could but read it, every human
being carries his life in his face, and is good-
looking or the reverse as that life has been good
or evil. On our features the fine chisels of
thought and emotion are eternally at work.
Beauty is not the monopoly of blooming young
men, and of white and pink maids. There is a
slow-growing beauty which only comes to perfection in old age. Grace belongs to no period
of life, and goodness improves the longer it
exists. I have seen sweeter smiles on a lip of
seventy than I ever saw on a lip of seventeen.
There is the beauty of youth, and there is also
the beauty of holiness—a beauty much more
seldom met, and more frequently found in the
arm-chair by the fire, with grandchildren around

its knee, than in the ball-room or the promenade. Husband and wife, who have fought the world side by side, who have made common stock of joy and sorrow, and aged together, are not unfrequently found curiously alike in personal appearance, and in pitch and tone of voice— just as twin pebbles on the beach, exposed to the same tidal influences, are each other's *alter ego. He* has gained a feminine something which brings his manhood into full relief. *She* has gained a masculine something which acts as a foil to her womanhood. Beautiful are they in life, these pale winter roses, and in death they shall not be divided. When Death comes, he will pluck not one, but both.

And in any case, to the old man, when the world becomes trite, the triteness arises not so much from a cessation as from a transference of interest. What is taken from this world is given to the next. The glory is in the east in the morning, it is in the west in the afternoon, and when it is dark the splendour is irradiating the realm of the under-world. He would only follow.

ON DREAMS AND DREAMING.

IN dealing with the curious phenomenon of Dreaming, the materialists and spiritualists are, as usual, in extremes: the one class regarding the phenomenon as mainly the result of indigestion, the other as one of the proofs of the immortality of the soul. In this matter it may be prudent to steer a middle course. One thing is certain, that whatever be the cause, the substance of a dream, whether it be beautiful or ghastly, depends entirely upon the dreamer. All men dream, just as all men live; but the dreams of men are as different as are their lives. You require opium and Coleridge combined before you arrive at *Kubla Khan:* few men have extracted such terrors from a pork chop as Fuseli. Every man has his own fashion of dreaming, just as every man has his own opinions, conceptions, and way of looking at things. While asleep a man does not in the least lose his personality. Dreams are the most curious *asides* and soliloquies of the soul. When a man recollects his dream, it is like meeting the ghost of himself. Dreams often surprise us into the strangest self-know-ledge. If a man wishes to know his own secret opinion of himself, he had better take cognizance of his dreams. A coward is never brave in his dream, the gross man is never pure, the untruth-ful man lies and knows he is lying. Dreaming is the truest confessional, and often the sharpest penance. In sleep the will is quiescent, and dreaming is like the talking in the ranks when the men are standing at ease, and the eye of the inspecting officer is absent for the nonce; it is like the chatting of the domestics round the kitchen-fire of the castle after the lord and the lady have retired—incoherent babblement for the most part; but the men in the ranks say things that the commanding officer might ponder on occasion, and the gossiping servants in the comfortable firelight downstairs, commenting on the events of the day, give their opinions on this thing and the other which has happened, and criticise not unfrequently the conduct of the master and mistress. You feel your pulse when you wish to arrive at the secret of your bodily

F

health; pay attention to your dreams if you wish to arrive at the secret of your health, morally and spiritually.

All men dream, and the most common experience of the phenomenon is the sort of double existence which it entails. The life of the night is usually very different from the life of the day. And these strange spectres and shapes of slumber do not perish; they live in some obscure ante-room or limbo of memory, and reappear at times in the most singular fashion. Most people have been startled by this reappearance. Something of importance to you has happened quite new, quite unexpected; you are sitting in a strange railway-station waiting for the train; you have gone to see a friend in a distant part of the country, and in your solitary evening stroll you come on a pool of water, with three pollard willows, such as you see in old engravings, growing beside it, and above the willows an orange sunset through which a string of rooks are flying; and all at once this new thing which has happened wears the face of an old experience; the strange railway-station becomes familiar; and the pool, the willows, the sunset with the undulating line of rooks, seem to have been wit-

nessed *not* for the first time. This curious feeling
is gone almost as swiftly as it has come; but
you are perplexed with the sense of a double
identity, with the emergence as of a former
existence.   The feeling alluded to is so swift
and intangible that often you cannot arrest it;
you cannot pin it down for inspection as you
would a butterfly on a card; but when you *can*,
you find that what has startled you with fami-
liarity is simply a vagrant dream—that from the
obscure limbo of the memory some occult law
of association has called a wandering wraith of
sleep, and that for a moment it has flitted betwixt you and the sunshine of consciousness,
dimming it as it flits.

One thing is worthy of remark, that in dreaming, in that reverie of the consciousness, men
are usually a good deal cleverer than when they
are awake. You may not be much of a Shakespeare in your waking moments, but you attain
to something of his faculty when your head is on
the pillow.   In dreams, whatever latent dramatic
power you may possess awakes, and is at work.
The dreamer brings far-separated people together, he arranges them in groups, he connects
them by the subtlest films of interest; and the

man who is in the habit of taking cognizance of his dreams soon learns that the phantoms of men and women whom he has once known, and who revisit him in slumber, are more life-like images—talking more consistently, and exhibiting certain little characteristics and personal traits which had never been to him the subject of conscious thought—than those he is accustomed to deal with during his waking hours. And then the strange persons and events one does dream about on occasions,—persons long dead, localities known in childhood, and never seen since; events which happened to yourself or to others, and which seem to have faded out of remembrance as completely as the breath of yesterday has faded from the face of the mirror. But these things have not so faded. There is a "Lost Office" in the memory, where all the waifs and strays of experience are taken care of. Word and act; the evil deed and the good one; the fair woman's face which was the starlight of your boyhood; the large white moon that rose over the harvest-fields in the September in which you were in love; the thrush that sang out in the garden betwixt light and dark of summer dawn, when the pressure of a hand at parting the night before kept you awake,—all these things, which you suppose to have perished as utterly as the clothes you wore thirty years ago, have no more perished than you have yourself. Memory deals with these things as a photographer deals with his negatives; she does not destroy them, she simply places them aside, for future use, mayhap. If you are a dreamer, you will know this. And in dreams the imagination does not always deal with experience; it frequently goes beyond that, and guesses at matters of which it cannot have any positive knowledge. There is no more common terror in dreams than that of falling over a precipice; and most dreamers are aware that in so dreaming they have felt the air *cold*, as they cut through it, in their swift rush earthwards. This, of course, cannot be matter of experience, as those who have been so precipitated are placed conclusively out of court. But it is curious that the dreamer should so feel; that the swift imagination should not only vividly realise the descent itself, but an unimportant accessory of the descent—the chilliness of the swiftly-severed air—as well. And then the all-absorbing fact of Death exercises an intolerable fascination over many a dreaming brain. A man dreamed once that he, along with sixteen others, had been captured on a field of battle, and that, by a refinement of cruelty, they were to be shot singly. It so happened that the dreamer was the seventeenth. The sixteenth man knelt, the levelled muskets spat fire, crackled, and he fell forward on his face. The dreamer was then conscious of the most burning feeling of envy of the dead man—he *had* died, he *was* dead ; he who was but a few yards distant a second ago, was now removed to an immeasurable distance ; he had gained his rest. And when the dreamer's turn came to kneel, and when the muskets of the platoon converged upon him, he found himself marvelling whether, between the time the bullets struck and the loss of sensation, he could interject the thought, " This is death." Of death this man knew nothing ; but even in the dream of sleep his imagination could not help playing curiously with the idea, and attempting to realise it ; and in his waking moments he could not have realised it so thoroughly. Altogether this vividness of the imagination in dreams is something to which nothing exactly corresponds in the waking state. A Scotch schoolboy dreams that he is being chased by the Foul Fiend, and as he flies along, he hears behind him a hard and a soft sound alternately ; and this does not surprise him, because he knows perfectly that the hard sound is the clang of the cloven hoof on the roadway. In thus unconsciously working the tradition of the cloven hoof into the body of his impression, the Scotch schoolboy has become a John Bunyan for the time being, and is far beyond his normal state of imaginative activity. If you are aroused from sleep by hearing your own name called, you start up in bed with an impression so vivid that you fancy the sound is yet lingering in your ears. I once heard a friend, and one not specially fanciful usually, tell how he had been one night tormented by the strangest vision. He was asleep, and on a curtain of darkness there hung before him a beautiful female face ; and this face, as if keeping time with the ticks of the watch under his pillow, the beating of his pulse, the systole and diastole of his heart, was alternately beautiful—and a skull. There, on the curtain of darkness, the apparition throbbed in regular and dreadful change. And this strange and regularly recurring antithesis of beauty and horror, with the spiritual meaning and significance under it—for the loveliest face that ever poet sang, or painter painted, or lover kissed, is but a skull beclothed with flesh : we are all naked under our clothes, we are all skeletons under our flesh—was as much out of my prosaic friend's usual way of thinking as crown, sceptre, and robe of state are out of a day labourer's way of life. He was a good deal astonished at his dream, and I, with my perhaps super-subtle interpretation of it, was a good deal astonished that he should have had *such* a dream. But the truth seems to be, that when the will is asleep the imagination awakes and plays. The most prosaic creature is a poet when he dreams. Every dreamer is, for the time being, in possession of the lamp of Aladdin — the world is ductile to be shaped as fancy wills. And this vividness of impression in dream—the realisation of strange situations, the recalling of dead persons—is not only singular, as showing the potency of imagination, which, perhaps unsuspectingly, we all possess—but out of the chaos of dreams a man may now and again extract a curious self-knowledge. The dreamer's belief in his dream is usually intense, and I

suppose the man who fancied himself the seventeenth man to be shot, and who saw the muskets
of the silent platoon converging upon him, felt
very much as the poor mutineer does, who,
seated on his coffin, sees the same thing of a
raw morning; and from his dream he might
discover, to some extent, how nature has steeled
his nerves, how he might comport himself in
deadly crises. In dream, better often than in
waking moments, a man finds out, as has been
said, the private opinion he entertains of himself; and in dreams, too, when placed in circumstances outside of his actual experience, and
which, in all probability, will never be evolved
in actual experience, he becomes in some sense
his own inspecting officer, and reviews his own
qualities. Through dreaming, a man is dual—
he is actor and spectator: and in dreaming, he
is never a hypocrite; the coward never by any
possibility can dream that he is brave, the liar
never that he is truthful; the falsest man awake
is sincere when he dreams.

Looking into a dream is like looking into the
interior of a watch; you see the processes at
work by which results are obtained. A man
thus becomes his own eavesdropper, he plays

the spy on himself. Hope and fear, and the other passions, are all active, but then activity is uncontrolled by the will, and in remembering dreams one has the somewhat peculiar feeling of being one's own spiritual anatomist. And as the dreaming brain concerns itself mainly with the ideas which stir the waking one, and as dreams are ruled by no known logic, conform to no recognisable laws of sequence, are stopped in career by no pale or limit, it is not in the least surprising that in remote unscientific periods these wild guesses of the spirit and bodyings forth of its secret wishes and expectations should have been credited with prevision. Even people in the present day, if any superstitious tincture runs in the blood, or if they are endowed with fineness of imaginative perception, find it hard to shake off the old belief. For, come how it may, dreams, in point of fact, often *do* read the future. We do not know what subtle lines of communication may radiate between spirit and spirit. If, a century ago, a man had sent a message from London to Edinburgh in ten minutes, he would have been looked upon as the blackest of magicians ; now such messages cost only a couple of shillings, and are matters of daily commerce. That a man in London should speak to a man in Edinburgh was just as astonishing and incredible to all practical minds a century ago, as that spirit should speak with spirit is incredible to the same minds at the present day. But the apparent prevision of dreams falls, of course, to be explained on quite other grounds than that of some supposed spiritual telegraphy. The dreaming brain is continually busying itself with the objects of fear or desire, and that it should occasionally make a lucky guess is not an unlikely circumstance. Suppose a man is a candidate for some office or post which he covets, the chances are that, while the bestowal of the post is yet in abeyance, he will dream either that he has obtained it, or that he has lost it; and should his dream jump with the ultimate result, he at once concludes it to have been prophetic. Suppose a man has a near relative at an Indian station, that for a couple of mails, contrary to custom, he has received no letter, and that he dreams a ship is bearing on through a sea of moonlight with the dead body of his friend on board (a result, as regards the friend, certainly on the cards, and a dream, as regards himself, not in

the least improbable — on the contrary, most
likely and natural, should his interest in his
friend be great), and that it proves true that
the friend has died—it would be difficult to
convince the man that his dream had not
something of prophecy in it. If dreams are
not fulfilled, they are naturally forgotten; if
fulfilled, they are just as naturally remembered.
That dreams, working continually in the stuff
of daily hope and fear, giving palpable shape and
image to desire and dread, should sometimes be
found to forestall the future fact, is not in the
least a matter for wonder. Such coincidences
are as certain to occur, by the law of chances,
as that a penny, if tossed up a hundred times,
will come down heads a certain number of
times. What concerns the dreamers more are
the hopes and fears, the desires and aversions
with which the dreaming fancy works ; looking
into these he may gain some information concerning himself not easily obtainable otherwise.

MR CARLYLE AT EDINBURGH.

SINCE the amendment of her constitution, seven or eight years ago, the University of Edinburgh has listened to some remarkable speeches—or at all events to speeches by some remarkable men. Lord Advocate Inglis's Act gave the University a Lord Chancellor and a Lord Rector ; and whatever duties might devolve on those high officials, that of delivering an address to the members of the University in the largest obtainable hall was one that could not be put by. At the first meeting of the General Council—a body consisting almost entirely of University graduates, and created by the Act referred to—Lord Brougham was elected Chancellor ; and in due time the old man, almost bowed down by the weight of his gorgeous robe, appeared before the University, and discoursed on things in general for over a couple of hours. The speech was attractive enough—to those at least who were near his Lordship, and were able to hear it—but the greater attraction lay in the speaker. The speech was heard by few, the speaker was visible to all. And positively, when he stood up before the University, a certain sense of awfulness possessed one, when one thought of his immense age and intellectual vitality. Lord Brougham lives in the printed Histories of England ; and here he was a contemporary. He rocked the cradle of the *Edinburgh Review.* More than thirty years ago Byron closed his career at Missolonghi ; but Brougham cut the pages of the new *Hours of Idleness*, and indited the famous critique—famous not in itself, but in its issues— which stung the author into a poet. He was Canning's arch foe in the House of Commons. He advocated the abolition of the slave trade. He was in his prime when that old shameful affair of Queen Caroline and her husband—what ages seem to have passed over English society since then !—was in everybody's mouth. Before many of the men who now listened to him were born, he had climbed into a peerage, had filled the highest offices of State—had culminated officially and intellectually—and still there he was, white and bent and shattered, yet with all his ancient vivid apprehensiveness and intellectual interests, and able to speak for a couple of hours. That his reception should be enthusiastic was, of all this, the most natural consequence. It was remembered that last century he was a scholar of the University; that he went out of the University into the world's battle, a sheet of maiden silk; and now, after more than fifty years, and while not only England, but an entire Europe had changed in the interim, he had returned to the University, creased and frayed and torn, but torn in honourable strife, and heavy with the emblazonries of many victories. He was a great speaker in a world which exists to the present generation by hearsay and in the printed page, and to hear him speak *now* was like witnessing some superannuated "Victory" —in the thickest of the fight at the Baltic and the Nile—firing a salute, the old port-holes flashing fire once more, the old cannon smoke curling around the decks. Of the matter of the speech itself not much need be said—not a single sentence of it probably remains in the memory of any one who heard it—but the sight of the old white Chancellor, who had seen and done so much, could not fail to impress itself indelibly on the memory and imagination. Lord Brougham was the elect of the General Council of the University; when their turn came round to choose a Lord Rector, Mr Gladstone secured the suffrages of the students; and before the University the present Chancellor of the Exchequer has delivered two addresses, the first some years ago, when he was installed, and the second at the close of last autumn, when he demitted office.

On both of these occasions the interest of the University was great, but it was of a different kind from that formerly manifested. Lord Brougham had the prestige of memory, Mr Gladstone the prestige of expectation. The one had finished his career long ago, the other was in the midst of his. Lord Brougham was the winner of past Derbys, Mr Gladstone was entered for the next, and the popular favourite. Lord Brougham interested the University seniors, Mr Gladstone the University juniors—the one represented the past, the other was the embodiment of the present. Critically speaking, Mr Gladstone's addresses, if more polished and graceful than Lord Brougham's, were not, on the whole, of greater mental calibre. They were

fluent, colourless, rhetorical, *expatiatory*—if one
may coin a word to express one's meaning in
the rough; and being devoid of every tincture of
individuality, and glancing rapidly over the sur-
faces of things, they gave one no idea what
manner of man the speaker was, or what quality
of mind he possessed. The only thing which
Mr Gladstone made sufficiently evident was,
that he could speak eloquently on any subject
for any given number of hours. The balanced
periods, as they fell on the ear, seemed to have
a meaning; the sentiments evoked applause
from the younger portions of the auditory, when
they were uttered; but when read in the newspapers next morning, and divorced from the
charm of voice, the whole thing seemed incre-
dibly flat and unprofitable. The truth is that,
before the University, Mr Gladstone did not
prove himself so much an orator, or a thinker,
as an elocutionist. And his elocution was really
something marvellous. His self-possession was
complete; he stood beside the reading-desk in
an easy attitude; his hands were not incum-
brances; the Rectorial robe lent him dignity;
the grave, severe, somewhat melancholy, almost
ascetic face, furrowed and lined " like the side of

a hill where the torrent hath been;" the finely-moulded mouth, with its immense capacity of scornful emphasis—of which perhaps Mr Disraeli is sufficiently aware—were worth study; and then the voice—silvery as Belial's,—now resonant in the higher passages, now solemn in the hortatory ones—of which passages there was perhaps a superabundance—who shall sing its praises? Mr Gladstone's voice is the finest to which I have ever listened; and during his valedictory address of nearly three hours, no hoarseness jarred the music of his tones, and his closing sentence was as clear and bell-like in its cadence as the first. One might suppose that, as a general rule, to speak for three hours is a more arduous task than to listen for the same space of time; yet when he sat down, Mr Gladstone seemed much less fatigued than any of his auditors. Mr Gladstone has the reputation of being the most accomplished speaker of his time; and if in these addresses before the University he did not quite fulfil popular expectation, the reason was perhaps to be discovered easily enough. His addresses were carefully composed beforehand, and if recited as only Mr Gladstone could recite them, they were recita-

tions all the same. On the occasions referred
to he was master of the situation just as a
preacher is on Sundays. There was no interruption to chafe, no opposition to excite, no heat
of debate to energise and spur the intellect to
an activity more than normal. Mr Gladstone,
speaking to the Metropolitan Scottish University
about the old Greek poets, and Mr Gladstone
on a grand field night in the Commons, carrying
fire and terror into the ranks of the Opposition,
are conceivably very different. There is the same
difference between rhetoric hot and rhetoric cold,
as between red-flowing lava and porous pumice-
stone.

Mr Gladstone demitted office, and then it
behoved the students of the University to cast
about for a worthy successor. Two candidates
were proposed, Mr Carlyle and Mr Disraeli;
and on the election-day Mr Carlyle was returned
by a large and enthusiastic majority. This was
all very well; but a doubt lingered in the minds
of many whether Mr Carlyle would accept the
office, or, if accepting it, whether he would deliver an address—said address being the sole
apple which the Rectorial tree is capable of
bearing. The hare was indeed caught, but it

was doubtful somewhat whether the hare would allow itself to be *cooked* after the approved academical fashion. It was tolerably well known that Mr Carlyle had emerged from his long spell of work on *Frederick*, in a condition of health the reverse of robust; that he had once or twice before declined similar honours from Scottish Universities—from Glasgow some twelve or fourteen years ago, and from Aberdeen some seven or eight; and that he was constitutionally opposed to all varieties of popular display, more especially those of the oratorical sort. But all suspense was ended when it was officially announced that Mr Carlyle had accepted the office of Lord Rector, that he would conform to all its requirements, and that the Rectorial address would be delivered late in spring. And so, when the days began to lengthen in these northern latitudes, and crocuses to show their yellow and purple heads, people began to talk about the visit of the great writer, and to speculate on what manner and fashion of speech the great writer would deliver.

Edinburgh has no University Hall—Mr Gladstone, holding high office therein for six years, and having the command of the purse strings

of the nation during the entire period, might
have done something to remedy that defect,
many think—and accordingly, when speech-day
approached, the largest public room in the city
was chartered by the University authorities.
This public room—the Music Hall, in George
Street—will contain, under severe pressure, from
eighteen hundred to nineteen hundred persons;
and tickets to that extent were secured by the
students and members of the General Council.
Curious stories are told of the eagerness on every
side manifested to hear Mr Carlyle. Country
clergymen from beyond Aberdeen came to
Edinburgh for the sole purpose of hearing and
seeing. Gentlemen came down from London by
train the night before, and returned to London
by train the night after. Nay, it was even said
that an enthusiast, dwelling in the remote west
of Ireland, intimated to the officials who had
charge of the distribution, that if a ticket should
be reserved for him, he would gladly come the
whole way to Edinburgh. Let us hope a ticket
was reserved. On the day of the address, the
doors of the Music Hall were besieged long before the hour of opening had arrived; and loitering about there on the outskirts of the crowd,

one could not help glancing curiously down Pitt Street, towards the "lang toun of Kirkcaldy," dimly seen beyond the Forth ; for on the sands there, in the early years of the century, Edward Irving was accustomed to pace up and down solitarily, and "as if the sands were his own," people say, who remember, when they were boys, seeing the tall, ardent, black-haired, swift-gestured, squinting man, often enough. And to Kirkcaldy too, as successor to Edward Irving in the Grammar School, came young Carlyle from Edinburgh College, wildly in love with German and Mathematics ; and the school-room in which these men taught, although incorporated in Provost Swan's manufactory, is yet kept sacred and intact, and but little changed these fifty years—an act of hero-worship for which the present and other generations may be thankful. It seemed to me that so glancing Fife-wards, and thinking of that noble friendship—of the David and Jonathan of so many years a-gone— was the best preparation for the man I was to see, and the speech I was to hear. David and Jonathan ! Jonathan stumbled and fell on the dark hills, not of Gilboa, but of Vanity ; and David sang his funeral song : "But for him I

had never known what the communion of man
with man means. His was the freest, brother-
liest, bravest human soul mine ever came in
contact with. I call him, on the whole, the best
man I have ever, after trial enough, found in
this world, or now hope to find."

In a very few minutes after the doors were
opened, the large hall was filled in every part;
and when up the central passage the Principal,
the Lord Rector, the Members of the Senate,
and other gentlemen advanced towards the
platform, the cheering was vociferous and
hearty. The Principal occupied the chair, of
course; the Lord Rector on his right, the Lord
Provost on his left. When the platform gentlemen had taken their seats, every eye was fixed
on the Rector. To all appearance, as he sat,
time and labour had dealt tenderly with him.
His face had not yet lost the country bronze
which he brought up with him from Dumfries-
shire as a student, fifty-six years ago. His
long residence in London had not touched his
Annandale look, nor had it—as we soon learned
—touched his Annandale accent. His countenance was striking, homely, sincere, truthful—
the countenance of a man on whom "the burden

of the unintelligible world" had weighed more heavily than on most. His hair was yet almost dark; his moustache and short beard were iron-grey. His eyes were wide, melancholy, sorrowful; and seemed as if they had been at times a-weary of the sun. Altogether, in his aspect there was something aboriginal, as of a piece of unhewn granite, which had never been polished to any approved pattern, whose natural and original vitality had never been tampered with. In a word, there seemed no passivity about Mr Carlyle; he was the diamond, and the world was his pane of glass; he was a graving tool, rather than a thing graven upon —a man to set his mark on the world—a man on whom the world could not set *its* mark. And just as, glancing towards Fife a few minutes before, one could not help thinking of his early connection with Edward Irving, so seeing him sit beside the venerable Principal of the University, one could not help thinking of his earliest connection with literature. Time brings men into the most unexpected relationships. When the Principal was plain Mr Brewster, editor of the *Edinburgh Cyclopædia,* little dreaming that he should ever be Knight of Hanover, and head of the Northern Metropolitan University, Mr Carlyle—just as little dreaming that he should be the foremost man of letters of his day, and Lord Rector of the same University—was his contributor, writing for said *Cyclopædia* biographies of Voltaire, and other notables. And so it came about that, after years of separation and of honourable labour, the old editor and contributor were brought together again—in new relations. The proceedings began by the conferring of the degree of LL.D. on Mr Erskine of Linlathen—an old friend of Mr Carlyle's—on Professors Huxley, Tyndall, and Ramsay, and on Dr Rae, the Arctic explorer. That done, amid a tempest of cheering and hats enthusiastically waved, Mr Carlyle, slipping off his Rectorial robe—which must have been a very shirt of Nessus to him—advanced to the table, and began to speak in low, wavering, melancholy tones, which were in accordance with the melancholy eyes, and in the Annandale accent with which his playfellows must have been familiar long ago. So self-centred was he, so impregnable to outward influences, that all his years of Edinburgh and London life could not impair, even in the slightest degree, *that.* The opening sentences were lost in the applause, and when it subsided, the low, plaintive, quavering voice was heard going on: "Your enthusiasm towards me is very beautiful in itself, however undeserved it may be in regard to the object of it. It is a feeling honourable to all men, and one well known to myself when in a position analogous to your own." And then came the Carlylean utterance, with its far-reaching reminiscence and sigh over old graves—Father's and Mother's, Edward Irving's, John Stirling's, Charles Buller's, and all the noble known in past time—and with its flash of melancholy scorn: "There are now fifty-six years gone, last November, since I first entered your city, a boy of not quite fourteen— fifty-six years ago—to attend classes here, and gain knowledge of all kinds, I knew not what— with feelings of wonder and awe-struck expectation ; and now, after a long, long course, this is what we have come to." (Hereat certain block- heads, with a sense of humour singular enough, loudly cachinnated!) "There is something touching and tragic, and yet at the same time beautiful, to see the third generation, as it were, of my dear old native land, rising up, and say-

ing: 'Well, you are not altogether an unworthy
labourer in the vineyard. You have toiled
through a great variety of fortunes, and have
had many judges.'" And thereafter, without
aid of notes, or paper preparation of any kind,
in the same wistful, earnest, hesitating voice,
and with many a touch of quaint humour by
the way, which came in upon his subject like
glimpses of pleasant sunshine, the old man
talked to his vast audience about the origin
and function of Universities, the Old Greeks
and Romans, Oliver Cromwell, John Knox, the
excellence of silence as compared with speech,
the value of courage and truthfulness, and the
supreme importance of taking care of one's
health. "There is no kind of achievement you
could make in the world that is equal to perfect
health. What to it are nuggets and millions?
The French financier said: 'Alas! why is there
no sleep to be sold?' Sleep was not in the
market at any quotation." But what need of
quoting a speech which by this time has been
read by everybody? Appraise it as you please,
it was a thing *per se*. Just as, if you wish a
purple dye, you must fish up the Murex; if you
wish ivory, you must go to the East; so if you

desire an address such as Edinburgh listened
to the other day, you must go to Chelsea for it.
It may not be quite to your taste, but, in any
case, there is no other intellectual warehouse
in which that kind of article is kept in stock.

Criticism and comment, both provincial and
metropolitan, have been busy with the speech,
making the best and the worst of it; but it will
long be memorable to those who were present
and listened. Beyond all other living men, Mr
Carlyle has coloured the thought of his time.
He is above all things original. Search where
you will, you will not find his duplicate. Just
as Wordsworth brought a new eye to nature, Mr
Carlyle has brought a new eye into the realms
of Biography and History. Helvellyn and
Skiddaw, Grassmere and Fairfield, are seen now
by the tourist even, through the glamour of the
poet; and Robespierre and Mirabeau, Cromwell
and Frederic, Luther and Knox, stand at present, and may for a long time stand, in the
somewhat lurid torchlight of Mr Carlyle's genius.
Whatever the French Revolution may have been,
the French Revolution, as Mr Carlyle conceives
it, will be the French Revolution of posterity.
If he has been mistaken, it is not easy to see

from what quarter rectification is to come. It will be difficult to take the "sea-green" out of the countenance of the Incorruptible; to silence Danton's pealing voice or clip his shaggy mane; to dethrone King Mirabeau. If, with regard to these men, Mr Carlyle has written wrongfully, there is to be found no redress. Robespierre is now, and henceforth in popular conception, a prig; Mirabeau is now and henceforth a hero. Of these men, and many others, Mr Carlyle has painted portraits, and whether true or false, his portraits are taken as genuine. And this new eye he has ʻbrought into ethics as well. A mountain, a daisy, a sparrow's nest, a moorland tarn, were very different objects to Wordsworth from what they were to ordinary spectators; and the moral qualities of truth, valour, honesty, industry, are quite other things to Mr Carlyle than they are to the ordinary run of mortals—not to speak of preachers and critical writers. The gospel of noble manhood which he so passionately preaches is not in the least a novel one; the main points of it are to be found in the oldest books which the world possesses, and have been so constantly in the mouths of men that for several centuries past they have

been regarded as truisms. That "work is worship;" that the first duty of a man is to find out
what he can do best, and when found, "to keep
pegging away at it," as old Lincoln phrased it;
that on a lie nothing can be built; that this
world has been created by Almighty God; that
man has a soul which cannot be satisfied with
meats or drinks, or fine palaces and millions of
money, or stars and ribands—are not these
the mustiest of commonplaces, of the utterance
of which our very grandmothers might be
ashamed? It is true they are most commonplace—to the commonplace; that they have
formed the staple of droning sermons which
have set the congregation asleep; but just as
Wordsworth saw more in a mountain than any
other man, so in these ancient saws Mr Carlyle
discovered what no other man in his time has.
And then, in combination with this piercing
insight, he has, above all things, emphasis. He
speaks as one having authority—the authority
of a man who has seen with his own eyes, who
has gone to the bottom of things and knows.
For thirty years this gospel he has preached,
scornfully sometimes, fiercely sometimes, to the
great scandal of decorous persons not unfre-

quently ; but he has always preached it sincerely and effectively. All this Mr Carlyle has done ; and there was not a single individual, perhaps, in his large audience at Edinburgh the other day, who was not indebted to him for something —on whom he had not exerted some spiritual influence more or less. Hardly one, perhaps— and there were many to whom he has been a sort of Moses leading them across the desert to what land of promise may be in store for them ; some to whom he has been a many-counselled, wisely-experienced elder brother ; a few to whom he has been monitor and friend. The gratitude I owe to him is, or should be, equal to that of most. He has been to me only a voice, some-times sad, sometimes wrathful, sometimes scorn-ful ; but when I saw him for the first time with the eye of flesh stand up amongst us the other day, and heard him speak kindly, brotherly, affectionate words—his first appearance of that kind, I suppose, since he discoursed of Heroes and Hero Worship to the London people—I am not ashamed to confess that I felt moved towards him, as I do not think, in any possible combina-tion of circumstances, I could have felt moved towards any other living man.

TO town and country Winter comes alike, but to each he comes in different fashion. To the villager, he stretches a bold frosty hand ; to the townsman, a clammy one. To the villager, he comes wrapt in cold clear air ; to the townsman, in yellow fogs, through which the gas-lamps blear at noon. To the villager, he brings snow on the bare trees, frosty spangles on the roadways, exquisite silver chasings and adornments to the ivies on the walls, tumults of voices and noises of skating-irons, smouldering orange sunsets that distain the snows, make brazen the window panes, and fire even the icicles at the cottage eaves. To the townsman, he brings influenzas, secret slides on unlighted pavements, showers of snowballs from irreverent urchins, damp feet, avalanches from the roofs of houses six storeys high, cab fares wofully be-grudged, universal slush. Winter is like a Red Indian, noble in his forests and solitudes, de-

teriorated by cities and civilisation. The signs of
his approach are different in the town and in the
village. To a certain northern city, whose spires
fret my sky-line of a morning, his proximity is
made known by the departure of the last tourist
and the arrival of the first student; by brown
papers taken from windows in fashionable streets
and squares; by the reassembling of schools
and academies; and by advertisements in the
newspapers relative to the opening of the University. By these signs, rather than by the
cawing of uneasy rooks, or the whirling away of
the last red leaf, the inhabitants know that the
stern season is at hand; a salvo of inaugural
addresses announces that he is in their midst,
and the reappearance of lawyers in the long-
deserted halls of the Parliament House, is regarded as a prophecy of snow. In that famous
northern city, winter is disagreeable, as in other
cities. Lawyers, doctors, and professors tumble
out of bed, and shave by gas-light. The entire
population catches cold, and the clergymen are
coughed down on Sundays. The falling snow
covers the pavements—except the spaces in front
of the bakers' shops, which are wet, and black,
and steaming; in due time it makes dumb the

H

streets, muffling every sound of wheel and hoof;
it slips its moorings, and hangs in icicles and
avalanches from the roofs of houses, but it does
not appear in any perfection; it has lost all
purity, and is dingy as a city sparrow. It is
regarded as a nuisance; shopkeepers scrape it
from their doors, deft scavengers build it in
mounds along the streets; in a couple of days
thaw sets in, and from roof, and eave, and
cornice, from window-sill, gargoyle, and spout,
there is a universal sound of weeping, like that
which was heard in the old Norse world, when
gods and men lamented the death of Balder
the Beautiful. On frosty mornings, cab-horses,
whose shoes are never sharpened in preparation, although the previous night every star was
sparkling like steel, are tumbling on the hilly
streets, and the fare gesticulates from the window, and one man holds down the head of the
terrified animal, whose breath is like a wreath of
incense, and the driver, clothed in a drab great-
coat, with a comforter up to his nose, is busy
with the girths, and small boys gather round,
and attempt to blow some warmth into their
benumbed fingers. Up from the sea comes a
wicked *harr*, shedding disastrous twilight; church

spires are visible half way up and disappear; the lights in shops are yellow smears on the darkness; at crossings, vehicles burst on you in a moment, and in another moment are swallowed up; and on the obscure pavement all ties of relationship and acquaintanceship are dissolved. Men are strangers for the time being; without a sinking of the heart, debtor brushes clothes with creditor; and with never a thrill Romeo steps off the pavement to let Juliet pass, quite unconscious that his divinity is near. Even on the more favourable days there is little to please one in a wintry city; over head the smoke hangs heavily and lazily; for an hour or so a small uninteresting sun is stuck on the murky sky, like a red wafer on a dirty letter, and the setting is accomplished as rapidly as possible, and without any attempt at pomp. The southwest will not even turn out a corporal's guard to present arms to such a visitor. The townsman does not care for Winter, although he may care for what Winter brings—the long lighted evenings in which he can read or work, the lectures, the dinner-parties, the concerts, the theatres, and, if very young, the sprig of mistletoe stuck under the chandelier of a Christmas night.

But in this quiet place—distant but a few miles from the city of which I have been speaking—Winter is as pleasant as summer in her prime. To this village, Winter sends other *avant couriers* than the taking down of brown paper from the windows of great houses, or the advertisement of college sessions. The rooks gathering in the coloured woods was one sign; the ploughing of the wheat-fields was another. The reddening of the beech hedges told me Winter was on his way. The Robin hopping along the shrubbery walks in his search for crumbs—remembering well they were scattered there last year—told me he was at hand. The rime of a morning on the old walls outside told me he was already come. One could feel the impalpable presence in the crisp air, in the clear blue distance with the Castle and city spires etched upon it, in the stillness broken only by the rustle of a withered leaf, in the bright yet sobered sunlight, in the quickened current of the blood as one walked. Sated whilom with foliage, in my rambles my eye delights in naked branches, and I please myself with noting how many objects become visible at this season which summer had kept secret; ragged nests high up

in trees, houses and farm-buildings standing
amongst woods, bridges, and fences, and the
devious courses of streams. These things are
lost and buried in the leafiness of summer, and
are only to be recognised now, as truths are dis-
cerned in age which youth never guesses of.
When I return, the sunset is burning away
behind the stripes of ancient pines that stand on
the scarped bank above the stream, making
their bronzed trunks yet more red—yet more
dark their undecaying verdure. And by the
last gleam on the distant hills, I notice that
their crests are hoary. Snow, then, has already
come, and will be with us anon.

Winter in the country, without snow, is like
a summer without the rose. Snow is Winter's
specialty, its crowning glory, its last exquisite
grace. Snow comes naturally in Winter, as
foliage comes in summer; but although one
may have been familiar with it during forty
seasons, it always takes one with a certain
pleased surprise and sense of strangeness. In
each Winter the falling of the first snow-flake is
an event; it lays hold of the imagination. A
child does not ordinarily take notice of the
coming of leaves and flowers, but it will sit at

a window for an hour, watching the descent of the dazzling apparition, with odd thoughts and fancies in the little brain. Snow attracts the child as the plumage of some rare and foreign bird would. The most prosaic of mortals, when he comes down stairs of a morning, and finds a new soft, white world, instead of the hard familiar black one, is conscious of some obscure feeling of pleasure, the springs of which he might find it difficult to explain. I do not care much for snow in town; but in the country it is ever a marvel: it wipes out all boundary lines and distinctions between fields; it clothes the skeletons of trees with a pure wonder; through the strangely transfigured landscape the streams run black as ink and without a sound; and over all, the cold blue frosty heaven smiles as if in very pleasure at its work. On such a day, how windless and composed the atmosphere, how bright the frosty sunlight, from what a distance comes a shout or the rusty caw of a rook! " Earth hath not anything to show more fair." And somehow the season seems to infuse a spirit of jollity into everything. As I walk about I fancy the men I meet look ruddier and healthier; that they talk in louder and cheerier

tones ; that their chests heave with a sincerer
laughter. They are more charitable, I know.
Winter binds " earth-born companions and fel-
low-mortals" together, from man to red-breast ;
and interior domestic life takes a new charm
from the strange pallor outside. The good creature Fire feels exhilarated, and licks with its
pliant tongue, as if pleased and flattered. Sofa
and slippers become luxuries. The tea-urn
purrs like a fondled cat. In those long warm-
lighted evenings, books communicate more of
their inmost souls than they do in summer ; and
a moment's glance at the village church-roof,
sparkling to the frosty moon, adds warmth to
fleecy blankets, and a depth to repose.

The white flakes are coming at last ! Stretch
out your hand—the meteor falls into it lighter
than a rose-leaf, and is in a moment a tear.
It is as fragile as. beautiful. How innocent
in appearance the new-fallen snow, the surface of which a descending leaf would dimple
almost ! and yet there is nothing fiercer, deadlier, crueller, more treacherous. On wild uplands
and moors it covers roads and landmarks, and
makes the wanderer travel hopeless miles till he
sinks down exhausted ; it steeps his senses in a

pleasing stupor, till he fancies he sees the light
of his far-off dwelling, and hears the voices of
his children, who will be orphans before the
morn; it smites him on the mouth and face as
he dies, and then covers him up, softly as with
kisses, tenderly as with eider-down, like a sleek-
white murderer as it is. In alliance with the
demon of wind, it will drift and spin along the
mountain-sides, and in a couple of hours a hundred sheep and their shepherd are smothered
in a corry on Ben Nevis. Welded by frost
into an avalanche, it slides from its dizzy hold,
and falls on an Alpine village, crushing it to
powder. A snowflake is weak in itself, but
in multitudes it is omnipotent. These terrible
crystals have stayed the marches of conquerors
and broken the strength of empires. The in-
numerous flakes flying forth on the Russian
wind are deadlier than bullets; they bite more
bitterly than Cossack lances. In front, behind,
on every side, for leagues and leagues they fall
in the dim twilight, flinging themselves in front
of the weary soldier's foot, clogging the wheels of
cannon, making the banner an icy sheet, stilling
the drum that beat the charge. O, weary soldiers of the Empire, eyes that saw the sun of

Austerlitz, hearts that love Napoleon—to this
grim battle with Winter, Lodi and Arcola were
holiday parades! The Loire will murmur from
antique town to town, through pleasant summer
lands of France, till it rests in the Spanish sea;
vines stretched from pole to pole will glow in
setting suns; girls will dance at village festivals;
but for you, never more the murmuring river,
nor the ripening grape, nor the dancing girl's
waist and smile. For you the deadly snow-kisses,
the sleep and the dreams that bring death,
the dreadful embalming of frosts, potent as
the spices that preserve Pharaoh.

At home, Winter is a terrible despot; but like
the wild Goths which he nurtured, he becomes
more civilised as he travels South. Like a travelled man of the world, he adapts himself to the
countries in which he sojourns. The ice, which
is misery at Labrador, is luxury at Naples. In
our country we know Winter chiefly in his mild
and fanciful moods. In England he is artist and
adorner. He brightens the bloom on the cheeks
of girls; he breathes the quaintest forests on our
bedroom windows; he beards cottage eaves with
icicles; he makes the lake a floor on which the
skater may disport himself; he fires the south-

west with sober sunsets; he gives star and planet a metallic lustre. But with all these pleasant qualities and obliging graces, he wears here, as at home, the old heart. Have you not seen him in our own streets pinch cruelly a poor child scantily clad? Do we not know how he maltreats the desolate widow and the unemployed artisan? Do we not hear of him in savage mood killing outright poor homeless wretches whom he has discovered asleep on stairs or in deserted cellars? Here, as I have said, he is partially civilised, but at home he is a despot; there he piles the iceberg that sails southward to crush ships; there he pinches the starved wolf; there he makes the Esquimaux shiver through all his furs. And the Arctic voyagers whom he takes prisoner and locks up in his immeasurable dungeons of snow and ice, *they* know what a Giant Despair he is; and friends at home who wait and wait, and to whom no news ever comes, know it too.

There is one more good thing about Winter,— he brings Christmas. Through the bleak December the thought of the coming festival is pleasant —like the reflection of a fire on our faces. We taste the cake before it is baked, and when it is ac-

tually before us we find that it is none the worse
for the fond handling of imagination. Christmas-
day is the pleasantest day in the whole year.
On that day we think tenderly of distant friends;
we strive to forgive injuries—to close accounts
with ourselves and the world—to begin the new
year with a white leaf, and a trust that the
chapter of life about to be written will contain
more notable entries, a fairer sprinkling of good
actions, fewer erasures made in blushes, and fewer
ugly blots than some of the earlier ones. And to
make Christmas perfect, the ground should be
covered and the trees draped with snow; the
bleak world outside should make us enjoy all
the more keenly the comforts we possess; and,
above all, it should make us remember the poor
and the needy; for a charitable deed is the best
close of any chapter of our lives, and the best
promise, too, for the record about to be begun.

We are accustomed to consider Winter the
grave of the year, but it is not so in reality.
In the stripped trees, the mute birds, the dis-
consolate gardens, the frosty ground, there is
only an apparent cessation of Nature's activi-
ties. Winter is a pause in music, but during
the pause the musicians are privately tuning

their strings, to prepare for the coming out-
burst. When the curtain falls on one piece at
the theatre, the people are busy behind the
scenes making arrangements for that which is to
follow. Winter is such a pause, such a fall of the
curtain. Under ground, beneath snow and frost,
next spring and summer are secretly getting
ready. The roses which young ladies will gather
six months hence for hair or bosom, are already
in hand. In Nature there is no such thing as
paralysis. Each thing flows into the other, as
movement into movement in graceful dances;
Nature's colours blend in imperceptible gradation; all her notes are sequacious. I go out to
my garden and notice that when the last leaves
have fallen off my lilac and currant-bushes, like
performers at the side-wings waiting their turn to
come on, the new buds are all ready. To-day I
beheld great knobs of buds on a horse-chestnut
of mine, liquored over with an oily exudation
which glittered in the sunlight. In my plants,
the life which in June and July was exuberant
in blossom and odour, has withdrawn to the
root, where it lies *perdue*, taking counsel with
itself regarding the course of action to be
adopted next season. The spring of 1864 is

even now under-ground, and the first snows will hardly have melted till it will peep out timorously in snowdrops; then, bolder grown, will burst in crocuses, holding up their coloured lamps; then, by fine gradations, the floral year will reach its noon, the rose; then, by fine gradations, it will die in a sunset of hollyhocks and tiger-lilies; and so we come again to withered leaves and falling snows.

LITERARY WORK.

IN every literary work there are two elements: there is the thought, or the thing to be said; there is the expression, or the manner of saying the thing. This latter element, especially when it takes any characteristic shape, we are accustomed to denominate style. And in every work of art the style is even of more importance than the thought: it is the artistic part, it is that through which the artist's personality becomes visible. The main body of the poem, or the novel, or the essay, consists necessarily of ideas which the writer did not originate, which he found ready-made to his hand, which have, in one shape or another, been used before; and his merit consists in the new forms into which he is able to work up the old·material. He calls in the worn coin of thought, melts it down in secret crucibles, and re-issues it, bearing a fresh super-scription and a new value. Thought is mine,

your's, everybody's; but the artist lays hold of
our thoughts, and works with them, as a sculptor
works with his clays. The world does not need
new thoughts so much as it needs that old
thoughts be re-cast. The artist is not required
to create his own materials. If a man makes
bricks, he is provided with clay; if a man paints
a portrait, he is allowed sitter, canvas, and pigments. To make a fine modern statue, there is
a great melting down of old bronze. Absolute
novelty of idea—in a poem, for instance—is felt by
many as a disturbance, because it is devoid of the
sweetness of acquaintanceship and association.
Absolute novelty, even if it could be procured,
the reader does not very much care about: what
delights him is the setting of a familiar thought
in a new light, the discovery of subtle links
and relationships between things with which
he is acquainted, but which he was in the
habit of considering disconnected and remote.
Approach from a new point a mountain with
which you are familiar, and it has all the charm
of strangeness; and this delight of strangeness
is felt all the more keenly from its unexpectedness, and from the mixture in it of the present
and the past. The pleasure lives in the mingling

of the old recognition and the new surprise. I
live—I love—I am happy—I am wretched—I
was once young—I must die, are extremely
simple and commonplace ideas, which no one
can claim as exclusive property; yet out of these
has flowed all the poetry the world knows, and
all that it ever will know. The "still sad music
of humanity" is simple enough, and may be
apprehended by any peasant; all that poets
have to do is to execute variations upon it, to
unwind its subtle sweetnesses, to pursue and
carry out its suggestions; and the important
matter is, with what amount of skill these variations, unwindings, and pursuings have been
accomplished. The thought is only a part of
the poem or the essay, and the commonest part.
What in a work of art is really valuable is the
art. The statue that is only worth the weight
of its metal is a very poor statue indeed. Take
an English classic—" The Castle of Indolence,"
or " The Vicar of Wakefield," for instance : strip
it of music, colour, epigram, wit, analyse the
residuum of naked ideas, and you will find
nothing very important nor yet very original.
The ideas which make up these works have
been gathered from far and near, and were as

much the property of a hundred contemporary persons, as they were the property of Goldsmith and Thomson. "Paradise Lost" proves nothing except that Milton was one of the greatest poets the world ever saw. And all this does not in the least detract from the merit of the poet or the novelist. The matter does not so much lie in the idea, as in the use made of the idea. Music sleeps in the strings of the harp, no doubt, but the skilful harper's hand has to come before it can be awakened. The architect is nothing without the services of the quarryman, brick-layer, and plasterer ; the general is nothing unless the recruiting-serjeant be preliminary. Yet we admire the great musician more than the artificer who built the instrument. We do not place Sir Christopher Wren and a hodman on the same level ; the recruiting-serjeant is gathered quietly to his fathers, and forgotten, while Wellington's war-horse snorts in bronze in every one of the British cities, and his fame fills an era in our history, as the sound of the billow Fingal's cave in Staffa.

A literary work of art is neither a mathe-matical demonstration, nor a "Pinnock's Guide to Knowledge," nor an argument. It is not

I

designed to prove anything, nor yet to dis-
seminate information useless or useful.   If
harshly questioned, it frequently can give no
very satisfactory reason for its existence.   It
is something above and beyond mere use, like
the colour and breath of a flower, or the burning breast of a humming-bird.   Incidentally, it
may subserve purposes tangible enough, but its
primary office is to please; at all events, if it fail
in *that*, it fails in everything.   If it cannot delight,
its existence is an impertinence for which no apo-
logy can be accepted, and the world gives it the
cold shoulder.   And here it is that the supreme importance of style becomes visible.   We
see at once the superlative value of concise-
ness, neat or cunning turns of sentence, colour,
cadence, the glitter of fancy and epigram ; we
see at once what room there is for the play of
all the weapons of rhetoric,—only in the using of
the weapons we must take lessons from Nature,
and not from the rhetorician.   For the lunge
that rids you of your adversary is the inspiration of the moment, never the remembered
lesson of the fencing-master.   In literature,
the *how* a thing is said is of as much importance as the thing itself.   Thought, if left to

itself, will dissolve and die. Style preserves
it as balsams preserve Pharaoh. Fine phrases
are, after all, the most valuable things. Epigrams are our most unquestionable antiques.
Out of the *débris* of the early world we have
raked a few poetical images, and they are as
fresh now as on the day on which they were
first uttered. The enamel of style is the only
thing that can defy the work of time. In virtue
of his style, Homer lives, just as Addison and
Jeremy Taylor live in virtue of theirs.

To define the charm of style is as difficult
as to define the charm of beauty or of fine
manners. It is not one thing, it is the result of
a . hundred things. Everything a man has is
concerned in it. It is the amalgam and issue of
all his faculties, and it bears the same relation
to these that light bears to the sun, or the per-
fume to the flower. And apart from its value
as an embalmer and preserver of thought, it
has this other value, that it is a secret window
through which we can look in on the writer. A
man may work with ideas which he has not
originated, which do not in any special way
belong to himself; but his style—in which is
included his way of approaching a subject, and

his method of treating it—is always personal and characteristic. We decipher a man by his style, find out secrets about him, as if we overheard his soliloquies, and had the run of his diaries, just as in conversation, and in the ordinary business of life, we draw our impressions, not so much from what a man says, as from the manner and the tone of voice in which the thing is said. The cunning reader draws conclusions from emphasis, takes note of the half-perceptible sneer, makes humour stand and deliver its secret, and estimates what bitterness it has taken to congeal into sharpness the icy spear of wit. After this fashion, in every book the writer's biography may more or less clearly be read. For a man needs not to speak directly about himself to be personally communicative. And, in truth, it is in the amount of this kind of personal revelation that the final value of a book resides. We read books, not so much for what they say as for what they suggest. A great writer's characters are not nearly so interesting as the great writer himself, and we take to them on account of their paternity, as we take to the children of our friends. There are books we read over and over again, and all the while we are striving to catch a glimpse of the author between the lines. The characters of the great writer take us back constantly to the great writer, as the sunbeam constantly takes us back to the sun. And by this relationship to something greater than themselves they are dignified, as an ambassador, in whatever country he may be placed, wears the dignity of the sovereign of whom for the time being he is the representative. If you desire information respecting the sovereign, it is to the ambassador you must apply. *Don Quixote* is not so great as Cervantes; *Hamlet* is not so great as Shakespeare; *Satan* is not so great as Milton; but through the characters we have named we learn more about the writers than we do from their professed biographies. Biography frequently can show us little more than the table a man sat at, the bed he slept on. In mere biographical value and pertinence, Lockhart's "Life of Burns" is not comparable for a moment with the poems of Burns; and what makes Mr Carlyle's essay on that poet stand almost alone in our literature as a masterpiece of full and correct delineation, is the way in which he makes this line or the other a transparent window of insight, through which he obtains the closest glimpses of his subject. It is only the books which contain this unconscious personal reference—and this comes out, not so much in what is said, as in the manner of saying it—that are worth much, or that can permanently interest.

Take up an essay of Montaigne's; you are startled by no remarkable breadth or weight of idea, but you are constantly encountering sentences through which you can look in on the author as through a stereoscopic lens. You take up an essay of Charles Lamb's, and in the quaint setting of his thoughts—like a piquant face in a Quaker bonnet—you are continually renewing and improving your acquaintance with the shiest, most delicate, and, in some respects, the noblest and purest of modern spirits. People never weary of reading Montaigne and Lamb, for while the thoughts they express have sufficient merit *as* thoughts, they are at the same time biographies in brief. They may have written finely or foolishly, seriously or with levity, but they have always written with a certain personal flavour. Take up, on the other hand, one or other of the novels which have recently acquired

a prodigious popularity, and while you find the
central secret hidden away in the cunningest
manner under fold on fold of incident, you find
nothing else in the least worthy of regard, and
a single perusal disposes of all the interest which
can arise from the unravelling of the plot. These
—in their own way extremely clever and exciting works—possess no reflection, no landscape,
no commentary on what is going on, and they
are entirely innocent of the personal revelation
of which we have been speaking. The characters
themselves are the merest films and shadows,
and the books in which we make their acquaintance seem written by people who have never
been in love, who have never stood by a friend's
death-bed, who have never seen the sun rise or
set—who have no biography, in short. Rising
from them, you have been enabled to form no
idea of the writer's personality, you have been
introduced to no experience with which you
can compare your own. You have only had
your curiosity piqued for an unconscionable
length of time; and when, at the close of the
third volume, the murder is out, you no more
think of reading the book over again, than,
reaching London by the night train from the

North, you dream of returning for the mere purpose of undergoing your journey a second time. You have found out the secret, as you have come to London. The carriage has been the instrument in the one case, the three volumes in the other, and your purposes with both have been entirely served. It is by their styles that writers are recognised, just as it is by their gait, their bearing, their tones of voice, and their numberless individual peculiarities that you recognise men in the street or in the drawing-room. Every sentence of the great writer is like an autograph. There is no chance of mistaking Milton's large utterance, or Jeremy Taylor's images, or Sir Thomas Browne's quaintness, or Charles Lamb's cunning turns of sentence. These are as distinct and individual as the features of their faces or their signatures. If Milton had endorsed a bill with half-a-dozen blank verse lines, it would be as good as his name, and would be accepted as good evidence in court. If Lamb had never gathered up his essays into those charming volumes, he could be tracked easily by the critical eye through all the magazines of his time. The identity of these men can never be mistaken. Every printed

page of theirs is like a coat of arms, every
trivial note on ordinary business like the impression of a signet ring.

As a whole, our literature, and especially our
periodical literature, is not distinguished at this
moment by style in any rich and characteristic
way. Much of the writing is commonplace, just
as a man's countenance is commonplace which
has no marked and prominent feature, which has
no individuality of expression, and which does
not differ in any material degree from the
countenances of his fellows. There is a certain weekly Review, which is much read, much
admired, and much feared. The writing is
extremely clever; but the odd thing is, that the
writing is throughout of equal cleverness, and of
the same kind of cleverness. Each number is
level, like a grassy lawn, yet each number must
be the production of at least twenty able quills.
Have these twenty writers identical tempers,
identical brains, and identical experiences? Or
is the editor a sort of grass roller, which keeps
everything smooth and level? There is a certain weekly journal, conducted by a master of
fiction, which seems to be entirely written by
the editor; certain portions when the editor is

at his best, other portions when his eyes were
weary. "Methinks there be six Richmonds in
the field"—one Richmond agile, and an able
swordsman ; five, who have received fencing
lessons from the master, who put continually in
practice his method of carte and tierce, but
who lack his stamina and dash. Such writing
is comparatively valueless, because it lacks individuality, and does not spring from any
peculiar personality. It is clever, of course ;
but the cleverness is acquired rather than native.
All the defects of our present literature may be
summed up in a word—want of style. And the
reason is not far to seek. Literature has become a profession. Books are written too
hastily, and to serve a purpose too immediate.
In the days of the old masters of style, the
writer adorned his thoughts for the mere love
of adorning his thoughts : in the present state
of things, it is hardly to be expected that he
should put himself to any considerable trouble
on that score. The market of the old writer
was with posterity ; the market of the present
writer is in the next street. The Gothic
cathedral, whose front, from base to pinnacle,
is a floral burst and laughter of stone, was not

built by estimate. The Gothic cathedral could wait a century or so for a congregation. Before our present churches are finished, the congregation are eager to enter and take their seats, to criticise the interior decorations, and to hear what the preacher has got to say. And yet in this world there is no such thing as entire and absolute loss. We cannot write so supremely now as did the old men ; but this we can say for ourselves, that while they served ten, we serve a thousand ; that while they ornamented sandals for nobles, we make boots and shoes for the multitude ; and that it is better for every man to have his beer in the pot, than that in the midst of need there should be spread at intervals a royal feast, with kings for guests, and golden vessels on the table. There are no dishes of peacocks' brains now, but there are wholesome wheaten loaves for all.

THE MINISTER-PAINTER.

IN glancing backward over the last century and a-half of Scottish history, it will be noticed that distinguished men have come in clusters, and that the intellectual products of these are visible in well-defined belts or zones. Nature there, as elsewhere, built capacious brains, and when her hand was in, it was her habit to build more than one; and so the clever Scotchmen of a generation have a family resemblance, and the works produced by them have a family resemblance also. Hume, Robertson, and Adam Smith came together; and through these we have the philosophic and historical belt. Scott and Galt created the imaginative belt; Jeffrey, Wilson, and Lockhart the critical belt. In any enumeration of eminent Scotchmen the name of Burns cannot be omitted, but then Burns has no place in any such loose generalizations. In his greatness he is the loneliest of all the northern geniuses. He had, strictly speaking, no predecessor, he had no companion, he has had no successor. Critics have delighted to point out that the " Farmer's Ingle" of Fergusson was the prototype of the "Cottar's Saturday Night," but the truth is, that Fergusson had no more share in the most exquisite of homely idylls than the leaves of the mulberry tree on which the silkworm feeds has a share in the silk which is produced. Putting Burns aside, as in some sense a special phenomenon, who must be considered by himself if considered at all, the three broadly-marked belts or zones of Scottish mental activity are indicated by the "Essays, Moral and Philosophical," and the " Wealth of Nations ;" the novels of Scott and Galt ; and the *Edinburgh Review* and *Blackwood's Magazine.* So much one can see looking back on the past ; but it would be extremely difficult to say what, since the establishment of the famous *Review,* and the still more famous *Magazine,* is the salient outstanding feature of Scottish intellectual life. And the difficulty lies in this, that, ecclesiastical matters apart, there has, during the last twenty or twenty-five years, been hardly any distinctive Scottish life at all. " Stands Scotland where it did ? " asks Macduff ;

and the answer to-day is, "No; if you seek Scotland, you must go to London for her." The old frontier line has been effaced by the railway and the post-office. The Tweed no longer divides peoples with different interests. Scotland and England have melted into each other and become Britain, just as red and blue melt into each other and become purple; and in the general intellectual activity of the empire, it would be as difficult to separate that contributed by north and south as to separate the waters of the Forth and the Humber in the German Ocean, or the taxes gathered on either side of the Tweed in the Imperial exchequer. John Bull and Patrick serve in the ranks of the Black Watch and the Greys, and Sandy is a sentry at the Horse Guards. An English professor is the most distinguished disciple of the Scottish Sir William Hamilton; and the representative of a metropolitan constituency—a Scot at least by extraction—is the intellectual descendant of the English Bentham. It is from this interconnection of the two peoples, that for the last quarter of a century there has been so little *distinctive* Scottish intellectual life. Scotland has overflowed its boundaries, and it has no longer a separate existence in thought or geography. It is not, however, to be supposed that, although working under different conditions, there is any diminution in the northern vigour. The Scot thinks as shrewdly and acts as prudently in Cheapside as at Aberdeen or at John o' Groat's; and when great things have to be done—when, for instance, a treaty has to be negotiated with China, when a revolted India has to be subdued, when a "Life of Frederick" has to be written—the doers of those feats of diplomacy, arms, and letters, are not unfrequently found wearing Scottish names. But the difficulty of pointing out any broad, salient, outstanding feature in Scottish intellectual life, does not altogether arise from the cessation of that life in the sense which has been explained, but in some degree from the fact that, since the establishment of *Blackwood's Magazine*, Scottish intellect and fancy have more and more sought a new manifestation and direction. For long, Scotland was the best educated and least æsthetic nation in Europe. Beauty and ornament had never specially been the denizens of the Scottish house or the Scottish street; and at the Reformation they were sternly thrust forth and forbidden to enter the ecclesiastical edifice. In Scotland, Beauty was churchless, and on Sundays had to abide with the daisy in the field, the cloud-shadow on the hill-side, and to consort with the Poet, who was a commoner of Nature like herself, and under the same social ban. Not the least religious nation in the world, the Scotch were content to worship in barn-like buildings, with windows hard in outline and innocent of colour as those of factories; and Music, suspected of Popish parentage, and of haunting the play-house and the opera, was turned away from the church-door, and had to go romp in the fields with Beauty and the Poet. Untouched by the softening influences of art, the Scottish nation was devout, deep-hearted, humorous, sincere; but it was harsh in manner, deficient in graciousness and suavity. The visitor, on coming to Scottish towns, was struck by the lack of politeness on the part of the inhabitants. He saw them, unyielding as tides, jostle each other on the pavement. If he asked to be directed to a particular street, he not unfrequently received a churlish response. He noted that in these towns statues and public monuments were rare, that they were disregarded and often ill kept;

and, if a travelled man, he drew disadvantageous comparisons between the Scottish towns and the French or Italian ones. This hardness and lack of graciousness, this lack of art and of regard for art, was attributable to a considerable extent to the national poverty and the national faith. There is no social civiliser like art, but art does not grow in poor countries any more than grapes on poor soils. You may keep a poet on £70 a year, and get a good deal out of him, just as our fathers for something like that sum got a tremendous deal out of Burns ; but you cannot so cheaply maintain painters and sculptors. If you will adorn your apartments with their works, they can at least claim upholsterers' wages. And, putting inspiration out of the question altogether, pigments and marble are much more expensive than pens and ink, and the backs of old letters, or excise schedules at a pinch. On Calvinism you can breed first-rate men, but not so easily first-rate artists. Art delights in minster and cathedral, in painted window and fuming incense, in gorgeous vestments and the voices of singing-men and singing-women, and finds but little sustenance in barn-like churches, discordant psalmody, rigid pews, and

K

intrepid, closely-knit, logical discourses. Scotland was a well-educated country, as countries went, but it wanted artistic susceptibility; and it was only when it became comparatively rich, and when its social atmosphere became a little more genial, that art began to develop itself in any general or unmistakeable manner. The picture and the statue came with wealth into the private apartment; the ornate church, the famous man in bronze or marble, came with wealth into the street ; and the public eye becoming accustomed to these things, gradually learned to enjoy them. The establishment of the *Edinburgh Review* and *Blackwood's Magazine* was the last distinct phase of Scottish—that is, of Scottish as distinct from British—intellectual life ; and at that time Scottish art was in its vigorous youth, and quite abreast of Scottish literature. Scotchmen, save in isolated instances, and generally out of their own country, have done nothing very remarkable in literature since ; but at home there has grown up a school of art, distinct, vigorous, individual, which has spread far and wide, and which has more than one representative amongst the Forty of the Royal Academy. The pen was long the favourite weapon of the clever Scot, but since

John Wilson's time the cleverest men in Scotland have wielded the brush rather than the pen.

The school of Scottish art had at first, as was
natural, a good deal in common with the more
favourite form of Scottish literature—of poetry
more especially. When the northern genius was
not piercingly lyrical—tingling to the very
marrow in song and ballad—it was for the most
part garrulous and manners-painting. Rustic
life, with its humours, its fun, its jealousies, its
petty passions, its coarsenesses even—when these
were reflected in some incident like a marriage,
a festival, a fair, or a wapinschaw—has always
had special attraction for the Scottish muse.
This vein of manners-painting is visible from
" Christ's Kirk on the Green," down through
the "Gentle Shepherd" of Ramsay, the "Leith
Races" of Fergusson, the "Jolly Beggars" and
" Hallowe'en " of Burns, to the "Anster Fair" of
Tennant ; and in the same way, and for the same
reasons, the Scottish school of painting abounds in
admirable representations of rustic life : witness
the best pictures of David Allan, the " Penny
Wedding," and a dozen others of Sir David
Wilkie, the " Curlers " of Mr Harvey, and the
works of many others less distinguished. The

Scottish painters have in an indirect, yet most sufficient manner, illustrated the Scottish poets. In this special department Scottish art will take rank with Dutch—with the advantage that it has more *esprit* and less of mere vulgar swilling and boorishness.   In the domain of highest art— just as there is no northern Spenser or Milton— Scotland is behind England, and has, perhaps, no proper representative, if we except the late Mr David Scott and the present Mr J. Noel Paton. In portraiture and landscape the Scottish school excels.   In the department of portraiture the Scotch are distinguished by a solidity of basis and treatment, and a direct going at essentials to the neglect of subsidiaries.   Any one look- ing at the men Sir Henry Raeburn, Sir John Watson Gordon, and Mr Macnee have painted, will see that, in the delineation of character- istic heads and faces, of men who are individual and not conventional, the national shrewdness, humour, biographical talent, and insight, have in the most mysterious way become mixed with the colours.   I say the *men* these artists have painted, for somehow they have not succeeded so well with women.   If the Scotch style has a specialty, it is that of robustness, of solid force and

character—elements which are much more masculine than feminine. Given a granite-faced
Provost of Peterhead, wrinkled all over with
shrewd, pawky, tell-tale lines, and there are
half-a-dozen Scotchmen who will paint him so
to the life, that the spectator will know what
kind of a voice he has, whether he has been
married twice, and what he usually takes for
breakfast. Given an elegant lady, and perhaps
Sir Francis Grant is the only Scotchman who
can paint her in her self-possession and easy
security—high bred to the finger-tips, and perfectly *comme il faut* in every least matter of detail. Sir Henry Raeburn struck the key-note of
Scottish portrait painting, and it is vibrating
still. In Scottish landscape again—which par-
takes of similar characteristics — the key-note
was struck by the Rev. John Thomson of Dud-
ingstone; and his influence is still observable, not
only in Mr Macculloch's "cold and splendour of
the hills," in the Wordsworthian repose of Mr
Harvey's pastoral hill-sides, but in Mr Peter
Graham's "Mountain River in Flood," amongst
the landscapes of the Royal Academy of this
year the observed of all observers.

Mr Thomson, while he lived, was the most

distinguished landscape painter of the Scottish
school ; and he was unique in this, that he was
clergyman as well as painter : that it was his
work to study the page of Nature and the page
of Revelation.   It would be interesting to know,
if it were at all now possible, how he conducted
this double life—if the artistic and clerical elements lived together, reciprocally enriching and
assisting each other—the one bringing reverence
and sanctity into his studio, the other bringing
pictures into his sermons.   When discoursing
on the Dead Sea, did he behold in imagination
the red hills of Moab looming low on the
horizon ?   If prelecting on the passage—as in
the course of his ministrations it is likely that
he would prelect—*And Abraham rose up early
in the morning, and saddled his ass, and took
two of his young men with him, and Isaac his
son, and clave the wood for the burnt-offering,
and rose up, and went unto the place of which God
had told him.   Then on the third day Abraham
lifted up his eyes, and saw THE PLACE
AFAR OFF*—one would like to know what
mental image he formed of the yet untempled
Moriah ; was it a Syrian mount, or the double-
peaked Benledi—the Hill of God of his own

country — with the Scottish morning spread
above it ? One would like to know, if one could,
whether Thomson brought the landscape painter
with him into the pulpit.   But of his quality
as a preacher no information can be obtained.
The people who bought his pictures did not
care for his sermons ; the people who listened
to his sermons did not care for his pictures.
His parishioners regarded his landscape painting as they regarded his violin playing — a
pretty amusement enough, but one not in the
least befitting the dignity of his cloth.   Thomson
was, no doubt, an excellent preacher, after a
quiet, elegant, unenthusiastic, charitable fashion.
He was in every way an accomplished man.   He
had a competent knowledge of literature, and,
when working on his landscapes, was in the habit
of reciting from the classical and English poets
passages that seemed to illustrate the scene he
was depicting ; he was an exquisite musician ;
he was well read in the natural sciences, and contributed several papers on such subjects to the
Edinburgh Review.   We know how he painted,
we can guess how he preached ; and the fact
that he was both preacher and painter takes
him out of the category of ordinary men.   A

solitary, sad-eyed, mediæval monk, illuminating missals in a cloistered silence, broken only by the tinkling of refectory or prayer bells, is familiar enough to the imagination; but a modern Presbyterian clergyman, painting pictures on week days, and preaching sermons on Sundays; writing papers on optics for the *Edinburgh Review*, and drawing tears in the evening in his drawing-room by his violin performances; throwing down his brushes of a forenoon, placing against the wall a picture of the Bass, with a thunder-cloud blackening over it; going out to see an ailing parishioner, noting on his way how a sunbeam made gleam the ivies on Craigmillar which a shower had just wet, and returning to receive to dinner Sir Walter Scott, fresh from the "Bride of Lammermoor;" or Sir David Wilkie, fresh from Spain and the study of Velasquez—this complex activity, this variety of duty, this fulness of noble life, is something not very frequently met with.

Young Thomson was born at Dailly in Ayrshire, of which parish his father was minister, in the latter half of the last century; and there, amid the beautiful scenery surrounding him, he nourished his taste for landscape. His father destined him for the sacred profession; and, in accordance with a Scottish fashion not yet obsolete, at a very early age he was sent to the University of Edinburgh, to attend literary and philosophical classes, preparatory to entering on the study of divinity. At the lodgings of his elder brother, who had come to Edinburgh some years before, and who, in after life, became distinguished as a feudal lawyer and an antiquarian, the enthusiastic young man made the acquaintance of Walter Scott, Francis Jeffrey, and others. He stuck to his work during the winter sessions; but in his summer vacations at home he devoted himself to painting and violin playing, to the no small consternation of his father, who could not help marvelling at the strange bird growing up in the quiet, orderly, clerical nest. All this while, whatever may have been his progress, he had no teacher but Nature, and it was only during the last year of his theological curriculum that he had the advantage of lessons from Alexander Nasmyth, and that only for the period of one month. At the age of twenty-one, he was licensed; and on the death of his father, in the first year of the century, he succeeded to the Dailly manse and the

Dailly pulpit.   A year after, he married ; and in a house rapidly filling with babies he composed his sermons, painted his pictures, and played on his violin.   In 1805 he was translated to the parish of Duddingstone, near Edinburgh—a place perhaps the best suited for him in Scotland—where he could walk out into the fields at eventide, like Isaac ; where he could watch the purple thunder-gloom gathering on the distant hills, like Claude.

In May, passing along the Queen's Drive in a south-easterly direction — sheep and lambs bleating above, the starling glistening as it sweeps past through the sunshine—you see Duddingstone Loch beneath you, with its stunted and pollard willows, whitey-green in the wind, its banks and promontories of rushes, its swans and beds of water lilies, its cloud-shadows crossed by the trail of low-flying teal.   Proceeding some twenty yards or so, you come in sight of the little village itself, and note its grey, low-roofed Norman-like church, its scattered houses, with garden-slopes behind filled with plum and apple blossom ; its yellow-faced inn, in which tradition mumbles Prince Charles slept the night before the battle of Prestonpans, or

else the night after; and the swiftly-greening
woods beyond, stretching towards Portobello
and the sea. As you look down upon it from
the Drive, 'tis a mere toy-village, breathing
soft smoke pillars, breathing fruit-tree fragrance.
The quietest place in the whole world, you
would say; not a creature to be seen in the
little bit of a street visible; silent as Pompeii
itself; motion only on the lake, when the coot
shoots across its surface, or when a swan, thrust-
ing its long neck under water, tilts itself upward in
its preposterous fashion. And this little clachan
of twenty or thirty houses is walled, too, like
a Babylon or Nineveh; its wall not one on
which six chariots could race abreast, but of
strictly modest pretensions. Descending on
Duddingstone, you find it retired, low-lying,
sunshiny, umbrageous; a place in which in
summer you may expect plenty of dust in the
narrow streets, plenty of drowsy bees around
the double-flowered white and purple stocks in
the gardens, plenty of flies buzzing in the sunny
parlour windows. You see the old low-roofed
Norman-looking church—several centuries old
some portions of it, antiquaries say—with its
pointed windows and flagged roof; the church-

yard heaped and mounded with generations on generations of village dead; the rusty "jougs" —an iron collar, in which malefactors did penance of old—hanging on the churchyard wall near the gate of entrance, with its "louping-on-stane," well worn by the hob-nails of dead farmers. Near the church is the manse, in which the minister-painter lived, looking out with all its windows on the lake; on ivied Craigmillar, in which Queen Mary dwelt; on the low hills of Braid, over which Marmion rode, and on which Fitz Eustace

> Raised his bridle hand,
> And made a demivolte in air,

at sight of the old Edinburgh of the Jameses, smoke-swathed; and beyond, on the lovely undulating line of the Pentlands, stained, as in these bright spring days, with the white uprolling vapour of the heather-burnings. Duddingstone is the prettiest place in the neighbourhood of Edinburgh in summer; and it is, if possible, still more worth seeing about Christmas. Then the swans are of course gone; the chestnuts have lost their broad drooping fans, and have donned their strange snow draperies; from out the frosty blue, white Arthur's Seat looks down on the little village. At that season Edinburgh flocks Duddingstone-wards. Pedestrians and carriages stand along the margin of the loch; carriages and pedestrians move slowly along the Queen's Drive above. The lake itself is crowded as Vanity Fair; skaters shoot hither and thither; while in a carefully-preserved circle, members of the Edinburgh Skating Club go through the most graceful evolutions, and interweave with each other the prettiest loops and chains. At a little distance the curlers are busy, their faces red with exercise, their eyes bright with excitement, the on-lookers stamping their chilled feet in the snow, and attempting to breathe a little warmth into their frost-bitten fingers. Elsewhere, on great belts of slides, people are working their arms like awkward windmills. Here skims a skate-shod Diana—fleet huntress of men!—yonder, in a sleigh driven by admirers, sits a lady enveloped in furs. Past your ear whizzes a shinty ball, and down upon you in hot pursuit thereof comes, with a noise like a troop of wild horses, a horde of young fellows, each armed with a cudgel, a long-haired Highlander leading the charge—as Murat was wont to do—

several lengths in front.   The Highlander is up
with the ball, as he turns on it his foot slips, and
in a moment the crowd are over him.   There is
a general *mêlèe*, and then out of the crowd, and
in an opposite direction, spins the ball, another
fellow leading the pursuit now, the eager crowd
streaming behind him like a comet's tail.   So
around Duddingstone the seasons come and go
—so they came and went while Thomson lived
there, with umbrageousness of summer, pallor
of winter; each differing from the other, yet
each aiding the painter's education.

In the pretty Duddingstone manse Thomson
established himself, and there, for thirty-five
years, his life flowed on peacefully, prosperously,
honoured by high and low.   As a clergyman,
he was much esteemed by his parishioners, consisting mainly of well-to-do folks who lived in
villas, small market-gardeners who brought
their produce into Edinburgh, and washerwomen
who worked for the inhabitants of the city, wash-
ing the clothes in the loch, and bleaching and
drying them on the slopes of Arthur's Seat,
where they caught the scent of the broom.   To
the former class, the minister commended himself
by his accomplishments, his gentlemanly man-

ners, and his distinction; to the latter by his
liberality and kind-heartedness, and his frank
ways of going in and out amongst them. The
price of many a landscape came to the poor
people, when sickness or distress was prevalent,
in the shape of bottles of wine or even of comforts more substantial. It was at Duddingstone
that Thomson first devoted himself to landscape
painting as a profession. Craigmillar was before
his eyes every time he looked out of his window,
and this subject he frequently painted—often
with grand effect by moonlight. While at Dailly
he distributed landscapes amongst his friends; at
Duddingstone he accepted payment. The first
picture was sold for fifteen guineas; and the
artist, it is said, was so startled by the mighty
sum, that it was only when Mr Williams, the
delineator of Greek scenery, whom he con-
sulted on the subject, told him that the work was
worth three times as much, that he could comfortably consign the coins to his breeches pocket.
As his reputation rose the demand for his works
increased, and in his heyday of health and artistic prosperity, he was in the receipt of £1800 per
annum. Some idea of Thomson's industry may
be gathered from the prices he received. For a

picture thirty inches long, and from twenty to
twenty-five inches broad, he got twenty-five
guineas ; for one forty-eight or fifty inches by
thirty-six, his price was fifty guineas.   These
were high prices for a Scottish artist at that date ;
and for the works executed for the Duke of
Buccleuch, and which may be seen at Bowhill, he
received still larger sums. His passion for his art
grew with his years, and he searched the country
for subjects for his easel with greater ardour, one
almost fears, than he showed in searching the
Scriptures for texts for his sermons. His pulpit at
Duddingstone had to be filled of course, but then
the capital was near and probationers were plenti-
ful. By the time the young artist left the manse on
Saturday afternoon, the probationer had arrived
with a couple of sermons in his carpet-bag.   In
company with his friend Mr Williams—"Grecian
Williams" he was called, familiarly and affectionately, from those pictures already alluded to on
which his reputation mainly rests—he explored
the country for ancient houses with trees round
them, picturesque glens, castles beetling over the
sea, and bare moors with a group of old Scotch
firs, their bronze trunks and black-green crowns
glowing in the fires of autumn sunset.   The

two friends sketched together and were each the other's critic. In these passionate sketching pilgrimages, extending over many years, Thomson visited the most picturesque districts of Scotland, and painted Dunstaffnage, Dunluce, Wolf's Crag, the Falls of Kilmorack, Glenfinlas, Lochs Awe and Etive; nay, he even penetrated as far as Skye and painted the magnificent peak of Ben Blaven, and the edges of Cuchullin holding dark communion with the cloud. Being a clergyman, Thomson, although urged to do so, would never become a member of any incorporated body of artists; but he always sent his pictures to the Exhibitions of the Royal Scottish Academy. From 1808 to 1840 he contributed to those exhibitions one hundred and nine works. He not the less was strangely disinclined to exhibit in London, and, as a rule, Englishmen are not acquainted with his pictures. In the beginning of the year 1840 his health began to fail; but though no improvement took place during summer, he still worked on at picture and sermon. Conscious that his end was nigh, on a lovely October afternoon he desired to be taken to a window, and propped up by pillows, that he might watch once more the setting sun. It was a last

L

interview between the ancient friends—an eternal
farewell-taking. The sun set ruddily. Thomson
was dead next morning. He was twice married
—happily both times—and his portrait, by his
son-in-law, Mr Robert Scott Lauder, hangs in
the Scottish National Gallery.

During Thomson's life, Duddingstone Manse
was not more remarkable for exquisite picture
painting and violin playing than for the distinguished men occasionally gathered under its roof.
When Thomson came up to Edinburgh as a student, he made the acquaintance of Scott and
Jeffrey, and during life his friendship with both
remained unimpaired. Sir Thomas Dick Lauder,
and John Clerk (Lord Eldin), who with a Homeric
conviviality, broad humorous speech, and eccentric manners, combined a love of art, and had
made an admirable collection of paintings, draw-
ings, prints, and etchings, were frequent visitors
at the manse. John Wilson, as great a landscape
painter in words as Thomson in colours, occasionally dropped in on the minister to discuss the
Greek and Latin poets with him, and to see what
landscape was smiling or glooming on his canvas.
I am indebted for the following note concerning
the painter's artistic friends, to Mr W. B. John-

stone, Curator of the Scottish National Gallery, and himself an admirable artist, the extent of whose information on such matters is only equalled by his courtesy in imparting it :—

" I think Thomson preferred the company of artists to that of literary men or lawyers, and after painters he liked to have musicians about him. During his earlier career there were few artists of sufficient standing to be associated with him on equal terms. I can only call to remembrance Alexander Naismith, Raeburn, and H. W. Williams, who could be ranked *pari passu*. But when Thomson was at his best, Naismith had become an old cynical man ; and although it is said that Thomson had taken lessons from him, their styles were wide apart, and Thomson's was more generally admired. Raeburn, engrossed with the study of character and expression in the human face, looked on landscape as a mere accessory to art. He was intimate with Thomson, admired his genius and general accomplishments, respected his social position ; but the congeniality of feeling between the men may be doubted from the following transaction : —They agreed to change pictures ; Raeburn was to paint Thomson's portrait, and in return

Thomson was to paint a landscape. Thomson
sat to Raeburn, and the portrait was painted;
and although Thomson repeatedly offered to fulfil
his part of the agreement, Raeburn declined to
give up the portrait, and, accordingly it has
never been out of the possession of Raeburn and
his family. "Grecian Williams" was a man after
Thomson's own heart. They were about the
same age, they were ardent worshippers of
Nature, which they looked on exactly in the
same preconceived idea or aspect, viz., the classic
form, and no petty jealousy could have place
between them, as the one worked in oils, the
other in water colours. Williams was possessed
of some literary taste, was quiet and gentlemanly
in his manners, and was, like Thomson, on terms
of intimacy with most of the principal Edinburgh men. William Allan and Andrew Wilson
were on friendly terms with the minister, and
were with him occasionally at the manse; but
Thomson had now achieved a high position,
and a number of clever young artists were
springing up, and he took pleasure in having
them rather than their elders around him. Of
the young artists, Robert Scott Lauder and
William Simson were most frequently at the

manse. Lauder was there almost daily; his admiration of Thomson was unbounded. The rich tones of colour he generally attained in his own pictures much resembled those Thomson often successfully produced, and Thomson's liking for the young artist was confirmed when he afterwards became his son-in-law. Simson's style was not what Thomson aimed at, yet the feeling for Nature and the admirable execution impressed Thomson most favourably; and many of the figures, vessels, etc., in Thomson's pictures are evidently the work of this artist's dexterous hand. Thomas Duncan was an occasional visitor. Thomson marked him as a rising man, and Duncan had a high respect for the talent of *Duddy*, as he styled the minister (who was rather slovenly in his dress, the front of his waistcoat being generally besmeared with snuff), but their aims in art were widely apart; Duncan could never get up, or cared to evince the same admiration for a landscape as for a figure picture. Thomson showed a great liking for Horatio Macculloch, and when he came up from Glasgow or Hamilton, where he then resided, to the opening of the Annual Exhibition at Edinburgh, he had him always to dine at the manse. Many other young artists—Sir Francis Grant, the President of the Royal Academy, then commencing his career, E. T. Crawford, Robert Gibb, and others—were kindly noticed by Thomson and asked to his house. He kept almost an open house; and when distinguished artists came from London—Wilkie or Turner, for instance—his young friends were always invited to dine at the manse, in order that they might meet and be introduced to the brilliant strangers."

All this shows a kindly, composed, generous disposition, far above professional vanity and rivalry, which is pleasant to contemplate. Turner was frequently at the manse, and we all know the story how when the minister took the *brusque* painter into his studio and showed him his works, he called out, "You beat me in frames, Thomson!" On another occasion, at Duddingstone, when Francis Grant and Mr Horsman, M.P., were present, Grant, who then resided in Regent's Park, near the Zoological Gardens, asked the great painter to dine with him. "I'll be very glad," cried Turner jocosely; "I often come to see the wild beasts feed."

Thomson, during his lifetime, was the greatest Scottish landscape painter, and even yet he is one of the greatest which the northern school has produced. His style was based on classic models, he was a devout student of Claude and the Poussins, but this study of the old masters of landscape was supplemented by a constant reference to Nature. He worked constantly in the open air, and face to face with his subject. While a young man, and living in his father's manse at Dailly, he would frequently go out at two o'clock an a summer morning, and walk several miles, to watch the effect of the early sunbeams penetrating the tree branches, retiring step by step to note the changes of the light. Many of the old fastnesses on the Scottish coast he sketched on the spot. Although defective in drawing, he was fond of colour, and by repainting on his pictures succeeded in producing a surface which increased the richness and lustre of his tints. But his gains in this way were not entirely clear. In the hurry and excitement of his task, he often worked over his surface before the under colours were dry; and as in laying on his colours he used various kinds of medium, or vehicle, to attain brilliancy and depth of tone, many of his pictures have suffered by contraction and cracking, and are now but the dim ghosts of themselves—the battle flag, shot-torn, and smoke-stained, as compared with the original silken sheet. An incomplete draughtsman, Thomson had yet fine general ideas of form and the effect of grand lines. His works are always bold, picturesque, vigorous, and they never fail to impress the imagination. He is always great in masses, and having by that means touched the soul of the spectator, he allows the spectator to supply the details. He pours himself, so to speak, on the key of the position in gloomy brigades of strength, and, having won that, is satisfied—he does not waste himself in skirmishing, however brilliant. There is no play in his pictures. The truth is, he was always a little divided in his allegiance between Nature and the Poussins. He was all for Nature in his sketch in the open air, he was all for Poussin while working in his studio. His pictures, with their incontestable fine qualities, are just a little too *like* pictures. Nature in them smells of oil, somehow. Bold and noble as was his imagination, able to cope with scenes of gloom and piled-up rocky wildness, he lacked a tender sense of beauty and an exquisiteness of colour. His picture of the Trossachs, in the Scottish National

Gallery, is ugly almost; the hills are lumpy and unrelieved by the grace of twinkling birch woods, and there are no distant peaks, as in Nature, softened by miles of airy azure. Light, which laughs and plays, and sleeps smilingly when it *does* sleep, is sad-visaged in this work as a mute at a funeral. In colour, again, Thomson, although often grand and imposing in a broad general way, is seldom what can be called exquisite—the world with a sun shining upon it is not cloaked in drabs, russets, dark-greens, and blacks, as the artist loved to attire her. Thomson's pictures have many of them lost their pristine brilliancy and freshness; but even when straight from his hand one can hardly conceive them to have been other than deficient in this respect.

The stranger entering the Scottish National Gallery, after he has passed Tintoretto's " Venetian Senators," Vandyck's " Italian Nobleman in Armour,"—who seems one of " God's spies," watching every person in the room, listening to every word they utter,—and the seven or eight glowing Ettys, will probably seek the works of the first great master of Scottish landscape. There are seven of them, four the bequests of the late Professor Pillans. "Bruce's Castle of Turnberry," a sunset, grand and sombre, but cracked through the use of some pestilent vehicle, will give some idea of what Thomson was at his best; while "The Frith of Clyde, with Benlomond in the distance," "Ravensheuch Castle, near Kirkcaldy, Sunset," are beautiful reminiscences of that richness and depth of tone which distinguished this artist's works when they were fresh from his hand. And, having satisfied himself with these, if he will step across the room and study Mr Horatio Macculloch's "Inverlochy Castle," he will see what progress in the painting of landscape has been made in Scotland during the last twenty years; how far it has receded from Claude and the Poussins, how much closer it has come to Nature.

SYDNEY DOBELL.

TEN years ago the readers of the magazines and critical reviews could hardly fail to encounter unfavourable strictures on what was called the "Spasmodic School of Poetry." The three or four writers supposed to constitute that "school" were, at the period referred to, passing through the fires of exhortation, reproof, and parody. The nickname was the invention of a brilliant poet and wit, recently gone to his rest; and it had a nickname's best prosperity—it stuck. That this said nickname had, in some rough obvious manner, hit off the salient characteristics and defects of the "school," was evident from the favour with which it was received. The quaint brain of Professor Aytoun shaped the happy phrase; and immediately thereafter the three or four writers were everywhere recognised as "spasmodists," just as, since Mr Bright, in his speech a short while ago, alluded to the cave of Adullam and its inhabi-

tants, Lords Grosvenor and Elcho, Messrs
Horsman and Lowe, have been "Adullamites,"
or "Dwellers in the Cave," to all the world.
Nothing tells like a nickname which catches the
popular ear, and which is called out at every
street corner. The nickname "Spasmodic School"
grew popular, and in a short time it became the
critical stock-in-trade of provincial newspapers,
just as if they had been its sole inventors, and
had taken out a patent for its exclusive use.
For a while, no one of the writers could air himself in public in a volume of verse, however staid
and hum-drum, without the cry of "spasmodist"
being raised, here, there, and everywhere, so
loudly that he was glad to retreat again into
his shell. All this is a matter of ten years ago.
For seven years past the magazine reader has
heard nothing of the "Spasmodic School,"—it
is the lost pleiad of the critical firmament.
Oblivion distributeth her poppies with an equal
hand. "Firmilian," too, has been forgotten in
these years. The nicknamed and the nicknamer
sleep in the same forgetfulness of reviews—like
foemen in one grave.

The reviews are powerful, but they are not
omnipotent; and a man's work exists, after the

reviewers have said their best and their worst about it, precisely as it is. On the whole, there is nothing more curious than the fluctuation of literary reputations. A poet comes into fashion very much as crinoline came into fashion, is universally quoted as crinoline was universally worn, and in due time makes way for a new favourite. Wordsworth's fame was of slow and cedar-like growth; but it attracted a larger number of pilgrims fifteen years ago than it does now. Byron sank after his death, and is slowly rising to be permanently recognised, not as the greatest poet, but as the greatest intellectual force and portent of his time. His poetry was but the brilliant hectic-coloured blossom; the wholesome fruit we were destined never to see. Had he lived, it is plainly visible in the closing cantos of "Don Juan," he would have deserted poetry for prose fiction, and been our second Fielding, and our greater. Keats culminated ten years ago, on the publication of his "Life" by Lord Houghton, and leads at present a sort of pale lunar-rainbow existence in the pages of his imitators. Several years since the *Quarterly Review* spoke of Robert Browning as a man possessed of some slight tincture of poetic individuality, and was

good enough to quote with approval passages
from "Paracelsus" and "Bells and Pomegranates;"
to-day he is regarded by many as the most original of living poets, original in merit and defect,
in music, thought, and dramatic instinct. The
Laureate has long been popular, but he is
popular not so much from the essential merits
of his verse as from his exquisite form, exquisite
finish, and the wonderful way in which he reflects
the culture, the sentiment, the refined lazy scepticism made amiable only by its sadness, the
vague aspirations of English society. He holds
the mirror up to the time, but it is an enchanted
one, and reflects but noble faces. People will
weary of his finish as they weary of pictures
executed on ivory ; and he will be succeeded by
some far stormier and less perfectly balanced
spirit. While noticing this ebb and flow of
poetical reputations, it may not be too much to
infer that the oblivion to which the "Spasmodic
School" has been consigned for the last few
years has been to a considerable extent undeserved. At all events, leaving the other writers
whom this matter may concern to shift for themselves, I am anxious to speak for a few pages
concerning Sydney Dobell, by far the most im-

portant member of the "school," and whom not a few fairly intelligent persons in England and America consider to have written some of the noblest poetry of our day. In the courts of law, when a man conceives that justice has not been done, it is competent for him to call for a new trial. In the interest of Sydney Dobell, I move for a new trial in the courts of criticism.

Originality, as it is called, is, in popular estimation, a first merit in a writer; but then this originality may either attract or repel. In itself, originality is not necessarily a merit. The colour-blind man is original in a world of men gifted with normal powers of vision. To a sane individual there is nothing more frightfully original than the seething brain of a madman. Our dreams are more original than our waking moments, but they are, on the whole, less wise. The feeling of strangeness with which one occasionally, for the first time, peruses a book, does not usually go for much. It frequently springs from the mere foreign-looking husks and wrappings of the matter—the wampum-belt and scalp-tuft of the Pawnee Indian, the bear-skin and snow-shoes of the Esquimaux—rather than from the matter itself. The highest beauty does not dazzle at first, it more frequently seems a simple plainness. The writers who strike you as original are never original enough, just as the man who strikes you as cunning, has not been cunning enough to hide his cunning. All the colours sleep in a beam of pure white light. The generations of books are like the generations of men, the one begets the other, and not unfrequently the features of an ancestor recur in a descendant of to-day. Absolute originality, even were it possible, would be of no effect. An absolutely original book would resemble the scenery of the moon. It would be a world without an atmosphere. In reading such a book one would be reft away from the mighty aids of association and use and wont. In the sense of newness and strangeness, Australia is the most original country on the planet, and it is the least interesting. In the same sense, Asia and Europe are the least original and the most interesting. The strange kangaroo of the one continent is as nothing to the homely sparrow of the other, which has been man's companion and chirped on his thatch during six millenniums. In poetry, the gaudy parrot is as nothing compared with the brown lark. It is astonishing when one reflects on it, to what few and simple root-ideas the entire poetry of the world may be traced. I am, I was, I love, I hate, I suffer, I am glad, I must die—these lie at the bottom of all song. After the death of Abel the first family had pretty nearly gone the round of all possible experiences. In the primordial elements of human experience there is nothing trite—except to the trite; the only fruitful originality comes out of an entire and noble apprehension of those primordial elements, and the man who can to that noble apprehension give musical utterance is a poet, and a sufficiently original one, too, for all purposes. The generations of singing birds pass, but the music of the spring mornings goes on, although it has hardly changed a note since Adam. Originality is not a thing which a man can put on like a cloak to masquerade in. It is, if he have it at all, the pure outcome of his personality—the clear, unobscured, unobstructed utterance of his nature—that which is to himself special and peculiar, like the tone of his voice and the play of his features—an undefinable something of which he is in the profoundest unconsciousness, but by which he is made recognisable and is set apart from other men. Thus it comes about that the original man is the least

M

conscious of being original. It is easy for a beauty to be beautiful, it is easy for an original man to be original. And the undefinable something which sets a man apart from his fellows is the most valuable thing in the world ; it is absolutely priceless. You cannot forecast its next manifestation any more than you can conceive of a new colour. It cannot be imitated, it can never be forged ; no counterfeit by any possibility can ever pass current ; and yet every man and woman is born into the world with some proportion of it more or less. To this pure, clear, natural note of the soul all the world listens— for a whole grove of clever mocking-birds no one cares. Nature makes the Koh-i-Noor, and Birmingham will turn you out a bushel of imitations. And it is this special and individual something in great writers which, above all things, subserves a noble culture. These men bring a new thing into the world with them, and when they die they leave it as an inheritance. Scott writes, and the historic past is no longer pale and cold, but warm and many-coloured. Wordsworth writes, and ever after the solitariest place breathes an austere contentment ; and to the thoughtful man there is no such thing as

utter loneliness in the world. Keats writes, and
the coldness of Greek marble is faintly tinged
with passion.

And in the sense of having something personal
and peculiar, some new thing to supplement and
enrich modern culture, Sydney Dobell is fairly
entitled to be considered an original poet. I
have remarked elsewhere that Chaucer and
Spenser are the fountain-heads of all succeeding
English poetry. Chaucer is the father of the
humorous, kindly, dramatic, genially-lyrical men;
Spenser of the intense, allegorical, didactic, remote, and, by comparison, unsocial men. Shakespeare, Dryden, Burns, Byron, Browning, draw
descent from Chaucer. Milton, Young, Wordsworth, Shelley, and Tennyson from Spenser.
Sydney Dobell, too, is of the line and stock of
Spenser. His mental constitution is high, solitary, disdainful. His genius is of an ascetic and
fakir kind. He stands apart from his fellows,
and wraps himself up in the mantle of his own
thoughts. He is terribly self-conscious; he is
the slave of ideas; he writes with a purpose, and
as if under a certain compulsion. There is
nothing he hates so intensely as commonplace;
nothing he loves so intensely as beauty—the

more ideal the better; and in his fine music a quick ear will not unfrequently detect a stridulous tone, as if the string from which it is drawn were a trifle too tightly strung. In whatever he writes, whether he is purely and simply beautiful, or haughty as Apollo conscious of glowing limbs, or grotesque or extravagant, you will find nothing done at hap-hazard; he knows precisely the why and the wherefore, and will be able to render you a sufficient reason for everything. If it be at all admissible, now that the word has been so foully fingered and misused, to call a man *earnest*, that man is Sydney Dobell. He is essentially a missionary. He has neither written for the mere enjoyment of writing, nor for money, nor for fame, but mainly because he has a doctrine to preach, a cause to plead; and this doctrine he has preached in ears too long accustomed to sounding brasses and tinkling cymbals to give heed to high discourse. Mr Carlyle preaches hero-worship, Mr Dobell preaches genius-worship. At bottom the two doctrines are essentially the same, only the one man abides in the practical, the other in the ideal. In Mr Dobell's conception, genius—poetic genius, more especially—is ever a new

revelation to man. To him the poet is the
Teacher, bringing to his fellows new ideas of
truth, beauty, and morality. In his mind the
great poet is the most perfect human being, and
as the greater includes the less, he is at the same
time the true legislator and ruler. If as such
he is not recognised by men,—why, then, the
worse for the men. Mr Dobell would have the
world sit at the feet of the poets, and shape
everything, not only private conduct, but Parlia-
ments, statute-books, home and foreign policies,
according to their behests. In his idea, a poem
should go forth like the proclamation of a king ;
adverse critics he regards as rebels against lawful
authority, and would probably have them executed forthwith. To such a writer it will be at
once evident that poetry is no holiday pastime,
but a most solemn and responsible duty, to the
proper discharge of which everything must be
brought of best, noblest, and bravest. To such
a man no labour can be too severe, no study too
intense, no experience too bitter : poverty, pain,
death itself would be even welcome, if so be he
could perfect his art, and thereby save, or help to
save, a world grievously out of joint. And the
poet must not only be true to other men, he must

be true to himself. Never arrogant, he should
be always dignified; he must remember that
there is no greatness beyond his own; that this
complex, visible world, with its capitals and
standing armies, is based upon ideas, and that
in the ideal department of things he is a king,
enforcing and abrogating laws at his pleasure.
Above all, he must remember that, as an apostle
of the Highest, it behoves him to take heed to
his walk and conversation. He has not only to
write poems, he must also live poems. The song
should be pure and noble, and so should also
the life of the singer be. As poetry is above
ordinary prose, so should his morality be above
ordinary morality.

This idea of the poet and the poetic life cannot be regarded otherwise than as a high one.
Without some such basement of belief one cannot see how, more especially in these times, the
poetic life can be conducted at all; but as, in
order that the tree shall leaf, and blossom, and
bear fruit, it is necessary that the root should
be hidden away under-ground, deep-sunk in
life-giving soil; so, in like manner, if the poet
would go on prosperously with his work, it is
essential that his belief and theories concerning

himself and his art should be buried in the silent
depths of his nature; that he should quietly
draw spiritual sustenance from these, and in no
wise obtrude them on the world. We have
nothing to do with the food which the athlete
devours, we have only to do with the results—
the mighty limbs, the iron sinews. There is
nothing with which a poet has less need to concern himself than with poets and poetry, and
here it is that Mr Dobell has to some extent
gone astray. Poetry is not, or at all events
should not be, a Narcissus in love with his own
shadow, and eternally gazing upon it. It has to
do with everything except itself; it is the Divine
light in which we see heroism, duty, love, beauty,
death. It is not the hero, it is only the song
which celebrates the exploits of the hero.
Women are not specially interesting to women,
poets are not specially interesting to poets ; Mr
Dobell seems to have forgotten this, and in
" Balder "—his longest book, and, with all defects,
this primal one included, his greatest—he concerns himself with a poet from first to last, gives
his soliloquies, his notions concerning his art,
quotes the songs he sung at intervals, the scraps
of verse with which he hung the walls of his

chamber, and tells us what books he purposed to write, through which to regenerate the world. "Balder" is the longest poem of our time, with the exception, perhaps, of "Festus;" and apart from the exquisite songs of "Amy," which, if extracted, would of themselves make a mournful anthology, there are not in its entire length a dozen pages of purely human interest. It contains wonderful things, it has passages of marvellous subtlety and music, but these fail to make pleasing the stupendous egotism. Now, it is evident that, if you wish to cure a sick man you must give him a medicine which it is possible for him to take; and if you wish, by means of a poem, to make the world better, you must needs write a poem which it will be possible for the world to read. "Balder" is, to the large majority of persons, simply unreadable, and this not from any defect of genius, but because it is based upon an erroneous theory. In "Balder," too, one is perpetually conscious of a certain strain and effort; there is a lack of spontaneity, of easy, unconscious, unsolicitous result, as of an Æolian harp sighing to the caprices of intermittent wind. At times the writer almost ceases to be a poet, and becomes a pamphleteer. In all Mr Dobell's books intellectual subtlety plays him false ; not unfrequently the dialectician overrides the poet. When opportunity offers, he ceases singing to argue

> Like some budge doctor of the Stoic fur;

and the matters over which he subtilises are often the most filmy and intangible : he will un-ravel you a thread of morning gossamer, he will dissect you an ephemeron, he will lay you bare the heart of a mote of the sunbeam. When he grapples with a subject, both he and it, like hawk and heron, disappear in the distance. He defines everything to the vanishing point, and beyond it. All this kind of thing seems labo-rious trifling to a reader of normal instincts. You can respect a whirlwind when it sinks a ship, or blows down a house ; you cannot when it merely makes a spire of dust and straws at the corner of a street. Mr Dobell's remarkable subtlety is in his art rather a hindrance than an aid, and is so for several reasons. In the first place, he has an entire and abiding horror of commonplace ; and although it may be seen leading easily and definitely to results, he can-not bear to walk, for ever so short a distance, in

a beaten path.   Above all things, he will be
independent, original, and self-sustained.   He
will lie under poetic obligations to no one.   He
will not only build his house after his own
plan, but he insists in providing his materials
out of his own quarries and forests.   Had it
been possible, he would have invented a language of his own.   He is continually " seeking
out a new path for himself," a task which Goethe
was happy in *not* having forced upon him.   He
will always stand on virgin soil ; and as the
Red Indian retires into his aboriginal forests
when he smells the watchfire of the white
settler, Mr Dobell, on the approach of the ordinary and commonplace, retires into the un-
pierced depths of his nature, where no one can
follow him, and where his subtlety is of none
effect, for the reason that it has no spectator.
Then, again, Mr Dobell is what Dr Johnson
would have ·called a "metaphysical poet ;"
he has much in common with Cowley and
Donne in past generations, and with Shelley
in our own.   Like these, he has a whole body
of ingenious theories, whimsies, and conceits on
every subject under the sun to enforce, illustrate, and uphold.   In all this his amazing

subtlety has ample play; but then in the work he is beyond the sympathies of his readers. There is such an entity, doubtless, as the pure spirit of life; but we have knowledge of it only through the form it assumes. There is such a thing as the spirit of poetry, but it is only recognisable in the concrete—in a flower, in a lark's song, in a beautiful woman, in some human experience more or less complex. Mr Dobell's verse is often not sufficiently "clothed upon;" it does not take palpable form and substance, but abides in vague guesses and shadows of things. It is too often like the night wind, a haunter of waste and solitary places in which there is no human dwelling; and deals with a something of which we are cognisant, but of which the imagination can form no picture. And as is not uncommon with earnest, eager, theoretical men, Mr Dobell's volatile impracticability of mind is unregulated by humour. He is defective in that quick sense of the ludicrous which is a man's best safeguard from absurdity, both in literature and in social life. He has plenty of wit, the brilliant sparks of collision,

> ————the light
> Struck out from clashing swords in fight;

but of humour, that other kind of love, with its tenderness and sadness, without its fiery passion and pain, there is, perhaps, not any very definite trace discoverable in his writings. He is, in consequence, always too trenchant and grimly in earnest; there is a lack of ease, of rapid lightness of touch, of graceful sportiveness. It is from this lack of humour, I take it, that Mr Dobell is too persistently dignified. The port of a king in a grand state ceremonial is simply laughable when transferred to his private apartment or to his palace grounds, as he walks in them of a morning before breakfast. Mr Dobell has not learned how to unbend; he is always in full uniform, never in *mufti.* Like Shelley, he is a great deal too constantly poetical. Genius is the most precious of mental gifts, gold is the most precious of metals; but as you cannot work gold without an alloy, you cannot make much use of genius without an intermixture of prosaic common-sense and mother-wit.

I have spoken thus frankly of what seem to me Mr Dobell's defects, in order that I may just as frankly speak of his merits. These are very much higher than the general public appear at all to be aware. For intellectual force, poetic

instinct and vitality, he may claim to be ranked,
pari passu, with Alfred Tennyson and Robert
Browning. He is, in the best sense, as has been
already indicated, an original man. He is a
poet ; but he bears to other poets such likeness
and difference as the birch bears to the elm
and the oak. He is of the same genus, but not
the same species. Of all recent writers, he seems
to bear the closest resemblance to Shelley.
He has much of Shelley's impracticability,
exaggeration, and hectic over-colour ; he has all
Shelley's subtlety, analytic habit and power,
splendour of imagery, dramatic instinct, and
rich-flowing lyrical impulse. There are as noble
passages in the "Roman" as you will find in
"Hellas;" there is as intricate searching of
dark bosoms and moods in "Balder" as in the
"Cenci;" there are lyrics in "England in Time
of War" which will mate with the "Sensitive
Plant" and the "Skylark." And as, when a man
is under strong emotion, there gleams on his
countenance an expression which is not ordinarily
there, a look of race, in which father, grandfather,
and great-grandfather are blended ; so in Mr
Dobell's finer passages one discerns a something
native to himself and to none other ; a some-

thing which finds its analogue in sculpture rather than in painting; a purity as of the undraped limbs of the marble nymph; a shining ethereal beauty, as of the cluster of white lilies which female saints wear, as they rise, with clouds of cherubs fluttering around their feet, into a heaven of blue and gold, in mediæval Italian altar-pieces.

The " Roman " was published—the author yet very young—in the after-swell of the revolutionary impulse of 1848. It had a great success, was admired by quick, vivid, impulsive Charlotte Brontë; and was regarded by all capable of forming a judgment in such matters, as the work of a man certain to leave a name amongst the poetical writers of his country. The work was thrown into a loose dramatic form, and its energy, enthusiasm, and eloquence were considered little less than marvellous. On·the top of the first page the author described his hero— " Vittorio Santo, a missionary of freedom. He has gone out disguised as a monk to preach the unity of Italy, the overthrow of the Austrian domination, and the restoration of a great Roman Republic;" and from its subject it naturally became a pendant to the " Deformed Trans-

formed" of Byron and the "Hellas" of Shelley.
The scenes are nine in number, and tell no very
closely-knit and connected story : the monk is
the main speaker throughout, and although there
is a monotony of eloquence inseparable somewhat from the conception and plan, vigour and
spirit never flag, and from beginning to close the
reader is carried stormily along. The tone is a
little too highly pitched all through ; now and
again there is a slight tendency to extravagance ;
but, apart from these defects of youth, born of
delight in the exercise of a newly-discovered
power, the style is unexceptionable—the English is clear, vivid, nervous, and without the
slightest haze of obscurity ; you are constantly
reminded of Byron in the swell and movement
of the verse. The first scene opens at evening
on an ancient Italian battle-field, on which a
number of young men and maidens are dancing
and singing. The monk is standing by, and at
length breaks in upon the dancers. He speaks
to them of Italy, his mother and theirs, and
how the ground they dance on is her grave.
The speech is too long to quote, but its drift
and character will be gathered from the following :—

I pray you listen how I loved my mother,
And you will weep with me.   She loved me, nurst me,
And fed my soul with light.   Morning and even
Praying, I sent that soul into her eyes,
And knew what heaven was though I was a child.
I grew in stature, and she grew in goodness.
I was a grave child; looking on her taught me
To love the beautiful: and I had thoughts
Of Paradise, when other men have hardly
Looked out of doors on earth.   (Alas! alas!
That I have also learned to look on earth
When other men see heaven.)   I toiled, but ever
As I became more holy, she seemed holier;
Even as when climbing mountain-tops the sky
Grows ampler, higher, purer as ye rise.
Let me believe no more.   No, do not ask me
How I repaid my mother.   O thou saint,
That lookest on me day and night from heaven,
And smilest, I have given thee tears for tears,
Anguish for anguish, woe for woe.   Forgive me,
If, in the spirit of ineffable penance
In words, I waken up the guilt that sleeps.
Let not the sound afflict thine heaven, or colour
That pale, tear-blotted record which the angels
Keep of my sins.   We left her.   I and all
The brothers that her milk had fed.   We left her—
And strange dark robbers with unwonted names
Abused her! bound her! pillaged her! profaned her!
Bound her clasped hands, and gagged the trembling lips
That pray'd for her lost children.   And we stood,
And she knelt to us, and we saw her kneel,
And looked upon her coldly and denied her!
Denied her in her agony—and counted
Before her sanguine eyes the gold that bought
Her pangs.   We stood——

Here the revellers, thinking that a veritable mother of the flesh is spoken of, break in on the monk and load him with reproaches and execrations. He undeceives them:

> You are my brothers. And my mother was
> Yours. And each man amongst you day by day
> Takes, bowing, the same price that sold my mother,
> And does not blush. Her name is ROME. Look round,
> And see those features which the sun himself
> Can hardly leave for fondness. Look upon
> Her mountain-bosom, which the very sky
> Beholds with passion; and with the last proud
> Imperial sorrow of dejected empire,
> She wraps the purple round her outraged breast,
> And even in fetters cannot be a slave.
> Look on the world's best glory and worst shame.
>
>   *   *   *   *
>
>   They are some souls
> That once took flesh and blood in Italy,
> And thought it was a land to draw free breath in,
> And drew it long, and died here; and since live
> Everywhere else.
>
>   *   *   *   *
>
> Look on that mother and behold her sons!
> Alas, she might be Rome if there were Romans!
> Look on that mother! Wilt thou know that death
> Can have no part in Beauty? Cast to-day
> A seed into the earth, and it shall bear thee
> The flowers that waved in the Egyptian hair
> Of Pharaoh's daughter!

In such eloquent fashion storms on the passionate monk, until, recovering from his enthu-

N

siasm, he finds that, with the exception of
Francesca, the revellers have one by one stolen
away. The monk perceives her, and she, with
all his words flaming in her heart, asks—

> I have heard much to-night
> Of Roman deeds, of sages, and of heroes,
> Of sons who loved, and sons who have betrayed.
> Hath Rome no daughters to repeat her beauty,
> Renew the model of old time, and teach
> Her sons to love the mother in the child?
> Was Rome, my father, built and peopled by
> One sex? The very marble of your ruins
> Looks masculine. In heart I roam about them;
> But wheresoe'er my female soul peers in—
> Even to the temple courts—some bearded image
> Gives privilege. Doth Salique law entail
> The heritage of glory? Is there nothing,
> Nothing, my father, in the work of freedom
> For woman's hand to do?

A long colloquy follows; *Santo* accepts her
services, and we have the result of it all in
Scene IV. *Francesca* is alone, and in her soliloquy she subtly and tenderly reveals a woman's
undevotion to abstractions, and her love for
Santo.

> And thou! Country!
> Thou stern and awful god, of which my reason
> Preaches infallibly, but which no sense
> Bears witness to—I would thou hadst a shape.

It might be dwarf, deformed, maimed,—anything,
So it was thine ; and it would stand to me
For beauty.   And my soul should wait on it,
And I would train my fancies all about it,
Till, growing to its fashion, and most nurtured
With smiles and tears, they strengthened into love.
But, Santo, this indefinite dim presence
I cannot worship.   O thou dear Apostle !
O what a patriot could Francesca be
If *thou* wert Rome !

      *   *   *   *

          Heart, have all thy will !
Santo, I love thee ! love thee ! love thee ! love thee !
Santo, I love thee !   O, thou wild word love !
Thou bird broke loose !   I could say on and on,
And feel existence but to speak and hear.
Santo, I love thee !   Hear, Francesca loves thee !
Santo, I love thee !   O, my heart, my heart,
My heart—thou Arab mad with desert thirst
In sight of water.

Immediately after this, Ceco, a friend, approaches and informs *Francesca* that *Santo* has been taken prisoner by the Austrians, and is sentenced to be shot at dawn.   What follows reads like a passage from the old masters of the English drama.   *Francesca* shows a poniard.

                    Ceco,
Tell me ; tell all, ah Ceco—nay, look here,
In the moonlight—Saints ! I can use it !
  Ceco.   Strange
Wild girl, how ?   Knowest thou not as well as I

Vittorio preaching to some Milanese
Who would be patriots if they knew but how,
Spent precious hours in which the German foe
Slipt from the snare?   Whereat brave Roderigo—
A gallant sword—the greatest libertine
In Milan—seized him.   In the castle dungeon
He lies since noon, and with the coming dawn
Dies.
   Francesca. Dies, dies—who dies?   Pray you, friend,
      say on ;
I am not wont to wander.
                This is well !
That last waltz spent me.   Let me see, what gallant
Danced young Francesca down?   Nay, he'll boast rarely !
Yet it seems long ago—long, long ago.
Such dreamless sleep !   Thou melancholy moon,
What ! have I caught my death damp of the dews ?
Death,—death—ah !—
A gallant sword—the greatest libertine
In Milan ?—yes, yes,—Roderigo,—yes—
He lies since noon, ay, in the castle dungeon,
And with the dawn—no, no, thou pitiless sun !
Thou durst not rise !   oh sea, if thou hast waves,
Quench him !
A gallant sword—the greatest libertine
In Milan—ah—the greatest libertine ?
Who says I am not fair?   Ye gods ! I curse you :
Why do ye tempt me ?
             It is over Ceco :
Ceco, I tell thee it is past, is past.
Santo is free.   Look thou that horses wait
Near the east gate by sunrise.

In the next scene we are introduced to a
number of students and burghers in the common

room, discussing the news of the day—notably,
the rescue of this monk by *Francesca.*

> *Lelio.*   At midnight—
> (Count Grassi's child hath a fair face).
>   *Several.*   At midnight
> Count Grassi's child hath a fair face ! Fie, Lelio ;
> Why, what a traitor art thou !
>   *Lelio.*   Attend, I say !
> Count Rossi's lewdness is a proverb—
>   *Several (pour badiner).*   Hold,
> Lelio, for pity—there are bachelors here—
> We are not all companions in misfortune !
> For pity Lelio !
>   *Lelio.*   You that shout for pity,
> If you be Pity's followers, do her now
> Your best allegiance. Good friends, I, her quæstor,
> Claim tribute for her. A few tears will pay it.
> Listen. The young Francesca, at the price
> Of her fair body, bought the captive's life ;
> The priest is free. Do not cry out. Young Rossi
> Craved instant payment. She, in her superb
> High loveliness, whose every look enhanced
> The ransom, sent him from her, glad to grant
> Another maiden hour for prayer and tears.
> Francesca wore a poniard. She is now
> A maid for ever.
>   *Hostess (to one standing by).* How is that, sir ?
>   *Student (aside.)*   Hush !
> Dead.

The reader capable of appreciating beauty,
passion, pathos, cannot fail to recognise all these
in the foregoing extracts ; and the same high

qualities distinguish the other dramatic scenes. At the close, the monk, tried by court-martial, is condemned to be shot; and beholds above the heads of the Austrian platoon, drawn out for his execution, the vision of a United Italy—the dream of so many martyrs.

"Balder" appeared some years after the publication of the "Roman," and was not nearly so well received by the critics. In truth, the gentlemen of the press did not seem to know very well what to make of this new candidate for their suffrages; and as abuse of the book was easier than laborious inquiries into its purport and meaning, it was abused more vigorously and universally than almost any other poetical effort of our time. And it must at once be admitted that "Balder" is very singular, puzzling, and obscure. It lacks the action, rapidity, and healthy human freshness of the "Roman." Nor is it written in the same vivid, simple English. The actors are few—*Balder*, a poet; *Amy*, his wife; *Dr Paul*, a medical man; an artist; a servant—these are all. There is no action in it; and with the exception of Scene XXIV., in which the poet and his wife pass out into the fields, the whole tragedy transacts itself in-doors. *Balder* is

continually writing or musing in his study, and
continually through the open door comes the
voice of *Amy—Balder* musing on his coming
poetic greatness, to which Nature had consented,
and the elements had set their seals—*Amy*
wailing of loneliness, of the departure of love, of
her dead child, of stagnant days and nights, and
madness creeping nearer and nearer. There is
the hard, selfish soliloquy of the proud, unami-
able man, alternating with the sigh of the
broken-hearted woman and the sound of her
falling tears. The book is designed to show
how fatally the egotism of genius clouds and
dwarfs the moral nature ; how, in the fierce thirst
for power, love dies out, and the man is left
with the strength of an archangel and the heartlessness and loneliness of a devil. But the book
is far too long, and the lesson might have been
enforced after some less painful fashion. *Amy's*
tortures are lingering and long-drawn-out ; she
is slowly broken on the wheel, as it were. *Balder*
himself is fretful, unsocial, incomprehensible,
and a bit of a prig as well. His communings
are with himself alone. At his open window,
or at his study-table, he will talk by the
hour about his feelings ; his ambitions ; of " his

having struck off one from the weary score of human tasks;" of his intention to make "his staff the solar centre of creation;" and of his "early-planned, long-meditated, and slowly-written epic." He is a monstrosity, and that most detestable of all monstrosities—polite, silvery-tongued as Belial—who will never get into a healthy human anger with any one; who will subtilize, argue, give a thousand exquisite reasons for everything, and, having made up his mind beforehand, will take his own way in the end. He will not get angry with you; he will sublimely pity you like a god. He may be cruel, but he is always pleasant of speech. Of *Balder* one does not know what to think,—one cannot conceive what motives actuate him, or forecast his conduct for a moment; he is utterly and hatefully inexplicable: and when at the close, like some rudderless ship, whose course is a series of accidents, he drifts into murder, or appears about to drift into it, you read on in a sort of stupid protesting bewilderment. Altogether, "Balder" is one of the most painful of books. There is in it an atmosphere of stagnant, formless woe, a crude misty misery, a selfishness that might be felt. In reading it you grope, as it

were, through some solid, stifling gloom. And
yet if any one would form a just estimate of the
power and originality of Mr Dobell's genius, of
the swift-cleaving character of his intellect, to
this book he must come and endure its pain.
With all its gloom and horror, I do not know
where else you will meet such sudden, unexpected,
exquisite sweetness; such radiant sunniness of
nature; such lovely lyrical trills, like the carol
of a bird from the blossomed apple-tree in the
orchard, heard through the silence of a house in
which a dead man is lying; such strokes of sharp
pathos at which the printed page disappears to
slowly glimmer back. Out of the heavy surrounding gloom *Amy* breaks into sudden song:

> Then came the cowslip
> Like a dancer in the fair,
> She spread her little mat of green,
> And on it danced she.
> With a fillet bound about her brow,
> A fillet round her happy brow,
> A golden fillet round her brow,
> And rubies in her hair.

There is nothing in Marlow, Webster, or
Dekker, more frightful than the close of this
book. *Balder* is reading a scroll, and talking to
himself of his "unthought of glory;" *Amy* rises

suddenly, snatches the scroll from his hand,
and throws it out of the open window into the
moat.

>   *Amy.*   Glory? see!
> Can it light up that pit down where I dwell
> Out of the light of day and of the stars?
> Out of the light o' the grave :—Ay, the dull earth
> Below the dead is not so black with night
> But the great day shall stir it! Is it well
> That the dull earth below the dead hath life
> And I am dark for ever? Is that well?
> Is that well, husband? Husband, is it well?
> O yes, thy glory; yes—he must have glory;
> Yes, he must have his glory; he can stand
> All day in the sun, but he must have his glory!
> He has walked here up in the sunshine world,
> He has been in the wind and the sweet rain,
> And none cried, "Upset the cup o' the honey time,
> Upset the cup o' the honey time,"
> And I am empty and dry.
>   *   *   *   *
>
> I am his wife! This is my murderer!
> Make way, make way, this is a murderer!
> I am in hell, slain, lost, robbed, murdered, mad,
> He did it, he!
>   *Balder.* He knows it.
>   *Amy.*   Mad, mad, mad!
>   (*Sinking in his arms in a swoon.*)
>   *Balder.* Now, now, my soul! it must be ere she wake,
> I will bear this alone; she shall not know
> The hand that strikes—This hand! Nor man nor fiend
> Would do thee harm but me! Now—now—yet O
> That it must be now! That it had been while
> The fire of madness burned her, and she swelled

And blackened like a burning house—once house,
Now but a house in flames.

    *   *   *   *

                              (Begins to divest her.)
                Heaving breast,
How oft have I undone thy weeds as now,
And very softly, very silently,
As now—and not more tenderly—no, not
More tenderly—no, on thy bridal night,
No, not more tenderly!   But oh, you heavens,
Wherefore and wherefore?
                        Here under her bosom
It cannot fail her.   Hide thee, hide thee, Heart,
Poor fluttering bird, why wilt thou stir the lilies?
Dost thou not know me, who I am!   Soft, soft;
Thou hast so often struggled in mine arms
Asleep, and I have wakened thee with kisses,
I pray thee do not struggle now, my child,
I cannot rouse thee from this dream.
                      O God,
If she should clasp her hands upon her breast
And moan!   If she should feel through this thin trance
The cold steel ere it pierce, and call on me
For help!—but I will hold thee fast, my child—
Fast in these arms, altho' thou start and cry—
And shield thee from myself!   If I strike ill
The first stroke, and she wake and strive for life;
If she should ope her eyes but once too late,
And go forth to believe for ever more
I struck unkindly—

                (Throws a kerchief over her face.)
           No, she shall not see me,—
And now thy living face is gone for ever,
And I have murdered thee before thy time.
Nor God nor demon could have wrung from me

This moment, the last moment, only thou,
O, only thou—

(*Frantically lifts the kerchief.*)
Amy.   Thou there, all there!
Help me, my child.   Ay, look so beautiful,
'Tis well; if this be heaven, this is not
To kill thee—Now.

The power of this is indisputable, but how it all comes about, how it evolves itself out of the body of the work, is not a little obscure.

"England in Time of War" is Mr Dobell's latest work, and it is in many respects his homeliest, simplest, and most delightful.   There is nothing of the enormous egotism of "Balder" about it, because, from the nature of the cases, it deals with a variety of characters, and touches on a multitude of interests.   The book is mainly composed of lyrics, but they are dramatic lyrics; only on one or two occasions the writer speaks in his proper person, and an attempt is made to give expression to every rank of English society in its relation to the war then raging.   In carrying out his idea, the writer necessarily passes from cot to castle, from milkmaid to merchant. The war lies at the centre of each of these lyrics, but there is remarkable variety in the people who utter them.   There is the market-

wife, who mixes Bible and newspaper, and who
imagines that the armies of Israel fought with
bayonets, and wore scarlet ; the merriment of
the recruits' ball ; the wail of the mad woman,
whose lover has been slain ; the sorely-wounded
officer slowly becoming convalescent, as he is
wheeled through the sunshine and over the
primroses of English spring. In very many of
these little songs there is an abounding free-
flowing music, a light, airy gracefulness of touch,
a sunny playfulness at times which is almost
humour, a homeliness and sincerity of pathos
which needs no fine words. Some of the
humblest, dealing with milkmaids and broken-
hearted, dying farmers, are more poetical than
the ambitious soliloquies in " Balder."

Here is an exquisite lyric, which has all the
charm, simplicity, and colour of an old ballad :

> The murmur of the mourning ghost
> 　That keeps the shadowy kine,
> O, Keith of Ravelston
> 　The sorrows of thy line !
>
> Ravelston, Ravelston,
> 　The merry path that leads
> Down the golden morning hill
> 　And thro' the silver meads.
>
> Ravelston, Ravelston,
> 　The stile beneath the tree,

The maid that kept her mother's kine,
　　The song that sang she !

She sang her song, she kept her kine,
　　She sat beneath the thorn
When Andrew Keith of Ravelston
　　Rode thro' the Monday morn.

His henchmen sing, his hawk-bells ring,
　　His belted jewels shine !
O, Keith of Ravelston,
　　The sorrows of thy line !

Year after year, where Andrew came
　　Comes evening down the glade,
And still there sits a moonshine ghost
　　Where sat the sunshine maid.

Her misty hair is faint and fair,
　　She keeps the shadowy kine;
O, Keith of Ravelston,
　　The sorrows of thy line !

I lay my hand upon the stile,
　　The stile is lone and cold,
The burnie that goes babbling by
　　Says nought that can be told.

Yet, stranger ! here, from year to year,
　　She keeps her shadowy kine ;
　O, Keith of Ravelston,
　　The sorrows of thy line !

Step out three steps, where Andrew stood—
　　Why blanch thy cheeks for fear ?
The ancient stile is not alone,
　　'Tis not the burn I hear !

> She makes her immemorial moan,
>> She keeps her shadowy kine;
> O, Keith of Ravelston,
>> The sorrows of thy line !

In this little poem, are not the palpable and the impalpable, the past and the present, subtly intermixed like day and night in twilight ?

If a man's literary success be judged by the number of editions his works have reached, and the number of readers he has secured, then, when compared with many of his contemporaries, Mr Dobell's literary success does not seem considerable. And, unquestionably, every sensible man must consider that popularity is an important element in literary success. If you sing a song in public, and if no one will listen to your singing, as a public singer you have most certainly failed. If you say that you don't care whether people listen or not, then why sing in public at all ? why not confine your melodious utterance to your private apartment, and dedicate it merely to your own delight ? The " Roman " and " Balder " have reached second editions; "England in Time of War " is yet in its first : Mr Tupper is at present advertising the Bijou Edition of " Proverbial Philosophy," being something like the

hundred and twentieth thousand. I do not put
these two statements together to point a barren
sneer at Mr Tupper—that has been a great deal
too much the custom of late, and many of the
writers who laugh the loudest at "Proverbial
Philosophy" would have been extremely puzzled
to write it—but I bring them together to
show that poetry of the highest class may not
find a public, while poetry of a far lower grade
is sometimes enormously successful in that respect. But then, if devotedness of attachment is
in these matters to be considered and valued,
the love of the six readers of the unpopular poet
may outweigh the love of a hundred readers of
the popular one. In the old Scottish days " The
King over the water" was pledged far seldomer;
but, when pledged, with a thousand times more
enthusiasm than was ever King George. In
the palmy days of Byron and the *Edinburgh
Review*, Wordsworth was the least read, but the
most intensely loved poet in England. It is
curious how unpopular books are loved by
the men who like them, and find in them
spiritual sustenance. Between the reading of
such books and of more popular ones, there is
all the difference between dining at an ordinary

and in a private room with select friends. The
" Phantastes" of Mr George MacDonald is a
book but little talked about; but I happen to
know some six men to whom admiration for that
most exquisite of modern prose poems is a sort
of bond of union. Mr Dobell has an audience,
not so large as many, but more devoted than
most. Whether he is to the full aware of that
devotedness, I cannot say; but I am certain,
knowing his serious and noble nature, that
whether his books are popular or the reverse,
is to him a matter of no very considerable moment. He is one of the few men who can say,
and that, too, without the slightest suspicion of
cant or insincerity, that having done his work
faithfully and well — this being the matter in
which he has strict personal concern—he is not
too anxious as to what reception his work may
meet with—that being more specially the concern of others.

VERY now and again it is asserted that our literature is being destroyed by the periodicals. Some hold that, under their baneful influence, we are losing all concision and polish of style, as well as all capacity for serious thought. Others, admitting that there may be as much intellectual wealth current now as there was forty or a hundred years ago, contend that, as the intellectual wealth of the former time was represented by a thousand gold coins, whilst that of the present day circulates in a million copper ones, the unprecedented distribution of pieces—the sordid material of which they are composed, the excess of bulk and weight—form serious deductions from the value actually in possession. The assertion that magazines and reviews are at present hurting literature, is one which, in virtue of being half truth and half falsehood, is likely to enjoy a long life. You cannot trample it quite out, on

account of the truth resident in it : you have an
uneasy suspicion of its falsehood even while
asserting it most loudly.   Every household in
the country has its periodical.   Henry of Navarre longed for the time when every Frenchman should have a hen in his pot.   That, he
conceived a better sign of the prosperity of a
country than certain big feasts in certain big
castles.   The magazines bring literature into
every home, just as aqueduct and pipe bring the
water of Loch Katrine into the homes of the
Glasgow citizens.   It is quite true that the
water occasionally tastes of iron, and wears a
rusty stain ; quite true that a perfectly pure
draught may always be had at the legendary
lake in the shadow of the hills ; but the water is
flowing in every house, and that, after all, is the
important matter.

And, to carry out the illustration, the water
is often as pure in the basin of the citizen as
beneath the trembling sedges that the wild duck
loves. The fact that so many of our books—and
so many of our best books, too—are reprints from
periodicals, proves that not only are periodicals
extensively read, but that they absorb much
of our best thinking and writing.   The best

written magazine naturally attracts the largest number of readers ; and this number of readers enables it to maintain its level of excellence, and to draw to its service the best men who may from time to time arise. When we say that our best periodicals are extensively read, we are simply saying that our best periodicals are attractive. No man who wishes to be amused will pay his money for dulness. No man who appreciates style will habitually peruse what cannot minister to his literary delight. The people who purchase the *Cornhill* may be presumed to be tolerably contented with the literature of the *Cornhill*. Their ordinary thinking is not quite up to the level of the thinking of the writers in that serial ; the articles it contains occasionally present them with a new fact, or with a new view of a fact already known ; and their ordinary conversation or correspondence does not exhibit the play of fancy and aptness of illustration which distinguish the writings of Mr Thackeray and Mr Lewes. So long as periodicals are read, we assume that they serve a very important purpose—that they amuse, instruct, and refine. Whenever they cease to do so, they will die, as the "Annuals" did. Nor

does this same literature affect writers in any
very disastrous way. It is frequently said that
periodical writing fritters away a man's intellectual energy ; that, instead of concentrating himself on some congenial task, devoting a whole
lifetime to it, and leaving it as a permanent
possession of the race, a man is tempted to
write hastily, and without sufficient meditation ;
that, in fact, we have articles now, more or less
brilliant, whereas, under different circumstances,
we might have had books. All this kind of
conjecture is exceedingly unprofitable. Doubtless, under different circumstances, the results
of a man's working would have been different
more or less ; but it does not of necessity follow
that the results would have been more valuable.
A man's power in literature, as in everything
else, is best measured by his accomplishment,
just as his stature is best measured by his coffin.
The man who can beat his fellows in a ten-mile
race is likely to maintain his superiority in a
race for a shorter distance. It is a mistake to
suppose that a man's largest work, or the work
on which he has expended the greatest labour,
is on that account his best. Literary history is
full of instances to the contrary. When mental

powers are equal, that is surest of immortality which occupies the least space ; scattered forces are then concentrated, like garden roses gathered into one bouquet, or English beauty in the boxes at the opera. Leisure and life-long devotion to a task have often resulted in tediousness. Large works are often too heavy for posterity to carry. We have too many "Canterbury Tales." The "Faery Queen" would be more frequently read if it consisted of only one book, and Spenser's fame would stand quite as high as it does. Milton's poetical genius is as apparent in "Comus" and "Lycidas" as in his great Epic, which most people have thought too long. Addison's "Essay in Westminster Abbey" is more valuable than his tragedy. Macaulay's Essays on Clive and Warren Hastings are as brilliant, powerful, and instructive as any single chapter of his "History"—with the additional advantage, that they can be read at a sitting. Certain readers have been found to admire Wordsworth's "We are Seven" more than the "Excursion," Coleridge talked of spending fifteen years on the construction of a great poem ; had he done so, it is doubtful whether his reader would have preferred it to the "Ancient Mariner." From all

this, it may be inferred that, if writers, instead
of " frittering themselves away " in periodicals,
had devoted themselves to the production of
important works, the world would not have
been much the wiser, and their reputations not
one whit higher. Besides, there are many men
more brilliant than profound—who have more
élan than persistence—who gain their victories,
like the Zouaves, by a rapid dash ;—and these do
their best in periodicals. These the immediate
presence of the reader excites, as the audience
the orator, the crowded pit the actor. Jerrold
sparkles like a fire-fly through the tropic night ;
Hood, in that tragic subject which his serious
fancy loved, emits, like the glow-worm, a melancholy ray. But they could not shine for any
continuous period, and had the wisdom not to
attempt it. Are they to blame that they did
not write long books to prove themselves dull
fellows ? It is of no use to cry out against
the present state of things in literature. The
magazines are here, and they have been produced by a great variety of causes. ·They
demand certain kinds of literary ware ; but
whether the wares are valuable or the reverse,
depends entirely upon the various workmen. It

is to be hoped, if magazine writers possess a specialty, that they will stick to their specialty, and work it out faithfully—that no one will go out of his way, like Mr Dickens, when he wrote "The Child's History of England," or Mr Ruskin, when he addressed himself to the discussion of questions in political economy.

To the young writer, the magazine or review has distinct advantages. In many instances he can serve in the house of a literary noble, as the squire in the fourteenth century served in the house and under the eye of the territorial noble. He may model himself on an excellent pattern, and receive knighthood from his master as the reward of good conduct. If otherwise circumstanced,—if, following no special banner, he writes under the cover of the anonymous, and is unsuccessful, — he may retire without being put to public shame. In the arena of the magazines he can try his strength, pit himself against his fellows, find out his intellectual weight and power, gradually acquire confidence in himself, or arrive at the knowledge of his weakness—a result not less valuable if more rarely attained. If he is overthrown in the lists, no one but himself is the worse ; if he distinguishes

himself, it is a little unreasonable to expect him
to keep his visor down when roses are shower-
ing upon him from applauding balconies. A
man eminently successful in the magazines
may fairly be forgiven for rushing to a reprint.
Actors who make a hit at Drury Lane, almost
immediately make a tour of the provinces. A
reprint is to the author what a provincial tour is
to the actor If he is an amusing writer, people
welcome him in his new shape with the gratitude which people always entertain for those
who have amused them ; if he is a great writer,
people desire to shake hands with him, as the
elector is proud to shake hands with the candidate whom he has elected as his representative.
And, indeed, the magazinists may fairly be
compared to the House of Commons—a mixed
audience, representing every class—stormy,
tumultuous, where great questions are being
continually discussed ; an assembly wherein
men rise to be leaders of parties ; out of which
men are selected to rule distant provinces ; out
of which, also, every now and again, a member
is translated to the Upper House, where he takes
his seat among his peers, in a serener atmosphere,
and among loftier traditions.

During the last year or two there has been a large number of reprints from the magazines, consisting chiefly of essays and novels. With the latter, at present, we have no concern. The essay has always been a favourite literary form with magazine writers; and in the volumes before us we have specimens of various kinds. Of the most delightful kind of essay-writing, that of personal delineation, which chronicles moods, which pursues vagrant lines of thought, Montaigne is the earliest, and, as yet, the greatest example. Montaigne is as egotistical in his essays as a poet in his lyrics. His subject is himself, his thinkings, his surroundings of every kind. He did not write to inform us about the events of his own time, though it was stirring enough; about his contemporaries, although he mingled much in society, and knew the best men of his day; about the questions which stirred the hearts and perplexed the intellects of the sixteenth century Frenchmen, although he was familiar with them all, and had formed his own opinions on them; these he puts aside, to discourse of his chateau, his page, his perfumed gloves;—to discuss love, friendship, experience, and the like, in his own way, half in banter, half in earnest.

Consequently, we have the fullest information regarding himself, if we have but little regarding anything else. Of course, Essays written after this fashion cannot, from the very nature of them, be expected to shape themselves on any established literary form. They do not require to have a middle, beginning, or end. They are a law unto themselves. They are shaped by impulse and whim, as emotion shapes the lyric. Montaigne wanders about at his own will, and has as many jerks and turnings as a swallow on the wing. He seems to have the strangest notions of continuity, and sometimes his titles have no relation to his subject-matter, and look as oddly at the top of his page as the sign-board of the Bible-merchant over the door of a lottery-office. He assails miracles in his " Essay on Criples," and he wanders into the strangest regions in his Essay " Upon some Verses of Virgil." In his most serious moods he brings illustrations from the oddest quarters, and tells such stories as we might suppose *Squire Western* to have delighted in, sitting with a neighbouring squire over the wine, after his sister and *Sophia* had withdrawn. These Essays, full of the keenest insight, the profoundest melancholy, continually playing with death as *Hamlet* plays with *Yorick's* skull, whimsical, humorous, full of the flavour of a special character—philosopher and eccentric Gascon gentleman in one—are, in the best sense of the term, artistic. There is a meaning in the trifling, wisdom in the seeming folly, a charm in the swallow-like gyrations. All the incongruous elements—the whimsicality and the worldly wisdom, the melancholy, the humour and sense of enjoyment, the trifling over articles of attire and details of personal habit, the scepticism which questioned everything, the piety and the coarseness—mix and mingle somehow, and become reconciled in the alembic of personal character. Oppositions, incongruities, contradictions, taken separately, are mere lines and scratches; when brought together, by some mysterious attraction, they unite to produce a grave and thoughtful countenance—that of Montaigne. He explains the Essays—the Essays explain him. Of course the writer's remoteness from the great French world, his freedom from the modern conditions of publication and criticism, his sense of distance from his reader—if ever he should possess one—contributed, to a large extent, to make himself his own audience.

He wrote as freely in his chateau at Montaigne, as Alexander Selkirk could have done in his solitary island. Had there been upon him the sense of a reading public and of critical eyes, he could not have delivered himself up so completely into the guidance of whim. As it is, the Essays remain among the masterpieces of the world. He is the first of egotists, because, while continually writing about himself, he was writing about what was noble and peculiar. No other literary egotist had ever so good a subject, and then his style is peculiar as himself. In his Essays, he continually piques the reader ; every now and then more is meant than meets the eye ; every now and then a great deal less. He plays at hide-and-seek with his reader round his images and illustrations. In reading Montaigne, we always think we are finding him out.

When the Essay became a popular literary form in England, the conditions of things had altogether changed since Montaigne's day. The Frenchman was a solitary man, with but few books except the classics, given to self-communion, constantly writing to please himself, constantly mastered by whim, constantly, as it were, throwing the reins upon the neck of impulse. He had no public, and consequently he did not stand in awe of one. The country was convulsed, martyrs were consumed at the stake, country-houses were sacked, the blood of St Bartholomew had been spilt, the white plume of Navarre was shining in the front of battle. Amid all this strife and turmoil, the melancholy and middle-aged gentleman sat in his chateau at Montaigne, alone with his dreams. No one disturbed him ; he disturbed no one. He lived for himself and for thought. When Steele and Addison appeared as English Essayists, they appeared under totally different circumstances. The four great English poets had lived and died. The Elizabethan drama, which had arisen in Marlow, had set in Shirley. The comedy of Wicherley and Congreve, in which pruriency has become phosphorescent, was in possession of the stage. Dryden had taken immortal vengeance on his foes. Fragments of Butler's wit sparkled like grains of salt in the conversation of men of fashion. English literature was already rich ; there was a whole world of books and of accumulated ideas to work upon. Then a public had arisen ; there was the "town," idle, rich, eagerly inquiring after every new thing, most

anxious to be amused. Montaigne was an
egotist, because he had little but himself to
write about ; certainly he had nothing nearly so
interesting. He pursued his speculations as he
liked, because he had no one to interfere with
him. He was actor and audience in one. The
English Essayists, on the other hand, had the
English world to act upon. They had its leisure
to amuse, its follies to satirise ; its books, music,
and pictures, its public amusements, its whole
social arrangements, to comment upon, to laugh
at, to praise. As a consequence, their Essays
are not nearly so instructive as Montaigne's,
although they are equally sparkling and amusing. We are introduced to a fashionable world,
to beaux with rapiers and lace ruffles, and
belles with patches on their cheeks ; there are
drums and card-tables, and sedan-chairs and
links. The satire in the " Spectator " is conventional ; it concerns itself with the circumference
of a lady's hoops, or the air with which a cox-
comb carries his cocked hat beneath his arm.
The Essayists of the eighteenth century were
satirists of society, and of that portion of society
alone which sneered in the coffee-houses and
buzzed round the card-tables of the Metropolis.

They did not deal with crimes, but with social foibles; they did not recognise passions in that fashionable world; they did not reverence woman, they took off their hats and uttered sparkling compliments to the "fair." Theirs was a well-dressed world, and they liked it best when seen by candle-light. They were fine gentlemen, and they carried into literature their fine-gentleman airs. They dressed carefully; and they were as careful of the dress of their thoughts as of their persons. Their epigrams were sharp and polished as their rapiers; they said the bitterest things in the most smiling way; their badinage was nothing if not gentlemanly. Satire went about with a coloured plume of fancy in his cap. They brought style to perfection. But even then one could see that a change was setting in. A poor gentleman down at Olney, under the strong power of the world to come, was feeding his hares, and writing poems of a religious cast, yet with a wonderful fascination, as if of some long-forgotten melody, haunting their theological peculiarities, which drew many to listen. Up from Ayrshire to Edinburgh came Burns, with black, piercing eyes, with all his songs about him, as if he had reft a county of the music of its groves; in due time a whole wild Paris was yelling round the guillotine where noble heads were falling. Europe became a battle-field; a new name rose into the catalogue of kings; and when the Essayists of our own century began to write, the world had changed, and they had changed with it.

The Essayists who wrote in the early portion of the present century—Lamb, Hazlitt, and Hunt—are not only different from their predecessors as regards mental character; . they differ from them also in the variety of the subjects that engaged their attention. And this difference arises not only from the greater number of subjects attracting public interest in their day, but also from the immensely larger audience they had to address. They were. not called upon to write for the town, but for town and country both. Society was reading in all its ranks, and each rank had its special interests. The Essayists' subject-matter had been vastly enlarged; great actors had trod the boards; great painters had painted; the older poets had come into fashion; outside nature had again reappeared in literature. The Essayist could weave an allegory, or criticise, or describe, or

P

break a social enormity on the wheel, or explode
an ancient prejudice, with the certainty of always
finding a reader. Lamb, the most peculiarly
gifted of the three—who thought Fleet Street
worth all Arcadia—confined himself for the most
part to the Metropolis, its peculiar sights, its
beggars, its chimney-sweeps, its theatres, its old
actors, its book-stalls; and on these subjects he
discourses with pathos and humour curiously
blended. For him the past had an irresistible
attraction; he loved old books, old houses, old
pictures, old wine, old friends. His mind was
like a Tudor mansion, full of low-roofed, wain-
scoted rooms, with pictures on the walls of men
and women in antique garb; of tortuous passages and grim crannies in which ghosts might
lurk; with a garden with plots of shaven grass,
and processions of clipped yews, and a stone dial
in the corner, with a Latin motto anent the
flight of time carved upon it, and a drowsy
sound of rooks heard sometimes from afar. He
sat at the India House with the heart of Sir
Thomas Browne beating beneath his sables. He
sputtered out puns among his friends from the
saddest heart. He laughed that he might not
weep. Misery, which could not make him a

cynic nor a misanthrope, made him a humorist.
And knowing, as now we all know from Serjeant
Talfourd, the tragic shadow which darkened his
home for years, one looks upon the portrait of
Elia with pity tempered with awe. Lamb extended the sphere of the Essay, not so much
because he dealt with subjects which till his
day had been untouched, but because he imported into that literary form a fancy, humour,
and tenderness which resembled the fancy,
humour, and tenderness of no other writer. The
manifestations of these qualities were as personal
and peculiar as his expression of countenance,
the stutter in his speech, his habit of punning,
his love of black-letter and whisky-punch. His
Essays are additions to English literature, just
as Potosi silver was an addition to the wealth
of Europe. Whatever his subject, it becomes
interpenetrated by his pathetic and fanciful
humour, and is thereby etherealised—made
poetic. Some of his Essays have all the soft-
ness and remoteness of dreams. They are not
of the earth earthy. They are floating islands
asleep on serene shadows in a sea of humour.
The "Essay on Roast Pig" breathes a divine
aroma. The sentences hush themselves around

the youthful chimney-sweep—"the innocent blackness," asleep in the nobleman's sheets— as they might around the couch of the sleeping Princess. Gone are all his troubles—the harsh call of his master, sooty knuckles rubbed into tearful eyes, his brush, his call from the chimney-top. Let the poor wretch sleep! And then, Lamb's method of setting forth his fancies is as peculiar as the fancies themselves. He was a modern man only by the accident of birth; and his style is only modern by the same accident. It is full of the quaintest convolutions and doublings back upon itself; and ever and again a paragraph is closed by a sentence of unexpected rhetorical richness, like heavy golden fringe depending from the velvet of the altar cover— a trick which he learned from the "Religio Medici," and the "Urn Burial." As a critic, too, Lamb takes a high place. His "Essay on the Genius of Hogarth" is a triumphant vindication of that master's claim to the highest place of honour in British art; and in it he sets forth the doctrine, that a picture must not be judged by externals of colour, nor by manipulative dexterity—valuable as these unquestionably are—but by the number and value of the thoughts it contains; a doctrine which Mr Ruskin has borrowed, and has used with results.

Leigh Hunt was a poet as well as an Essayist, and he carried his poetic fancy with him into prose, where it shone like some splendid bird of the tropics among the sober-coated denizens of the farm-yard. He loved the country; but one almost suspects that his love for the country might be resolved into likings for cream, butter, strawberries, sunshine, and hayswathes to tumble in. If he did not, like Wordsworth, carry in his heart the silence of wood and fell, he at all events carried a gilly-flower jauntily in his button-hole. He was neither a town poet and essayist, nor a country poet and essayist; he was a mixture of both,—a suburban poet and essayist. Above all places in the world, he loved Hampstead. His Essays are gay and cheerful as suburban villas,—the piano is touched within, there are trees and flowers outside, but the city is not far distant, prosaic interests are ever intruding, visitors are constantly dropping in. His Essays are not poetically conceived; they deal—with the exception of that lovely one on the "Death of Little Children," where the fancy becomes serious as an angel, and wipes the tears of mothers as tenderly away as an angel could—with distinctly mundane and commonplace matters; but his charm is in this, that be the subject what it may, immediately troops of fancies search land and sea and the range of the poets for its adornment—just as, in the old English villages on May morning, shoals of rustics went forth to the woods and brought home hawthorns for the dressing of door and window. Hunt is always cheerful and chatty. He defends himself against the evils of life with pretty thoughts. He believes that the world is good, and that men and women are good too. He would, with a smiling face, have offered a flower to a bailiff in the execution of his duty, and been both hurt and astonished if that functionary had proved dead to its touching suggestions. His Essays are much less valuable than Lamb's, because they are neither so peculiar, nor do they touch the reader so deeply; but they are full of colour and wit. They resemble the arbours we see in gardens—not at all the kind of place one would like to spend a lifetime in, but exceedingly pleasant to withdraw to for an hour when the sun is hot and no duty is pressing. He called one of his books, "A Book

for the Parlour Window;" all his books are for
the parlour window.

Hazlitt, if he lacked Lamb's quaintness and
ethereal humour, and Hunt's fancifulness, possessed a robust and passionate faculty which
gave him a distinct place in the literature of his
time. His feelings were keen and deep. The
French Revolution seemed to him—in common
with Southey, Wordsworth, and Coleridge—in
its early stages, an authentic angel rising with
a new morning for the race upon its forehead;
and when disappointment came, and his friends
sought refuge in the old order of things, he, loyal
to his youthful hope, stood aloof, hating them
almost as renegades, and never ceasing to give
utterance to his despair. "I started in life with
the French Revolution," he tells us; "and I have
lived, alas! to see the end of it. My sun arose
with the first dawn of liberty, and I did not
think how soon both must set. We were strong
to run a race together, and I little dreamed that,
long before mine was set, the sun of liberty would
turn to blood, or sink once more in the night of
despotism. Since then, I confess, I have no
longer felt myself young, for with that my hopes
fell." This was the central bitterness in Hazlitt's

life ; but around it were grouped lesser and more personal bitternesses. His early ambition was to be a painter, and in that he failed. Coleridge was the man whom he admired most in all the world, in the light of whose genius he stood, like an Arcadian shepherd in an Arcadian sunrise, full of admiration—every sense absorbed in that of sight ; and that genius he was fated to see coming to nothing. Then he was headstrong, violent, made many enemies, was the object of cruel criticism ; his financial affairs were never prosperous, and in domestic matters he is not understood to have been happy. He was a troubled and exasperated man, and this exasperation is continually breaking out in his writings. Deeply wounded in early life, he carried the smart with him to his death-bed. And in his Essays and other writings it is almost pathetic to notice how he clings to the peaceful images which the poets love ; how he reposes in their restful lines ; how he listens to the bleating of the lamb in the fields of imagination. He is continually quoting Sidney's Arcadian image of the *shepherd-boy under the shade, piping as he would never grow old,*—as if the recurrence of the image to his memory brought with it silence, sunshine, and waving trees.

Hazlitt had a strong metaphysical turn ; he was an acute critic in poetry and art, but he wrote too much, and he wrote too hurriedly. When at his best, his style is excellent, concise, sinewy—laying open the stubborn thought as the sharp ploughshare the glebe ; while, at other times, it wants edge and sharpness, and the sentences resemble the impressions of a seal which has been blunted with too frequent use. His best Essays are, in a sense, autobiographical, because in them he recalls his enthusiasms and the passionate hopes on which he fed his spirit. The Essay entitled "My First Acquaintance with Poets" is full of memorable passages. To Hazlitt, Coleridge was then a divinity. They walked from Wem to Shrewsbury on a winter day, Coleridge talking all the while ; and Hazlitt recalls it after the lapse of years : "A sound was in my ears as of a syren's song : I was stunned, startled with it as from deep sleep ; but I had no notion then that I should ever be able to express my admiration to others in motley imagery and quaint allusion, till the light of his genius shone into my soul like the sun's rays glittering in the puddles of the road. . . . My soul has indeed remained in its original bondage—dark, obscure, with longings infinite and unsatisfied ; my heart, shut up in the prison-house of this rude clay, has never found, nor will it ever find, a heart to speak to ; but that my understanding also did not remain dumb and brutish, or at length found a language to express itself, I owe to Coleridge." This testimony, from a man like Hazlitt, to the worth of Coleridge's talk, is interesting, and contrasts strangely with Carlyle's description of it, when, in later years, the silvery-haired sage looked down on the smoky London from High-gate. Nor is it without its moral. Talk which, in his early day, came like a dawn upon another mind, illuminating dark recesses, kindling in-tellectual life, revealing itself to itself—became, through personal indulgence and the will's in-firmity, mere swathes of glittering mist in which men were lost. Hazlitt's other Essay, on the "Pleasures of Painting," is quite as personal as the one to which we have referred, and is perhaps the finest thing he has written. It is full of the love and the despair of art. He tells how he was en-gaged for blissful days in painting a portrait of his father ; how he imitated, as best he could, the rough texture of the skin, and the blood circu-lating beneath ; how, when it was finished, he

sat on a chair opposite, and with wild thoughts
enough in his head, looked at it through the long
evenings ; how, with a throbbing heart, he sent it
to the Exhibition, and saw it hung up there by
the side of a portrait " of the Honourable Mr
Skeffington (now Sir George)." Then he charac-
teristically tells us that he finished the portrait
on the same day that brought news of the battle
of Austerlitz : " I walked out in the afternoon,
and, as I returned, saw the evening star set
over a poor man's cottage, with other thoughts
and feelings than I shall ever have again. O for
the revolution of the great Platonic year, that
these times might come over again ! I could
sleep out the three hundred and sixty-five thousand intervening years very contentedly." He
was a passionate, melancholy, keen-feeling, and
disappointed man ; and those portions of his
Essays are the least valuable where his passion
and his disappointment break out into spleen or
irritability, just as those portions are the most
valuable where bitter feelings are transfused
into poetry by memory and imagination. With
perhaps more intellectual, certainly with more
passionate force, than either Lamb or Hunt, Hazlitt's Essays are, as a whole, inferior to theirs;

but nearly all of them contain passages, which not only they, but any man, might be proud to have written.

These men wrote in a period of unexampled literary activity, and in the thick of stupendous events : Scott, Moore, and Byron were writing their poems ; Napoleon was shaking the thrones of the Continent. Looked back upon from our days, the conquests of the poets seem nearly as astonishing as the conquests of the Emperor. He passed from victory to victory, and so did they. When quieter days came, and when the great men of the former generation had either passed away or were reposing on the laurels they had earned so worthily, other writers arose to sustain the glory of the English Essay. The most distinguished were Lord Macaulay and Mr Carlyle. They began to write about the same time,—Lord Macaulay's Essay on Milton appearing in the *Edinburgh Review* in 1825, and Mr Carlyle's first Essay on Jean Paul Richter in the same *Review* in 1827. The writings of these men were different from those of their predecessors. Mr Carlyle's primary object was to acquaint his countrymen with the great men whom Germany had recently pro-

duced, and to interest them in the productions
of German genius. His plans widened, however, as his way cleared ; and the eye which had
, looked into the heart of Goethe, Schiller, and
Richter, was in course of time turned on the
Scottish Burns, the English Johnson, and the
French Voltaire. It is not too much to say that
he has produced the best critical and biographical
Essays of which the English language can boast.
And it is in the curious mixture of criticism
and biography in these papers—for the criticism
becomes biography, and the biography criticism
—that their chief charm and value consist. Mr
Carlyle is an artist, and he knows exactly what
and how much to put into his picture. He has
a wonderful eye for what is characteristic. He
searches after the secret of a man's nature, and
he finds it frequently in some trivial anecdote or
careless saying, which another writer would have
passed unnoticed, or tossed contemptuously aside.
He hunts up every scrap of information, and he
frequently finds what he wants in a corner. He
judges a man by his poem, and the poem by the
man. To his eye, they are not separate things, but
one and indivisible. A man's work is the lamp
by which he reads his features. And then he so

apportions praise and blame; so sets off the jocose
and familiar with a moral solemnity; makes anecdote, and detail of dress, and allusion to personal
grace or deformity, subserve, by intricate suggestion, his ultimate purpose, and so presents to us
life with eternity for back-ground, that we not only
feel that the picture is the actual presentment
of the man as he lived—a veritable portrait,—
we feel also that the writer has worked in no
light or careless mood, that the poorest life is
serious enough when seen against eternity, and
that we ourselves, however seldom we may remember it, are but momentary shadows pro-
jected upon it.   Mr Carlyle does not write
"scoundrel" on one man's forehead, and "angel"
on another's: he knows that pure scoundrel and
pure angel have their dwellings in other places
than earth; he is too cunning an artist to use
these mercilessly definite lines.   He works by
allusion, suggestion, light touches of fancy,
spurts of humour, grotesque imaginative ex-
aggerations; and these things so reduce and
tone one another down, that the final result is
perfectly natural and homogeneous.   It is only by
some such combination of intellectual forces that
you can shadow forth the complexity of life and

character. In humanity there is no such thing as a straight line or an unmixed colour. You see the flesh colour on the cheek of a portrait: the artist will tell you that the consummately-natural result was not attained by one wash of paint, but by the mixture and reduplication of a hundred tints, the play of myriad lights and shadows, no one of which is natural in itself, although the blending of the whole is. These Essays are the completest, the most characteristic portraits in our literature. Mr Carlyle is always at home when his subject is man in the concrete.

Lord Macaulay also wrote Essays critical and biographical, and has been perhaps more widely popular than his great contemporary; but he is a different kind of thinker and writer altogether. He did not brood over the abysses of being as Mr Carlyle continually does. The sense of time and death did not haunt him as they haunt the other. The world, as it figured itself to Lord Macaulay, was a comparatively commonplace world. He cared for man, but he cared for party quite as much. He recognised men mainly as Whigs and Tories. His idea of the universe was a Parliamentary one. His insight into man was not deep. He painted in positive colours. He is never so antithetical as when describing a character; and character, if properly conceived, sets the measured antitheses of the rhetorician at defiance. It is constantly eluding them. His criticism is good enough so far as it goes, but it does not go far; it deals more with the accidents than the realities of things. Lord Macaulay, as we have said, lived quite as much for party as for man; and the men who interested him were the men who were historical centres, around whom men and events revolved. He did not, as Mr Carlyle often does, take hold of an individual, and view him against immensity; he takes a man and looks at him in connection with contemporary events. When he writes of Johnson, he is thinking all the while of Goldsmith, and Garrick, and Boswell, and Reynolds; when he writes of Clive and Warren Hastings, he is more anxious to tell the story of their Indian conquests than to enter into the secrets of their spirits. And for this posterity is not likely to blame Lord Macaulay. He knew his strength. His pictorial faculty is astonishing; neither pomp nor circumstance cumbers it; it moves along like a triumphal procession, which no weight of insignia and banner can oppress. Out of the past he selects some special drama, which is vivified and held together by the life of a single individual, and that he paints with his most brilliant colours. He is the creator of the Historical Essay, and in that department is not likely soon to have a successor. His unfinished History is only a series of historical pictures pieced together into one imposing panorama, but throughout there is wonderful splendour and pomp of colour. Every figure, too, is finished, down to the buttons and the finger nails.

A generation has passed since Mr Carlyle and Lord Macaulay wrote their essays, and during the interval new men have come into the field, and won deserved laurels. " Notes from Life," by the author of " Philip Van Artevelde," is a volume every way remarkable. Mr Taylor is a fine and thoughtful poet, and he has brought with him into the essay the poet's style and the poet's wisdom. In his essays you find no cheap and flashy sentiment, no running after the popular manias of the day ; the eye is never offended by a glare of colour : on the contrary, there is a certain ripeness about the thought, as of autumn tints ; a certain stillness and medita-tive repose, as of an autumn evening ; a certain

Q

remoteness and retiredness from modern strife and bustle, as of autumn woodlands. These essays are born of wisdom and experience; and of a wisdom and experience that has ripened in solitude and self-communion. No sound reaches you from the market-place—you cannot catch the tang of any literary coterie. The style, too, is peculiar in these days, from its leisurely movement and old-fashioned elaborateness. It has an Elizabethan air about it. It is far from being unornamented: but the ornaments are worn proudly, as heir-looms are worn; and these never glare,—they are far too precious for that, in price of gold and gem and sacredness of memory,— and are but seldom manufactured at Birmingham. The style has not been formed on the fluent and hasty moderns, but on Bacon, Jeremy Taylor, and such old men, and is about the best that has ever been written by poet.

Mr Helps has the credit—apart from what may fairly attach to his exquisitely pellucid English, and the intrinsic value of his thinking —of introducing a novelty into essay writing. Naturally subtle-minded and tolerant, most courteous to everything that comes to him in the name of truth, conscientious, disposed to listen to every witness, to hesitate and weigh, he does not take up an opinion suddenly ; and when he does take up one, he does not cling to it as a shipwrecked sailor to his raft—said raft being his only chance of escape from drowning. Superficially, at least, an unimpassioned man, fond of limitations and of suggesting "buts," knowing that a good deal may not only be said on two sides, but on a dozen sides of a thing, Mr Helps, when he began to write, found himself beset with an artistic difficulty. He had, of course, on subjects in which he was interested, and which he wished to write about, certain definite opinions ; but as he was big enough and clear-eyed enough to see all round the matter in hand, he was conscious that each of the opinions, which he accepted as a whole, was subject to limitations, that each of them was intersected and eaten into by its opposite, like the map of Scotland by branching sea-lochs, and that, if he gave expression to all his doubts and hesitations in the work of essay-writing, he would make no sort of direct progress. He would only be painting above his picture. His one foot-print would obliterate the other. And yet, to be faithful to himself and to the work in hand, these limitations of broad statement must be indicated in some way. It is from this particular difficulty felt by Mr Helps that we are indebted for the machinery of the " Friends in Council." From the necessity which lay on him of setting forth in fulness his views of things, he was forced to the artistic device of creating around the central essay a little drama — one character reading the essay which contains the broad view, whilst other characters listen and criticise, suggest the subtle difficulty, point out the hazardous spot, define the inevitable limitation. By this device the writer's subtlety has a field to display itself in; for the objections brought forward by the listeners are not men of straw, raised up for the purpose of being knocked down again—they are other views of the central truth or opinion under discussion. The listeners do not argue; they converse amicably and thoughtfully. And more is gained than this: the author has an opportunity of introducing some admirably dramatic by-play—for Ellesmere, Dunsford, and Lucy really live; and although the subject under discussion may be as old as evil or ignorance itself, by letting in outside nature and English life upon it, the thinking is not only charmingly relieved, but it takes an essentially modern air. The subject may be old, but English gentlemen talk over it, and set forth their ideas of it from their peculiar points of view. By this method Mr Helps is enabled to discuss his subject thoroughly, and to utter all 'that occurs to him of value. The essay which Milverton reads is a crystal; but, by means of the other characters, the crystal is held up towards the sun, and turned slowly round, so that every facet catches the ray, and flashes it back.

Considered as a literary form, the Essay is comparatively of late growth. The first literary efforts of a people consist of song and narrative. First comes the poet or minstrel, who sings heroic exploits, the strength and courage of heroes. These songs pass from individual to individual, and are valuable, not on account of the amount of historic truth, but of the amount of passion and imagery, they contain. Explode to-morrow into mere myth and dream the incidents of the Iliad, and you do not affect in the slightest degree the literary merit of the poem. Still for all men Achilles shouts in the trenches,

Helen is beautiful, the towers of Ilium flame to heaven. Prove that Chevy Chase cannot in any one particular be considered a truthful relation of events, and you do it no special harm. It stirs the blood like a trumpet all the same. After the poet comes the prose narrator of events, who presents his facts peering obscurely through the mists of legend, but who has striven, as far as his ability extends, to tell us the truth. When he appears, the history of a nation has become extensive enough and important enough to awaken curiosity ; men are anxious to know how events did actually occur, and what relation one event bears to another. When he appears, the national temper has cooled down—men no longer stand blinded by the splendours of sunrise. The sunrise has melted into the light of common day. The air has become emptied of wonder. The gods have deserted earth, and men only remain. Long after the poet and the historian comes the Essayist. Before the stage is prepared for him, thought must have accumulated to a certain point ; a literature less or more must be in existence, and must be preserved in printed books. Songs have been sung, histories and biographies have been writ-

ten; and to these songs, histories, and biographies, he must have access. Then, before he
can write, society must have formed itself, for in
its complexity and contrasts he finds his food.
Before the Essayist can have free play, society
must have existed long enough to have become
self-conscious, introspective; to have brooded
over itself and its perplexities; to have discovered its blots and weak points; to have become critical, and, consequently, appreciative of
criticism. And as the Essay does not, like the
poem, or the early history or narration of events,
appeal to the primitive feelings, before it can be
read and enjoyed, there must exist a class who
have attained wealth and leisure, and a certain
acquaintance with the accumulated stores of
thought on which the Essayist works, else his
allusions are lost, his criticism a dead letter,
his satire pointless. All this takes a long time
to accomplish, and it is generally late in the
literary history of a country before its Essayists
appear. Then, the Essay itself has its peculiar
literary conditions. It bears the same relation
to the general body of prose that the lyric bears
to the general body of poetry. Like the lyric,
it is brief; and, like the lyric, it demands a

certain literary finish and perfection In a long epic, the poet may now and then be allowed to nod ; in a history, it is not essential that every sentence should sparkle. But the Essayist, from the very nature of his task, is not permitted to be dull or slovenly. He must be alert, full of intellectual life, concise, polished. He must think clearly, and express himself clearly. 'His style is as much an element of his success as his thought. The narrow limit in which he works demands this. In a ten-mile race it is not expected that the runners shall go all the way at the top of their speed ; in a race of three hundred yards it is not unreasonably expected that they shall do so. Then, besides all this, the Essay must, as a basis or preliminary, be artistically conceived. It is neither a dissertation nor a thesis ; properly speaking, it is a work of art, and must conform to artistic rules. It requires not only the intellectual qualities which we have indicated, but unity, wholeness, self-completion. In this it resembles a poem. It must hang together. It must round itself off into a separate literary entity. When finished, it must be able to sustain itself and live. The Essayists of whom we have spoken fulfil these conditions more or less; and the measure of their fulfilment is the measure of success. These writers indicate in what directions the Essay has manifested itself, and they may be roughly arranged in groups and clusters. There are the Egotists—the most delightful of all—who choose for subjects themselves, their surroundings, their moods and phantasies, whose charm consists not so much in the value or brilliancy of thought as in revelation of personal character: these are represented by Montaigne and Lamb; the satirists of society, manners, and social pheno-mena, by Addison and Steele; the fanciful and ornamental Essayists—they who wreathe the human porch with the honeysuckles of poetry— by Hunt, and by Hazlitt to some extent; the critical and biographical Essay, by Mr Carlyle; the historical Essay—the brilliant and many-coloured picture of which some single man's life is the frame—by Lord Macaulay; the moral and didactic Essay, by Bacon in old time, and recently by Mr Henry Taylor and Mr Helps. Of course, this is but an arrangement in the rough, and will not stand a too critical examina-tion, for several of the writers mentioned belong now to one cluster and now to another; but it is sufficiently strict for our present purpose. Essay writing is a craft vigorously prosecuted in England at present; and generally the writers will be found to belong to one or other of the groups which we have indicated. It is our duty now to see of what stuff these men are made, and how as Essàyists they have acquitted themselves.

Mr Hannay, whose "Essays from the *Quarterly*" appeared some eighteen months ago, has been before the world as a writer for twelve or fourteen years. Born among Galwegian moors and moss bogs, where the shells of old fortresses yet stand, their red walls clothed with ivies, their crannies inhabited by starlings and jackdaws— a native of the district to which Lord Maxwell bade "good night" in the famous ballad, and which adjoins the Ayrshire which Burns has consecrated from pastoral hill-top to valley-daisy— his first spiritual food was naturally song, ballad, tradition. For in that region—quite as much as in the regions north of the Grampians—

"The ancient spirit is not dead."

Sent into the navy at an early age, he spent several years in the Mediterranean, visited the

Grecian Isles and the Syrian coast, alternating his native Scottish traditions with older classical and sacred associations. The Acropolis succeeded to Drumlanrig Fair; the far-seen snowy Lebanon to blue Criffel and the Solway; Horace and the Old Testament displaced the ballad-monger. On leaving the navy, and while yet a very young man, he flung himself into London literary life, while London literary life was more brilliant, socially and conversationally, than it is at present. For a literary man, Mr Hannay may be said to have started with a fair variety of experience as a preliminary basis. It is not every man that, into the first twenty years or so of his life, has crushed grey Scotland and the glowing East, the Mediterranean and the Solway, the classical poets and the Scottish ballads, the discipline and routine of duty on board a man-of-war; nay, something of the splendour and terror of war itself. His first literary efforts consisted of sketches of naval life, which met with considerable success. In 1851 he published his first novel, " Singleton Fontenoy;" and in 1854 his first volume of Essays, entitled "Satire and Satirists" appeared. These Essays, in all probability suggested by Mr Thackeray's " English

Humorists," were originally delivered in the form of lectures. Whether as lectures they were successful, we cannot say; but in that form their merits were discovered, and they made their appearance in a volume shortly after.

In the six Essays which the book contains, Mr Hannay gives an account of European satire from Horace to Jerrold; and although somewhat slight, as was inevitable from its narrow limits, the work is thoroughly well done. From the polish of the suave old Roman to the wit of the Englishman, whose epigrams are yet ringing in our ears, is a journey which, if accomplished in a little book of two hundred pages, can allow but little loitering on the way. But for his task Mr Hannay possessed abundant knowledge, and his special liking for his subject is everywhere evident. He lingers over the good things of his heroes; he relates their immortal revenges with the same pride with which the member of a regiment become historical recalls the battle-fields on which it gathered its renown. He speaks of Erasmus, Dryden, Pope, and Byron, as the art student copying in the galleries speaks of Michael Angelo and De Vinci —appreciating their excellences, and hoping one day to emulate them. Mr Hannay was not only qualified to write on the Satirists from taste, enthusiasm, and loving study, but from the possession of a power somewhat akin to their own. He writes clearly, criticises soundly when occasion arises; yet one can see at a glance that the sovereign faculty of his own mind is wit. His thought is continually condensing itself into epigram. And then his wit has a certain something of poetry about it, which makes it all the more delightful; it is continually going about with a flower of fancy in its hand. In "Satire and Satirists," Mr Hannay, like all very clever young men, is somewhat spendthrift of his means. He is always giving sovereign "tips," so to speak. Some of his pages are as brilliant and dangerous with squib and serpent as a London pavement on Coronation night. He cracks his satirical whip for the mere pleasure he has in hearing it. If the occasion requires it, he fires off his rockets, and he fires them off frequently when there is no occasion whatever: there is a large stock on hand, and, after all, rockets are a very pretty sight. The following passage on the "Simious Satirist" will illustrate what we mean :—

"The Simious Satirist is distinguished by a deficiency of natural reverence mainly. His heart is hard, rather; his feelings blunt and dull. He is blind to everything else but the satirical aspect of things; and if he is brilliant, it is as a cat's back is when rubbed in the dark! He has generally no sentiment of respect for form, and will spare nothing. He is born suspicious; and if he hears the world admiring anything, forthwith he concludes that it must be 'humbug.' He has no regard to the heaps of honour gathered round this object by time and the affection of wise men. He cries, 'Down with it!' As his kinsman, when looking at some vase, or curious massive specimen of gold, sees only his own image in it, our satirist sees the ridiculous only in every object, and forgets that the more clearly he sees it, the more he testifies to its brightness. Or, as his kinsman breaks a cocoa-nut only to get at the milk, *he* would destroy everything only to nourish his mean nature. He prides himself on his commonest qualities, as the negroes who rebelled called themselves Marquises of Lemonade. He would tear the blossoms off a rose branch to make it a stick to beat his betters with. He employs his gifts in ignoble objects, as you see in sweetmeat shops sugar shaped into dogs and pigs. He taints his mind with egotism, as if a man should spoil the sight of a telescope by clouding it with his breath. He overrates the value of his quickness and activity, and forgets that, like his kinsman, he owes his triumphant power of swinging in high places to the fact of his prehensile tail."

Mr Hannay, we have said, is fond of epigram; and it seems to us that in "Satire and Satirists" epigram is used at times somewhat vaingloriously. The epigram does not always arise naturally from the matter in hand; it is rather stuck upon it, like a bit of tinsel; and this is, perhaps, the chief blot on the book. It is too clever, and it is too clever wilfully. This literary ornament, like all others, should be used sparingly. A gentleman gains nothing by covering his fingers with rings; and at any time one sole diamond is worth a dozen inferior stones. Yet it must be said that the writer is often exceedingly happy in his epigram. Take the following, for instance, on Theodore Hook: "They"—his noble patrons—"set him down to the piano, even before he had had his dinner sometimes, according to one biographer.

This was too bad. He was proud, however, of the equivocal distinction he attained, and was inclined to swagger, I understand, among his equals. The plush had eaten into his very soul. Ultimately he ruined his heart, his circumstances, and (what was a still greater loss) his stomach, and so died. The biographer above mentioned observes, that his funeral was ill attended by his great friends. But we need not wonder at that—a funeral is a well-known 'bore;' and, besides, the most brilliant wag cannot be amusing on the occasion of his own interment." The closing sentence of this extract is perfect, and quite equal to the best thing of any epigrammatist. On the face of it, it is amusing. But it is more than that. It is a biography and a moral judgment in a single sentence. It reveals the relation which the wit bore to his patrons far more clearly than whole pages of writing, or any amount of moral declamation. And in the book there are many sentences equally memorable.

"Essays from the *Quarterly*," is, in every way, a better and riper book than its predecessor: the writing is always excellent; and if there is less epigram, there is more matter. The sub-

jects of several of these Essays lie in a region
somewhat remote, not frequently visited by the
modern man of letters ; and on these subjects
Mr Hannay has written, not on account of their
novelty, but because he was already acquainted
with them, and had a special affection for them.
In these Essays there is little trace of " reading
up ;" he writes from the fulness of knowledge.
Certain of the Essays contained in the volume
—as those on " Table Talk," on " English Political Satires," on " Electioneering," and on
" Horace and the Translators " — are, in the
very nature of them, akin to " Satire and
Satirists," and may be considered as supple-
mentary to that work. These he has treated
everywhere with the old lightness, grace, and
knowledge, but—having more space and leisure
at command—with greater fulness and elabora-
tion. It would be difficult to find pleasanter
reading than these. The town is well worth
seeing, and the cicerone knows every turn and
winding, and is familiar with the best stand-
points. It is a discourse on " good things," by
a writer who not only can appreciate them, but
who can say them. It is a wit talking about
wits. In these Essays there is abundance of

R

knowledge and sound sense, but the knowledge and the sense go about in sparkle and epigram.,

There are two things which Mr Hannay specially admires—genius, wit, scholarship—literary distinction, in fact—and good blood. If you are a wit or a poet, he will take you to his heart; if you are neither wit nor poet, he will take you to his heart equally enthusiastically if you can prove to him that your great-great-great-grandfather was ruined in the wars of the Roses. His admiration for wit, scholarship, and song, he has set forth in "Satire and Satirists," and in his "Essays from the *Quarterly;*" his admiration for ancient and historical names airs itself in the papers on "British Family Histories" and "The Historic Peerage of England." These Essays are quite peculiar in their way. It is not often that the reflected colours of *or* and *gules* lie on the popular page. But seldom have genealogical trees greened with the spring, and put forth blossoms of fancy. Genealogy indeed has been the favourite pursuit of Dr Dryasdust. But poetic association can do almost anything. An old china cup may be uninteresting enough in itself; but when one remembers the fair lips that once touched it, the dead scandals that were talked over it, it becomes at once an object of interest. An old Roman coin may be quite useless for the purchase of modern beef or bread; but when you gaze imaginatively on the half-obliterated effigy of the Roman Emperor, the intervening centuries collapse; England becomes green waste and forest; up springs the triumphal arch, the conqueror passes through it with all his captives, you hear the shouts of the populace. And so, to Mr Hannay, a great name recalls a thousand memories; he sees the chivalric and wise faces of the men, and the beautiful eyes of the women, that bore it of old. An old castle is sacred in his eyes, for noble memories grow upon it as thickly as its shrouding ivies. He sees the modern earl standing, but Agincourt is in the back-ground, and there is always "a pomp of fancied trumpets on the wind." He traces the stems of ancient families, and lingers over the flowers of valour, wit, genius, personal beauty, which generation after generation they put forth, and which brighten yet the air of history. He values a sprig of ivy or a wild flower from a castle wall over which a banner once flapped, more than the wealth of Rothschild. To be embalmed in a

ballad is the fame which he would covet most.
He is fond of crests and coats of armour, and all
the insignia of the herald ; but he cares nothing
for these in themselves—his affection goes out
towards what these symbols represent. He
reverences the Bloody Heart, and cares not on
what material it may be worked—the standard's
silken folds, or the gaberdine of the beggar.
He laughs openly at the chivalric device and
motto blazing on the coach-panels of the successful coal-merchant. The past moves him
mightily—he is attracted by the deeds, the wit,
the splendour of long ago ; and on the past he
continually feels that the present is based, as
its natural outcome and result. Instinctively
he feels that in history there is sequence and
progression ; in the face of the son he seeks to
discern something of the high features of the
father. And it is his belief that the ancient
feudal hardihood did not die out on feudal
battle-fields ; that wit did not expire for ever in
the poem or the epigram in which it made itself
visible ; that beauty did not cease finally in
wrinkles and grey hairs. He thinks that the
virtues of race are the truest heirlooms, descending from father to son, and from mother to

daughter, far more certainly than broad lands
and castles. He holds that the courage which
kept the trenches in the Crimea, and which
subdued the Indian mutiny, is directly transmitted from the men who fought at Bosworth
and Marston Moor, and that the beauty which
charms us to-day is a reminiscence of the beauty
which charmed the cavaliers. Thus, by per-
petuation of valour and beauty, he knits century
with century, and generation with generation ;
thus to his mind does epoch flow out of epoch.
And this theory—which, doubtless, many will be
inclined to dispute—Mr Hannay supports by
numerous instances :—

" Few writers in our day have a word of decent
civility for the family of Stewart. It would be
curious to trace its hereditary character in the
chief line; our present purpose is only to remark
on the greatness attained by some men who
descended maternally from it. We need scarcely
say that the mother of William of Orange was
a Stewart princess. The mother of Cromwell
was, as we believe, of one branch of the family.
So was the mother of the Admirable Crichton;
and of the famous soldier Alexander Leslie, first

Earl of Leven. Chatham was nearly and directly from the royal stem, through his grandmother—a descendant of the Regent Murray. Fox's mother, Lady Lennox, was immediately descended from Charles II. Byron had the blood in his veins. How interesting to see eminent families sharing in this kind of way in a great man's renown! The gifted Shaftesbury's mother was a Manners; Algernon Sidney's, a Percy; and his famous kinsman, Philip's, a Dudley; the poet Beaumont's, a Pierrepont. The mother of Marshal Stair was a Dundas; and the brilliant Peterborough was the son of one of the brilliant Carys. The Ruthvens and Carnegies gave mothers to Montrose and Dundee. The Villierses gave a mother to Chatham; the Granvilles, to Pitt; the Douglases of Strathhenry, to Adam Smith. Nelson inherited the blood of the Sucklings and Walpoles; Collingwood that of the Greys and Plantagenets. From the Hampdens came the mother of Waller, and also Mary Arden (of that ancient Warwickshire family), the mother of Shakespeare. The literary talent runs through female lines like other qualities: Swift's mother was a Herrick, and his grandmother a Dryden. Donne, derived through his mother, from Sir Thomas Moore; and Cowper in the same way from the Donnes. Thomson had the Hume blood in his veins. A daughter of Becaria produced Manzoni. The late Bishop Coplestone evidently got his playfulness from the Gays, as Chesterfield his wit from Lord Halifax. The relationship between Fielding and 'Lady Mary' is well known. Sometimes, when a notable man comes from a family never before heard of, it happens that he just comes after a marriage with a better one: Thus, the mother of Seldon was of the Knightly Bakers of Kent; Camdens, of the ancient Curwins of Workington; and Watts of the old stock of Muirhead. . . . . Philosophers, like Bacon, Hume, and Berkeley; poets, like Spenser, Cowper, Shelley, and Scott; novelists, like Fielding and Smollett; historians, like Gibbon; seamen, like Collingwood, Howe, Jervis; Vanes, St Johns, Raleighs, George Herberts, and many other men of the ancient gentry, amply vindicate the pretensions of old families to the honour of producing the best men that England has ever seen."

Holding the theory that families can only rise to distinction through superiority of some kind—

that, having arisen, they intermarry with families on their own social level, who have also arisen through superiority of some kind—consequently that the offspring of such marriages have a double chance of possessing an unusual share of brain or of general power, and that the virtue of race thus built up is perpetuated in the descendants, and is continually making itself visible in them—Mr Hannay is in politics inevitably a Conservative. A nation must be ruled by its best men, and the best men must be sought in the old houses. If a man wishes to enter into public affairs, the best letter of introduction he can bring with him is his ancient descent. We know what his family has been in the past ; and as he inherits the virtues and the traditions of his race, we can form some idea of how he will turn out. His good conduct is guaranteed by a hundred ancestors. Holding these doctrines, Mr Hannay naturally detests democracy, looks upon universal suffrage with no favourable eye, is quite the reverse of an adherent of Mr Bright's, and does not think that America has solved the problem of how a nation can best be governed. He does not consider that a cheap government is necessarily the best, and he expects nothing

but disorder from an extension of the franchise.
He thus expresses himself in the Essay on "The
Historic Peerage:"—"This—'the great difference
between the vulgar and the noble seed'—was an
article of faith among the gentlemen of the kingdom. They held the old Greek doctrine, that
'nobility is virtue of race,' and believed that
those who possessed it were naturally superior
to other men. Their portraits—calm, stately,
brave, and wise faces—justify their creed to the
eye ; and the men they produced—the Sidneys,
Raleighs, Bacons—justify it to the understanding. By and by there will be a hearing again
for this side of affairs in Europe, after the total
failure of the revolutionary party to produce
governing intellects has had a still wider scope
to show itself in."

So, argues Mr Hannay—the men of the old
houses possessed calmness, dignity, bravery,
wisdom; they were leaders, they were states-
men ; and when we wish these qualities to bear
on the work of government, we cannot do better
than seek them in the persons of their descendants. There is at least *one* chance more
that the governing intellect will be found there
than in other regions. The quarter of the wood

in which you gathered strawberries six summers ago, is the likeliest place to find strawberries when they are again wanted.

This view of the virtue of race, and its transmission in the blood from father to son, is rather indicated than formally argued out in these Essays. Of course many objections will be taken to it ; and as a theory, it cannot be accepted *in toto.* Its truth ends when its chapter of instances ends. Grant that a family rises above the level of mankind through superiority of one kind or another, that superiority is not transmitted perpetually. Even when a family which has been potent does not actually die out, the superiority which it once possessed, and by virtue of which it arose, seems at times to die out. There were historical families which have disappeared entirely from history, just as there were stars known to the ancient astronomers which are not now visible in our heavens ; certain families, too, seem to lose, after a generation or so, their ancient pith and force, and to lose themselves as a stream loses itself in a morass. Mr Hannay hints that, as Cromwell had a dash of the Stewart blood in his veins, the Stewart blood should have the credit of his

greatness; but Cromwell's son, Richard, had the
Stewart blood also, and he let the reins of
government slip from his grasp through weakness and ineptitude. Then, admitting the theory
of general force in a race, you never can tell what
shape that general force will take in a descendant. Every now and again, in a historical line,
an alien character seems to blossom out, as the
spiritual, saintly face of Edward VI. gleams
among the strong-willed and masterful Tudors.
Mr Hannay tells us that many men of the
"ancient gentry" amply vindicate the pretensions
of old families to the honour of "producing the
best men that England has ever seen." The
phrase "ancient gentry" is a misleading one.
How ancient? Mr Hannay does not limit the
ancient gentry to the descendants of the men
who came over with the Conqueror. In every
generation certain families rise out of the people
into the position of gentry; and if the theory is
correct, that a family only rises into eminent
station through general superiority, and that that
superiority is to some extent perpetuated, the
governing intellect is as likely to be found in the
descendant of the gentleman of one century's
standing as in the descendant of the gentleman

of ten. And, in point of fact, it *is* as readily found. Within the last seventy years the Buonapartes have become occupants of thrones, the Peel family rose into eminence quite lately, the Gladstone family yet more recently. But, putting cavil aside, Mr Hannay's view of blood contains much truth, and is essentially poetic besides. He looks back with reverence and affection on the generations of dead Englishmen and Englishwomen. The eyes of the Countess of Salisbury haunt him. He cannot forget Sidney's chivalric face; he enjoys the wit of Charles II. quite as much as did any of his courtiers. He walks back into history, and he is greeted by wit, and song, and beautiful women, and fine manners, and splendid furniture and array. The old time, with its colour and high spirit, lives again for him; again the feast is spread in the feudal castle; again the feudal banners unroll themselves on the breeze; again on the battle-field old war-cries are shouted. And, in a country like England, so full of the past, not only in its political constitution and its unparalleled literature, but in objects which appeal directly to the eye—in mighty castle ruins, where nobles lived who mated once with kings;

cathedrals in which the sound of chanting is heard no more; Westminster Abbey with its dead; the world's first sailor and soldier beneath the dome of St Paul's; dwellings of nobles sequestered in oak woods, which for two hundred autumns now have shed their acorns; princely colleges, endowed by liberal and pious men of old; guns and banners captured in every quarter of the globe—this reverence and affection for the remarkable families who have headed its efforts in every direction, are most natural and befitting. English history was not built up by knaves and scoundrels, and men hungry for wealth and advancement, but mainly by good and noble men and women. The virtues had more to do with it than the vices. Mr Hannay loves his land, but it is with a love

> " Far brought
> From out the storied past."

And although his readers may not go all the way with him in his theories of descent, yet it may be said that even in these theories there is a great proportion of truth, and a side of the truth which has perhaps not been sufficiently dwelt upon of late. We need to be reminded

at times that worth is older than the steam-
engine, that the present is moored upon the past,
and that a great deal of what we are proudest of
is drawn directly from our ancestors.   Mr Hannay has lived in close intellectual companionship
with great Englishmen—the nobles, the wits, the
cavaliers who could turn a stanza on the pleasures
of the wine cup and the beauty of woman, as
well as, on battle mornings, fling themselves
bravely on the foemen's pikes; and from his
intercourse with these worthies he has gained
much, for into his own writings he has imported
the grace, the polish, and the wit for which they
are so remarkable.

Readers of *Fraser's Magazine* have, for the
last six or seven years, been familiar with
critical and descriptive papers to which the signature of "Shirley" was appended—papers which,
considered as literature, rose considerably above
the average contents of a periodical which has
always been distinguished for literary excellence.
Having read these papers with singular pleasure
as they appeared month by month, we are glad
to see them collected in a volume, which, if it
gets its deserts, will find a place in many a

private as well as in many a circulating library.
Shirley is a pleasantly vagrant writer; his
thought gads and wanders around his subject
like the wild convolvulus, taking colour and fragrance with it wherever it goes. If, for the most
part, he avoids profound subjects, and never
attempts exhaustive treatment, he is always
eminently readable, charming his reader with an
unusual grace of presentment and the light of
pleasant fancies. He has a laudable horror of
dulness; he is a bookish man, well read in the
poets and prose writers—a little too indolently
inclined, perhaps, to quote the poets;—tasteful,
acute, picturesque; and the Essays now re-
published are the mere play and recreation of
his mind. He takes up his pen from the same
motive, and with the same enjoyment, with which
he puts his foot in the stirrup and rides into the
country—down the quiet lane scented with white
and red dog-roses, out to the headland which
gazes upon the azure world of the Atlantic, up to
the red ruin on the hill, patched with ivies. In
these papers there is no plodding, no burden or
heat of the day; he infects the reader with his
own freshness of feeling; everything is light,
airy, graceful. He yachts over the shining seas

of criticism and speculation.   He is fond of out-door life, of bare and level sands through which the slow stream stagnates to the main, of worn and fantastic northern rocks around which sea-birds wheel and clamour, and on which the big billow smites itself into a column of foam.   The sea-side he is never tired of painting ; yet we feel that at the sea-side he does not spend his days. We almost fancy that Shirley writes‚ only in vacation.   His Essays do not seem to have been produced in a study littered with books ; rather they seem to have been composed in Tweeds and "wide-awake" in a clover field ; for the shadows of the tall grasses are constantly chequer-ing his pages, and the summer breeze and the lark's song seem to get entangled and mingled with his sentences somehow.   He is fond of framing his criticisms with a border of landscape or incidents of country life ; and it not unfre-quently happens that the frame is more valuable than the picture it contains.   And this constant intrusion of the outside world into the critical and more serious papers, which is at best a pretty irrelevance, symptomatic perhaps of volatility of mind and purpose, suggests the main defect of these Essays, which consists in a certain lack of

body and thoroughness. They have but little spe-
cific gravity. There is too much holiday and too
little work in them. They are brilliant enough, but
their brilliance is rather that of nebulous vapour
than of the condensed and solid star. They lack
personality, and the definite edge of intellectual
character. They are of the stuff that dreams are
made of. If a writer professes to give us a critical estimate of a book or an author, we naturally
expect that he shall at once proceed to do so; if
he begins with a description of a trouting stream,
tells us how a girl fords it with kilted petticoats,
then relates how he captured a fish, and gives
the exclamation of a certain "Bob Morris" from
the opposite bank on witnessing the feat, then
diverges on a yellow bee which comes humming
along seeking honey on the heathery bent, we
begin to suspect either that he is conscious that
he has nothing critically important to say, or
that he is terribly afraid of the trouble of saying
it. To write critically may not be so easy as to
write descriptively; but it must be done, nevertheless; and especially should it be done by a
writer who professes to do it. Why should not
criticism be criticism and nothing else? When
you have a book to review, what necessity is

S

there for running into Arcadia with it to accomplish the task? Arcadians do not compose the modern reading world. Shirley spars prettily enough; but it is all sparring, with no close and wrestle. Before he arrives at his subject, he has to walk into the country for a couple of miles, and has his fish to catch. In the "Sphinx," certainly one of the best of his Essays, and which, as dealing with the impotence of history, might be supposed to demand a uniform seriousness of treatment, he starts off in the following manner:

"We sat on the Devil's Bridge, and swung our legs over the parapet, Reginald de Moreville and I.

"The De Morevilles were a fine Norman family in the reign of David I., 'that sair sanct for the Crown.' The present representative inherits the feudal tastes of his house, without the burden of its acres.

"The arch of a royal dome that hangs above the blue sea! Down the storm-stained sides of the precipice we can see the marrots standing like sentries along the slippery ledges, crowding around their fantastically-coloured eggs, indulging in expressions of uncouth fun and uncouth endearment. Farther off, the skua gulls, 'white as ocean foam in the moon,' 'white as the consecrated snow that lies on Dian's lap' [choose between Shakespeare and Tennyson], float along the face of the cliffs, or hover above their nests on noiseless wings. Yet lower, the blue and shining deep beats against the iron bàses of the hills, and moans among the caverned fissures where the seal and the otter lodge."

Now, considered merely as writing, the sentences we háve quoted have distinct and substantial merits; they póssess music and colour, and a firm, consistent movement. But it seems to us that a man properly possessed with his subject, and with an instinct for the heart of it, would not have chosen to begin after this fashion. Especially would he have avoided the poetical extracts and the sentence contained in brackets; for that kind of by-play—that irrelevant thinking within thinking—does not occur to one whose loins are sufficiently girt for his work. When a man is in haste, or is impelled onward by a strong motive, he does not gather the flowers that grow by the wayside, and compare their beauties. All this kind of thing is a literary iniquity, and a face of flint should be set against it. It has become far too common of late. It increases the bulk of books without increasing their value. It obstructs the literary thorough-fare as crinoline obstructs the material one. Shirley is too frequently a sinner in this way; and it is no palliation of his fault that he sins gracefully, fancifully, eloquently, because lesser men, who have neither his grace nor his fancy, may be tempted to follow his example.

Having indicated what seems to us the de-fect of the book, we are prepared now to give "Nugæ Criticæ" our warmest welcome. It is thoroughly fresh, genial, and pleasant; and that portion of it which directly relates to out-door life—happily no inconsiderable portion—is uni-formly excellent. Shirley is a sportsman; he is fond of the aquatic tribes of birds; he is familiar with the scenery of our eastern and northern coasts; and his opening paper, "At the Seaside," is written with humour, vividness, spirit, and a quite unusual power of picturesque presentment. It is a true vacation paper. As we read, the hum of the city dies away, and we are trans-ported to the chalky cliffs, on whose scalps are corn fields with scarlet poppies intermixed, and beyond a whole horizonful of ocean, sleek and blue in the lazy summer day. Although everything is silent, the silence does not arise from absence of life. A gun, and the rocks are clamorous with startled sea-fowls. Shirley has affectionately watched the habits of gulls, ducks, divers, loons, herons, and cormorants, and the swan that comes out of the northern twilight ; and since Christopher North dropped his pen, we have had no better ornithological writing. Take this photograph of the cormorant, or *scrath*, as he is locally called :—

"The *scrath* is not by any means a lively bird; he entertains serious, not to say gloomy, views on most of the questions of the day. I have seen the cormorants who frequent this rock sit together for hours without uttering a syllable to each other—in a kind of dyspeptic dejection. Apart from his sentiments upon serious subjects, this is probably the result of a system of over-feeding ; for, even with the most perfect digestion, such excessive eating must tell upon the spirits. They are, moreover, somewhat speculative birds, and employ their leisure in various impracticable experiments. They seem, in par-

ticular, to entertain a theory that they are intended by Providence to live upon invisible
pinnacles, where a titmouse could not find foot-
ing. The consequences may be easily foreseen.
No sooner is the unwieldy monster seated than
he loses his balance, and a fierce and violent
flapping of his sable pinions is required to pre-
vent him from falling to the bottom. Nothing
can convince him of the fallacy of the notion;
and it would be difficult to determine what satisfaction or enjoyment he can derive from an
insane proceeding like this, which so ill consorts,
moreover, with the sepulchral gravity of his
appearance."

Nothing can well be better in its light way
than this; and the affectionately-humorous exaggeration brings out, far more vividly than any
cold and exact description could do, the characteristics of the grave, funereal fowl. Shirley enters
into the heart of his cormorant as Mr Carlyle
enters into the heart of his hero, and works out
from that. And this peculiar kind of humorous and picturesque presentment is not confined to the passage we have quoted. It per-
vades more or less every page of the opening

paper, which, as we have said, is the pleasantest and ablest of his Essays.

The most important papers in the book, so far, at least, as actual substance and gravity of treatment are concerned, are the three entitled, " People who are not Respectable ;" "A Lay Sermon on Nonconformity, a plea for Liberty ;" and " William the Silent, the earliest Teacher of Toleration." The first deals with Lola Montez, Heine, and the Abbé Domenech, and reveals an audacious generosity of sentiment ; the beauty and the poet are tenderly dealt with ; and, when rebuked, there is a sneaking kindness in the rebuke. The second is a reply to two questions —" In the first place, How is the State, and in the second place, How is the Church, to treat Nonconformity ?" while the third relates in a rapid way—somewhat after Lord Macaulay's fashion— the career of Orange the taciturn, and rises into panegyric towards the close on that prince's tolerant and unpersecuting spirit in the midst of an intolerant and persecuting time. These Essays depend one upon the other; and, however diverse in subject, they form one argument. This age, it appears, is not tolerant enough ; the persecuting spirit is as virulent as ever, the

methods of martyrdom are only changed. Hear
Shirley on the matter: "In many circles you
would incur more odium if you told its members
that you read 'Maurice' and 'Jowett,' and believed them to be good and honest men, than if
you picked their pockets. Holy hands are lifted
in pious horror; an inquisition is held upon the
condition-of-your-soul question; your opinions,
which you have always supposed to be at least
harmless, charitable, and good-natured, if nothing better, are pronounced 'unsound' and
'unsafe' (words of evil import) by the assembled
saints; and you are then solemnly tied to the
stake and burned—fortunately in effigy only."
"The victim may indeed retreat from the family
and the sect, sever local ties, which daily become
more oppressive and unmanageable, and calmly
appeal to a wider tribunal. But the rent is very
trying to mortal nerves; the heartstrings sometimes crack in the venture." So much for social
martyrdom. Now for the question between
Nonconformity and the Church. "A national
Church, in the largest sense, is the development
of the devotional side of the national mind.
. . . . If this definition be accurate—and we are
convinced that it is—then it follows that such

an institution, maintained it may be out of the
public purse, should be devoted to the service of
the public ; and that any limitations of *caste*, or
of doctrine, when not absolutely indispensable,
are inconsistent with its design, and with the
purpose for which it exists. Any condition which
prevents any religious citizen from becoming a
minister (and thereby partaking of the emolu-
ments to which he would otherwise be entitled),
or a member (and thereby partaking of the privi-
leges which communion confers), is, *prima facie*,
imperious and indefensible. A clear necessity
alone can justify its retention. Is there, then, to
be no limitation ? Are men of all opinions and of
no opinions to find shelter within the sanctuary ?
To such a question the reply is obvious. A
national Church cannot be permitted to lose its representative character. The national Church of a
Christian people must remain distinctively Christian, just as the national Church of a Mahometan
people must remain distinctively Mahometan."
Elsewhere, we find that "the clergyman, when
he has once 'taken' the Articles, undergoes a
species of petrifaction ; he becomes a fossil
thenceforth to the day of his death. The rich
and invaluable lessons which experience teaches

must not be learned by him ; he must close his
eyes upon the growing light ; his moral and
intellectual nature, like Joshua's sun at Ajalon,
' must come to a full stop.' "

In a paper like the present, it is not advisable
to enter into these deep matters of controversy,
and all the less advisable that they have already
been discussed at length elsewhere. It may be
permitted to be said, however, " that a national
Church, in the largest sense, is the development of the devotional side of the national
mind," just as a standing army is the development of the fighting side of the national character ; and that Church and army, to be effective,
must possess identity of purpose and uniformity
of discipline. To have persons of peculiar
doctrinal views within the national Church,
who give expression to these peculiar doctrines,
would be quite as hurtful, and would lead to a
like confusion, as to have persons in the ranks
who have peculiar notions as to how marching
is to be conducted, and who assert their individuality in the method of discharging their fire-
locks. If persons of peculiar notions on certain
doctrinal points are to be admitted into the
Church, you turn the Church itself into a bear

garden ; it immediately begins to fight within itself, instead of fighting against the evil which is in the world. Shirley very properly says, "that the national Church of a Christian people must be distinctively Christian ;" but who is to be the judge of *what is* distinctively Christian ? The disbeliever in the Divinity of Christ calls himself a Christian ; the person enjoying the gift of the unknown tongues calls himself a Christian ; the believer in purgatory and transubstantiation calls himself a Christian ; and as all these accept the Scriptures, to some extent at least, as an authority, and are certainly neither Mahometans, Pagans, nor Jews, it would be difficult to rob them of the appellation. But could a Church exist with these discordant and inflammable elements in its bosom ? What is "distinctively Christian" must, like every other dispute in the world, be decided practically by the majorities. And if men holding peculiar notions of doctrine or discipline shall have entered the Church, or if, after entering, they find that, from whatever reason, they cannot conscientiously give intellectual adherence to the standards of the Church, and if, in consequence of this discordance between themselves and their brethren, they are uncomfortable, and ill at ease, what is the course they should adopt? They have placed.themselves, or they find themselves, in a false position, and their duty is to get out of that false position with as little delay as possible. Honesty, comfort, reverence for their own consciences and for the consciences of others, alike counsel resignation of their positions in the Church.

With respect to the social martyrdom to which Shirley refers, it may be said that, from the very constitution of things, such martyrdoms have always been and ever will be. The man who acts in the teeth of public opinion—and it matters nothing whether that opinion is local or general—must, as a matter of necessity, meet opposition : he is like a ship sailing against a head wind. A certain conformity with the existing order of things is required of all men, under penalties of discomfort. A man cannot even take mustard to his mutton, or eat peas with his knife, with impunity. This is very intolerant, it is true ; but tolerance to the man who chooses to eat peas with his knife is *in*tolerance to twenty people who may be sitting at dinner with him. Shirley tells us that there are certain circles in which a man incurs odium by reading " Maurice " and "Jowett." It is unquestionably true. And if a man chooses to attire himself in the jacket of a harlequin, he will incur odium in every circle he enters. If a man acts in opposition to the opinions, the prejudices, the traditions of the people with whom he mixes, he is just as certain to incur opposition and pain as he is to hurt himself if he runs his head against a wall. The nonconformist never did tread on róses ; and till the constitution of human nature changes, on roses he will never tread. And this fate awaits not only the nonconformist in religion, but all nonconformists alike. The nonconformist in hats is liable to be stared at in the street ; and it is possible that he may overhear the remarks of irreverent urchins as he passes by. The nonconformist in politics has his own annoyances : Peel had hard words and ungenerous insinuations to bear when he split with his party. The nonconformist, if he has any knowledge of men, will expect some little trouble and misrepresentation to fall to his lot, and he will not care to make a noise about it. If the path of the nonconformist were perfectly smooth, what merit would there be in his nonconformity ?

Several essays in Shirley's book, other than

those we have mentioned, are of great merit, especially " The Last Word on Lord Macaulay," which indicates with clearness the limitations and defects of the great writer—altogether the best piece of critical writing which he has produced. " Terra Santa ; a Peep into Italy," contains reading of the pleasantest kind ; and the allusions it contains to Mr Hawthrone and Mrs Browning are characteristic—for, after all, this writer sees the world clearest through the window of books. On whatever subject he writes, you are sure to come into contact with the writers he most admires. In " Nugæ Criticæ," Shirley touches on many subjects, and always with grace and true literary skill ; but we confess that we like him best " at the sea-side :" his vagrant, desultory, yet always pleasant and picturesque vein, flows freest when he has the eastern coast to deal with—the sea and the sea-fowl. He is always at his best when out of doors.

A. K. H. B. gathered his reputation in *Fraser;* is, we understand, exceedingly popular in England, and prodigiously so across the Atlantic. That this popularity arises from a certain merit discoverable in his Essays, there can, of course, be no matter of question ; he is an exceedingly clever writer, he has a happy knack of putting things, he is always readable. Yet it would be difficult to explain by what charm he leads us along his pages. One only feels that the charm exists. A. K. H B. is as egotistical as Montaigne, but in no other particular does he resemble him. There is great sameness in his papers : reading them is like walking on an American prairie ; green undulation follows on green undulation, beginning nowhere, ending nowhere, without prospect, without outlook. He starts on his subject without a pocket-compass, and, after a long circuit, he arrives at the place from which he set out ; and the worst of it is, he arrives as empty-handed as when he started. He could perform the feat of voyaging round the world and bringing home nothing. A great element of success in a writer is peculiarity, and A. K. H. B. has his peculiarities. Once possessed of an idea, he can make it go farther than any of his contemporaries. Give him a bit of gold, and no man living will beat it out into a broader and thinner leaf. Mount him on a platitude, and he will make it carry him across a county. In his Essays he laughs occasionally at Mr Martin

Farquhar Tupper; but he is related to the body of contemporary prose very much as Mr Tupper is related to the body of contemporary verse, and the popularity of each arises from similar causes. For the mass of readers, it is a pleasant thing to feel that they are as wise as the author they are reading, and the mass of A. K. H. B.'s readers are made happy in this way.

A. K. H. B. is an egotist; he is continually writing about his Essays, his sermons, his methods of composition, his garden, his children, his man-servant—if that functionary dips furtively into *Fraser's Magazine* when his master is done with it, he must be gratified by the manifold recognition of his existence—his own horses, or the horses of his friends. Now, to egotism in itself no man will object, provided the egotist is great or peculiar. We never weary of Montaigne or of Charles Lamb when they are speaking about themselves. Unhappily, however, A. K. H. B. is neither great nor peculiar; he is simply a clever, fluent man, well read up in current literature, conversant with its "slang," in the dexterous use of which one-half of his smartness consists, perfectly ready to kick a man when it is the fashion to kick him—witness his frequent sneers at Mr Tupper and *Mr Wordy*—and who can prattle in a pleasant way enough "Concerning Hurry and Leisure," "Tidiness," and certain "Blisters of Humanity." Egotism of the light, trifling kind, which A. K. H. B. indulges in, is apt to weary one after a little. In a very little while, one gets irritated at his familiar, hail-fellow-well-met, dawdling, sauntering ways, disgusted rather with his man-servant and horses, and a little inclined to request him, in a somewhat peremptory manner, to say his say "concerning" whatever subject he may have in hand, in a direct, straightforward fashion, and have done. He cannot, without protest, be permitted to take the airs of a Montaigne. If he writes "Concerning the Paring of Nails," let him discuss the general subject with what light may be given him, and cease to linger so lovingly over his own.

And yet, after all, there is a certain charm in A. K. H. B.'s Essays. He writes for the most part with grace and purity; he possesses fancy, liveliness, and his papers have now and again touches of shrewdness, insight, and common sense. If some savage critic would but lay hold of him, and whip the pestilent coxcombry out

T

of him, he would do the world some service, and confer on A. K. H. B. himself the greatest benefit he will ever receive from a fellow-mortal. For in him the elements of an excellent writer do incontestably exist. He possesses "faculties" which hitherto "he hath not used," or only in a perfunctory way and at long intervals. He can be direct, suggestive, pathetic even, when he chooses, but the misfortune is he so seldom chooses. The best thing which he has written is a little paper entitled "Gone," absolutely without grimace or wilful irrelevance, and into the pathetic undertone of which neither himself, nor his garden, nor his next Sunday's sermon, nor even his man-servant, does for one moment intrude. In the following passage, A. K. H. B. is at his best, perhaps :—

"Every one knows what Dr Johnson wrote about 'The Last.' It is, of course, a question of individual associations, and how it may strike different minds; but I stand up for the unrivalled reach and pathos of the short word 'Gone.'

"It is curious that the saddest and most touching of human thoughts, when we run it up to its simplest form, is of so homely a thing as a material object existing in a certain space, and then removing from that space to another. *That* is the essential idea of 'Gone.'

"Yet, in the commonest way, there is something touching in that: something touching in the sight of vacant space, once filled by almost anything. You feel a blankness in the landscape where a tree is gone that you have known all your life. You are conscious of a vague sense of something lacking where even a post is pulled up that you remember always in the centre of a certain field. You feel this yet more when some familiar piece of furniture is taken away from a room which you know well. Here that clumsy easy-chair used to stand: and it is gone. You feel yourself an interloper, standing in the space where it stood so long. It touches you still more to look at the empty chair which you remember so often filled by one who will never fill it more. You stand in a large railway station: you have come to see a train depart. There is a great bustle on the platform, and there is a great quantity of human life, and of the interests and cares of human life, in those twelve or fourteen carriages, and filling that little space between the rails. You stand by and watch the warm interiors of the carriages, looking so large and so full, and as if they had so much in them. There are people of every kind of aspect, children and old folk, multitudes of railway-rugs, of carpet-bags, of portmanteaus, of parcels, of newspapers, of books, of magazines. At length you hear the last bell ; then comes that silent, steady pull, which is always striking, though seen ever so often. The train glides away : it is gone. You stand and look vacantly at the place where it was. How little the space looks —how blank the air! There are the two rails, just four feet eight and a half inches apart ; how close together they look ! You can hardly think that there was so much of life, and of the interests of life, in so little room. You feel the power upon the average human being of the simple, commonplace fact, that something has been here, and is gone."

There is not very much in this, perhaps, but it is nicely felt ; and the illustration, if familiar to all, cannot fail to be felt by all. Most of us have seen a railway train depart, and when nothing remains but bare rails and empty space, have been conscious, in an obscure way, of the subtly mingled strangeness and regret which A. K. H. B. so tenderly indicates.

Mr Patterson's "Essays in History and Art" contain less of the personal element than the writings of Shirley or A. K. H. B., and are on that account perhaps less interesting. We hear nothing of his peculiar moods, of the house he lives in, or the places he visits. He does not begin a paper on the banks of a trouting stream, or seated on the parapet of the Devil's Bridge, with his legs dangling over, like Shirley; nor does he haunt stables, and make a writing-desk of a horse's face, like A. K. H. B. He has nothing of the lightness, jauntiness, and holiday feeling of these gentlemen. He means work; he desires to inform rather than to amuse. The more important papers in the volume—on the "Ethnology of Europe," "Our Indian Empire," "The National Life of China," "India, its Castes and Creeds"—are laboriously and solidly done. Into these Essays he has gathered the pith and essence of many books; and to people wishing to be informed on these matters we do not know a volume more entirely to be recommended than

Mr Patterson's. The style is always clear, if at times a little ornate ; and evidences of conscientiousness and care are everywhere manifest. Mr Patterson, when he has a solid, useful information-subject on hand, is at his best. Certain of the lighter papers—as, for instance, "Youth and Summer," "Genius and Liberty"—are spoiled by an Asiatic floridity of taste. A passage like the following rather provokes a smile in the judicious :—

"But the genius of Greece is rising in beauty everywhere on land and sea—the blue Ægean, gemmed with the 'sparkling Cyclades,' bearing, like floating flower-baskets, the isles of Greece on its calm surface. On the lovely bay-indented shores of Iona, where the vines are trailing in festoons from tree to tree, lighting the emerald woods with their purple clusters, sits merry Anacreon, singing of love and wine in undying strains. Light-hearted old man, sing on !—until, in luckless hour, the choking grapestone end at once thy lays, thy loves, and thy life. The lofty strains of Alcæus and Simonides make the Ægean shores to re-echo their undying hatred of a tyrannic power ; while on her Lesbian isle, hapless Sappho, weary of a fame that cannot bring her love, leaps from the cliffs of Leucus into the sea, but lives for ever in her country's memory as the Tenth Muse."

This is a kind of eloquence which convulses the debating societies of young men in their teens, and the frequency of its appearance in these Essays proves that Mr Patterson retains in middle life all the juvenility and freshness of his youthful spirit.

It is with a certain proud sorrow that we regard "Essays, Historical and Critical," by Hugh Miller. Six years have passed since the writer was borne to his grave, and his place in literature is as well defined now as it was on the day in which he was laid in "The Grange;" and future years, with a sense of the sacredness of their task, will keep clear from all intrusion Miller's place in the literature of his country. The British Valhalla will be crowded indeed when room cannot be found for him. Miller was not only an accomplished journalist and able geologist, a writer singularly acute and picturesque, but he was something beyond all these

—a great man. He possessed, in some degree, that largeness of limb and majesty of mental lineament which distinguished Burns and Scott, Chalmers and John Wilson. He came up from the red sandstone quarries of Cromarty into his fame, as Burns came into his from the Ayrshire harvest fields. Scotland is proud to think that she is peculiarly the mother of such men; and if Burns was her first-born and greatest, Hugh Miller was her second, and only in stature a little lower than the first. The present volume of Essays is entirely selected from the file of the *Witness* newspaper; consequently it does not so much represent Miller at his best, as in his usual working attire. These papers were not written by him with a view to separate publication; they were composed in his usual course of duty as a journalist; and, as newspaper articles, their concision, their wit, their fancy, their richness of sentence, are quite wonderful. The opening Essay, on "The New Year," is an exquisite poem. The visit of her Majesty to Edinburgh in 1842 was an interesting event, but it is doubly so when we see it through the medium of Mr Miller's graphic and picturesque prose. In the opening sentences—so exquisite in their natural analogies

—of the article entitled "The Echoes of the World," an article which concerns itself with the death of Dr Chalmers, we have the truest poetry as well as the most impressive statement of fact :—

"Has the reader ever heard a piece of heavy ordnance fired amid the mountains of our country? First, there is the ear-stunning report of the piece itself—the prime mover of those airy undulations that travel outwards, circle beyond circle, towards the far horizon; then some hoary precipice, that rises tall and solemn in the immediate neighbourhood, takes up the sound, and it comes rolling back from its rough front in thunder, like a giant wave flung far sea-ward from the rock against which it has broken ; then some more distant hill becomes vocal, and then another, and another, and anon another ; and then there is a slight pause, as if all were over—the undulations are travelling unbroken along some flat moor or across some expansive lake, or over some deep valley, filled, haply, by some long, wide, and roaring arm of the sea ; and then the more remote mountains lift up their voices in mysterious mutterings, now lower, now louder, now more abrupt, anon more prolonged, each, as it recedes, taking up the tale in closer succession to the one that had previously spoken, till at length their distinct utterances are lost, in one low, continuous sound, that at last dies out amid the shattered peaks of the desert wilderness, and unbroken stillness settles over the scene as at first. Through a scarcely voluntary exertion of that faculty of analogy and comparison, so natural to the human mind that it converts all the existences of the physical world into forms and expressions of the world intellectual, we have oftener than once thought of the phenomenon and its attendant results as strikingly representative of effects produced by the death of Chalmers. It is an event which has, we find, rendered vocal the echoes of the world, and they are still returning upon us, after measured intervals, according to the distances."

This is wonderful writing; and when Miller proceeds to complete his analogy by describing how, from every quarter of the world, there came back here, in a murmur of grief and admiration, the report of the death of Chalmers, the effect of the whole is singularly grand and complete. It is contemplated, we notice from the preface, that should the present collection of Essays meet with success, other and similar volumes may be gathered from the file of the *Witness*. Of the success of the book there can be no manner of doubt; so that we presume we may soon look for a second volume, and, perhaps, a third.

A SPRING CHANSON.

TO the amber east the happy merle
    From tree-top whistles clear—
  "What Love is to young man and girl
    Spring-time is to the year."
While in the wind the poplar bent
    Like a torch of emerald flame ;
'Neath the flowering currants' coloured light
    A brilliant chaffinch came :
And he hardly alit, ere away he flew
In a twinkle of yellow, green, and blue,
And when I saw him, I knew, I knew
That Spring, bringing favour to bird and beast,
    Mosses to thatches of cottage and shed,
Iris to mirrors of morning dew,
Sunset colours to west, sunrise colours to east,
    New green to old furrows of churchyard dead,
Would bring an ode to the poet too,
Or a chanson at the least.

When Spring came to my garden

(The wintry world's retriever!)
The crocuses stood in their ranks, like a guard
　Of honour to receive her.
And now in Spring's inconstant smile,
　In Spring's inconstant light,
One rebus bush is a rosy cloud,
　Its neighbour a cloud of white.
The ivies have clomb o'er the cottage rafter:
　The gummy buds of the chestnut glitter:
　On the southern wall I mark a titter
Of bloom—in a month, or so, hereafter
'Twill be all covered o'er with a blossoming
　　laughter,
　And the ground beneath an exquisite litter
Of shed pink and white—and I know who
　Will then sit in the noon, the patientest
　　knitter
(My dearest, my dearest, who is it but you!)
Sunshine-kissed, blossom-powdered; and, while
　　the wind blows
　Warm and warmer, around her the hyacinth
　　swells
　To break into clusters of coralline bells,
Princess rose-bud, green-hooded, to open to rose.

In the Spring-time's lovely thronging

Lurk a sacred thirst and longing.
Every deep earth-hidden root
Yearns to turn to flower and fruit;
Every hen-bird east and west
Pines for eggs beneath her breast;
On all harmless creeping things
Comes desire of painted wings;
And the brightest vision hovers
In the eyes of happy lovers;
The burst of apple-blossom brave
Hides the newly-mounded grave;
The voice of happy bird in brake
Soothes the oft-recurring ache.
Spring is breathing through my hair,
Spring is smiling in the air;
And in her deep delight I share
    With far-removèd things—
The solitary-mining mole,
The lark, a disembodied soul
    That, lost in heaven, sings.

O Spring that bids the crocus
    Uplift its coloured lamp,
That with the wind-flower lights the wood,
    With marigold the swamp,
That woos from out the apple-bough

The perfumed white and red—
Breaks the sod to daisies under my foot,
Hangs a musical heaven o'er-head—
Oh Spring, Spring, I would meet thee
The happiest man alive
If—as once—I could but greet thee
With the heart of twenty-five,
Which was hermit of its sweetness
As of honey is the hive !

Oh youth, youth, youth,
More beautiful than truth—
The truth that checks the blood, and makes the
temples grey :
The light of thy sunrise
Dwells deep in memory's eyes,
And I feel as bare as winter in the thick leaf-
coming May.
Oh youth, youth, youth,
Time has neither rest nor ruth.
Spring enkindles wood and plain
But it passes heart and brain.
Spring, above the mountain crag,
Waves the morning's fiery flag,
Draws the evening amethyst,—
Time has staled the lips I kissed

In such passion undissembled
That its very rapture trembled.
Spring may walk o'er daisies spread,
With a skylark over head ;
Her garments scented with the May ;
Round her footsteps lambs at play.
But she is alien, she is foreign :
Her delight I have no store in.
I regard her as a child
Singing in her spirits wild,
Dancing in the sheer excess
Of a thoughtless happiness.
Her smile is bright, but very shallow.
More I love September's yellow :
Morns of dew-strung gossamer,
Thoughtful days without a stir,
Rooky clangours, brazen leaves,
Stubbles dotted o'er with sheaves,
More than Spring's bright un-control
Suit the Autumn of the soul.
Who would choose the giddy girl,
In her spirits' endless whirl,
Before the calm, deep-thoughted woman,
With a heart entirely human ?

From summit of thy slowly-greening tree,

Sing to the breaking east, oh happy merle,
Scatter rich jewel and melodious pearl,
Then close in a thick-warbled ecstasy !
Sing to the Spring—but through the Spring I
look
And see, when fields are bare, the woodlands
pale,
And hear a sad un-mated redbreast wail,
In beechen russets by a leaden brook.
For I am tortured by a boding eye
That, gazing on the morning's glorious grain,
Beholds late shreds of fiery sunset stain
The marble pallor of a western sky.
Sweet is thy song, oh merle ! and sweetly sung
Thy forefathers in our forefathers' ears ;
And this—far more than all—thy song endears
In that it knits the old world with the young.
Men live and die, the song remains ; and when
I list the passion of thy vernal breath,
Methinks thou singest best to Love and
Death—
To happy Lovers and to dying Men.

MAY, 1866.

U

EDINBURGH.

[ON the following piece, Alexander Smith was occupied in some
intermittent way, when seized by fatal illness. He intended
it as a companion poem to his fine Lyric "Glasgow." As
the one City had been treated of, as endeared to him by
associations of youth and early passion, the other was now
to be dealt with as the home of his manhood and mature
affections, the place where essentially his life was lived,
where in all probability he might look for the solemn advent
of death. Thus it was that he himself spoke of it. In the
verses as left, this scheme of the poem seems scarce even
indicated. As in many parts exceedingly imperfect, I had
some hesitation as to here including them; but finding my
own strong feeling that they should be given approved by
the advice of friends on whose judgment I could rely, I
decided they should be inserted. Certain omissions were
suggested; but as to these there was no clear unanimity of
opinion; and, on the whole, it has seemed best to give the
piece just as it was left by the Poet. It is to be judged as
merely a fragment, and first rude, hasty, draught. As
such, it is hoped it will be thought to have merit enough to
justify its appearance; the true lyrical life and movement,
and the undefinable touch of the Poet are perhaps throughout sufficiently marked in it, with all its obvious sins of
imperfection and incoherence.

Had the writer lived to complete his plan, a great deal
more would have been written; the whole being then re-

garded as a sort of quarry, out of which was to come the finished work. A vigorous recast would have been made; weak or superfluous verses would have been excised; the general arrangement—pretty much at first left to itself— would have been fixed, links of connection being furnished where such were needed; and the whole poem would in much have altered its aspect. As it stands, it would be plainly unfair to subject it to anything like rigour of criticism; sufficient if, as a rude sketch, it is held of interest enough as the last fragment from the pen of the Poet, to justify its insertion here.—ED.]

AH me, the years they come and go!
  Twelve times the snowdrop o'er the snow
   Hath shiver'd; June hath sway'd
Rich rose-branch, full-blown rose and bud;
Broad sun-flower from its disc of blood
   A sun-like glory ray'd—
Since, urged by passionate unrest,
  I sang the City of the West.

Grown staider, somewhat now I scorn
The mavis of my early morn,
   Clear-singing 'gainst the sheen;
Care, that sleeps late, and early stirs,
Like daily feet of villagers
   Across the village green,
Hath worn its track—and youth's delight
An Autumn swallow, taken flight.

Another and a nobler Me
Dwells in regretful memory,
　　Bright-eyed, and golden-hair'd ;
No more I breathe melodious song ;
Yet to these later years belong
　　Moods, passions, unimpair'd :
Still lives the rapture of the eye,
Dim city, hanging in the sky !

The dazzling cataract, strong and loud ;
The reddening of the morning cloud ;
　　Ben-Blaaven's craggy spears,
And ridge, half lost in misty steam ;
Brown tangle-beds, that heave and gleam
　　Idly round stony piers ;
Rude turf hut, girl in scarlet cloak
Set in an azure film of smoke—

I love, as I did long ago ;—
Yea, better ; for I've come to know
　　The loveliest space of sky
Is that which silently o'erbends
Old apple-blossom'd gable-ends,
　　Wherein men live and die.
The world is lovely ; but the sight
Of man adds pathos to delight.

Girt with thy cloudy equipage,
Swart city, thou wert once the cage
　　In which I sang—Afar
I cannot hear thy solemn roar
Ascending, when day's toil is o'er,
　　To meet the evening star.
My later home is still and fair
With mournfulness of sunset air.

Edina, high in heaven wan,
Towered, templed, Metropolitan,
　　Waited upon by hills,
River, and wide-spread ocean—tinged
By April light, or draped and fringed
　　As April vapour wills,
Thou hangest, like a Cyclop's dream,
High in the shifting weather-gleam.

Fair art thou when above thy head
The mistless firmament is spread ;
　　But when the twilight's screen
Draws glimmering round thy towers and spires,
And thy lone bridge, uncrown'd by fires,
　　Hangs in the dim ravine,
Thou art a very Persian tale—
Oh, Mirza's vision, Bagdad's vale !

The spring time stains with emerald
Thy Castle's precipices bald ;
    Within thy streets and squares
The sudden summer camps, and blows
The plenteous chariot-shaken rose ;
    Or, lifting unawares
My eyes from out thy central strife,
Lo, far off, harvest-brazen Fife !

When, rain-drops gemming tree and plant,
The rainbow is thy visitant,
    Lovely as on the moors ;
When sunset flecks with loving ray
Thy wilderness of gables grey,
    And hoary embrasures ;
When great Sir Walter's moon-blanch'd shrine,
Rich carved, as Melrose, gleams divine,

I know thee ; and I know thee, too,
On winter nights, when 'gainst the blue
    Thy high, gloom-wilder'd ridge
Breaks in a thousand splendours ; lamps
Gleam broadly in the valley damps ;
    Thy air-suspended bridge
Shines steadfast ; and the modern street
Looks on, star-fretted, loud with feet.

    *   *   *   *   *   *   *

Once, on a Royal Nuptial Eve,
I saw thy bulk of Castle heave,*
   In fire and vapour roll'd ;
St Giles wore strange and gem-like light ;
St George's dome, aloft in night,
   Hung like a fleece of gold ;
Sir Walter's shrine, 'mid rubies, beryls,
Glow'd with the chasten'd glow of pearls :

March wind in fitful gusts that came,
Made stream the wild padella flame ;
   Dull came the cannon's boom :
Past all thy fronts of blazing pride,
Through streets that shone, a jubilant tide
   Rolled, hued with sudden bloom,
As rainbow-like, through festal air,
Passed emerald gleam and crimson glare.

*   *   *   *   *   *   *

Fair art thou City, to the eye,
But fairer to the memory :
   There is no place that breeds—

---

* The allusion is to the grand illumination throughout the country on the occasion of the marriage of the Prince of Wales. The natural advantages of Edinburgh for such a *spectacle* are quite unequalled ; to the utmost they were made available ; and the splendour of the total effect was such, I understand, as can never be forgotten by any one who witnessed it.

Not Venice 'neath her mellow moons,
When the sea-pulse of full lagoons
    Waves all her palace weeds—
Such wistful thoughts of far away,
Of the eternal yesterday.

Within thy high-piled Canongate
The air is of another date ;
    All speaks of ancient time :
Traces of gardens, dials, wells,
Thy dizzy gables, oyster-shells
    Imbedded in the lime—
Thy shields above the doors of peers
Are old as Mary Stuart's tears.

Street haunted by the step of Knox ;
Darnley's long, heavy-scented locks ;
    Ruthven's blood-freezing stare :
Dark Murray, dreaming of the crown—
His ride through fair Linlithgow town,
    And the man waiting there
With loaded fuse, undreamed of—wiles
Of Mary, and her mermaid smiles !

Thou saw'st Montrose's passing face
Shame-strike the gloating silk and lace,
    And jeering plumes that filled

The balcony o'erhead; with pride
Thou saw'st Prince Charles bare-headed ride,
 While bagpipes round him shrilled,
And far Culloden's smoky racks
Hid scaffold craped, and bloody axe.

What wine hast thou known brawl be=spilt!
What daggers ruddy to the hilt!
 . What stately minuets
Walked slowly o'er thy oaken floors!
What hasty kisses at thy doors!
 What banquetings and bets!
What talk, o'er man that lives and errs,
Of double-chinned philosophers!

Great City, every morning I
See thy wild fringes in the sky,
 Soft-blurr'd with smoky grace:
Each evening note the blazing sun
Flush luridly thy vapours dun—
 A spire athwart his face:
Each night I watch thy wondrous feast,
Like some far city of the East.

But most I love thee faint and fair,
Dim-pencill'd in the April air,
 When in the dewy bush

I hear from budded thick remote
The rapture of the blackbird's throat,
  The sweet note of the thrush ;
And all is shadowless and clear
In the uncoloured atmosphere.

*   *   *   *   *   *   *

APPENDIX.

PLAGIARISMS OF ALEXANDER SMITH.

THE great majority of these so-called Plagiarisms are, as instances, so frivolous, that in themselves they could have won no attention. As here—

TENNYSON.	SMITH.
"The shattering trumpet shrilleth high. They reel, they roll in clanging lists."	"His voice that shivered the mad trumpet's blare, A new raised standard to the reeling field."

In the first case of parallelism, it is to be admitted that, by both Tennyson and Smith, mention is made of a trumpet—otherwise, neither in idea nor expression, does Smith's really nervous and noble line in the least come in contact with Tennyson's, whose "shattering trumpet," by the way, is somewhere to be found in Scott. In both of the next pair, the word "reel" is used, the inference against Tennyson being clear— Smith supposed convicted—of his having purloined a beauty from the author of "The Reel of Tulloch-gorum." Again—

COLERIDGE.	SMITH.
"To free the hollow heart from pain-ing."	"To ease the empty aching of her heart."

MARLOW.	SMITH.
"Shallow rivers, to whose falls Melodious birds sing madrigals."	"A shallow river breaks o'er shallow falls."

TENNYSON.	SMITH.
"The long brook falling down the cloven ravine."	"The torrent raging down the long ravine."

BAILEY'S "FESTUS."	SMITH.
"If that's called lively, or in part, or wholly, The gods preserve me from your melancholy."	"If short and merry, Heaven speed your tongue; If long and sad, the Lord have mercy on us."

These, and quantities of others not less ridiculous—the mass being indeed of this character—are called "instances of appropriation, simple and direct." As I said, had such things been set forward by themselves, they could only have brought ridicule on the person adducing them. But interspersed were a considerable number of cases of true indebtedness in way of suggestion, in the light of which only could the others seem of any significance even to a careless reader.

Firstly—in regard of *these*, Mr Helps' distinction is to be signalised "between the man who *conquers* and the man who *steals*." In adapting an image from a previous Poet, and in so doing, ennobling it, genius as true may be shown, as in the invention of an original image. As instance

KEATS.	SMITH.
"Gold vase embossed With long-forgotten story."	"Dropt in my path like a great cup of gold All rich and rough with stories of the gods."

The *suggestion* admitted probable here, the man is, I venture to say, out of court as an incompetent, who does not see with trenchant clearness, how, taking from Keats the mere abstract notion of a vase embossed, or with reliefs on it, Smith has concreted and visualised it, as Keats had not done, into a genuinely poetical image—has *conquered* his image from' Keats, not picked his pocket of it. In nearly all the other instances, it will in like manner be found, that in taking an image from another Poet, he proves his right to do so, by some happy art of adaptation; "conveys" the gold coin, so to speak, and proves his right so to do in its re-issue with the stamp and signature of his own mind upon it. And the man—as Mr Helps in his happy way put it—who cannot distinguish between *conquest* of this kind, and the baser "conveyance" called *theft*, had greatly better, as a Critic, keep himself as much as possible out of the eye of the Public.

Secondly—such things are to be condoned, for the most part, as unintentional; reminiscences under a condition of obliviscence, to no one so much to be excused as to a young Poet, reading fiercely and uncritically, and blessed or cursed with "a memory at once tenacious and treacherous," in virtue of which the thing he remembers is *bona fide* reproduced as his own. Farther, there is absolutely *no* Poet—of whatever undenied originality—from whom numerous instances of this very thing might not be cited. This unconscious Commerce of Minds covers so large a space in Literature, that only a rather rash man, as probably a rather ignorant one, would care to stake the reputation of any Poet whatever on the originality of a special beauty or image. The odds would really be, that if he did so, some curiously read person would be able to massacre his pet beauty for him, by showing how the Poet had come by it. To give an instance from Burns, commemorated by Carlyle as supreme in force and effectiveness: "Our Scottish forefathers in the battle-field struggled forward *red-wat-shod;* in this one word, a full vision of horror and carnage, perhaps too frightfully accurate for art." Well, it is fine, doubtless ; but it is taken direct from the old Ballad of Otterbourne—

> " The Gordons gude, in English *blude*
> They *wat* their hose and *shoon.*"

There it is, nearly *verbatim,* Burns only packing the thing a little closer. Various others of the finest, and almost, it might be said, most characteristic strokes in Burns have, in like manner, been traced to their source. Such are—

> " The rank is but the guinea-stamp,
> The man's the gowd for a' that."

> " A king can mak' a belted knight," etc.

> " Her 'prentice han' she tried on man,
> An' syne she made the lasses, O !"

These and others have been clearly shown to have been " conveyed " by Burns. Here is an instance, so far as I know, unnoticed hitherto, and curious enough to be given :

> " An' my fause lover stole the rose,
> But ah ! he left the thorn wi' me."

Compare Shakespeare, *Diana* in " All's Well that Ends Well : "

> " Ay ! so you serve us
> Till we serve you ; but when you have our roses,
> You basely* leave our thorns to prick ourselves,
> And mock us with our bareness."

---

* In all editions "barely ;" but surely *basely* must almost needs be what Shakespeare wrote.

Can plunder be more palpable than here? and suppose twenty or thirty cases of the like could be rapidly indicated, would our sense of the essential Genius of Burns be in the very least disturbed?

Perhaps in Mr Tennyson's superb "Tithonus" there is nothing more beautiful than the following; and in fact I have seen it quoted by an admiring critic, as eminently Tennysonian in beauty:

> " And the wild team
> Which love thee, yearning for thy yoke, arise,
> And shake the darkness from their loosened manes,
> *And beat the twilight into flakes of fire.*"

Yet here it is pretty accurately in the germ from old Marston, as given in Lamb's Specimens:

> " But see, the dapple-grey coursers of the morn
> *Beat up the light with their bright silver hoofs,*
> And chase it through the sky."

And I think it will almost be ruled that the modern Poet in conveying it—no doubt in deep unconsciousness—has lost a little of the life of the image. Nobody for such a thing as this, repeated ever so, would denounce Mr Tennyson as mere Plagiarist and no Poet. And I suppose what is permitted to one man is, in fairness, to be excused in another.

If from any Poet of his time we should have looked for immunity from this kind of thing, Wordsworth is perhaps the man; but not even an originality so towering as his, so determined and wilful, one might almost say, could avail at all times to preserve him from it. Seldom, indeed, is he to be caught stealing from a contemporary writer. He admired Wordsworth too much to care for any of his contemporaries, and, in his serene and haughty self-opinion, was little at pains to read them—in this by so much unwise, that precisely as he thus isolated himself from the best influences of his time, he tended to narrow the range and mar the flexibility of his genius. Yet here is something in him pretty boldly pilfered from a Poet, whose debt to *him* is considerable, yet to whom he would not have greatly liked to consider himself indebted :

BYRON.	WORDSWORTH (IN 1826).
" He who has loved not, here may learn that lore, And make his heart a spirit ; he who knows [more." That tender mystery, will love the	" Yes ! where Love nestles thou canst teach The soul to love the more ; Hearts also shall thy lessons reach That never loved before."

Not often, as I said, will he be found thus indebted to a modern writer ; but to Milton his obligations for suggestions of the kind are frequent, and have been indicated, as in " The child is Father of the Man," which is merely Milton in " Paradise Regained :"

> " The childhood shows the man,
> As morning shows the day."

Two instances only—for brevity's sake—I select, as quite indubitable :

WORDSWORTH.	MILTON.
"She comes—behold ! That figure like a ship with snow-white sail ! Nearer she draws ; a breeze uplifts her veil." —*The Triad.*	" Who is this, etc. That so bedeck'd, ornate, and gay, Comes this way, sailing like a stately ship, With all her bravery on, and tackle trim, Sails filled, and streamers waving." —*Samson Agonistes.*
"And angels to his sight appeared, Crowning the glorious hills of Paradise ; Or through the groves, *gliding like morning mist.* Enkindled by the sun." —*Excursion.*	" The heavenly bands Down from a sky of jasper lighted now In Paradise, and on a hill made halt, A glorious apparition ! * * * The cherubim descended, on the ground *Gliding, meteorous as evening mist,* Risen from a river, o'er the marish glides." —*Paradise Lost* (last page).

Here we have a very noble instance of an image

conquered, not *stolen;* as glorified in the act of appropriation. Wordsworth might be held here to somewhat improve on Milton; whose soberer version is yet
felt, for his own purpose, to have subtle grace of pro-
priety. In that solemn close and twilight, so to speak,
of his mighty Poem, who does not instinctively feel
that the gay morning image of Wordsworth—finer as
angel-likeness in the abstract—would relatively have
been felt an incongruity and splendid irrelevance?
And yet, in the interest of imaginative truth more
absolute, the Poet, in the epithet "meteorous," per-
mits himself an insinuation of the brightness which
his nice sense of keeping and harmony forbids him
more obtrusively to thrust upon us.

Desultory illustration of this kind might to almost
any length be prosecuted. Enough has perhaps been
said to suggest that, in seeking to convict a writer of
Plagiarism, care will be very necessary, together with
a pretty wide range of close and accurate reading.
For the risk must be always considerable that the
Poets from whom the things are alleged to be stolen
may be proved to be not the lawful proprietors, but
really themselves thieves of the property in dispute.
In which case, one would think, the gentleman ten-
dering the accusation must needs look a little foolish.
The writer who thus attacked Smith had plainly some
little reading. With a very little *more* he would have
known that frequently his charges were in this way
self-stultified. If this can be shown; if it be proved
beyond dispute that, of the articles which Smith was
maligned for stealing from certain Poets, these very
Poets had commonly themselves pilfered from other
Poets, I think it must in fairness be admitted, there
was never very much in the charge against him. Let
us see, then, a little as to this.

X

The lines of Smith being quoted about

> "Mysterious voids,
> Throbbing with stars, like pulses,"

it is said they are "dangerously near akin" at once to Keats'

> "Etherial, throbbing like a star,"

and to Wordsworth's

> "Galaxy displayed
> Her fires, that like *mysterious pulses beat.*"

One might have fancied it could not but occur to the writer here that—as things which are equal to the same thing are equal to one another—if Smith here was "dangerously near akin" to *two* Poets, these two Poets must be pretty near akin to each other—as, in fact, they are; the "throbbing" star of Keats, and the "beating" or "pulsing" stars of Wordsworth being, in truth, identical. Wherefore Keats must have taken the *beat* or *throb* of his star from Wordsworth. And when subsequently in "Maud" Mr Tennyson made *his* stars "*Beat* to the noiseless music of the night," he also did felony on Wordsworth. I do not see how we can well send Smith here to the pillory, without sending such excellent company with him as Messrs Keats and Tennyson. Again—

TENNYSON.	SMITH.
"The leader wild swan in among the stars Would *clang* it."	"Long strings of geese came *clanging* from the stars."

Now, admitting that this expression *clang*, as applied to the wings of the larger waterfowl, is fine, bold, peculiar, and so little obvious as not likely to be independently hit upon by two poets—what of Burns in his "Lines to Waterfowl on Loch Turit?"

> "Swiftly seek on *clanging* wings
> Other lakes and other springs."

If Smith stole his "clanging" from Tennyson, by parity of reason, Tennyson must have stolen *his* from Burns. Both are plagiarists, or neither is.* Farther—

KEATS.	SMITH.
" *Enskied* ere this."	" White *enskied* soul."

This is somewhat too frivolous; but meaning anything, the writer must mean that the word "enskied," as first minted by Keats, is of the nature of exclusive property to him. It is not, however, so; *vide Lucio*, of *Isabella*, in "Measure for Measure," "a thing *enskied* and sainted." Wherefore, what Smith stole from Keats, Keats must have stolen from Shakespeare.

---

* On the very first page of the "Life-Drama" occurs an instance, to myself highly curious, which the minute diligence of the critic has failed to note—

SMITH.	BROWNING.
" As a torrid sunset boils with gold Up to the Zenith. "	" Faster and more fast O'er night's brim day boils at last, Boils pure gold o'er the cloud-cup's brim." Opening of *Pippa Passes*.

This seems to me curious; inasmuch as I certainly know that Smith when he wrote this, knew of Browning—afterwards one of his first favourites—precisely nothing whatever; his absolutely first acquaintance with him being got from a copy of "Paracelsus," which I remember his friend John Nichol one evening presenting to him. What is the explanation? Both Poets had read Shelley—

> " Sudden the sun uprose; his beams were lying
> *Like boiling gold* on ocean fair to see—"

and both would seem unawares to have transferred his effect of ferment from the water to the sky; finely, yet a little irregularly, and perhaps with some sacrifice of absolute truth; the sky of sunset or sunrise, as it runs through its successions of swift and subtle change, being at every particular instant, a distinctly *stationary* splendour.

Another instance :

SHELLEY.	SMITH.
" A power Girt round with weakness— A breaking billow; even whilst we speak, Is it not broken?"	" Thou art a rock ; I a weak wave would break on thee and die."

Here it is only necessary to cite Wordsworth's

" Come hither in thine hour of strength,
Come *weak as is a breaking wave*,"

which Shelley has in the most shameless way appropriated. Also, in this relation there is a certain pertinence in a touching passage from Scott's " Journal," written when prostrated by his wife's death, in aid of other dire griefs: " For myself I scarce know how I feel ; sometimes as firm as the Bass Rock, sometimes *as weak as the water that breaks on it.*" Against an accusation in which Scott and Shelley are thus included with him, it is not necessary to defend Smith. To proceed :

LEIGH HUNT.	SMITH.
" Ghastly prison that eternally Holds its blind visage out to the lone sea."	" An old fort, like a ghost upon the hill, Stare in blank misery through the blinding rain."

This is produced, not so properly as a plagiarism but a " Parallelism " of a class so abject, that " every reader of sense—and more especially every writer of sense—knows the trick of such transformations." Pity that *this* " writer of sense " did not think—the thing being so mere and easy a trick—of giving us some specimens of *such* on his own account ! Had he done so with good effect, they would have been much the best things produced by him to prove his case. But I think he showed here more *sense*, than elsewhere he succeeded in doing, when he declined any such attempt. What, as to this instance, is the exact state of the matter? Neither Poet is, in *feeling*, to be held original; both are plainly dominated by the genius of Shelley, and have caught for the moment his weird way—morbid but strangely fascinating—of identifying aspects of Nature with bewildered modes of human emotion. This at a glance will be obvious to every one of ordinary critical intelligence; and besides this identity of feeling, as derived from a common source, there is between the passages no relation whatever.

Let us go on a little:

> " 'A lofty scorn I dared to shed
> On human passions, hopes and jars.
> I—standing on the countless dead,
> And pitied by the countless stars.' "
> *Smith.*

Here is the original in Mrs Browning:

> " ' O man, thy hate with stars o'erhead,
> Thy love with graves below.' "

And here from Goethe is the original of Mrs Browning:

> "Solemn before us
> Veiled the dark portal !
> Goal of all mortal !
> *Stars silent rest o'er us,*
> *Graves under us silent,*"

familiar to every one, as quoted by Carlyle in his "Past and Present." If Smith be here a plagiarist, Mrs Browning also is.

Farther—for there can be no lack of instances:

SMITH.	COVENTRY PATMORE.
"Chanticleer that struts Among his dames; faint-challenged claps his wings, And crows defiance to the distant farms."	"A shrill defiance of all to arms, Shrieked by the stable cock, received An angry *answer* from three farms."

Summarily disposed of by Wordsworth's*

> " On tiptoe reared, he strains his clarion throat,
> Threatened by faintly *answering farms* remote,"

from which plainly Mr Patmore has with frank auda-
city stolen. No sin to Mr Patmore in this; and what
is innocent license in Mr Patmore, cannot be sin in
Mr Smith. To go on with what almost gets to be a
weary business in the positive surfeit of instances :

SMITH.	EDGAR A. POE.
"This Pantomime	"An angel throng, bewinged, be-
* * *	dight
At which mayhap an angel audience sits,	In veils, and drowned in tears,
Mixing strange comment with its wildness."	Sits in a theatre to see
	A play of hopes and fears.
	* * *
	The play is the Tragedy ' Man.' "

Surely it is not difficult from Shakespeare to convict
Poe here—

> " All the world 's a stage,
> And all the men and women merely players."
> —*As You Like it.*

---

* On the same page of Wordsworth, from which this is taken,
I find

> " In the rough fern-clad park the herded deer
> Shook the still twinkling tail and glancing ear,"

which is as nearly as possible Tennyson, in " The Brook "—

> " In copse and fern
> Twinkled the innumerable ear and tail."

This I have seen expressly cited as an instance of the true
Tennysonian nicety; yet, as we see, it comes direct from Wordsworth ; as by plain suggestion, the

> " Far up the *solitary* morning smote
> The peaks of virgin snow,"

in the opening lines of "Œnone," also comes from Wordsworth's
fine and peculiar

> " In the broad open eye of the *solitary* sky."

But no one, on account of such things, would think the less of
Tennyson ; and frankly permitted to *him*, they cannot be forbidden to another.

One is a little ashamed to have to quote such a thing. Again :

> " Life's but a walking shadow, a poor player
> That frets and struts his hour upon the stage,
> And then is heard no more."—*Macbeth*.

And if the " angel throng drowned in tears" be wanted to complete his conviction, here they expressly are in " Measure for Measure"—

> " But man, proud man,
> Drest [for his poor part presumably] in a little brief authority,
> Plays such fantastic tricks before high heaven
> As make the angels weep."

Now, on what ground shall we acquit Poe here, and condemn Alexander Smith ? Yet another instance :

SMITH.	W. ALLINGHAM.
" The firth was throbbing with glad *flakes* of light."	" The liquid thrills to one gold *flake*."

The similarity here, of course—the only one—is in the use of the word *flake*, to express an effect of sunlight on water. This, it is alleged, Smith stole from Mr Allingham. But what of Wordsworth :

> " Strong *flakes* of radiance on the tremulous stream."

Mr Allingham could not the least, if he thought it worth while to try, substantiate a claim here of original and exclusive property. And how should Mr Smith be bound on penalties to be more original than he ?

SMITH.	TENNYSON.
" The drowsy steeples tolled the hour of one."	" The heavy clocks knolling the drowsy hours."

One is almost ashamed to treat seriously of such puerilities, for really this is poor piddling ; but as the critic had choice of his weapons, the degradation of meeting him with them seems inevitable, if he is to be met at all. What, then, of Shakespeare here—

> " If the midnight bell
> Did with his iron tongue and brazen mouth
> Sound one unto the *drowsy race of night*."

Smith being condemned, clearly Tennyson is condemned along with him. As also in this other case—

SMITH.	TENNYSON.
"Upon the salt sea must I ever roam ; Wander for ever on the *barren foam.*"	"Most weary seemed the sea, weary the oar, Weary the wandering fields of *barren foam.*"

This epithet "barren," as applied to the sea, Smith is accused of stealing from Tennyson ; with equal reason may Tennyson be accused of stealing it from Shelley's

"For this ye plough
The *barren* waves of ocean."

Both are plagiarists, or neither is.
Again—

SMITH.	COLLINS.
"Draw o'er the world a veil of dewy grey."	"Thy fingers draw dewy, The gradual dusky veil."

But Shelley's

"Gentle darkness, and the hills and woods
Distinctly seen *through that dusk airy veil*"

is rather nearer to Collins than Smith is ; and the charge preferred against the one, we must extend to include the other.

One more specimen, and as it is to be the last, it will be well to make it a good one :

SMITH.	TENNYSON.
"Bring me love's honied nightshade, fill it high, I know its madness." *City Poems.*	"The cruel madness of love, The honey of poison-flowers." *Maud.*

The resemblance is somewhat striking. But Mr Tennyson's "Maud" was published in the interval between the "Life-Drama" and the "City Poems ;" and the "Life-Drama" Mr Tennyson is known to have read. Here is a passage from it (p. 133) :

"O God, I 'd be the very floor that bears
Such a majestic thing ! now feed, mine eyes,
On *beauteous poison, Nightshade, honey-sweet.*"

This, in his " Maud," Mr Tennyson unawares utilises ;
and when Smith, in his " City Poems," very closely re-
peats *himself*, he is arraigned as a base plunderer of
Tennyson. In all these instances—and they form a
very large proportion indeed of the things alleged
against Smith not on the very face of them ridiculous
—his justification may be held complete in the crimina-
tion under the same rule of the very poets he is said
to have plundered; nor is it, I should say, to be
doubted that if others, who read and remember under
conditions of taste and association different from
mine, were called on for their contributions, the list
might be indefinitely extended, so as to neutralise
in the same way very nearly all the main items of
the charge. And perhaps the helpless futility of it
could scarce in any way be more conclusively shown.
Nothing being proved against Smith more than is also
proved against these other Poets whose property he
is accused of making free with, wherein is he to be
held in the matter any whit more culpable than they?

Before quitting the subject, I am almost obliged to
remark on the oddity of this gentleman's notions as to
what may constitute an almost absolute *verbal identity*
between two passages of Poetry. The following lines
from Smith are quoted :

> " The rain which I had heard so often weep
> Alone, within the middle of the night,
> Like a poor, beaten, and despised child,
> That has been thrust out from its father's door."

And they are thus summarily set aside—" Copied
from Coleridge almost word for word !" The writer
did not care to quote the passage of Coleridge, from
which Smith, according to him, " almost word for
word copied." I will now do so. Smith's passage
refers to the weeping of the Rain. That of Coleridge
is part of a wild *fantasia*, in which the " mad Lutanist,"

the Wind is exhibited in various functions.   Having
told several other tales, it *now* is supposed to tell

> " A tale of less affright,
> And temper'd with delight,
> As Otway's self had framed the tender lay ;
> 'Tis of a little *child*,
> Upon a lonesome wild,
> Not far from home, but she hath lost her way ;
> And now moans low, in bitter grief and fear,
> And now screams loud, and hopes to make her mother hear."
> *—Dejection—An Ode.*

The reader will be good enough to take my word for
it that this is the *only* passage in Coleridge to which,
by any possibility reference can be intended.   And
what of Smith, in *his* lines, having " copied it almost
word for word?"   The verbal identity asserted absolutely resolves itself into *this*—that the word *child*
is to be found in both passages.   In a case of this
kind it would be idle to mince one's terms.   While
willing to suppose a general *bona fides* in the writer, I
not the less boldly assert, what to every reader must
be obvious, that *here* he was, with full knowledge,
merely trading on the presumed ignorance of his
public.   The question, be it observed, is not *here* as
to possible *suggestion*, but as to a distinctly asserted
" *copying* of a passage *almost word for word.*"   And
even as to any " suggestion " of the one by the other
passage, the inference seems surely of the slightest.
  For farther conviction to the reader, I had prepared
a list of the Plagiarisms precisely such as those here
cited against Smith—the really weighty ones, that is,
not the mass of mere rubbish amid which they were
imbedded—which, simply as fruit of one person's never
more than merely desultory reading of him, could be
brought home to a writer of genius so high, peculiar,
and original as Shelley ; but I find it extends to such
length that I must needs exclude it.   And after all, if
given—though in itself perhaps curious more or less—

it could scarce have had real importance in regard of
the matter in hand. It is already sufficiently shown—
and it did not need to be shown except for behoof of
people entirely uninstructed—that this unconscious
reproduction of material in reading assimilated, is
simply more or less inevitable to every poet who has
read in the least widely. It is sufficiently known,
moreover, that if there be sin in it, some of our
greatest Poets must be held the chief of sinners.
Byron, for instance (whom I venture to think something of a Poet, however, nowadays, creatures whom
he could have eaten by the dozen to breakfast, think
it clever to express contempt for him), was one of the
most audacious pirates who ever roamed the high
seas of literature; and against Shelley, as I said,
whose sins in this kind are less suspected, a considerable case can be made out. How, then, can we
legitimately impeach any one Poet for the sin of
which all are guilty? All, it may be said, are not
equally guilty; but the thing at all permitted as innocent, where is the line to be drawn, on the one side
of which is innocence or permitted laxity, on the other
guilt or unpermitted? No such line can possibly be
drawn; and nothing can be more ridiculous than to
say—to Wordsworth we excuse his Plagiarisms; there
are only two of them—Shelley, with his three or four,
also we excuse—here is Byron with his five or six;
him also we pass—Alexander Smith is guilty of seven
or eight; on this sole ground, down with him as
Plagiarist and not Poet. This is, on the face of it,
arbitrary, and merely irrational. The sole question
must in every such case be—is this stuff before us
Poetry? If so, we may be sure no one not a Poet
could have written it, with the whole of English
literature to help him in this way of pillage and suggestion; and if admitted Poetry, it will never, as such,

be discredited by being shown to contain here and
there a thought or an image inadvertently appropriated from other writers. Nevertheless, it is well
and of interest that such things, when they occur,
should sharply be pointed out. In the "Life-Drama"
they occur in such numbers, that had the critic to
whom I have been alluding been at all a proficient in
his business, he might readily have made out against
Smith a considerably stronger case. And had he done
so, his inference from it in favour of himself as having
demolished Smith's claims as a Poet would no whit
the less have been àn absurd one. But had what he
essentially did been a little better done, and done in
the right spirit, as without this ridiculous inference,
there was no harm in his doing it; and, indeed, it
would have been a clearly good ahd useful thing to
do. Done as it was, it was not only useless, but
mischievous, at once to the Poet and the Public, to
whose mere ignorance its appeal was made. The
sins—so call them—of the "Life-Drama" in this kind,
are sufficiently accounted for and excused, as result
of youth, a somewhat turbulent course of wide and
half-mastered poetical reading, and a memory, as I
have before called it, at once tenacious and treacherous. Neither of his after volumes lie open to the
same objection in nearly the same degree, or indeed
in any degree the least worthy to be specially remarked upon.

Smith's Poetry admitted as such, and he himself
therein admitted as Poet, there may yet very well be
question of the claims supposed made for him by
some of his more ardent admirers. Poet! it may be
said; Poetry! admitted; but how much, and in what
sense, Poetry, as guarantee of Poet? Poetry may be
very genuine, and, as such, even delightful, yet, as
merely *imitative*, as distinct from *original* poetry, and

no product of the man's clearly distinct individuality, it may yet be fairly set aside as naught. The music he makes is pleasant,—it may be said,—but he is really no. more than a pipe which Tennyson or some other Poet "commands to utterance of harmony." And of Smith this is the view by some critics latterly taken. ·While admitting that something is to be said for it, I do not admit it as a correct or conclusive judgment of the whole matter. A man might very well be an original, and even a *great* original Poet, though his verse should include an imitative element. As notably Byron,* of whom

---

* The truth is, that in Byron's later poetry—most notably in the Third Canto of " Childe Harold "—the imitation—and at times something more—of Wordsworth, is such as would have compromised the claim to originality of any less potent and versatile spirit than he. In Shelley also may be traced imitative elements —a colouring influence—from Wordsworth almost continuously —from Byron at times, and less distinctly. He himself was well aware of this—*vide* Prefaces to the " Revolt of Islam" and " Prometheus," in which he wisely says that if a man *could* keep himself free from the influence of men of genius, his contemporaries, it would be foolish in him to do so—as Wordsworth unquestionably tried to do, entirely, I must think, to his detriment. An " imitative element " in his verse—which after all may mean no more than that, as himself a child of his Time, he cannot be divorced in feeling from those who are its highest representatives—will thus never, in itself, distinctly discredit any poet. The question of proportion and degree, however, not the less remains to be discussed ; and in regard of Smith it is, I think, a perfectly fair subject of discussion. Had the man still lived, such a discussion, if started, might have had some interest for me. Seeing he is dead, if vehemently debated to-morrow, it could not have much, if any. One single word of it and no more. The "imitative element" in him is chiefly to be noted in his first work, the "Life-Drama," which includes frank imitation of every poet with whom he was familiar — of Keats, Tennyson, Bailey, Wordsworth, Byron, and specially—though this and justly, we scarcely stigmatise as imitation—of Shakespeare and the Elizabethans. But if there was *nothing* in it *but*

Coleridge said that he was like the mocking-bird, which can imitate every songster of the grove, and has yet a sweet note of its own. This "note of his own" is, *me judice*, throughout to be caught in Smith, interfused in the admitted imitation. Is it to such an *extent* interfused as to save his Poetry, as a whole, from being disposed of as imitative? My own opinion, which cannot be of the least importance, would distinctly be given in the affirmative. Again, admitting his Poetry in a sufficient sense original, or *his own*, is there in it such a forceful vitality as might possibly suffice to maintain it in "the struggle for existence" which goes on among poems as elsewhere? Such questions as these intelligent people might be supposed to discuss, in regard of Smith, or of another poet. That *other* question of "Plagiarism" will never be discussed at all—except to be set aside with contempt—among men of any intelligence and also of competent knowledge. It is not for readers of that class, I have thought it might be well to discuss it a little here. But considering the impression which, undoubtedly with the Public, was produced by the attack in question, it seems reasonable to suppose there must be another class of readers, to whom the remarks I have ventured to make on the subject—supposing them to give, as I hope they do, the just *rationale* of the matter—may more or less be found of service.

---

such imitation—no clear individual distinctive "note of the Poet's own "—how enormous was the folly of the general British public (critics included) in giving it the reception they did as the work of a great "New Poet" *in esse*, and *in posse* who could tell what? So enormous was the folly, as to discredit for evermore the verdict of the British public and Critics, as given on any poet whatever, either in applause or censure.